From the Pages of
The Secret Agent

Mr. Verloc would have rubbed his hands with satisfaction had he not been constitutionally averse from every superfluous exertion. His idleness was not hygienic, but it suited him very well.

(page 18)

History is made with tools, not with ideas; and everything is changed by economic conditions—art, philosophy, love, virtue—truth itself!   (page 48)

"Ah! Here it is. Bomb in Greenwich Park. There isn't much so far. Half-past eleven. Foggy morning. Effects of explosion felt as far as Romney Road and Park Place. Enormous hole in the ground under a tree filled with smashed roots and broken branches. All round fragments of a man's body blown to pieces."   (page 64)

The way of even the most justifiable revolutions is prepared by personal impulses disguised into creeds.   (page 72)

"Give it up. You'll find we are too many for you."   (page 83)

"I mean to say, first, that there's but poor comfort in being able to declare that any given act of violence—damaging property or destroying life—is not the work of anarchism at all, but of something else altogether—some species of authorised scoundrelism. This, I fancy, is much more frequent than we suppose."   (page 118)

"It would be an easy way for a young man to go down into history! Not so many British Ministers have been assassinated as to make it a minor incident."   (page 122)

"I have been mad for a month or more, but I am not mad now. It's all over. It shall all come out of my head, and hang the consequences."   (page 171)

"What pleased me most in this affair," the Assistant went on, talking slowly, "is that it makes such an excellent starting-point for a piece of work which I've felt must be taken in hand—that is, the clearing out of this country of all the foreign political spies, police, and that sort of—of—dogs. In my opinion they are a ghastly nuisance; also an element of danger. But we can't very well seek them out individually. The only way is to make their employment unpleasant to their employers."   (page 186)

Dark drops fell on the floorcloth one after another, with the sound of ticking growing fast and furious like the pulse of an insane clock. At its highest speed this ticking changed into a continuous sound of trickling. Mrs. Verloc watched that transformation with shadows of anxiety coming and going on her face. It was a trickle, dark, swift, thin. . . . Blood!   (page 214)

He stared, his face close to the glass, his eyes protruding out of his head. He would have given anything to get away, but his returning reason informed him that it would not do to let go the door handle. What was it—madness, a nightmare, or a trap into which he had been decoyed with fiendish artfulness? Why—what for?
                                                                           (page 230)

Such were the end words of an item of news headed: "Suicide of Lady Passenger from a Cross-Channel Boat." Comrade Ossipon was familiar with the beauties of its journalistic style. "*An impenetrable mystery seems destined to hang for ever. . . .*" He knew every word by heart. "*An impenetrable mystery. . . .*" And the robust anarchist, hanging his head on his breast, fell into a long reverie.
                                                                    (pages 246–247)

THE SECRET AGENT

A Simple Tale

Joseph Conrad

With an Introduction by Steven Marcus
and Notes by Tatiana M. Holway

George Stade
Consulting Editorial Director

x

x

BARNES & NOBLE CLASSICS
NEW YORK

ß

BARNES & NOBLE CLASSICS

NEW YORK

Published by Barnes & Noble Books
122 Fifth Avenue
New York, NY 10011

www.barnesandnoble.com/classics

The Secret Agent was serialized from October to December 1906 in *Ridgway's: A Militant Weekly for God and Country*, an American journal. Conrad expanded and revised the work for publication as a single book volume in 1907 by British publisher Methuen and, a little later, in America by Harper's. The current edition is based on the 1921 republication by William Heinemann in the English Collected Edition of Conrad's works.

Published in 2007 by Barnes & Noble Classics with new Introduction, Note on this Edition, Notes, Biography, Chronology, Inspired By, Comments & Questions, and For Further Reading.

The Secret Agent
ISBN-13: 978-1-59308-305-2
ISBN-10: 1-59308-305-X
LC Control Number 2006923255

Produced and published in conjunction with:
Fine Creative Media, Inc.
322 Eighth Avenue
New York, NY 10001

Michael J. Fine, President and Publisher

Printed in the United States of America

QM

1 3 5 7 9 10 8 6 4 2

FIRST PRINTING

THE SECRET AGENT

A Simple Tale

Joseph Conrad

*With an Introduction by Steven Marcus
and Notes by Tatiana M. Holway*

George Stade
Consulting Editorial Director

JB

BARNES & NOBLE CLASSICS
NEW YORK

$\mathcal{B}$

BARNES & NOBLE CLASSICS

NEW YORK

Published by Barnes & Noble Books
122 Fifth Avenue
New York, NY 10011

www.barnesandnoble.com/classics

The Secret Agent was serialized from October to December 1906 in *Ridgway's: A Militant Weekly for God and Country*, an American journal. Conrad expanded and revised the work for publication as a single book volume in 1907 by British publisher Methuen and, a little later, in America by Harper's. The current edition is based on the 1921 republication by William Heinemann in the English Collected Edition of Conrad's works.

Published in 2007 by Barnes & Noble Classics with new Introduction, Note on this Edition, Notes, Biography, Chronology, Inspired By, Comments & Questions, and For Further Reading.

The Secret Agent
ISBN-13: 978-1-59308-305-2
ISBN-10: 1-59308-305-X
LC Control Number 2006923255

Produced and published in conjunction with:
Fine Creative Media, Inc.
322 Eighth Avenue
New York, NY 10001

Michael J. Fine, President and Publisher

Printed in the United States of America

QM

1 3 5 7 9 10 8 6 4 2

FIRST PRINTING

Joseph Conrad

Józef Teodor Konrad Korzeniowski was born on December 3, 1857, in a Polish province in the Ukraine to parents ardently opposed to the Russian occupation of eastern Poland. From his father, Apollo, Conrad developed a great love of literature, and he read the works of Shakespeare, Sir Walter Scott, James Fenimore Cooper, Charles Dickens, and others in Polish and French translations. After he lost his parents to tuberculosis in 1865 and 1869, respectively, Conrad was cared for by his uncle, Tadeusz Bobrowski, who oversaw the education of the often sickly boy and arranged that he be privately tutored.

At the age of seventeen, Conrad left for Marseilles to begin a career at sea that would span twenty years. Working first on French ships, he then joined the British merchant marine in 1878, climbing the ranks and passing his captain's examination in 1886—the same year he became a British subject. Conrad's voyages took him all over the world and provided inspiration for many of the works he produced in his subsequent writing career.

This career began in 1886, when Conrad started writing fiction in English, a language he learned only as a young adult. With the help of Edward Garnett, an influential publisher's reader and literary critic who would encourage Conrad for many years to come, he published his first novel, *Almayer's Folly*, in 1895 under the pen name "Joseph Conrad." There followed, in rapid succession, many more works inspired by his life at sea, including *The Nigger of the Narcissus* (1897), *Heart of Darkness* (1899), and *Lord Jim* (1900). *Nostromo* (1904), *The Secret Agent* (1907), and *Under Western Eyes* (1911) are among Conrad's other major novels and have overtly political themes. Although critics reviewed many of his works favorably, financial success eluded Conrad for many years, and it was only with the publication of *Chance* (1914) that the fifty-seven-year-old author found popular as well as critical acclaim. Suffering from a variety of physical and psychological ailments throughout his life, Conrad nevertheless produced a substantial body of work consisting of many more novels, as well as collections of stories and memoirs, and he is now regarded as one of the premier prose stylists and writers of psychological fiction in the English language. He died of a heart attack on August 3, 1924.

Table of Contents

The World of Joseph Conrad and
The Secret Agent

1857 Józef Teodor Konrad Korzeniowski is born on December 3 in a province of the Russian-occupied Ukraine to Polish parents, Ewa (née Bobrowska) and Apollo Korzeniowski. A poet, dramatist, and translator, Apollo is also an ardent Polish nationalist, active in a movement seeking Polish independence from Russia.

1859 Charles Darwin publishes *On the Origin of Species by Means of Natural Selection.*

1861 Apollo is arrested by Russian authorities for his nationalist activities and imprisoned in Warsaw for a year. Serfs are emancipated in Russia, and the American Civil War begins (1861–1865). Charles Dickens publishes *Great Expectations.*

1862 The family is forced into exile in northern Russia, where they remain for six years. There, the young Conrad has a haphazard education, but becomes an enthusiastic reader, absorbing himself in the work of Dickens, Fenimore Cooper, Marryat, and others, which he reads in Polish and in French. He later encounters Shakespeare through Apollo's translation.

1865 Ewa Korzeniowski dies of tuberculosis.

1866 Fyodor Dostoevsky's *Crime and Punishment* is published.

1867 The first volume of Karl Marx's *Das Kapital* is published.

1868 Apollo and his son are permitted to leave Russia. They return to Poland, settling first in Lwów and then in Cracow.

1869 Apollo dies, also of tuberculosis, and Conrad is adopted by his maternal uncle, Tadeusz Bobrowski. For the next four years, Conrad remains in Cracow, where the often sickly boy is educated mainly by a private tutor. Nonetheless, he forms a desire to pursue a life at sea. The Suez Canal opens.

John Stuart Mill publishes *The Subjection of Women.*
Gustave Flaubert publishes *L'Education sentimentale.*

1870   Charles Dickens dies. The Franco-Prussian War begins (1870–1871).

1871   Bismarck becomes chancellor of the German Empire.

1872   George Eliot's *Middlemarch* is published.

1873   Conrad tours Switzerland and northern Italy with his tutor.

1874   Conrad leaves Poland for Marseilles to become a trainee seaman. Working for a French banking and shipping firm, he sets sail for Martinique first as a passenger and then as an apprentice on the *Mont Blanc.* His career at sea will last twenty years.

1875   Leo Tolstoy's *Anna Karenina* begins serialization. Alexander Graham Bell demonstrates the telephone.

1876   Queen Victoria is proclaimed Empress of India.

1876–1878 Conrad serves as a steward on the *Sainte-Antoine,* bound for the West Indies, and has a brief stint as a gun-runner on the *Tremolino,* which carries illegal arms to the supporters of Don Carlos, the Spanish pretender. Back in Marseilles and plagued with gambling debts, he shoots himself in the chest, but escapes serious injury.

1878   Conrad joins the *Mavis,* his first British ship, and lands in England for the first time, knowing only a few words of English. He subsequently becomes an ordinary seaman and serves on *The Skimmer of the Sea,* which sails the coastal waters of Britain. Henry James publishes *The Europeans.* Following Russia's defeat of Turkey, the Congress of Berlin is held, resulting in the partitioning of areas previously held by the Ottoman Empire as well as the emergence of Serbia, Romania, and Bulgaria as independent states.

1879   King Leopold II of Belgium founds a private company to develop the Congo, the Comité d'Etudes du Haut Congo; he will assume title of King of the Congo Free State in 1885.

1878–1886 Conrad voyages extensively. He serves as an ordinary seaman on the *Duke of Sutherland* to Australia and on the *Europa* to the Mediterranean; as third mate on the *Loch Etive*, which also sails for Australia; and as second mate on the *Palestine*, the *Riversdale*, and the *Narcissus*, bound for Southeast Asia and India. During his voyage on the *Palestine*, the ship's cargo of coal catches fire and the ship must be abandoned; Conrad navigates an open boat and lands safely in Singapore. Passing examination for first mate in 1884, he then serves as second mate on the *Tilkhurst*, sailing to Singapore and Calcutta.

1886 Conrad becomes a British citizen and earns his Master's Certificate from the Board of Trade. He writes his first story, "The Black Mate," and submits it to a competition in a journal; it is not accepted. Friedrich Nietzsche publishes *Beyond Good and Evil*. Henry James publishes *The Princess Casamassima*.

1887–1889 Conrad sails as first mate on the *Highland Forest*, bound for Java, is injured, and then hospitalized in Singapore. Upon recovery, he serves as first mate on the *Vidar*, sailing to the East Indies, and then has his first command, of the *Otago*, sailing to Australia and western Africa.

1889 After resigning from the *Otago*, Conrad settles briefly in London and begins writing his first novel, *Almayer's Folly* (completed in 1894).

1890–1894 Conrad travels to Poland for the first time since 1874. He then sails for the Congo, where he is initially second in command and then commander of the river steamer *S. S. Roi de Belges*. Following a period of illness and recovery in Brussels, he works for a year managing a warehouse in London and then sails as first mate on the *Torrens*, where he meets John Galsworthy. His last voyage is as second mate on the *Adowa*.

1894 Tadeusz Bobrowski dies, leaving Conrad £1,600. Conrad meets Edward Garnett, as well as Jessie George. Nicholas II becomes tsar of Russia.

1895 *Almayer's Folly* is published under the pen name "Joseph Conrad." H. G. Wells publishes *The Time Machine*. Stephen Crane publishes *The Red Badge of Courage*.

1896 Conrad's second novel, *An Outcast of the Islands*, is published. He marries Jessie George, and they settle in Essex. He also becomes acquainted with H. G. Wells and initiates a correspondence with Henry James.

1897 A third novel, *The Nigger of the Narcissus*, is published. Conrad's circle of literary friendships grows to include R. Cunninghame-Graham and Stephen Crane. Queen Victoria's Diamond Jubilee is celebrated.

1898 *Tales of Unrest*, a collection of stories, is published. The Conrads' first son, Borys, is born. The family moves to Kent, to a house leased to them by Ford Madox Hueffer (later Ford), who will collaborate with Conrad.

1899 *Heart of Darkness* is serialized in three parts in *Blackwood's Edinburgh Magazine* (February–April). Two years later, when it appears in book form (in *Youth: A Narrative, and Two Other Stories*), Edward Garnett reviews it favorably. The Second Boer War, fought by the British and the Boers for control over South Africa, begins (1899–1902).

1900 *Lord Jim* is published in book form after appearing as a serial. J. B. Pinker becomes Conrad's agent. Sigmund Freud publishes *The Interpretation of Dreams*.

1901 *The Inheritors*, the first collaborative work by Conrad and Ford, is published. Others will include *Romance* (1903) and *The Nature of Crime* (1924). Queen Victoria dies and is succeeded by Edward VII. The first transatlantic Morse code signal is transmitted. Rudyard Kipling publishes *Kim*.

1903 *Typhoon, and Other Stories* is published. Making the first of several forays into the theater, Conrad adapts "Tomorrow," one of the stories in the *Typhoon* volume, for the stage; it will appear in London as *One Day More* in 1905. The Wright Brothers make their first successful flight. Henry James publishes *The Ambassadors*.

1904 *Nostromo* is serialized and then published in book form. Jessie Conrad suffers knee injuries that leave her partly crippled for life. The Russo-Japanese War begins (1904–1905).

1905 Freud publishes *Three Essays on the Theory of Sexuality*.

1906 The Conrads spend several months in Europe, as they had the previous year. John Alexander is born. *The Mirror of the Sea*, a collection of sketches, is published. The first version of *The Secret Agent* is serialized in an American journal.

1907 Conrad revises *The Secret Agent* for publication in book form. After another sojourn in Europe, the Conrad family moves to Bedfordshire.

1908 *A Set of Six*, a collection of stories, is published.

1909 Conrad breaks with Ford. The family moves to Kent.

1910 Conrad suffers a nervous breakdown after completing *Under Western Eyes*, which will be published in 1911.

1912 *Some Reminiscences*, a memoir later titled *A Personal Record*, is published, followed by *'Twixt Land and Sea*, a collection of stories.

1913 D. H. Lawrence publishes *Sons and Lovers*.

1914 With the publication of *Chance*, his thirteenth work of fiction, Conrad achieves financial success for the first time. The family travels to Poland and is trapped there for several weeks by the outbreak of World War I.

1915 Another collection of stories, *Within the Tides*, is published, as is the novel *Victory*.

1916 James Joyce publishes *A Portrait of the Artist as a Young Man*.

1917 *The Shadow Line* is published. The Russian Revolution begins.

1919 *The Arrow of Gold* is published. A dramatization of *Victory* is staged in London, and Conrad sells film rights to four novels. He also begins writing the Author's Notes for the Collected Edition of his works, which will be published by Heinemann in London and Doubleday in New York, starting in 1921. The Treaty of Versailles effectively ends World War I.

1920 *The Rescue*, a novel begun in 1898, is published.

1921 *Notes on Life and Letters* is published.

1922 A dramatization of *The Secret Agent* has a brief run on a London stage. T. S. Eliot publishes *The Waste Land*.

1923 Conrad visits the United States, where he is lionized. *The Rover* is serialized and then published in book form.

1924 A sickly Conrad declines knighthood several months before his death from a heart attack on August 3. His posthumous publications include *Tales of Hearsay* (1925), *Suspense* (1925; incomplete), *Last Essays* (1926), and *The Sisters* (1927; a fragment).

Introduction

Ever since the terrorist destruction of the World Trade Center in September 2001, Joseph Conrad's *The Secret Agent* has figured prominently as an object of exemplary reference. In the incessant stream of published commentary, analysis, opinion, and moralizing reflection that such a devastating event inevitably brings forth, Conrad's novel has been repeatedly annexed as both illustration and in support of a wide range of interpretative perspectives. For the most part, journalistic commentary has focused upon the figure of the Professor, and has included incidental references to the more bloodthirsty utterances of the other anarchist characters. In 1906–1907, so this line of discussion goes, Conrad had clairvoyantly perceived the catastrophic consequences that the European traditions of radical and revolutionary political theory, ideology, and practice were to bring about, and *The Secret Agent* is to be understood by us today as in this sense both prophetic and minatory.

Other readings of a more "centrist" persuasion stress the symbiotic relation between the police and the terrorists, that they often "come from the same basket" (p. 64). The elaborate "game" in which continuous surveillance by the police authorities and toleration of radical political dissent are simultaneously played off against one another creates a situation of stress and conflict in which government, imperfect enough as it is, tends to overrespond on the side of security. In doing so the state violates the liberties of freedom of opinion and expression that it has also been mandated to sustain and that the radical dissenters claim as rights belonging to them as equal members of a democratic, liberal society. Encroachment on or invasion of such rights serves chiefly to expose the substantial elements of untruth and hypocrisy in liberal ideology, reinforces dissident and radical fixed opinion as to the wholesale illegitimacy of prevailing political and social institutions, and prompts those already in opposition to further measures of "resistance."

A bit further along on the spectrum of interpretation is the contention that the political society attacked and wounded by the terrorists is itself in considerable part responsible for the destruction brought down on its head—this may be called the chickens have come home to roost hypothesis. Finally, there are a number of far-out or advanced readings. There is, first, the inference that the entire scenario was masterminded by the host-victim itself or by one of its surrogates. Just as the scheme against the Greenwich Observatory is the brainchild of the First Secretary of the Russian Embassy, so too the "non-appearance" of Jewish employees at the World Trade Center on the morning of September 11 clearly points to . . . etc. And in addition, exactly as the scenario in Conrad was deliberately cooked up to inspire repressive official action against the anarchists, so too in our time the subsequent administration fantasy of weapons of mass destruction was part of a concerted authoritarian effort to bamboozle the public and justify aggressive military intervention in Iraq.*

Such diverse readings—most of them containing at least a few granules of insight—suggest both the force and complexity of Conrad's imaginative vision along with the force and complexity of the events of recent history, as well as the urgency that actuates our responses to both. In point of fact, ever since its first appearance *The Secret Agent* has acted as a special screen for the projection by readers of varying interpretations of the modern world. As culture and society change, and the minds and sensibilities of readers change in some inexact but correlated dimension, so too, apparently, do great works of art. That is one crude and incomplete way of describing how it is that such works both require and sustain continuous and repeated new interpretations.†

---

*There is even the peculiar contention that 9/11 in some important sense never happened: the world experienced the events through television and other media of mass communication. These representations are continually manipulated and repeated so that everything that appears in and through them becomes a pseudo-event, evacuated of whatever referential actuality it might once have had. It all becomes part of the global imaginary, a controlled and censored region of collective mental existence, generated by technology and the prefabricated "reality" that such technology and the institutions which command it require.

†Augmented public interest in the phenomena of terrorism, however, preceded by many years the traumas of September 2001. As early as the late 1960s, organized

But of course terrorism, being as it is a form of political behavior and not an ideology or political theory or set of doctrines, can occur almost anywhere—wherever or whenever a group of conditions that include both personal and transpersonal (that is, social, cultural, political, economic, religious) components, circumstances, and motives coincide. Here in the United States, one recalls such disparate and relatively recent phenomena as the Weathermen, the Symbionese Liberation Army, the Oklahoma City bombing, and the Unabomber. The last of these, Theodore Kaczynski, holed up in his cabin in Montana, kept a copy of *The Secret Agent* handy to his bedside.

Moreover, terrorism has a long history and is protean in the forms of its occurrence. The historian Walter Laqueur regards it as an "insurrectional strategy that can be used by people of very different political convictions," and at the same time asserts that "a comprehensive definition of terrorism" does not exist and is not, at least for the foreseeable future, likely to be found.* He does not mean that terrorism cannot be analyzed or understood. What he implies is that terrorism exists in too many shapes and occurs in too many dissimilar contexts for it to be adequately or usefully captured in a single universal description. It follows from this consideration that apart from certain very general features, it tends to be characterized by particular and changing constellations of causal influences and intricate, unstable correlations of circumstances and motives.

The kind of terrorism that Conrad dramatizes in *The Secret Agent* was affiliated with the anarchist movement in European and

---

academic study was well under way, and government and foundation support for research and related collateral activities was visibly forthcoming. As the Third World mutated conceptually into both the developing and the post-colonial worlds, forms of terrorist behavior associated with movements of national independence or ethnic separatism became familiar features of the international political scene. Such disturbances were duly integrated as subsidiary elements in the Cold War strategies of both adversarial blocs. With the effective dissolution of the Soviet-led confederation, the now unipolar and globalized set of arrangements found new foci in local and regional conflicts, in which terrorist outbreaks were regularly foregrounded.

*Walter Laqueur, *A History of Terrorism* (New Brunswick, NJ: Transaction Press, 2001), pp. 4–5. See also by Laqueur, *The Age of Terrorism* (Boston: Little, Brown, 1987); and *No End to War: Terrorism in the Twenty-First Century* (New York: Continuum, 2004).

American political life and thought. This movement found its origins in the after-consequences of the French Revolution. From about 1840 and for a century thereafter, it existed as part of the nineteenth- and twentieth-century radical and revolutionary political and cultural universes. And anarchism itself, in common with other historical revolutionary tendencies, was anything but uniform or unitary.* A movement that includes at one end desperate conspirators and terrorists and at the other pacifists, or at yet a third boundary extreme collectivists and communitarians and at a fourth rabid egoists and individualist libertarians seems to have found a means of stretching ideological consensus out of reasonable recognition. And indeed anarchists divided into schisms, factions, and groupuscules as readily and obsessively as other radical political sects. Like other messianic conventicles, they often dedicated as much energy and aggressiveness to internal and intramural disputes as they did in opposition to the great, oppressive arrays of capitalism and the state against which they had originally recruited themselves. In compact, concise strokes, Conrad in *The Secret Agent* manages distinctively to suggest the rancor and sourness of atmosphere and discourse that were frequently characteristic of such small, splintered, oppositional, and minority groups.

This narrative representation of radical sectarian political and ideological existence is set by Conrad within the conventions of what was already the popular and rapidly expanding genre of the detective or police novel. This category of fiction naturally extends to include stories about spies and espionage, international conspiracies and intrigues, agents, double agents, *agents provocateurs*, police spies and counter-spies, secrets of state and military plans, all of these matters of the utmost sensitivity or confidentiality. Such covert goings-on, many of them illegal or criminal as well as surreptitious, involve the handling of and trafficking in information that is incendiary or incriminating; those whose employment

---

*The sociologist Irving L. Horowitz has identified at least eight different subtypes of anarchist beliefs and factions, these differing among themselves not so much as to fundamental doctrine as to priorities and strategies of action. See *The Anarchists* (New York: Dell, 1964), pp. 28–55. See also George Woodcock, *Anarchism* (Harmondsworth: Penguin, 1962); and James Joll, *The Anarchists* (New York: Grosset and Dunlap, 1966).

requires dealing with such material are placed perforce in a situation that entails trust, responsibility, and danger. These conditions are balanced off against numerous countervailing pressures toward betrayal, infidelity, and self-interest. Such stipulations are equally inseparable from both the conventions of this genre of narrative and the referential context of circumstances in the historical world upon which these narratives construct their dramatized model of how such a world, or that part of it, is experienced—from the inside. Part of Conrad's achievement in *The Secret Agent* has to do with his success in transforming narrative substance that was for the most part ephemeral in both quality and the material conditions of its production into modernist fiction of a high and demanding order.*

The London that is the closely enveloping *mise-en-scène* of *The Secret Agent* is very much a prototype of the modern metropolis. In the Author's Note of 1920, Conrad recollects how

> the vision of an enormous town presented itself, of a monstrous town more populous than some continents and in its man-made might as if indifferent to heaven's frowns and smiles; a cruel devourer of the world's light. There was room enough there to place any story, depth enough there for any passion, variety enough there for any setting, darkness enough to bury five millions of lives (p. 7).

It is big, too big, monstrous in its extensiveness. And in its density as well, more than the population of continents being crowded into its built-up quarters. Such compression renders the city's size even more monstrous. The experience of compaction and confinement nullifies whatever idea of spaciousness the city's sheer magnitude may at first suggest. It is all our own doing and seems "as if indifferent" to nature's (or super-nature's) disapproval or assent—as we see in the final charge that the city is "a cruel devourer of the

---

*In doing so, Conrad prepared the career-paths for such later novelists as Graham Greene and John le Carré, along with regiments of journeymen storytellers who have sustained the police or spy novel in its popular, formulaic appeal. See also, Barbara Melchiori, *Terrorism in the Late Victorian Novel* (London: Croom Helm, 1985).

world's light." This deliberate ambiguity affirms on one side that
urban existence is anti-natural, that London's darkness, fog, and dirt
are cruel and voracious, violations of some natural norm. But on
the other it refers to "the world's light," civilization itself, reason
and the Enlightenment—which the great urban settlements were
once thought to embody, but which have transformed themselves
into agglomerative entities of anti-human oppression. London is as
much a place of darkness as the Congo, and hence it is an appropriate site for "any story," even one that wryly announces itself as "A
Simple Tale."

Such a state of suspended, hovering, and apparently unresolv-
able contradiction is in its sustained emphasis deeply characteristic
of *The Secret Agent*. It is to be found throughout, permeating the
local details of the prose, and it persists even in the later Author's
Note. It is to be observed as part of the internal drama of the individual characters, each of them carrying about unacknowledged
secrets, conflicts, and incoherences. The political and personal
hostilities among and between the sub-groups of characters (anarchists, police, Winnie's family, etc.) recurrently represent both
conceptual antagonisms and perplexities that arise as a result of
irreparably adverse tendencies of thought coming on occasion to
virtually identical conclusions (as for example with Vladimir and
the Professor). Conrad's imaginative grasp is working at this pitch
of complexity: he has constructed a novel upon such principled
thematic problematicalities as arguments that are self-contradictory, purposes that are incoherent, and conflicts of motives that are
unconscious. At the same time, these unreconciled oppositions are
realized in a formal narrative design of exceptional symmetry and
fullness of execution, and a narrative prose whose unremitting
irony is both poised and controlled.

Urban existence as it is represented in *The Secret Agent* has as its
chief locus of interest Verloc's shop, in particular its shop-window,
with which the text itself opens. The articles on display belong for
the most part to the tawdry and semi-suppressed world of the sexual
market-place. What today is called soft pornography is openly offered, and the plain paper wrapping and closed envelopes pretty
clearly suggest additional degrees of explicitness within such tempting enclosures—these may be graphic or written, and some of them

may also contain contraceptives or other devices associated with sexual activity. Verloc describes his business as selling "Stationery, newspapers" (p. 36), and along with an assortment of miscellaneous items that seem to have no particular reference apart from their being in the window of a shop that deals with written and printed material, there are the "apparently old" copies of "obscure newspapers," as "badly printed" as the pornographic matter on offer side by side with them. The titles of the erotic books hint "at impropriety," and these news-sheets have such equally "rousing titles" as *The Torch* and *The Gong*. They are in fact connected with radical, revolutionary activities, and specifically with anarchism. The stress falls on the contiguity of the socially marginal, morally disreputable, and more or less illicit trade in sexual commodities and the similarly marginal, semi-covert, and abject but incendiary representations in prose and print of the revolutionary presses. Both of them are also clearly earmarked as "foreign" in provenance and inspiration.*

As is the Soho where Verloc's shop and home is planted. Both central and marginal at once, Soho was known for its resident foreigners, for its drinking places and cheap hotels, for its prostitutes and sex shops, and for its continental and other foreign restaurants.† And here too, in the most minor details, Conrad detects, and

---

*The association between sexual and political dissent, radicalism and subversiveness goes back considerably in time. See chiefly the work of Robert Darnton, for example, *The Forbidden Best-Sellers of Pre-Revolutionary France* (New York: W. W. Norton, 1965). Contemporary with *The Secret Agent* is the scandal that surrounded the publication of the first volume of Havelock Ellis's *Studies in the Psychology of Sex* (1897). Ellis ran into an imposter and con man who went by the name of Dr. De Villiers, who brought out the volume under the imprint of the "University Press of Watford." De Villiers also published a periodical entitled *The Adult Review*, which was itself the organ of a group called The Legitimation League, a gathering of persons opposed to legal marriage, who affirmed what was then known as "free love" and who campaigned against the stigmas that attach to children born outside of legally sanctioned unions. Its subscribers and members were anarchists, and they sold Ellis's volume along with other, related works of sexual and moral dissent and/or deviance—the subject of Ellis's first volume was "inversion," or homosexuality as it was just then beginning to be called. For an account of the episode, see Phyllis Grosskurth, *Havelock Ellis: A Biography* (New York: Alfred A. Knopf, 1980), pp. 184–204.
†Both Dr. Manette and Karl Marx, among many others, found places to live in Soho. Mr. Hyde, sprung temporarily free from Dr. Jekyll, rents luxurious, "decadent," and "aesthetic" rooms in Soho, outside of which prostitutes parade their wares.

makes us see, unsettling contradictions. When the Assistant Commissioner, on his way to Verloc's shop, stops for a "short meal" at a "little Italian restaurant round the corner," he annotates the place as "one of those traps . . . baited with a perspective of mirrors and white napery" (p. 124). The perspective of mirrors is, of course, a falsifier—as in the current "it's all done with smoke and mirrors." And the Italian restaurant itself discharges an "atmosphere of fraudulent cookery" (p. 124). Moreover, the Assistant Commissioner observes in ironic puzzlement, although "the Italian restaurant is such a peculiarly British institution," yet "the patrons of the place had lost in the frequentation of fraudulent cookery all their national and private characteristics." They were as "denationalised as the dishes set before them with every circumstance of unstamped respectability." Very respectable but equally inauthentic. "They seemed created for the Italian restaurant, unless the Italian restaurant had been perchance created for them." But this chicken-and-egg hypothesis is "unthinkable," an offence to reason and the laws of causality. Still, he goes on, "One never met these enigmatical persons elsewhere. It was impossible to form a precise idea what occupations they followed by day and where they went to bed at night. And he himself had become unplaced" (p. 125).

Something seems to be occurring in urban life that cannot be adequately described by such upbeat terms as "internationalization" or "the melting pot" or "multicultural plurality" or "ethnic diversity." The particular venue is neither distinctively Italian nor British. It seems rather to be denatured and decontextualized—in the text's happy word "unstamped." Although the Assistant Commissioner appears to himself and others as more than slightly "foreign," by virtue in part of class, the attenuation of personal and inner specific gravity that he perceives may be diagnosed as a mild case of the anomic jitters.* Mild enough so that he can also

---

*The Assistant Commissioner is rather humorously supplied with some of Conrad's own personal traits. In addition to being perceived as foreign, he also began his career as a police officer in "a tropical colony" (p. 87)—Conrad's career at sea was largely spent in tropical waters. The cultural figure of the detective was from the beginning an irresistible urban stand-in or surrogate for the mid- and late-nineteenth-century novelist. Moreover, the narrator regards the Assistant Commissioner as "looking like the vision of a cool, reflective Don Quixote, with the sunken eyes

experience a "pleasurable feeling of independence . . . when he heard the glass doors swing to behind his back" (p. 125). Even more, when he first sits down in the "immoral atmosphere" of the restaurant and reflects "upon his enterprise, [he] seemed to lose some more of his identity" (p. 124), the loss here being evenly distributed as to influence between the general atmosphere and his specific, overdetermined mission (that is, undercutting Heat, collaring and neutralizing Verloc, undoing the Russians). But this falling away too is qualified by another dialectically complementary bearing:

> He had a sense of loneliness, of evil freedom. It was rather pleasant (p. 124).

Conrad needed no urging to re-read *The Strange Case of Dr. Jekyll and Mr. Hyde*, since the comparison of him with Robert Louis Stevenson as two novelists of "romance," of adventure and faraway places had been adduced too frequently for him to feel gratified by it. Nevertheless, the concatenation of loneliness, evil freedom, and pleasure is precisely what Jekyll and Hyde compositely experience when the former disinhibits his double out of himself.*

When about an hour or two later, the Assistant Commissioner takes a hansom for the short drive from Soho to Westminster, he passes through an unbroken medium, "an immensity of greasy slime and damp plaster interspersed with lamps . . . oppressed, penetrated, choked, and suffocated by the blackness of a wet London night, which is composed of soot and drops of water" (p. 125). He alights "at the very center of the Empire on which the sun never sets" (p. 176). Despite the broad and obvious irony, this is also London, the imperial, international city, a world center of power and an epicenter of civil and political liberties, combined with settled public order and general social stability. It had for many decades

---

of a dark enthusiast and a very deliberate manner" (p. 123). This paradoxical delineation doesn't make a great deal of sense in relation to Cervantes—or to the usual illustrations that represent Don Quixote. But it is a very good description of the pastel drawing of Conrad made by William Rothenstein in 1903.

*It is also difficult not to suspect a fleeting allusion in this entire passage to *The Picture of Dorian Gray*.

now figured as a place of refuge and asylum for radicals and revolutionaries of every description. Fleeing for the most part from
illiberal and oppressive continental regimes, they had found both
secure exile and toleration in England. They gathered in considerable numbers in London. Safe from persecution, they were able to
pursue their political activities of propaganda, publishing radical
sheets and papers in both English and their native languages, arranging for such printed matter to be smuggled back to the Continent, organizing political associations and convening public
meetings, plotting various protests and actions, peaceful and violent, and then sending agents back to their homelands to put such
plans into effect, raising funds to support such small but not inexpensive projects, and keeping themselves afloat with whatever
means they could scrape together.*

It is also the London of high society, of distinguished and very
wealthy great ladies, one of whom takes up the paroled anarchist,
Michaelis, and sends him abroad to take the waters at Marienbad
(p. 41). This "lady patroness" (p. 90) also welcomes him along with
other "notabilities and . . . notorieties of the day" (p. 91) into her
drawing-room, which provides an unrivaled perspective on the
continual shift and flow of persons and tendencies in the social and
cultural worlds. Because her "social prestige" is of inordinate power,
she has attracted to herself

> everything that rose above the dead level of mankind, lawfully or un-
> lawfully, by position, wit, audacity, fortune or misfortune. Royal
> highnesses, artists, men of science, young statesmen, and charlatans
> of all ages and conditions, who, unsubstantial and light, bobbing up

---

*Russian expatriate anarchists in England roughly fell into two groups. There were
the Russian-speaking political exiles who were by and large drawn from the middle
and upper levels of Russian society. But there were also from the mid-1880s onward
large numbers of Yiddish-speaking Russian and Polish Jews who settled in the East
End of London, many of whom formed their own anarchist clubs and circles.
These made up, according to anarchism's historian, "the largest group of Russian
anarchist exiles in Western Europe." See George Woodcock, *Anarchism*, pp. 413f.
For an account of these socio-linguistic and class-status differences and discrepan-
cies as they played out among the communities of immigrant anarchist and socialist Jews in New York, see Irving Howe, *The World of Our Fathers* (New York: Simon
and Schuster, 1976), pp. 101–109.

like corks, show best the direction of the surface currents, had been welcomed in that house, listened to, penetrated, understood, appraised, for her own edification. In her own words, she liked to watch what the world was coming to. . . . Her drawing-room was probably the only place in the wide world where an Assistant Commissioner of Police could meet a convict liberated on a ticket-of-leave on other than professional and official ground. . . . The notabilities and even the simple notorieties of the day brought each other freely to that temple of an old woman's not ignoble curiosity. You could never guess whom you were likely to come upon being received in semi-privacy within the faded blue silk and gilt-frame screen . . . (p. 91).

This scene acts as an anticipated or premonitory counterweight to the fraudulent Italian restaurant in Soho, to be sure, but the pressure of judgment is to be observed in more than the stimulating and bazaar-like variety of the human and cultural wares on offer. It is the "charlatans" young and old who make the best indicators of the shifting currents of cultural fashion. These currents are on the "surface"; where or how the deeper currents are to be found goes, in this passage, uncommented on—unless there is a presumption that, being deep, they tend not to fluctuate. Still, life is lived amid those surface streamings and pushings, and one has to steer one's way among them, deceptive and superficial as they and what they indicate may be.

And even amid this apparent diversity of types, when the grand old lady makes her shrewd and sympathetic comment on Michaelis and his pathetic situation (" 'The poor creature is obviously no longer in a position to take care of himself. Somebody will have to look after him a little' " [p. 94]), the narrator directs our attention to the responses of her immediate audience— "the banal society smiles hardened on the worldly faces turned towards her with conventional deference" (p. 94). Those faces are about as vivid and sociably communicative as what the Assistant Commissioner sees in the Soho restaurant: "the long back of a tall, not very young girl, who passed up to a distant table looking perfectly sightless and altogether unapproachable. She seemed to be an habitual customer" (p. 125). If she is a local prostitute (as the surrounding context

strongly suggests), then her apparent sightlessness and unap-
proachability are component parts of the wintry contradictions that
at once beset and signal the advertisement in this sector of society
of a commerce in illicit sexuality—it must be of an "unstamped respectability," as repellent, marmoreal, and depersonalized as society smiles hardened with conventional deference on worldly faces.
Such details are as well early manifestations of the blank walls that
come increasingly to populate this text—though in these instances
the blank walls are, additionally, human.

It is also the London of the police—constables in uniform, detectives as Chief Inspectors in mufti, evolving according to need
into Special Branches assigned to follow radical organizations and
keep their adherents under silent surveillance. The work of these
public servants is directed toward safely monitoring and "containing" the behavior of revolutionary groups—Irish nationalists (Fenians as they were then called), as well as violent anarchists and other
assorted dissidents. The efforts of the police to corral and confine
radical behavior within certain "tolerable" limits applies by reflex
as well, and with some nicety, to their own operations and methods.
In the prosecution of these tasks, they can count on the ambiguous
resources of the increasingly omnipresent, omnivorous, and prepo-
tent mass daily press.

Along with its overwhelming numbers—the abstract and undif-
ferentiated millions that comprise the lower and middling ranks of
turn-of-the-century London—the city is also the capital seat of government, the radiating nucleus of imperial power, and along with
Paris an archetype of modern, international urban massification, as
well as a center for the conduct of world-wide political relations
by all means as well as by diplomacy. In *The Secret Agent* nations
regard one another as semi-friendly, semi-hostile inhabitants of a
fundamentally Hobbesian state of nature. The Russian Embassy
occupies the attention of the London police almost as much as the
despised anarchists. And for good reasons: the leading anarchists
originally emerged from Russia, and Russia itself was one of the
most notorious centers of political violence in Europe. The violence was shared by both the retrogressive and inflexible autocratic
regime and by the movements of resistance and rebellion—the various underground populist organizations, among them, ultimately,

socialists, anarchists, and communists. All of these existed in local sub-groups and splinters, consisting mostly of students, largely unemployed numbers of the intelligentsia, and disaffected members of the gentry and nobility—who, when they weren't forcibly put down by the Russian police (for illegal association and publishing forbidden material), sooner or later and for the most part resorted to underground meetings, conspiracies, assassination, bombing, and general incitement to peasant uprisings or insurrections (*Jacqueries* as they were known). Large numbers of these mostly young and idealistic protesters ended up dead, or in prison or Siberia, both of which were virtual express trains to death. Others found their way to escape, to exile and a more or less intermittently fugitive existence—in Germany, in Paris, in Switzerland, above all in England (and slightly later in America).

It was in the interest of the Tsar's government to subvert and disrupt exiled revolutionary groups abroad. To this end they employed spies, double agents, and *agents provocateurs* to stage acts of public violence and outrage and hence bring down the repressive force of the police upon the revolutionaries whose principal (though not exclusive) project was the overthrowing of the Tsar's government. The British authorities were well aware of this covert Russian policy of manipulation, and they were equally cognizant of its corrupt and corrupting tendencies. Not only did such practices aim to pass off fraudulence and untruthfulness as realities; they also confounded blamelessness and guilt, undermined public confidence in government and the authority of law, indeed public confidence in the public itself. Moreover, the phrase from a newspaper with which *The Secret Agent* ends, "This act of madness or despair," connects the novel with the circumstance that in fewer than ten years Europe was to engulf itself in an extended nightmare of madness and despair. The catastrophe of the First World War was not the chief causal result of the injustices and oppressions that the revolutionaries had indicted and broadcast their propaganda against. It was primarily a failure of the system of nation-states who had controlled Europe's destiny for more than a century. It was a functional consequence of the contradictions, corruptions, follies, and unconstrained self-destructive tendencies of that system, along with the nationalist and related ideologies that rationalized and justified it, and the economic institutions that fueled it. England and the British Empire were full partners in that system, as was, eventually, the United States. The anarchists and other revolutionaries had not foreseen this cataclysm, much less its extent and duration. They had diagnosed some of the symptoms that had led to it, and the Russian Revolution coming toward the end of the war was indeed a partial confirmation of what they had argued and preached. But they were at the same moment themselves manifestations of the larger and multiple series of conflicts and crises that they had tried to analyze, had denounced, and had promised themselves to resolve. As much could be said about the nation-states who were tearing themselves and each other to pieces in a convulsive effort to purge themselves of a deadly endosomatic infection and make themselves whole again.

How symmetrical both elements in this historical confluence appear can be suggested by the mottoes or slogans that were borne by each. The apostles and agents of world revolution referred to the one final act of violence that would end all further acts of violence. And the nation-states (or at least some of them) spoke with passion of the war to end all wars. We are still living today amid the dispersed echoes of such phrases. Noble as the impulses behind them and the ideals they express may be, their influence as operational goals or strategic directives has not been unambiguously benign. If one wants to regard Conrad as something of a prophet (as do a number of current commentators), it is as a prophet of the general modern European and Western crises of the twentieth century and beyond, rather than as the prophet of terrorism, that he should figure. Terrorism has its rightful place in such an understanding, but that place is as part of a larger conception.

II

When it came to acknowledging the sources in the real world which he imaginatively annexed and worked over for his narratives, and to which he was to that limited extent indebted, Conrad tended as a rule to be tight-lipped and parsimonious, noncommittal or even misleading, anxiously elusive. *The Secret Agent* is a striking instance of this mingling of misdirection and retentiveness. The incident which forms its nucleus, the setting off of a bomb in the near vicinity of the Royal Observatory in Greenwich, took place in 1894. It was the one sensational anarchist "outrage" committed in England during the latter decades of the nineteenth century, when "dynamite outrages" occurred with alarming frequency, and it was botched and bungled. The only thing the bomb destroyed was the man who was carrying it, who happened to be the brother-in-law of a known anarchist writer of pamphlets. The incident came up ten years later in the course of a "casual conversation" about anarchism between Conrad and his friend and collaborator, Ford Madox Ford. They both recalled the incident and its bizarre character, and Ford then remarked that the exploded bomber was " 'half an idiot. His sister committed suicide afterwards.' " Conrad then goes on to register his doubts about Ford's direct knowledge of anarchists, and passes on to his own recollected construction that "about a week later, I came upon a book which as far as I know had never attained any prominence, the rather summary recollections of an Assistant Commissioner of Police . . ." (p. 6). It is once more rather casual and accidental—like Coleridge's "person from Porlock" or Browning's "the old yellow book." And it is rather less than entirely true.*

But if these minor deviations from openness and candor bear saliently on remarks put down by Conrad in 1920, they are as nothing to the disavowals he sent forth at the earlier time of writing and publication. In September 1906, he wrote to John Galsworthy, who had read part of the manuscript and had responded to it positively:

> In such a tale one is likely to be misunderstood. After all you must not take it too seriously. The whole thing is superficial and it is but

---

*Ford knew more about anarchist politics than Conrad allows; for example, he provided Conrad with the material for "The Informer," a short story about anarchists in London. The materials themselves came from Ford's personal and family experiences. For accounts of Conrad's sources for *The Secret Agent*, see Norman Sherry, *Conrad's Western World* (Cambridge: Cambridge University Press, 1971), pp. 205–334 and 379–394; Ian Watt, "The Political and Social Background of *The Secret Agent*," *Essays on Conrad* (Cambridge: Cambridge University Press, 2000), pp. 112–126; Jacques Berthoud, "*The Secret Agent*," *The Cambridge Companion to Joseph Conrad*, ed. J. H. Stape (Cambridge: Cambridge University Press, 1996), pp. 81–121.

a tale. I had no idea to consider Anarchism politically—or to treat it seriously in its philosophical aspect: as a manifestation of human nature in its discontent and imbecility. The general reflections. . . . come in by the way and are not applicable to particular instances—Russian or Latin. . . . As to attacking anarchism as a form of humanitarian enthusiasm or intellectual despair or social atheism that—if it were worth doing—would be the work for a more vigorous hand and for a mind more robust, and perhaps more honest than mine.*

This kind of smoke-screen might be more helpfully described if we translated it into the idiom employed by observers of infra-human creatures—they call it the behavior of "flight." The anxiety that almost palpably rises off the page is true anxiety, a signal and warning of danger. Conrad's awkward or precautionary defensiveness has been generally read as an index of the apprehensiveness he must have felt in light of the liberal and left-wing beliefs of many of his literary friends. That may in fact be part of the case. But the intensity of assertion (along with its slightly opaque sequences of reasoning) leads one to suppose that the danger and its accompanying emotion of fear also arise from interior sources. Conrad's insistence that the narrative is "but *a tale*"—a pure disavowal if there ever was one—was carried over in elaborated form in the novel's subtitle, "A Simple Tale," and repeated with further upholstery in the dedication to H. G. Wells.

Responding to the praise of his radical friend R. B. Cunninghame-Graham, Conrad wrote:

But I don't think I've been satirizing the revolutionary world. All these people are not revolutionaries—they are shams. And as regards the Professor I did not intend to make him despicable. He is incorruptible at any rate. In making him say "madness and despair—give me that for a lever and I will move the world" I wanted to give him a note of perfect sincerity. At the worst he is a megalomaniac of an extreme type. And any extremist is respectable.†

---

*The Collected Letters of Joseph Conrad, ed. Frederick R. Karl and Laurence Davies (Cambridge: Cambridge University Press, 1988), vol. 3, pp. 354–355.
†Letters, vol. 3, p. 491.

They are all "shams," but then again the Professor is not (and Michaelis?). And after all what is satire up to if it is not in some considerable measure the exposure of shams? As for the respectability of "any extremist," does Conrad really believe in the unqualified inclusiveness of such an abstraction—is he really prepared to endorse such a decontextualized generality as "extremism in the defense of freedom is no offence"? Or to move back a bit further in historical time, is he up to affirming that in the name of Liberty, Equality, and Fraternity, everything is permitted?

Conrad's uneasiness and ambivalence are expressed in his letter to Algernon Methuen, the publisher of *The Secret Agent*. This new novel, he writes,

> is based on the inside knowledge of a certain event in the history of active anarchism. But otherwise it is *purely a work of the imagination*. It has no social or philosophical intention.*

He gives with one hand and takes back with the other. Yes, it begins with privileged knowledge of something, perhaps something of importance, that actually happened, although that circumstance is really of no consequence. In all events, the novel itself is a purely aesthetic phenomenon; any connections that may turn up between it and things that matter in the real world are coincidental and of no account. In the face of such denials, what are we to make of such apparently sincere and discordant statements as Conrad's vivid recollection that the pages of *The Secret Agent* "emerged one after another from a mood as sincere in feeling and thought as any in which I ever wrote a line" (p. 7)? Or his conviction beyond any doubt that "there had been moments during the writing of the book when I was an extreme revolutionist, I won't say more convinced than they, but certainly cherishing a more concentrated purpose than any of them had ever done" (p. 8)? And how are we to take the concluding lines of the Author's Note, written after the end of the war? In Conrad's view, that interval of historical time had compelled him to regard *The Secret Agent* in a still more grim and grisly light. The novel had reached its conclusion with the

---

*Letters, vol. 3, p. 371.

story of Winnie Verloc, the story which in its terrible closure seals up the narrative structure of *The Secret Agent* and brings it to "its anarchistic end of utter desolation, madness, and despair." That end is correlative in the sphere of personal, domestic existence to the domains of social and political revolution and ideology and of war which make up the counterpart source of the violent anarchistic impulses and urgings represented in the narrative. As a whole, Conrad concludes, deliberately and with calculation, in constructing the narrative as he did, "I have not intended to commit a gratuitous outrage on the feelings of mankind" (p. 9).

Revolutionary and terrorist assassinations and bombings were called at the time "outrages." Conrad allows by implication that *The Secret Agent* is an offence against our sentiments of common humanity. He denies, however, that the outrage it commits is "gratuitous." In this, he dissociates himself again from Vladimir, the instigator of the bombing, who insists that " 'the attack must have all the shocking senselessness of gratuitous blasphemy' " (p. 34). It is to the deliberately gratuitous quality of the violent and transgressive scheme that Conrad takes notable exception. Human existence is sufficiently senseless, purposeless, and ungrounded as it is. There is no need to pile absurdity on top of meaninglessness. Blasphemy is understandable when it is uttered by Lucifer or by a Blake or a Byron. But having declared that God is dead and then to continue on with one impiety after another is not merely unseemly and indecent. It is to compound, without sufficient motive, our irredeemable situation. One of Conrad's earliest French admirers was André Gide. In 1914 Gide published *Lafcadio's Adventures*, a novel in which a character commits a murder for no reason at all—it is described as an *acte gratuit*. This phrase represents in itself a sharp modernist turn on Coleridge's "motiveless malignity." Coleridge invented the term to describe the perplexing villainy of Iago. Gide applies *"acte gratuit"* to any of us—we do not have to be malevolent villains to behave, in an almost random sense, destructively and murderously. All any of us has to do is to assert our free will, and for its own sake. Conrad, great modernist that he is, was still sufficiently attached to nineteenth-century attitudes and forms of intellectual conduct; confronted by the abyss and tempted to dive into it, he stepped back instead.

Are we then at a juncture where we can invoke the useful critical rule that we must trust the tale and not the teller? Not altogether, for Conrad, as we have already seen, was as likely to provide comments of heuristic value as he was ready to supply copious misdirections. Besides in his instance, the connections between tale and teller are so intimate that there is at least as much loss as there is gain in striving to achieve a surgical or formal separation of the two. His example prompts an analogy with that of one of his masters—Flaubert, who wrote: "*Mme Bovary, c'est moi.*" In this profession, Flaubert was declaring more than that he had imagined Emma out of himself. He was asserting that the two were, all the way down, indivisible, that she was the artist's life and his life's blood, and that in constructing her imaginary biography—her desires, ideas, loves, sorrows, follies, desperations, and self-destruction—he was at the same time living his life, suffering his own sorrows and failures, and regarding with a cold, sympathetic eye his own fatuities.

Conrad's example prompts an analogy as well with another master, in respect of whom Conrad expressed pronounced distaste. Dostoevsky brought forth in him expressions of animus and scorn. Dostoevsky's writing was for Conrad a mess and a chaos—he was, he repeatedly declared, repelled by it. And yet when one thinks about it, Conrad seems closer to Dostoevsky than to any other European novelist of comparable genius. I do not refer to such matters as the probable influence of *Crime and Punishment* on *Under Western Eyes*. What I have in mind is a striking analogical resemblance at the internal site at which psychic structure, sensibility, and attitudes toward authority intersect. Both Dostoevsky and Conrad were committed to conservative views: Dostoevsky to Slavophilia, orthodox Christianity, and anti-rationalism; Conrad to the idealized moral order of rank, command, and fellowship on board a ship, and by extension to the organic bonds of community, loyalty, and mutuality that support civilized life elsewhere. Both were equally alert and responsive to the increasing forces in modern European society that had marshaled themselves in dedicated resistance to the traditional social abuses of rank, privilege, and money, and that defended every inequity and inequality in the established order. These forces of insurrection looked back to the French Revolution, and forward to a future in which science,

rationality, social and political liberty, and democratic equality
would replace the stagnation and corruption of the entrenched traditional institutions of order. For all their affirmative and humane
ideals, many of the forms through which these values came to be
expressed, considering the circumstances of adversity in which they
were composed, took on the impression, often the very features, of
those same conditions of narrow constraint. Nevertheless, the angry
and corrosive character of much radical and revolutionary style and
rhetoric, the abrading and acidulous effects upon their audiences,
were often effective and affecting in proportion to their crudeness
and hyperbole.

The responses of Conrad and Dostoevsky to these radical critical challenges and demystifications were simultaneously deep unconscious identifications with the forces of resistance and protest and
a backing away and repulsion from the anticipated consequences of
what such views in operation might lead to, what kind of a social
world such ideas might in their execution entail. The striking capacity of being able to give authentic expression to both sides of this
conflict—although neither even-handedly nor even in the same
register or inclusive category of discourse—is one of the qualities
that makes for the distinctive creative ambivalence of both
novelists. Their combative conservatism was in multiple senses a
derived function of the primitive intensity and authenticity of their
intimate responses to the appeal made by these aggressive and
negating impulses and conceptions—indeed it was a testimony to
them.*

I began this discussion with material taken on the whole from locations that are not central to the text of *The Secret Agent*. Some of
it comes from our present in the twenty-first century, some from
Conrad's own historical epoch, some from his correspondence, and
some from passages that involve the police, official politics, and
London high society. These constitute what might be thought of as
outer circles of the narrative and its contexts, if we take them

---

*In this unusual compounding within a single sensibility of pronounced conser-
vatism and revolutionary negation and innovation, Conrad and Dostoevsky join
such figures as Hegel and Burke.

together as a heterogeneous whole. One attribute that almost all this disparate textual matter has pervasively in common is its quality of instability: we recognize this in the diction we select to describe scenes and passages. Such terms as ambiguousness, uncertainty, contradictoriness, ambivalence, opposing or oppositional, conflicting, shifting, inconsistent, on the one hand and on the other, taken together suggest the character of complexity offered by this narrative text. It has to do in the first instance with its insistent irony—the overarching irony of the narrator throughout, in addition to the ironic utterances and attitudes ascribed to different characters. Conrad himself recognized the enabling distance and perspective that irony permitted him to sustain (pp. 7–8). Irony works in other senses as well. It presupposes that statements are made with at least a double intention of sense or meaning, and that such messages are also received by different agents or audiences in both different ways and at varying degrees of understanding. It thrives upon paradox and contradiction and consistently implies that things are more complex and less certain than at least one or some (or even most) of us consciously reckon. It makes for compression and concentration since it assumes a disjunction between how a statement is mistaken by one hearer—is taken for example literally—while the genuine, intended sense of the statement passes him by; and this genuine sense is also understood often enough by a second listener who in addition appreciates the disparity in pitches of understanding that characterize such "communications" in language.*

The Secret Agent is a novel in which almost any theme or representation, any idea or affirmation or opinion finds a qualifying and destabilizing counterpart put forth, in the service of a sustained uncertainty, somewhere else in what is nonetheless an exceptionally coherent narrative text. The dramatization of these dialectically mobile entities is so pointed as to render dubious or inaccessible one-sided explanations or settled, univocal conclusions. Everything is multiple and elaborated; conclusions are provisional and no

---

*For a general discussion of irony in Conrad, see Laurence Davies, "'The Thing Which Was Not' and The Thing That Is Also: Conrad's Ironic Shadowing," in Carola M. Kaplan, Peter Mallios, and Andrea White, eds., *Conrad in the Twenty-First Century* (New York: Routledge, 2005), pp. 223–237.

more than momentarily decisive.* The restless, rotating ironic perspective and insistent multi-angularity of the text compels the
reader into continually revising his or her judgments—right up to
the last page. Almost the only matters one can settle on are the
darkness and portentousness of the narrative's vision. The sense of
general contingency which the reader experiences directly in the
concrete details of text, in the macro- and micro-structures of the
narrative, and in the unresolved conceptual drama of conflicts,
equivocations, non-sequiturs, and other dissonances all contribute
more than any epistemological theory of representations can to the
claim that this novel is a classic of modernism and modernist sensibility.

Conrad asserts and creates his modernism, in this instance, and
in part, by way of his appropriation of Dickens. It is Dickens's
London that figures as the dense allusive ground for this single
novel of Conrad's that is set in modern London. It is also the Dickens of the second half of his career that Conrad has turned to new
use—the Dickens of *Bleak House, Little Dorrit,* and *Our Mutual
Friend.* In these novels of vast textual and temporal extension,
Dickens creates what amount almost to musical or symphonic com-
positions in metaphoric or figurative terms. These extraordinary
arrays of textual figures in quasi-systematic motion operate symbolically and as cognitive and conceptual elements in the narrative
structure of each work. In other words, Conrad's assimilation of
Dickens's London was not limited to the scenery or atmosphere.†

---

*Conrad's dry and paradoxical sense of his own entangled procedures of thinking
and writing was expressed to his friend Edward Garnett: "I am long because my
thought is always multiple—but it is to the point anyhow." *Letters*, vol. 3, p. 492.
†Not that he was indifferent to the scenery. In the "Author's Note" Conrad recalls
that when he was in the process of imagining the London surrounding of the narrative: "I had to fight hard to keep at arm's length the memories of my solitary and
nocturnal walks all over London in my early days, lest they should rush in and overwhelm each page of the story" (p. 7). Such walks were, to be sure, taken in the footsteps of Dickens. Conrad described his very first experience of London, in 1878, as
Dickensian. It was a walk to find "one of those courts hidden away from the charted
and navigable streets . . . approached by an inconspicuous archway as if by a secret
path; a Dickensian nook of London, that wonder city, the growth of which bears no
sign of intelligent design, but many traces of freakishly sombre phantasy the Great
Master knew so well how to bring out by the magic of his understanding love.

The presence of Dickens in *The Secret Agent* is palpable as well in the poetic compression of its prose and the mastery of interlocking detail achieved in its narrative structure. The "explosive" events of the narrative are all compressed into fewer than twenty-four hours. Within that narrow temporal interval, Conrad intercalates the death of Stevie, Verloc's doings both before and after the explosion, the various activities of the police, the return home and murder of Verloc, and the account of the behavior of Winnie and Ossipon thereafter. Conrad also inserts narrative and dramatic episodes that are located in the near and less than near pasts of Verloc and Winnie and her family. The flawless interweaving of anterior narrative material, not as reminiscences of one or another character but as dramatic occurrence on the same temporal plane of representation as the narrative present, has among other things the effect of condensing and occasionally conflating past and present and of further ratcheting up the almost hallucinatory intensity with which each of the chief characters is presented as experiencing his or her distinct consciousness. It also tightens the focus of a narrative in which motion often appears to be temporarily suspended or takes place with paralytic slowness and delay. The sense of alternate compression and expansion of the experience of temporality is peculiarly appropriate for a novel whose central event symbolically represents an effort to destroy time.

III

The Secret Agent has been the object of commentary and critical reflection on more occasions than one can easily summarize—such occasions preceding by many years the recent topicality of terrorist

---

And the office I entered was Dickensian too." See "Poland Revisited," *Notes on Life and Letters* (New York: Doubleday, Page, 1921), p. 152. And of *Bleak House*, he maintained that it is "a work of the master for which I have such an admiration, or rather such an intense and unreasoning affection, dating from the days of my childhood, that its very weaknesses are more precious to me than the strength of other men's work. I have read it innumerable times, both in Polish and in English; I have read it only the other day. . . ." See *A Personal Record* (New York: Harper, 1912), p. 124.

Conrad referred to Dickens as "the master," a term of veneration that he also reserved for Flaubert and Henry James.

activities and commentaries upon them. Moreover, in a text of such intentional depth and thickness of reference, in which almost everything seems to be connected with everything else, analysis must focus on a limited number of topics, in the hope that such discussions will act as general guides to readers and suggest additional lines of enquiry. We might begin, for example, with Mr. Verloc himself as we first see him framed by the door that opens into his shop and that leads as well to the parlor of the house in which he

> carried on his business of a seller of shady wares, exercised his vocation of a protector of society, and cultivated his domestic virtues. These last were pronounced. He was thoroughly domesticated. . . . He found at home the ease of his body and the peace of his conscience, together with Mrs. Verloc's wifely attentions . . . (p. 12).

Verloc has a business: he keeps a shop in a nation of shop-keepers. He also has a vocation or calling: he is a professional spy, in the pay of the Russian Embassy, embedded among revolutionary circles in London, working to keep the Russians informed of anarchist plans for assassinations, bombings, and anarchist comings and goings. The plans in question are projected for sites on the Continent, from and to which the conspirators ordinarily shuttle. He is also, unknown to his Russian spymasters, an unpaid but highly useful informant for Chief Inspector Heat of the Special Crimes Department. Heat in turn regards Verloc as a source of "private information," and has built up for himself another layer of secrecy, keeping all knowledge of Verloc back from his superiors. This privileged information keeps Heat abreast of covert radical doings and, presumably, of Russian clandestine behavior as well. Hence Verloc plies his vocation as a "protector of society" by supplying inside information against the anarchists to the Russian Embassy, as well as the same information on demand to the English police along with intelligence about covert Russian anti-anarchist schemes in London. One might suggest as well that by conducting his trade in pornography under the regular surveillance of the London police, he is also, in an unacknowledged sense, doing his bit to protect society.

Verloc is also "thoroughly domesticated." He is in the first instance a domesticated animal, a barnyard creature, and the references to him as a pig ("he had an air of having wallowed, fully dressed, all day on an unmade bed" [p. 11]), along with other less than flattering animal comparisons, establishes him ineffaceably in a bodily sense. Tamed, like other domesticated beasts, he finds peace, security, and satisfaction within his home: he believes in and exemplifies family values. Although he and his wife are childless, he is uninflectedly uxorious, and the narrator makes it plain that sexually Verloc's married life (at least as far as *he* is concerned) is active and more than satisfactory. The Verloc household is hence, on several of its sides, a bastion of British upper-working-class/lower-middle-class respectability. And even though Verloc is half-French, and his goods come largely from Paris and Brussels, and his associates from elsewhere in Europe, his style of living is insular and domestic, and in some peculiarly ironic and twisted sense blameless, responsible, and law-abiding, gathering for him a gratifying "peace of his conscience."

That is one side of Verloc. Another is almost at once revealed as the narrator describes him walking toward his appointment at the Russian Embassy. "Fat pig" as he may appear to be, Verloc gets himself up in the manner of "a well-to-do mechanic in business for himself." The style of dress is that of an artisan or craftsman who has succeeded and become "an employer of labour in a small way." But there is about Verloc "an indescribable air" that no mechanic "could have acquired in the practice of his handicraft, however dishonestly exercised" (p. 18). It is

> the air common to men who live on the vices, the follies, or the baser fears of mankind; the air of moral nihilism common to keepers of gambling hells and disorderly houses; to private detectives and inquiry agents; to drink sellers and . . . to the sellers of invigorating electric belts and to the inventors of patent medicines. But of that last I am not sure. . . . For all I know, the expression of these last may be perfectly diabolic. . . . What I want to affirm is that Mr. Verloc's expression was by no means diabolic (pp. 18–19).

Not even a dishonest and cheating craftsman could be so permeated. If, as Gibbon remarked, history is "indeed, little more than the register of the crimes, follies, and misfortunes of mankind,"* then Verloc has been drenched in and dredged through the mediums of those who make their livings from such offscourings. These are agents who batten on our weaknesses, vulnerabilities, and shames, who exist on the social margins and sometimes off them. Furtively sought out, they nonetheless supply certain social needs, as they are always the first to tell you. When Verloc sells some item of pornography over the counter, he does so with "a firm, steady-eyed impudence" (p. 11). His customer is there of his own free will; if there were no market demand for these goods, Verloc would be out of business. Activities of this kind indefeasibly put the mark of "moral nihilism" on those who traffic in such material. They are also, however, foreshadowings in the realm of personal and individual circumstances of the more inclusive and consequential moral nihilisms that color, if they do not altogether contaminate, the political and social worlds that we also perforce inhabit. Verloc is actively engaged and committed in both of these domains. And yet his expression is "by no means diabolic." He also does not seem diabolic. Indeed he is not, as an individual person, diabolic. No more is he demonic, like Mr. Kurtz. He is nonetheless involved up to his eyeballs in the demonic matrices of social behavior in which revolution, oppression, large-scale violence, and terrorism and war are fomented. He is involved and he is responsible. He may in some final analysis be a pawn of uncontrollable historical circumstances, but he remains responsible. He is in addition a telling early instance of the banality of evil, a manifestation of one of its lesser sides. And he is also a shop-keeper and family man and wants no trouble.

Another plane on which the juxtaposition of the extreme and the banal is brought to expression is disclosed in the foregathering of anarchists in the parlor behind Verloc's shop. Verloc himself is " 'one of the Vice-Presidents' " of The Future of the Proletariat, an organization, as he explains to Vladimir, " 'not anarchist in principle, but open to all shades of revolutionary opinion' " (p. 29). This society puts its imprint on publications variously described as leaflets, pamphlets, tracts, and newspapers—one of the truisms of

---

*Edward Gibbon, *The Decline and Fall of the Roman Empire*, vol. 1, chapter 3.

revolutionary legend and tradition holding that without a printing press (or its equivalent) revolutions get nowhere. The three associates who attend the meeting are Michaelis, Karl Yundt, and Comrade Alexander Ossipon, each of them a "special delegate of the more or less mysterious Red Committee . . . for the work of literary propaganda" (p. 45). Since the activities of radical groups are necessarily projected toward the future, much of their energies are directed toward changing opinion, upon educating, raising, and clarifying the conscious minds of those whom they wish to recruit and retain. In the word "propaganda," whose history refers back to the Catholic Church and its mission to propagate faith and doctrine, the secular revolutionaries of the modern era, and particularly the anarchists, touched upon sensitive ground, since it seems to be in the nature of things that most revolutionary aims and plans never get beyond propaganda.

If there appears to be a certain overlapping or redundancy between The Future of the Proletariat and the Red Committee, that circumstance as well was and still is characteristic of small, sectarian, covert movements. When Ossipon mistakenly concludes that Verloc has blown himself up at Greenwich, he immediately and fearfully anticipates

> the blame of the Central Red Committee, a body which had no permanent place of abode, and of whose membership he was not exactly informed. If this affair eventuated in the stoppage of the modest subsidy allotted to the publication of the F.P. pamphlets . . . (p. 69).

Among many radical groups, the word "Central" functioned from the outset as essentially a figure of speech—a circumstance that suggests once again an ironic discrepancy between the portentous title or office and a banal actuality. The anarchists in particular had virtually as a matter of principle no real central directorate. It followed that the membership of any executive body would be occult and transient and—perforce for such subversive and illegal collaborative undertakings—generally withheld, however inchoate or even illusionary the existence of such a body might be. These amorphous entities, however, were at the same time the nominal source of whatever uncertain funds trickled down for the purposes of publication and support of those who were the ideological voices of the movement.

The organizations, or perhaps only their names, continue to multiply. Inspector Heat learns from a colleague in the Paris police that Verloc is "a rather well-known hanger-on and emissary of the Revolutionary Red Committee" (p. 110), even as the French suspect that he is simultaneously secretly employed by one of the embassies in London. And the international character of the revolutionary movements is further underscored when Heat confides to the Assistant Commissioner that

> he did not suppose Mr. Verloc to be deep in the confidence of the prominent members of the Revolutionary International Council, but that he was generally trusted, of that there could be no doubt (p. 111).

That there were actual revolutionary international organizations is beyond question: that the Working Men's International Association (or First International) was founded in London in 1864 under the leadership of Marx and Engels and that it continued to exist through conflicts, challenges, resignations and expulsions, and other vicissitudes (including changes of names) is equally certain. But that Bakunin, for example, succumbed to the temptation to invent imaginary international associations and conspiracies, and that he wrote out constitutions for some of these phantom bodies as well as membership cards that he gave to actual people, seems beyond dispute as well. The police themselves, it should also be noted, were not above fabricating revolutionary and terrorist cells for their own purposes. And it isn't clear from the text of *The Secret Agent* what grade of "reality" is to be accorded to any of these obscure, spectral bodies.

At the gathering in Verloc's parlor, Michaelis begins by affirming his "realism," his respect for complexity, his disregard for "moralists." "History is made by men, but they do not make it in their heads," he declares, closely paraphrasing Marx.* He is a

---

*"Men make their own history, but they do not make it just as they please; they do not make it under circumstances chosen by themselves, but under circumstances

materialist, an economic determinist, and an anarchist-socialist. At the same time he is convinced that " 'no one can tell what form the social organisation may take in the future. Then why indulge in prophetic phantasies?' " (p. 41). Having spent fifteen years in prison for his role in a terrorist jail-break in which a policeman was killed, Michaelis has been released on parole. In prison he has become enormously fat.* Confinement and isolation have given him time to think things out for himself. Despite the uncertainty of the social future, nothing has shaken his revolutionary optimism. The "end of all private property [was] coming along logically, unavoidably." The "inherent viciousness" of private property can lead only to further oppression and internecine warfare: "Yes. Struggle, warfare.... It was fatal. Ah! he did not depend upon emotional excitement to keep up his belief.... Not he! Cold reason, he boasted, was the basis of his optimism" (p. 43). In the "solitary reclusion" of prison he had acquired the habit of thinking aloud; released, he continued talking "to himself, indifferent to the sympathy or hostility of his hearers, indifferent indeed to their presence." His existence is figured as an extension of "the solitude of the four whitewashed walls of his cell, in the sepulchral silence of the great blind pile of bricks near a river, sinister and ugly like a colossal mortuary for the socially drowned" (p. 44).

The pronounced modification in the narrator's tone continues in what immediately follows.

> He was no good in discussion, not because any amount of argument could shake his faith, but because the mere fact of hearing another voice disconcerted him painfully, confusing his thoughts at once— these thoughts that for so many years, in a mental solitude more barren than a waterless desert, no living voice had ever combated, commented, or approved (p. 44).

The alternations throughout this extended passage from irony to sympathy and then back again to irony in a slightly different

---

directly found, given and transmitted from the past." Karl Marx, *The Eighteenth Brumaire of Louis Bonaparte* (1852), paragraph 2.

*Bakunin was also obese. However, a number of characters in *The Secret Agent* are very bloated.

register are characteristic of the modulated and fluid mobility of assessment that Conrad brings to bear on the representation of something as contingent and complex as the momentary state of the human mind and soul. One can, however, suggest the process through which Conrad might have arrived at this shift in articulation. The change begins when the narrator invokes the punitive solitude of the "four whitewashed walls of his cell" in which Michaelis has been so to speak "buried alive." It continues on from there, as the narrator, in Conrad's persona, finds himself identifying with the evoked representation of an isolated human spirit. He does so, I believe, by way of a semi-conscious recollection or echo of one of the most influential and recurrent passages of prose of the later Victorian era—Pater's Conclusion to *The Renaissance*:

> the whole scope of observation is dwarfed into the narrow chamber of the individual mind. Experience, already reduced to a group of impressions, is ringed round for each one of us by that thick wall of personality through which no real voice has ever pierced on its way to us, or from us to that which we can only conjecture to be without. Every one of those impressions is the impression of the individual in his isolation, each mind keeping as a solitary prisoner its own dream of a world.*

The pathological extremity of Michaelis's mental state is for the interval of a prolonged moment presented to us as being in addition a special case of a condition which in the rest of us constitutes the generality or norm. In this non-trivial measure, Michaelis is also "one of us."

Gripped by his revelation and vision, Michaelis continues to talk to himself amid the not exactly friendly audience made up by his fellow-revolutionaries.

> He saw Capitalism doomed in its cradle, born with the poison of the principle of competition in its system. The great capitalists devouring the little capitalists . . . and in the madness of self-aggrandisement

---

*Walter Pater, *The Renaissance: Studies in Art and Poetry*, ed. Donald L. Hill (Berkeley: University of California Press, 1980), pp. 187f.

only preparing, organising . . . making ready the lawful inheritance of
the suffering proletariat (p. 47).

He has been seized by one of the meta-narratives of Western civilization. It is the master narrative of the salvation of humanity
through Progress, as revised by the post-Enlightenment Hegel and
additionally rotated (if not spun) by the secular revolutionary Marx.
It supplies the inheritance plot of the tragic and comic stage and
the enduring narrative template for countless novels. And it is the
family romance *cum* Bildungsroman of all "the young men from
the provinces," that is to say of all of us, male and female alike,
who, like the suffering proletariat, look forward to just rewards.*
    But, Michaelis continues with "seraphic trustfulness," one must
exercise "Patience." The "great change would perhaps come in the
upheaval of a revolution." Perhaps not. In any case, "revolutionary
propaganda," as the education of the future masters and sovereigns
of the world, must be cautious, even timid, in the tenets it ad-
vances. We cannot foretell the certain effects of "any given economic change. . . . For history is made with tools, not with ideas;
and everything is changed by economic conditions—art, philosophy, love, virtue—truth itself!" (p. 48). Everything is inevitable, and
by a similar token everything is contingent. But Michaelis is in no
situation to take account of the circumstance that his argument has
run itself into the sands. Preparing to leave, he stands up and bears
witness to his certitude:

"The future is as certain as the past—slavery, feudalism, individualism, collectivism. This is the statement of a law, not an empty
prophecy" (p. 48).

The "gentle apostle" then grasps the feeble arm of "the old terrorist"
Karl Yundt and "with brotherly care" assists him out of the room.
    We are subsequently to learn that Michaelis has become some-
thing of a celebrity. When he was originally imprisoned, "popular

---

*For the young man from the provinces, see Lionel Trilling, "The Princess
Casamassima," in *The Liberal Imagination* (New York: Viking Press, 1950), pp.
58–92.

sentiment" had "applauded the ferocity of the life sentence" passed
upon him, even though his complicity in the crime was limited
and had nothing to do with the killing of the policeman (p. 91). Fifteen years later, the same "popular sentiment" had undergone a revulsion. And just as his severe sentence made for his "groundless
fame . . . the fame of his release was made for him on no better
grounds by people who wished to exploit the sentimental aspect of
his imprisonment either for purposes of their own or for no intelligible purpose" (p. 92). These latter are in large measure journalists
"in want of special copy" (p. 103). They have taken him up, as has
society in the semi-public theater of the great old lady's drawing-
room. A fashionable publisher has offered him five hundred
pounds for a book. In short, we recognize at work the deplorable
process that has come to be known as "radical chic." But the self-
less Michaelis, like Peter Kropotkin on whom he is partly mod-
eled,* lets it all occur

> in the innocence of his heart and the simplicity of his mind. Noth-
> ing that happened to him individually had any importance. He was
> like those saintly men whose personality is lost in the contemplation
> of their faith. His ideas were not in the nature of convictions. They
> were inaccessible to reasoning. They formed in all their contradic-
> tions and obscurities an invincible and humanitarian creed, which
> he confessed rather than preached, with an obstinate gentleness, a
> smile of pacific assurance on his lips, and his candid blue eyes cast
> down . . . (p. 92).

Withdrawn to a pastoral retreat which is at the same time an improved reproduction of his life behind bars, he is "writing night and
day in a shaky, slanting hand that 'Autobiography of a Prisoner'
which was to be like a Book of Revelation in the history of mankind"

---

*Kropotkin came to be universally thought of as "saintly." His visit to the United
States in 1897 came at moments to resemble a royal "progress." In Cambridge,
Massachusetts, he stayed as the houseguest of Charles Eliot Norton, the icon of
American liberalism and liberal education, who described Kropotkin affectionately
as "the mildest and gentlest of anarchists." See James Turner, *The Liberal Education of Charles Eliot Norton* (Baltimore: Johns Hopkins University Press, 1999),
p. 389.

(p. 102). Urged on by a "delightful enthusiasm," he experiences "the liberation of his inner life" (p. 102). He has never been so happy.

Michaelis is dead to the world, literally incommunicado, knows nothing of what has happened, but sits in his " 'tiny cage in a litter of manuscript,' " and looks " 'Angelic.' " His autobiography has now been divided in

> "three parts, entitled—'Faith, Hope, Charity.' He is elaborating now the idea of a world planned out like an immense and nice hospital, with gardens and flowers, in which the strong are to devote themselves to the nursing of the weak" (p. 244).

His Marxian/Utopian/Christian/anarcho-socialism has taken a "natural" curve of historical evolution, and he is now writing in the spirit of the later Tolstoy. He has also taken to living " 'on a diet of raw carrots and a little milk' " (p. 244), allying himself not merely with the vegetarian wing of the movement but, more significantly, with the Gandhi who was soon to make his appearance on the international scene. His chiliastic vision of the world as an institution for the care and feeding of the weak is not all that remote from William Morris's rendering in *News from Nowhere*, nor from H. G. Wells's ironic reversal of that "dream" in *The Time Machine*. But it is also an anticipation of the therapeutic culture whose advent was just around the corner, as well as of the revisionist orthodox Christianity that represented a reflux against it.* In sum, Conrad may not have been sufficiently fair to the anarchists, and

---

*For example:

The wounded surgeon plies the steel
That questions the distempered part;
Beneath the bleeding hands we feel
The sharp compassion of the healer's art
Resolving the enigma of the fever chart.

Our only health is the disease
If we obey the dying nurse
Whose constant care is not to please
But to remind of our, and Adam's curse,
And that, to be restored, our sickness must grow worse.

may not have known enough about them—which were the two prongs of Irving Howe's well-known critical deprecation of *The Secret Agent*—but it seems to me, at this later date, that his seaman's nose had picked up more of what was in the wind than Howe and some others have given him credit for.*

As for the other revolutionaries, a few comments may prove helpful. Karl Yundt, superannuated, toothless, moribund, calls himself "the terrorist." Derived in part from such figures as Bakunin and Johann Most, Yundt is largely made up of bloodthirsty rhetoric and verbal expressions of incendiary outrage:

> "I have always dreamed . . . of a band of men absolute in their re-
> solve to discard all scruples in the choice of means, strong enough
> to give themselves frankly the name of destroyers, and free from the
> taint of that resigned pessimism which rots the world. No pity for
> anything on earth, including themselves, and death enlisted for
> good and all in the service of humanity . . ." (p. 42).†

Having acquitted himself of such sentiments, he goes on at once candidly to reflect that he " 'could never get as many as three such men

---

The whole earth is our hospital
Endowed by the ruined millionaire,
Wherein, if we do well, we shall
Die of the absolute paternal care
That will not leave us, but prevents us everywhere. (T.S. Eliot "East Coker" [1940], part 4, in *Four Quarters* [1943].)

*Irving Howe, *Politics and the Novel* [1957] (New York: Meridian, 1987), pp. 95–100.
†These sentiments are variations on familiar passages from Bakunin, in which, for example, he calls for revolutionary action which "spares nothing and stops at nothing," or praises bandits and brigands; or from Most's editorials and articles in *Freiheit* or *Revolutionaere Kriegswissenschaft* (1884), in which he gives instructions on how to concoct poison at home (for use against police spies and informers), create letter bombs and more substantial explosives for larger targets, etc.
Yundt's black "toothless mouth" may also be attributed to Bakunin, whose teeth fell out during his imprisonment in Russia and Siberia, though there were doubtless many other toothless anarchists. His gouty hands may be a reflexive ironic allusion to Conrad himself, who suffered from gout in both his lower and upper limbs. The expression of "underhand malevolence . . . in his extinguished eyes" (p. 42) is his alone.

together.' " But he then turns on Michaelis and snarls, " 'So much for your rotten pessimism,' " which suggests that he too, like Michaelis, has lost his capacity for listening to other voices. Not entirely, however, for when Ossipon mentions Lombroso, Yundt breaks in at once with ' "Lombroso is an ass,' " and follows this with " 'idiot' " and ' "imbecile,' " voicing the unlimited rancor, contempt, and disdain for others that he shares with Vladimir and the Professor. Searching for such physical markings as would infallibly identify congenital criminals, Yundt declares, Lombroso has got it all upside down. He would do better by attending to the scars of burned and branded prisoners, markings of the sadistic law by which criminals are made. Yundt is all bloodthirsty indignation:

> "Do you know how I would call the nature of the present economic conditions? I would call it cannibalistic. That's what it is! They are nourishing their greed on the quivering flesh and the warm blood of the people—nothing else" (p. 48).

This "terrifying statement," as if it had been itself a piece of poisoned meat, is "swallowed" by poor Stevie, who sinks at once to the floor. Although the venomous hyperbole of the old terrorist consists exclusively of revolutionary clichés, Conrad is going to renew the vividness of such worn-thin metaphorical phrases through their literalization in the fate of Stevie. Thus even the hackneyed viciousness of Yundt's utterances is pressed into the cycle of rotating and mutating images through whose means the thematic substructure of the narrative is both built up and moved forward.

Yundt's foreign accent along with his "dried throat and toothless gums" combine to make his "enunciation . . . almost totally unintelligible" to those who are not familiar with him (p. 42).* Nevertheless, the physical impression of his presentation of himself in speech preserves "his historic attitude of defiance . . . . There was an extraordinary force of suggestion in this posturing."

---

*Conrad's spoken English was also according to observers idiosyncratically odd and frequently difficult to understand.

The all-but-moribund veteran of dynamite wars had been a great actor in his time . . . on platforms, in secret assemblies, in private interviews. The famous terrorist had never in his life raised personally as much as his little finger against the social edifice. He was no man of action; he was not even an orator of torrential eloquence, sweeping the masses along in the rushing noise and foam of a great enthusiasm (p. 46).

He has been no "propagandist of the deed."* He is nonetheless an instigator of activism in others. In speech and writings he has performed with "a more subtle intention":

he took the part of an insolent and venomous evoker of sinister impulses which lurk in the blind envy and exasperated vanity of ignorance, in the suffering and misery of poverty, in all the hopeful and noble illusions of righteous anger, pity, and revolt (p. 46).

He is the tempter who works upon our raw resentments; but he appeals in the same breath to our unmerited oppression and our noble and non-self-serving imaginations of rebellion that arise from the anger and pity that, as human beings, we properly feel. He is Milton's Satan, and he is Camus's Rebel, man in revolt, as well. And because he is a propagandist, an agent of language—like the novelist himself, he has a "gift" of expression and a power of persuasiveness—his responsibility to guide and educate his fellows is coordinate with his capacity to misdirect and corrupt them. They are correlative endowments. The narrator has gone out of his way to tell us that Verloc's expression was "by no means diabolic"; he also lets us know that Yundt's "evil gift" is only a "shadow" of what it once was, "like the smell of a deadly drug in an old vial of poison" (p. 46). But he also subsequently remarks that when Yundt takes his morning "constitutional crawl" in Green Park, it is as a "spectre." It is difficult to believe that Conrad in this charged verbal context could be less than aware of what his insertion of this descriptor signified.†

---

*"Propaganda of the deed" was one of best-known slogans of anarchist activists.
†The claim being advanced is that the narrator is referring to the opening sentence of the *Communist Manifesto* (1848): "A spectre is haunting Europe—the spectre of Communism."

Comrade Alexander Ossipon, the third professional revolutionary, is the youngest of them. He is an "ex-medical student" and also the "principal writer of the F.P. leaflets." He too is very much an embodied presence. A "bush of crinkly yellow hair" along with a "red, freckled face" and "flattened nose and prominent mouth . . . in the rough mould of the negro type" are completed by "high cheekbones" over which "almond-shaped eyes" "leered languidly" (p. 43). This former student of science is ironically depicted in terms lifted from a number of the popular pseudo-sciences of the latter part of the nineteenth century. These all had to do with physical features or inherited characteristics; such signs were studied and classified according to a suppositious, meaningful correlation with non-physical—that is, mental and behavioral—tendencies. Phrenology, craniology, "racial science," comparative anthropology, along with applications of evolutionary theory to almost anything began to fly around. Conrad's sardonic and parodic notation of Ossipon clearly makes him out as a "mongrel" physical type. Moreover, there is a strong admixture in Ossipon of "lower breeds," the Negro and the Mongoloid.* Since his name suggests origins that are Slavic, he makes an interesting contrast to Vladimir, whose visage, "clean-shaved and round, rosy about the gills . . . with the thin sensitive lips formed exactly for the utterance of . . . delicate witticisms" (p. 35), suggests, with no relief from irony, breeding of a finer, higher order of selection.

So it comes as no surprise that when Ossipon looks at Stevie's chaotic drawing of "innumerable circles," he should remark, " 'Typical of this form of degeneracy. . . . That's what he may be called scientifically. Very good type, too, altogether, of that sort of

---

*In *Der Einzige und sein Eigentum* (1845), one of the canonical works in the early history of anarchism, Max Stirner uses the racial types of the Negroid and the Mongoloid to represent early phases in the evolution of the individual, society, and the human race. The Negro represents childhood or antiquity, the time of "dependence on things." The Mongoloid (or Chinese) represents youth, the time of dependence on "thoughts," on rules and permanent institutions. See *The Ego and Its Own*, trans. Steven Byington (London: Rebel Press, 1993), pp. 67ff. Stirner clearly swiped these categories from Hegel's *Philosophy of History*, where Hegel employed such speculatively inclusive cultural categories to express extremely general attitudes toward experience.

degenerate. It's enough to glance at the lobes of his ears. If you read Lombroso——' " (p. 45). The parodic "typing" of Ossipon himself indicates to us in advance how seriously we are to take Ossipon's own typing (as we would say today "labeling") of Stevie. Lombroso was one of a small host of medical and "scientific" writers who, in the wake of Darwin, set out to apply evolutionary science, theory, and speculation to human and social problems. Evolution allowed for uneven development, for atavisms or "throwbacks," and for de-volution or degeneracy. Criminals and other deviants could be readily classified—"profiled" in the current lingo—as degenerate biological types, as could whole other races and even nations. Ste-vie's ears, whatever they are, are to be read as the clue to both his drawings and his mental retardation, all of these being intertwined stigmata, warrants of his inherited, congenital degeneracy.*

Equipped with this kind of science (but with no degree!), Ossipon has become a part-time "wandering lecturer to working-men's associations upon the socialistic aspects of hygiene" (p. 45). "Hygiene" was code at the time for matters that concerned sexual behavior and health and comprehended such subjects (properly euphemized) as masturbation and contraception and a certain amount of assorted information and misinformation about venereal disease, sexual anatomy and physiology, and the functioning of the organs of the body. The "socialistic aspects" would focus on various methods of birth control, on such alternatives to marriage as free or non-contractual unions, which might entail either non-punitive separations or allowances for one or both of the pair to choose oc-casional or temporary extra-conjugal partners. Ossipon has also written a "popular quasi-medical study . . . entitled *The Corroding Vices of the Middle Classes.*" This "cheap pamphlet," having been "seized promptly by the police" (p. 45), was in overwhelming like-lihood a series of largely narrative accounts that reviewed such much-rehearsed subjects as middle-class morality as hypocritical and untruthful, the truth lying in the vicious freedom exercised by bourgeois men and sometimes even women. Marriage was repre-sented as slavery and/or prostitution, as was the middle-class family.

---

*Lombroso's studies had led him to conclude that jug-handled ears were one of the identifying features of the average criminal.

Prostitution was described, with truth, as the enslavement of working-class girls and women, and their exploitation in the service of bourgeois infidelity, convenience, and greed. Female domestic servants were the prey of young and old male members of the middle-class family, who treated them without consideration or mercy. Venereal diseases, homosexuality, and rape, with accompanying illustrative stories that combined titillation and moralizing, were also commonly featured. The clergy and the police were regularly represented as enthusiastically sharing such vices, participating in them while protecting the offending bourgeois horde of predators. Anecdotal extracts of varying degrees of explicitness, from "confessions" of prostitutes and young girls sold into slavery, to interviews with pimps, brothel toughs, and bullies, and to recollections of representatives of medicine and the law were common features of such publications, and the police were never up to confiscating more than a minority of them. Ossipon is also "the principal writer of the F.P. leaflets," but the meager compensation he receives for these efforts is insufficient to keep his "robust" form in working order. So he has transformed his previous theoretical interests into practice and makes much of his living out of "silly girls with savings-bank books," romancing and seducing nurses, nannies and domestic servants, along with an occasional "elderly nursery governess" (p. 249). He has turned his medical and scientific studies to good account, and is now a semi-successful practitioner of the middle-class vices that he had once, to no profit, denounced as a writer.

Verloc regards his guests and associates with dissatisfaction and distaste. They are for him a "lazy lot." Although his own "kindred temperament" (p. 49) facilitates this recognition, what irks him in addition about his fellows is that they are all supported by women: Yundt by an old mistress, Michaelis by his "wealthy old lady," Ossipon by a cohort of doubly exploited working women. The style of life they have without apparent purpose gravitated into is that of the urban bohemian and pseudo-artist, a style in which male, middle-class education and consciousness consort with working-class location, dress, manners, and personal moral habits. By contrast, Verloc is the sole means of support of his wife and her family. His strong instinct of "conventional respectability" reassures him of his superiority to his colleagues, while the impulses of indolence and antipathy to "all kinds of recognised labour" (p. 43) that he shares with them is an element in the unexpressed envy of them that he also feels, which expresses itself in his sentiments of moral disapproval.

IV

Conrad's imagination of Verloc's situation entails a veritable web of moral sentiments. As householder, shopkeeper, purveyor of both pornography and revolutionary publications, and as participant in revolutionary circles, he engages in an array of roles each of which involves particular moral presumptions and choices, each of which has its specific moral gravity. His vocation as a spy has specific resonances as well—in itself, as a way of being in the world, and as it affects and ramifies all his other roles and undertakings. In order to be a spy, one must build up relations of trust with numbers of people and parties.

Verloc's career began when as a youthful conscript in the French army he contracted, in the anesthetized idiom of melodrama and popular romance that he often uses, " 'a fatal infatuation for an unworthy——' " (p. 24). He stole the designs for an improved piece of artillery that the French had developed.* He sold the designs to the Russians, gave the money to the unworthy object of his fatal infatuation, who in turn promptly " 'sold' " Verloc " 'to the police' " (p. 25). What he "got" for his successful theft of the plans was " 'Five years' rigorous confinement in a fortress' " (p. 24). Verloc's surprising access to abrasive irony intimates that he is not altogether the fat wooden Indian that Vladimir and others take him for. He is aware that he got off on the wrong foot as he entered upon his predestined path through life. The elements that he was called upon to manipulate—guarded and restricted knowledge, privileged access, betrayal—were correct, but he had mistakenly gotten them turned around or upside down. Following his

---

*Although this kind of thing went on (and goes on) all the time, the allusion to France, military secrets, and spying was in the nature of things bound to bring up associations with the Dreyfus case.

release from prison, he successfully contrived to enlist himself in the clandestine services of the Russian embassies in both Paris and London and has been in their pay for eleven years. He gained the special confidence of the ambassador in both capitals, "the late Baron Stott-Wartenheim," and was transmuted in good time into "the famous and trusty secret agent . . . never designated otherwise than by the symbol Δ" in the late Baron's "official, semi-official, and confidential correspondence" (p. 30). Vladimir, whose unremitting scorn for humanity is unsurpassable, regards in retrospect the former Ambassador as at best an anachronism, a pathetic relic of the Congress of Vienna. He had "the social revolution on the brain," and was notorious for his "pessimistic gullibility" (p. 30). He labored under the fantasy that he had been sadly elected "to watch the end of diplomacy, and pretty nearly the end of the world, in a horrid democratic upheaval." It is reported that on his deathbed, being visited by the Tsar, he exclaimed: " 'Unhappy Europe! Thou shalt perish by the moral insanity of thy children!' " These dismissive reflections pass through the mind of Mr. Vladimir and are followed by his insight that the late Baron "was fated to be the victim of the first humbugging rascal that came along" (p. 30), meaning Verloc.

It happens that nearly every conclusion that the energetic and clever Mr. Vladimir arrives at is wrong. It is true that the huggermugger about agent Δ is about as silly as 007, but Verloc has not served the Ambassador and the old regime badly. He has given timely warning of plotted assassinations which were in fact not fabricated in his imagination, and which were through his intervention avoided, foiled, or otherwise aborted. He has also put his stentorian voice to diligent use, and over the years in speeches at "open-air meetings and at workmen's assemblies in large halls" built up "his reputation of a good and trustworthy comrade. . . . It had inspired confidence in his principles. 'I was always put up to speak by the leaders at a critical moment,' " he proudly confesses (p. 27). He has earned the confidence of the anarchists as one of their own, and he is in some senses one of them almost as much as he is their betrayer. And as for the old and defunct Baron, his apprehensions of approaching cultural disaster and moral psychosis were in the decades before 1914 closer to the real ground than anyone else's in this novel. And Verloc had gained the inside track in his confidence as well.

In addition, Verloc has been "turned" by Inspector Heat, and is his informant on both the anarchist revolutionaries and the Russian embassy's efforts to thwart them. He has proved himself reliable in this connection as well. Moreover, he continues to be trusted by his anarchist associates and most of all by Winnie and her mother and Stevie. The characters who place their faith in Verloc, however provisional that confidence may have to be, all have good reasons to be skeptical of such an investment. The police and the Russians by virtue of the nature of their work and its goals must exercise caution, discretion, tentativeness, and neutrality of commitment as matters of course. The anarchists in their special, occluded underworld must be constantly watchful against the police and other instruments of order, and against the infiltration among them of police spies and other undercover agents or hostile informants. And Winnie and her family, without resources, independence, or autonomy, have reasons to be suspicious of Verloc's open-handed and unpremeditated generosity. Given the nature of this society, with its rules and rituals of class behavior and differential, unequal rights and freedoms, they have sufficient causes to feel anxiety about the uninterrupted benignity of his interest in them. Yet they too, like the others in both degree and quality appropriate to their circumstances, place their trust in him.

The occupation of a spy, we are reliably informed, is "to betray trust."* The capacity to relate to others, and indeed to the non-human world as well, with a sense of trust, to endow others with an aura of reliability and trustworthiness, is one of the fundamental human aptitudes.† Our faculty to invest the world and others in it

---

*The source of this information is a veteran intelligence official who, when he retired, was serving as the executive officer of the Counterintelligence Staff of the CIA. "Like war, spying is a dirty business. Shed of its alleged glory, a soldier's job is to kill. Peel away the claptrap of espionage and the spy's job is to betray trust. The only justification a soldier or a spy can have is the moral worth of the cause he represents." See William Hood, *Mole* (Washington: Brassey's, 1993), p. ix.

†Psychologically this capability begins to develop virtually at birth and is constituted out of the bond created between mother and infant. It is fostered and sustained by the interaction of the mother's nurturing care and attention and the infant's lively demands, responses, distresses (and their assuagements), and gratifications—as these are both prolonged and developed throughout this early phase of

with the qualities of stability, constancy, and dependability are practical preconditions for the carrying forward of collaborative undertakings. In Conrad's novels, trust and its betrayal are recurrent engrossing themes. In making the life and work of a political police spy the focal center of this narrative, Conrad has chosen to enlarge dramatically on how the betrayal of trust is carried into effect in both personal life and the larger social world and how the two are joined and interanimated.

How explicitly conscious Conrad was of these matters is in part disclosed in the narrator's comment on the "practice," the shape of behavior, of Verloc's life,

> which had consisted precisely in betraying the secret and unlawful proceedings of his fellow-men. Anarchists or diplomats were all one to him. . . . His scorn was equally distributed over the whole field of his operations. But as a member of a revolutionary proletariat—which he undoubtedly was—he nourished a rather inimical sentiment against social distinction (p. 200).

He makes no apologies for his operations as a spy, double agent, or *agent provocateur*. He feels as guiltless about them as he does about his trade in pornography. They are irremissible parts of his world and indeed of the more spacious social worlds which have called them into existence, upon which they batten, and without whose sponsorship they could not flourish.* But Verloc is at the same time ablaze with rage at the "disloyalty" of Vladimir. By a kind of not unfamiliar double-think he regards himself as having "exercised his secret industry with an indefatigable devotion. There was in [him] a fund of loyalty. He had been loyal to his employers, to the cause

---

life. The psychoanalyst Erik Erikson, in *Childhood and Society* (New York: Norton, 1950), chapter 7, made the inner establishment of what he called "basic trust" the central achievement of this first stage in the construction of human identity. It does not require an intricate train of inferences to recognize how indispensable to social and communal existence extensively elaborated derivatives of this functional capacity truly are.

*"'There isn't a murdering plot for the last eleven years that I hadn't my finger in at the risk of my life. There's scores of these revolutionists I've sent off, with their bombs in their blamed pockets, to get themselves caught on the frontier'" (p. 195).

of social stability—and to his affections. . . ." (p. 195). As for those affections, he has also betrayed Stevie and Winnie, and in this connection as well he is unwilling or unable to own up to his responsibility and culpability, much less to disloyalty.

Verloc has been terrorized and traumatized by the sadistic Vladimir. He must "do" something, carry out some propaganda of the deed. Vladimir has in mind the execution of a " 'bomb outrage' " that must " 'go beyond the intention of vengeance or terrorism. It must be purely destructive' " (pp. 33–34). It must in other words be nihilistic. Since the Greenwich Observatory represents the sacred, secular values of science and astronomy, and since it sets standards for the measurements of time and longitudinal space throughout the world, an effort to blow it up would be the next best thing to throwing " 'a bomb into pure mathematics' " (p. 35). It would be a demonstration against a building, an object, an outrage that " 'combines the greatest possible regard for humanity with the most alarming display of ferocious imbecility' " (p. 35). It would be " 'absurd . . . incomprehensible, inexplicable . . . mad' " (p. 34). Senseless and gratuitous, its "madness alone is truly terrifying, inasmuch as you cannot placate it either by threats, persuasion, or bribes' " (p. 34). By the time Vladimir has finished this riff, Verloc appears to have been reduced to a "state of collapsed coma," so bewildered and stricken has he been rendered. That condition had set in as soon as Vladimir began to lecture him about his work. With autocratic "scorn and condescension" and with equally alarming autocratic

> ignorance as to the real aims, thoughts, and methods of the revolutionary world. . . . [h]e confounded causes with effects . . . the most distinguished propagandists with impulsive bomb-throwers; assumed organisation where in the nature of things it could not exist; spoke of the social revolutionary party one moment as of a perfectly disciplined army . . . and at another as if it had been the loosest association of desperate brigands that ever camped in a mountain gorge (p. 32).

Since one of Verloc's implicit functions is to be an *agent provocateur*, Vladimir in effect tells him to go and provoke (pp. 28, 37). If he needs help, Vladimir continues, he has the gang of stalwart propagandists at his disposal. Moreover, he menacingly reminds Verloc, " 'If you imagine that you are the only one on the secret fund list, you are mistaken' " (p. 36). He gives Verloc a month to provoke—that is, to execute—a " 'dynamite outrage.' " If Verloc fails to produce within that time, he is fired.

The scene in Verloc's parlor with Michaelis, Yundt, and Ossipon immediately follows, and the despondent Verloc inevitably recognizes that these three, as far as any propaganda of the deed may be concerned, add up to mission impossible. Verloc goes abroad for ten days, presumably in an effort to recruit some help, and returns without result. Winnie notes that Stevie, missing his mother (who has betaken herself to a charity home), has "moped a good deal" while Verloc has been gone. She urges him to spend more time with Stevie; the boy trusts and idealizes him. It is at about this point that Verloc silently begins to hatch the absurd, insane, and wickedly ruinous notion that he will employ Stevie as the agent of the deed of terrorist outrage. Accordingly Verloc warms to Winnie's suggestion and takes Stevie along with him on his regular walks through the city streets. But Stevie is understandably disturbed by all the violent political talk that he hears while he is in Verloc's company; and so Verloc suggests that he take his easily upset brother-in-law to the country, where he can stay with Michaelis. Winnie approves of the pacific Michaelis, and Verloc takes Stevie away. Verloc also approaches the Professor, who builds a bomb for him. On the fatal morning, Verloc catches an early train down to the country, picks up Stevie, and the two take another train to Greenwich. Verloc has brought Stevie there several times previously, and his plan is to have Stevie deposit the bomb at the walls of the Observatory and then rejoin him "outside the precincts" of Greenwich Park. The bomb was set to explode after fifteen minutes. "But Stevie had stumbled within five minutes of being left to himself" (p. 188). Verloc, on his way out of the park, has heard the premature explosion and has taken promptly to his heels. With the additional help of fog, he has made good his escape undetected (p. 172).*

---

*The weather on the appointed day was "very trying . . . choked in raw fog to begin with" and later "drowned in cold rain" (p. 87).

Returning to London, he has withdrawn all the money from an account he keeps in the name of Prozor. He has spent most of the rest of the afternoon "sitting in the tap-room of an obscure little public-house," brooding on his darkening fate, thinking vaguely about flight and emigration, and, he tells Winnie, " 'made myself ill thinking how to break it to you' " (pp. 173, 189). Although he does not yet know all the details that he will soon learn from the Assistant Commissioner and Inspector Heat, he cannot evade the serious realization that he is enveloped in catastrophe—and if he has seen the afternoon papers or heard the news-hawkers' cries, he knows that the scene was filled with "fragments of a man's body blown to pieces" (p. 64). Verloc, the narrator remarks, "was shaken morally to pieces" (p. 188). He makes his way home at dusk, and sits down almost inside the fireplace: "His teeth rattled with an ungovernable violence, causing his whole enormous back to tremble at the same rate" (p. 158). It is almost as if Stevie's dismemberment had operated with sympathetic magic on Verloc, as if he has responded symbolically and unconsciously with his own mimetic somatic disintegration. Yet he is not altogether undone, for he reasons that he has conducted himself as well as he possibly could. He did not make allowance for Stevie falling over a root almost at once— "He had foreseen everything but that." Moreover, that Winnie should have sewn their address inside Stevie's overcoat "was the last thing that Mr. Verloc would have thought of. One can't think of everything" (p. 189).* Mr. Verloc, "peripatetic philosopher" and walker in the streets of London, had been converted by the "unexpected march of events . . . to the doctrine of fatalism. Nothing could be helped now" (p. 189).†

---

*Even as the walls figuratively close in on him, Verloc has not entirely lost his own sense of slightly out-of-kilter irony. Winnie "had assured him that the boy would turn up all right. Well, he had turned up with a vengeance" (p. 189).

†As if to stress the ironic Q.E.D. of such dramatic fatality, the text prompts us to recall that on the very first page of the narrative, in the description of Verloc's shopwindow, "bottles of marking ink" are singled out for enumeration. They are there of course for Winnie to use in writing the identifying tag (the shop's address) that she sews beneath the collar of Stevie's coat. This expression of her "maternal passion" for Stevie's safety is at the same time the material fragment that leads to the unraveling of the entire plot and its ending in further "tragic" mayhem and destruction.

Still, he feels called upon to affirm the innocence of his intentions to Winnie: " 'I didn't mean any harm to come to the boy,' " and to add the assurance that " 'I didn't feel particularly gay sitting there [in the tap-room] and thinking of you' " (p. 189).* Moreover, almost as soon as he gets home, Verloc finds the occasion to say, forcefully, to Winnie, " 'You know you can trust me' " (p. 159). Winnie assents, and everything that follows demonstrates the inevitable, unstoppable, fatal disintegration of that faith. Her existence falls apart. This is one of the associated connotations of the Assistant Commissioner's grimly ironic comment that " 'From a certain point of view we are here in the presence of a domestic drama' " (p. 182). He says this to the Great Personage, Sir Ethelred, in the latter's private office in the buildings of Parliament, the House, the narrator states, "which is *the* House *par excellence* in the minds of many millions of men" (p. 176).† To be sure, the house of

---

Like Oedipus's lameness or similar physical markings or other associated objects that point to personal or original identity, this symbolic shred of matter also suggests Conrad's explicit awareness of the reverberations with classical tragic works that his text sets in motion.

*These statements are delivered in the course of a protracted scene that extends from Verloc's homecoming to his murder. Into this episode, Conrad interpolates a chapter that details the Assistant Commissioner's second meeting with the Great Personage, his subsequent attendance at the great lady's drawing-room, where he comes across Vladimir and eventually disposes of him in front of the Explorers' Club, at which point he looks at his watch and notes that it is "only half-past ten." (p. 187). In the chronological time traced by the narrative, Verloc has been dead since 8:50 (p. 214); in the time that is measured out by the reader's experience of that narrative, however, Verloc will remain alive until Winnie stabs him at the end of the following chapter. In a narrative so focused upon time in several of its dimensions, Conrad's experimental maneuverings with inversions, foreshortenings, and dislocations of the experience of time—and of the asymmetry between a narrated temporal account and the reader's temporal experience of reading such an account—take on more than formal meanings. Such innovations are enlisted themselves to become part of the unmoored, ungrounded, continually shifting and alternating series of narrative and cognitive perspectives by means of which Conrad represents the equally complex, ambiguous, and unresolved array of issues and ideas, of motives and contexts, of beliefs and conclusions that in *The Secret Agent* he heroically tries to bring off all at once and together.

†When, earlier in the narrative, the Professor and Inspector Heat accidentally come across one another in "a narrow and dusky alley" running out of "a populous street," it was "like a meeting in a side corridor of a mansion full of life" (pp. 73 and 74).

Verloc is not really to be compared to the House of Atreus, nor with its fall. But the analogy, set in motion by the text itself, is teasingly suggestive. At the very least, the two are comparably bloody, and invoke cannibalism. And just as the fragments of Stevie's exploded body "might have been an accumulation of raw material for a cannibal feast" (p. 70),* so the fat, bloated bodies of Verloc, Michaelis, and the Great Personage himself suggest something stuffed and overripe, something going rotten in the state of the body politic. For the state is Leviathan, the "artificial man," and its specific means are a monopoly of the legitimate means of violence—a monopoly and legitimacy that the anarchists and terrorists explicitly deny and contest.

V

But the point of such an analogy is, in respect of *The Secret Agent*, not to bring out by comparison the similarities and differences between private and public realms of experience, or how they resonate and interpenetrate. It is rather to gesture toward some third plane of implication, pervasive and inclusive. This dimension exerts its presence in the connected chains of figures, metaphors, and images that circulate through the text and work to effect its special, poetic density. For example, characters in *The Secret Agent* do not look at things. They "stare." The word occurs with such frequency that counting is superfluous. To stare means to look directly and fixedly, often with a wide-eyed gaze. It can be applied to the behavior of a person, or to the action of the eyes alone. It can be a sign of rudeness: "Don't stare!" or of embarrassment or puzzlement: "What are you staring at?" It can refer to the obvious: "It's staring you in the face." It can imply anger, astonishment, amazement, or disbelief in the evidence of one's chief sense. It can imply as well horror, or alternatively, fixity, paralysis, non-presence, as in "staring blindly" or "staring blankly." In *The Secret Agent* the reiterated

---

One may note here the alteration in register of the narratorial comment on London. In addition, the scriptural allusion is not to be overlooked (John 14:2).
*And look back to Yundt's remarks in chapter 2.

contexts in which "stare" or "staring" occurs belong largely to these latter shadings of usage. Characters stare, but it is neither clear nor self-evident what it is they are looking at or what they see. They and their eyes are fixed on something, though we are usually not told what that might be.

Winnie Verloc, for example, has conducted her life on the pre-conception that "things do not stand much looking into." When Verloc sees her in bed, "her big eyes stared wide open, inert and dark. . . . She did not move" (p. 147). These physical features contribute to the impression that she has "an equable soul"—she may stare, but she doesn't much look into things. Indeed she herself is not to be much looked into. She impresses others with a uniform "impenetrable calmness" (p. 155), which can be otherwise interpreted as an "air of unfathomable indifference" (p. 11) or the "fixed, unabashed stare and the stony expression" with which she both disconcerts and intimidates the younger men who seek to purchase the shop's illicit articles (p. 166). In the Author's Note, Conrad observes that Winnie's rule of behavior, that "life doesn't stand much looking into," is a "tragic suspicion" and bears less on her "psychology" than it does on her "humanity" (p. 7). When she learns about Stevie's death in all its details, her world too is torn apart. Her immediate "rage and despair" freeze her into a pose of "perfect immobility," while with her hands pressed against her face and her fingers contracted against her forehead, it seemed "as though the skin had been a mask which she was ready to tear off violently" (p. 174). The mask is of course the visage of expressionless composure with which she has confronted life; it also, in the nature of the case, refers to the mask of tragic drama, which that visage had concealed, and which it now strives to throw off, even as it is itself revealed as yet another tragic mask.

Verloc, who has never had a clue about Winnie's feeling for her brother, says with some impatience, " 'You might look at a fellow,' " and Winnie answers with a "deadened" " 'I don't want to look at you as long as I live' " (p. 191). But she does take her hands down, and when Verloc next looks up,

he was startled by the inappropriate character of his wife's stare. . . . its attention was peculiar and not satisfactory, inasmuch

that it seemed concentrated upon some point beyond Mr. Verloc's
person. . . . Mr. Verloc glanced over his shoulder. There was nothing behind him: there was just the whitewashed wall. . . . [Verloc]
saw no writing on the wall (p. 196).

Winnie also sits there in "a frozen contemplative immobility addressed to a whitewashed wall with no writing on it" (p. 197).
Verloc glances at her again and sees her gazing "at the whitewashed wall. A blank wall—perfectly blank. A blankness to run at
and dash your head against" (p. 199). We have met these walls before. Michaelis has spent fifteen years in "solitary reclusion,"
thinking aloud to himself "in the solitude of the four whitewashed
walls of his cell, in the sepulchral silence of the great blind pile of
bricks" (p. 44). If his revolutionary optimism had ever forsaken
him, " 'there were always the walls of my cell to dash my head
against' " (p. 43). Such blank surfaces are also, of course, the wall
of Belshazzar's unholy feast, upon which the finger of God in-
scribes the message that Daniel translates: the days of thy kingdom
are numbered; thou art weighed in the balance and found wanting. No such messages from the beyond—neither condemnations
nor assurances—appear on the walls of *The Secret Agent*. They remain unmarked, not to say "unstamped."

Those empty white surfaces are in addition the sheets of paper
on which Stevie, a hallucinatory image of the figure of the artist,
draws his "innumerable circles . . . a coruscating whirl of circles
that by their tangled multitude of repeated curves, uniformity of
form, and confusion of intersecting lines suggested a rendering of
cosmic chaos, the symbolism of a mad art attempting the inconceivable. The artist never turned his head . . ." (p. 44). And they are
by irresistible inference the blank sheets of paper that confronted
Conrad every day as he sat down to take up again the life and death
struggle that he had contracted for in his self-chosen vocation as a
writer. Those walls and their repelling featurelessness simultaneously anticipate and recall the writings of Sartre and Camus, both
of whom regularly and centrally deploy these and allied metaphorical figures. The walls have nothing written on them; there is no
code to decipher, no esoteric meaning. There is, as far as anyone
can tell, nothing on the other side of them, no beyond. They are

mute and dumb; there is no getting around or over them. We suspect that they are an intimation of *le Néant* that surrounds human
existence, but even that knowledge is reserved from us. While he
was writing *The Secret Agent*, Conrad compared himself to Sisyphus—unfavorably and to his own disadvantage. Sisyphus, he remarked, "was better off. He did get periodically his stone to the top.
That it rolled down again is a mere circumstance—and I wouldn't
complain if I had his privilege."* Sisyphus is also, of course, the
"absurd hero" of Camus's existentialist mythology; his rebellious-
ness against the gods has "won for him that unspeakable penalty in
which the whole being is exerted toward accomplishing nothing."
Toiling with his face against the stone, Sisyphus is also aware that
his face has become stone itself.†

Such linked groupings of images are actively present in the text
from the outset. They form a sort of perfused medium through
which the narrative both constitutes itself and moves; and their continuous presence is indispensable to the elaboration of the novel's
thematic plurality. They cluster together in the opening account of
Verloc's walk from Soho to the Russian Embassy in Knightsbridge.
He turns out of the noise and rush of traffic into a street so expen-
sive and exclusive that it could "with every propriety be described as
private. In its breadth, emptiness, and extent it had the majesty of inorganic nature, of matter that never dies" (p. 19). Inorganic nature,
rocks, stones, mountains, oceans, the solar system, and interstellar
space are all majestic because of their magnitude, their semi-per-
manence and stability, their apparent uniformity and monumental-
ity. A mountain-scape, the Alps or Rockies, is also in large measure
a rock-scape. But the sublimity of inorganic nature, of matter that
never dies, has also to do with the circumstance that it has never
lived—that it is inhuman. When Winnie and others "stare" or when
paralyzed by rage and grief Winnie's head appears "as if it had been
a head of stone" (p. 211) or her body in the dark seems "like a figure half chiselled out of a block of black stone" (p. 226), she and
they are succumbing to a process of mineralization. They become

---

*Letters, vol. 3, p. 350.
†Albert Camus, *The Myth of Sisyphus and Other Essays* (New York: Vintage,
1960), pp. 88–91.

like statues or sculpture, monumental, enduring, god-like, but im-
mobile, insensate, inanimate, not alive. As Vladimir and the Assistant Commissioner depart from the great lady's house and go down
into the street, they come upon

> a couple of carriages ... by the curbstone, their lamps blazing
> steadily, the horses standing perfectly still, as if carved in stone, the
> coachmen sitting motionless under the big fur capes, without as
> much as a quiver stirring the white thongs of their big whips (p. 185).

Although placed as a counterpart to the earlier episode of the gla-
cial carriage ride toward death undertaken by Winnie's mother, this
vignette tends to stress the recalcitrance of the social world as a virtual materialization or petrification—a densifying and mineraliz-
ing of organic objects as if to demonstrate resistance to the human
will or purpose to make things happen, to get them moving, to get
them to change. As Vladimir himself has remarked earlier, in the
minds of the dominant middle classes, " 'Property seems ... an
indestructible thing' " (p. 35).

After his guests have left, Verloc, anxious, dissatisfied and frus-
trated,

> leaned his forehead against the cold window-pane—a fragile film of
> glass stretched between him and the enormity of cold, black, wet,
> muddy, inhospitable accumulation of bricks, slates, and stones,
> things in themselves unlovely and unfriendly to man (p. 53).

And Winnie faces Ossipon,

> under the falling mist in the darkness and solitude of Brett Place, in
> which all sounds of life seemed lost as if in a triangular well of as-
> phalt and bricks, of blind houses and unfeeling stones (pp. 223–224).

The walls in Knightsbridge come in for thematic notation as well.
Verloc walks along "the side of a yellow wall which, for some
inscrutable reason, had No. 1 Chesham Square written on it in
black letters. Chesham Square was at least sixty yards away."

Unfazed, he makes for the Embassy, whose address is number 10. He enters, through

> an imposing carriage gate in a high, clean wall between two houses, of which one rationally enough bore the number 9 and the other was numbered 37; but the fact that this last belonged to Porthill Street . . . was proclaimed by an inscription placed above the ground-floor windows. . . . (p. 20).

The walls in Knightsbridge, if they are not blank, are at least misleading. A disjunction has occurred between sign and signified. An otherwise blank wall asserts incomprehensibly that it is the address of a building on a square some distance away, and a house on that square numbered 37 on its wall belongs to another street altogether, from which it has mysteriously "strayed." Whatever information one wishes to take from these other-than-rational entities has to be handled with circumspection.

But humanity and organic life lay claim to an intrusive presence in this desert of inorganic splendor. The sole "reminder of mortality" at first is "a doctor's brougham arrested in august solitude close to the curbstone." The doctor is of course an intermediary between life and death, between the organic and its long passage back toward final decomposition into inorganic matter. The doctor is behind doors and walls, tending discreet services to matter in distress. "And all was still."

> But a milk cart rattled noisily across the distant perspective; a butcher boy, driving with the noble recklessness of a charioteer at Olympic Games, dashed round the corner sitting high above a pair of red wheels. A guilty-looking cat issuing from under the stones ran for a while in front of Mr. Verloc, then dived into another basement; and a thick police constable, looking a stranger to every emotion, as if he, too, were part of inorganic nature, surging apparently out of a lamp-post, took not the slightest notice of Mr. Verloc (p. 19).

Signs of energy appear in humble forms. The wheels and cans on the milk cart carry their own noisy message about the life-enhancing substance they convey. The butcher boy in a fantasy of heroic

vitality and athletic conquest—Ben-Hur and Stirling Moss at
once—guns his hot rod through the elegant neighborhood. He will
recur at least twice in the narrative. He is also the young butcher's
son of Winnie's youthful love, whom she renounced because of
poverty and her responsibility to her crippled mother and the hand-
icapped Stevie (pp. 40, 223). For Winnie he was a "fascinating companion for a voyage down the sparkling stream of life" (p. 198). But
before we register this vision in the narrative, we are brought up
short when Inspector Heat examines in the hospital at Greenwich
the "heap of nameless fragments" that had once been Stevie's body
and Stevie himself.

> The Chief Inspector went on peering at the table with a calm face
> and the slightly anxious attention of an indigent customer bending
> over what may be called the by-products of a butcher's shop with a
> view to an inexpensive Sunday dinner (p. 78).

The butcher boy is vitality and exuberance, but he is at the same
time associated with slaughter and dead meat, with the cannibal's
feast of social life. This collocation is brought home to us by Winnie's and Verloc's business over the carving knife and "the cold
beef" to which she draws his attention. " 'You should feed your
cold,' " she recommends (p. 159). And later on that piece of roast
beef "laid out in the likeness of funereal baked meats for Stevie's
obsequies" does become the object of Verloc's raging appetite: "He
partook ravenously, without restraint and decency, cutting thick
slices with the sharp carving knife, and swallowing them without
bread" (p. 206). The quotation from *Hamlet*, the allusions to totem
feasts as well as to cannibalism again, clinch such a demonstration
of Conrad's procedures in this novel. For every affirmation there is
a negation; for every asseveration a cloud of incertitude and dubi-
ety—and the reverse. These alternations do not add up to an even-
handed determination or balance, as if the writer were making an
effort to split the difference or achieve the better part of both worlds
by compromising with each of them. Rather they suggest perpetu-
ated imbalance, uncertainty, and irresolvability. They suggest as
well the expectation that any conclusion momentarily attained will
be subverted by annulling, negating considerations. This continual

cycling of mutually cancelling conceptual images—themselves bearing both positive and negative valences—is in considerable measure responsible for the peculiar density and authentic complexity of *The Secret Agent*.

The guilty-looking cat rising silently from some basement may be on his stealthy way to the butcher shop, where he will scrounge some offal or, as it was called at the time, "cat's meat." In any event, he is another sure sign of life, illicit life to be sure, stealing as he does from one subterranean location to another. And he is a second reminder in advance of Stevie, to whom Verloc "extended as much recognition . . . as a man not particularly fond of animals may give to his wife's beloved cat" (p. 39). Verloc's notice of these two cats and of Stevie may be taken as habitually minimal. The final element in this remarkable composition is the

> thick police constable, looking a stranger to every emotion, as if he, too, were part of inorganic nature, surging apparently out of a lamp-post, [who] took not the slightest notice of Mr. Verloc (p. 19).

The police constable, like the doctor an agent of an institution and of intermediation, and also like the doctor conventionally impassive to the point of inertness, is assimilated to the "majesty" of the inorganic (as well as embodying the "majesty" of the law).* He seems like a sardonic, futurist sketch of the classical centaur or satyr. These older figures combined man and beast; this modernist variation fuses man and mineral or man and metallic, machine-made object. Although he "surges" out of the lamp-post, he takes no more notice of Verloc than Verloc apparently takes of the cat. Guardian of civil order and peace, he has steadfastly stood his post until he has at last

---

*The butcher and the policeman have been summoned up together before this by Conrad. In *Heart of Darkness*, Marlow responds with asperity to the discounting comments of his listeners: "Absurd! . . . Here you all are, each moored with two good addresses, like a hulk with two anchors, a butcher round one corner, a policeman round another, excellent appetites and temperature normal . . . normal from year's end to year's end. And you say, Absurd! Absurd be—exploded!" (chapter 2). The butcher and the policeman figure as the norm, the average expectable base of settled civilized existence, from which the tellingly significant modern experiences radically depart.

become one with it.* These paradoxical and sometimes contradictory tropes and figures explode from this passage as it were and are dispersed non-randomly throughout the entire narrative. They seem to have been released or set going by the narrator's remarking of Verloc as he walks purposefully toward the Embassy that he proceeded "steady like a rock—a soft kind of rock" (p. 19). His respectability and his corpulence together set off this collocation, which is oddly like a joke. Organic nature tends toward softness; most rocks tend in the other direction. Just before Winnie stabs him, Verloc, who is tired after his long day, reflects that "A man isn't made of stone" (p. 210). A soft rock, one surmises, is penetrable. And when Winnie's carving knife "met no resistance on its way," the narrator merely notes that "Hazard has such accuracies" (p. 213).

Winnie, herself a blank wall, staring with "far-off fixity" at the same, is absorbed by the thought that Verloc had taken "the 'poor boy' away from her in order to kill him" (p. 203). The universe that she had constructed out of a series of presumptions has vanished. Everything has altered, "even the aspect of inanimate things" (p. 203). If Stevie can be annihilated ("they had to fetch a shovel") (p. 172), then inanimate nature itself is perishable, the very ground one stands on can give way. In this disintegration she feels "released from all earthly ties," launched into space. "Her contract with existence," as represented by Verloc, "was at an end. She was a free woman" (p. 204). Her freedom is so new-found, perhaps, that she "had really no idea where she was going to" (p. 205), nor does she "exactly know what use to make of her

---

*The policeman and the post return to the text when the Assistant Commissioner, having finished his first interview with the Great Personage, pauses on his way out to have a word with that marvelous minor character, the great man's unpaid private secretary, the young and "revolutionary" Toodles. This is the early evening of the day of the outrage, and Toodles is concerned for his Minister's sake about the safety of the streets. Westminster seems to be covered with security: " 'There's a constable stuck by every lamp-post, and every second person we meet between this and Palace Yard is an obvious ' "tec" ' (p. 122). The name Toodles alerts us that Dickens is in the neighborhood. (Toodle being the name of a family in *Dombey and Son*.) And indeed Conrad in this developed and acute ironic trope of the policeman and the post is making exemplary use of *Little Dorrit*. The Barnacles are a great political family, no strangers to Westminster and beyond: "wherever there was a square yard of ground in British occupation under the sun or moon, with a public post upon it, sticking to that post was a Barnacle" (book 1, chapter 24). This species of appropriation is the way that one great creative artist pays tribute to another.

freedom" (p. 206). Following the "characteristic reasoning" which has informed her entire relationship with her husband and had "all the force of insane logic," she thinks that Verloc will now "want to keep her for nothing" and from there her "disconnected wits" lead her to the carving knife (p. 206). Hence, having murdered Verloc—

> She had become a free woman with a perfection of freedom which left her nothing to desire and absolutely nothing to do, since Stevie's urgent claim on her devotion no longer existed. . . . she did not think at all. And she did not move. She was a woman enjoying her complete irresponsibility and endless leisure, almost in the manner of a corpse (p. 211).

The freedom she has for a moment attained is an absurd freedom, in a sense not directly canvassed by Camus. It is the liberty of total independence, of nullity without ties or connections. It is absolute, it is a void of solitude, and it is death itself.

Although Winnie had cohabited with Verloc "without distaste" of either body or mind (p. 203), her idea of getting away from him (if not of "perfect freedom") is expressed in the thought " 'I would rather walk the streets all the days of my life' " (p. 207). Moreover, she was "capable of a bargain the mere suspicion of which would have been infinitely shocking to Mr. Verloc's idea of love" (p. 210). The bargain refers both to the "contract" she has made with Verloc (and herself) and to the fantasy bargain she has just imagined she will strike with Ossipon. Such dealings constitute in substantial measure her metaphorical identity as a secret agent as well and suggest that her moral capacities are situated on a different plateau than her husband's.

Although Verloc is a professional betrayer of trust, his duplicity does not extend to his sexual life. He "was inclined to put his trust in any woman who had given herself to him. Therefore he trusted his wife" (p. 200). Such ill-founded credulity had originally got him going on his career of illegality and deception. This preconception was both gratuitous and a vanity, and Verloc had entered all his "affairs of the heart . . . with no other idea than that of being loved for himself." In this self-deception "he was completely incorrigible. . . . He had grown older, fatter, heavier, in the belief that he lacked no

fascination for being loved for his own sake" (p. 205). This unarticu-
lated piety constitutes Verloc's "secret weakness." But it is also central
to the account that sums him up as "a human being—and not a
monster, as Mrs. Verloc believed him to be" (p. 208). These clandestine and unvoiced purposes that are nonetheless expressed in the
personal and marital conduct of the Verlocs are self-contradictory
and mutually destructive. They are also structurally analogous to the
motives and cross-purposes that are dangerously at play in English
and European society.

   Chief Inspector Heat, for example, has gotten himself into a
pickle by assuring the Great Personage only recently that no anarchist outrage was conceivable in the near future. He expressed himself unconditionally because he knew that this was what the
Minister wanted to hear, and that he, Heat, was "the great expert of
his department" on anarchists and terrorism. He was also moved by
silent urgings of self-interest. Heat had risen very rapidly in his departmental career. A more measured and candid report "would have
alarmed his superiors, and done away with his chances of promotion." His ambition had led him to speak with unwarranted assurance. But that is not truly wise. "True wisdom, which is not certain
of anything in this world of contradictions, would have prevented
him from attaining his present position" (p. 75). True wisdom is
skeptical because the contingencies and unpredictabilities of practical experience make certainty an unsound operational assumption.
Such blurring of lucidity does not sit well with the "official" wisdom
of the Great Personage, which has to do with an "idea of the fitness
of things"—that is, that things in the world are running quite as they
should. He takes no account of the "close-woven stuff of relations
between conspirator and police" in which "there occur unexpected
solutions of continuity, sudden holes in space and time" (p. 75). Instead of clarity and unity, which speak to the fitness of things, there
are gaps, broken connections, logical ruptures, and loose ends, all of
which speak to circumstances that fall short of transparency and coherence. But had Inspector Heat adhered to such a prudent and realistic perspective, he would not have gotten very far—which is itself
a part of another group of unresolved contrarieties.

   Another instance of such antinomies is to be found when Verloc, goaded by Winnie's protracted and ominous silence, flares out,

" 'Don't you make any mistake about it: if you will have it that I killed the boy, then you've killed him as much as I' " (p. 209). We may leave to one side any analysis of the mixture of truth, self-deceit, and misunderstanding such an utterance requires, since the narrator's comment on it claims priority on our attention:

> In sincerity of feeling and openness of statement, these words went far beyond anything that had ever been said in this home, kept up on the wages of a secret industry eked out by the sale of more or less secret wares—the poor expedients devised by a mediocre mankind for preserving an imperfect society from the dangers of moral and physical corruption, both secret, too, of their kind (p. 209).

Here the analogy between the personal situation of the Verlocs and the customary behavior of nations between and among themselves is pressed sharply home. The Verloc household has been kept afloat by covert payments earned from spying and eked out with proceeds from the sale of pornography and related items. Both of these are unattractive and unsatisfactory expedients arrived at by our defective condition as a civilized species. They weakly serve the intention of assisting a poorly conceived and executed set of collective arrangements for living in its efforts to survive the hidden forces that beset and menace its inner and its bodily well-being. Spying on anarchists for the Russians and being a double agent in the service of England do not appear to be the most straightforward, principled, intelligent, or even most effective means of dealing socially and politically with subversives and terrorists. Pornography is not the most useful contrivance for controlling or deflecting unsanctioned sexual behavior; it leads neither to happier marriages, less infidelity, reduced frustration, nor to decline in prostitution; and contraceptive devices do not guarantee immunity from disease. Still more, such expedients themselves are corrupting. They add to and become another element in the distresses and evils they were at least in part intended to alleviate—they become in their own turn integral attributes of this universe of contradictions.*

---

*In *The Human Factor* (1978), Graham Greene reshuffles these elements. Spies, double agents, and counter-intelligence officers, a Soho bookshop that sells

Is this, then, where *The Secret Agent* comes to a halt? Do these multiple contrarieties of persons and purposes, of interests and institutions, of action and counteraction all the way down to the strange opposition and intermingling of inorganic and organic substance at last fill up the narrative space and arrest further conceptual or narrative development? Are all these opposing vectors brought to a standstill in the annihilation of Stevie, Verloc, and Winnie, or in the ironic representations of the police and the ministerial offices, in the provocation and then frustration of Vladimir, and in the ineffective rancor of the anarchists? It seems so until we turn our attention to the Professor.

VI
—

We first encounter the Professor when he and Ossipon meet in the "underground hall" (p. 57) of the "renowned Silenus," a restaurant and beer hall well-known to the police as "frequented by marked anarchists" (p. 71). The walls of the beer hall are covered with frescoes depicting scenes that could be taken from William Morris's communist-anarchist Utopia, *News from Nowhere.* The Professor is an extreme solitary. Grotesquely dwarfed, undernourished, and unhealthy, he is yet "supremely self-confident"; in his presence Ossipon "suffered from a sense of moral and even physical insignificance" (p. 58). He is a corporealization of some negative field of force, and Conrad describes him in terms that recall the Martians of *The War of the Worlds.*

> these round black-rimmed spectacles progressing along the streets
> on the top of an omnibus, their self-confident glitter falling here and
> there on the walls of houses, or lowered upon the heads of the un-
> conscious stream of people.... the walls nodding ... people run-
> ning for their life at the sight of those spectacles.... What a panic!
> (p. 59).

---

pornography and is part of the espionage circuit, along with a despondent and mostly cynical set of characters are combined in a narrative world that, in contrast to *The Secret Agent,* is unable to sustain the play of such exacting contrarieties.

Those spectacles confront Ossipon "like sleepless, unwinking orbs flashing a cold fire" (p. 60). Although he is no extra-terrestrial life-form, he is like Wells's creatures an agent of destruction. He is in fact a human bomb, defying the police to arrest him, his hand never leaving the rubber ball that actuates the detonator of the explosive that he always carries about with him. He is also a scientific technician, working to improve the "weak point" of bomb-making, which is the mechanism that ignites the explosion.

> "I am trying to invent a detonator that would adjust itself to all conditions of action, and even to unexpected changes of conditions. A variable and yet perfectly precise mechanism. A really intelligent detonator" (p. 61).

What he has in mind is a self-acting, self-regulating device, a piece of machinery that would by means as yet undiscovered be set to operate, as it were, autonomously. What he has in mind, in point of fact, is either a human being or a computer. This vision is both duplicated and burlesqued in the Silenus's player-piano, which "executed suddenly all by itself a valse tune with aggressive virtuosity. The din it raised was deafening. . . . it ceased, as abruptly as it had started" (p. 57). Until he achieves the "perfect detonator" (p. 63), he has to get along on his improvisations and tinkerings. What he can utterly rely upon, however, is his " 'force of personality.' " He has managed to instill in the police " 'the belief . . . in my will to use the means. That's their impression. It is absolute. Therefore I am deadly.' " He is superior to them because he " 'stands free' " from " 'conventional morality' " (p. 62). Ordinary, mediocre people " 'depend on life, which . . . is . . . open to attack at every point; whereas I depend on death, which knows no restraint and cannot be attacked' " (p. 63). He is indeed absolute for death. Into such passages Conrad has packed allusions to the literature of nihilism, terrorism, anarchism, and rebellion—to Bakunin and Nechaev, to Heinzen and Most, to Nietzsche and Dostoevsky. In this salute to oblivion, the Professor also appears as a manifestation of the aggressive, destructive drive that Freud was to call the death instinct. Ossipon, in his turn, reminds the Professor that Karl Yundt also holds forth in such a grandiose and " 'transcendental' " manner, to which the Professor responds that Yundt is a typical bag of wind. His terrorism is all propaganda, words that lead to nothing. While the Professor labors to invent the perfect detonator, the others " 'can't even bear the mention of something conclusive.' " Something conclusive is something certain, unconditioned, absolute, final—a detonator that will blow everything away, a "clean sweep" (p. 67). The other anarchists and the police—Yundt and Inspector Heat—" 'come from the same basket' " (p. 64). The police work to defend " 'social convention' " (p. 63), anarchists to " 'revolutionise it,' " that is, to turn it around, reform, renovate, remake, and then preserve it.

> "Revolution, legality—counter moves in the same game; forms of idleness at bottom identical. He plays his little game—so do you propagandists. But I don't play; I work fourteen hours a day, and go hungry sometimes" (p. 64).

The Professor is not for revolution in any ordinarily accepted sense: he is for destruction. What will happen thereafter in the way of creation or regeneration is not his business. In this manner, he concludes, he is the " 'true propagandist' " (p. 64). In the universe framed by the propaganda of the deed, he is the genuine article, and hence he is the true terrorist as well. He has gladly given Verloc the bomb, as he would to almost anyone else who asked him. He cares nothing for personal consequences.

> I would see you all hounded out of here, or arrested—or beheaded for that matter—without turning a hair. What happens to us as individuals is not of the least consequence (p. 65).

In the annals of historic terrorism, two names stand out among many—Robespierre and Nechaev. In these brief declarations, the Professor makes clear his lineage and affiliation.*

---

*"By a revolution, the society does not mean an orderly revolt according to the classic western model—a revolt which always stops short of attacking the rights of property and the traditional social systems of so-called civilization and morality. Until now, such a revolution has always limited itself to the overthrow of one political

His humble origins notwithstanding, the Professor, as he is uniformly known, did achieve some actual academic standing. He became "an assistant demonstrator in chemistry" at a technical institute. His sense of what was owing to his talents led him to complain of "unfair treatment," and his subsequent employment in the laboratory of a dye-making factory led only to additional injustice and another departure.* He is entirely self-made, and his sense of his own merits, achieved through hard work and privation, have made him hypersensitive to anything that even remotely touched his *amour propre*. He "had genius," no doubt, but neither "patience" nor "resignation." His inflamed sense of injury had resulted in full-scale insurrection. Almost nothing can affect his confidence in his own superior competence and power. Explaining to Ossipon how the bomb he constructed for Verloc could have accidentally exploded, he lamely concludes: " 'The system's worked perfectly. . . . You can't expect a detonator to be absolutely foolproof' " (p. 69). Yet he also knows precisely that a "perfect detonator" would be just that—absolutely fool-proof. This combination of denial and insensate indifference is disclosed from another angle when, referring to the supposedly widowed Winnie, he advises Ossipon to " 'Fasten yourself upon the woman for all she's worth' " (p. 71). The "sedate scorn" of his expression conveys his contempt for Ossipon, who is no more than a leech, as well as his complete cynical disregard for Winnie, who is literally "nothing" to him.

Nevertheless, and above all else, he regards himself as a "moral agent of destruction" (p. 74), and in his embittered way takes enormous pride in his "power." What regularly gives him pause, however, is his recurrent perception of the city, its streets, its throngs of vehicles, the crowds of men and women.

---

form in order to replace it by another, thereby attempting to bring about a so-called revolutionary state. The only form of revolution beneficial to the people is one which destroys the entire State to the roots and exterminates all the state traditions, institutions, and classes in Russia." See Sergey Nechaev, *Catechism of a Revolutionist* (1869), paragraph 23.

*In *The Princess Casamassima* (1886), Henry James makes Paul Muniment, the young English anarchist and conspirator, an employee in a chemical company.

He was in a long, straight street, peopled by a mere fraction of an immense multitude; but all round him, on and on, even to the limits of the horizon hidden by the enormous piles of bricks, he felt the mass of mankind mighty in its numbers. They swarmed numerous like locusts, industrious like ants, thoughtless like a natural force, pushing on blind and orderly and absorbed, impervious to sentiment, to logic, to terror too, perhaps (p. 73).

This repeated impression of the resistant magnitude and weight of the city, its unambiguous massive substantiality, renders him impotent. Although he generally manages to avoid going out, when he does, "when he happened also to come out of himself, he had such moments of dreadful and sane mistrust of mankind. What if nothing could move them?" (p. 73). It is at such a moment that the Professor runs into Inspector Heat.

This meeting between "the perfect anarchist" and the detective policeman demonstrates just how incapable of understanding his antagonist Heat is. Indeed, he is patently out of his depth. Heat is accustomed to dealing with decent, sane, straightforward burglars and thieves, with whom he shares a universe of assumptions. "The mind of Chief Inspector Heat was inaccessible to ideas of revolt" (p. 81). A metaphysical rebel is conceptually *terra incognita* to him. For him, as for Durkheim, crime is a "normal" element in the constitution of society, as "normal as the idea of property" (p. 82). When the Professor taunts Heat about playing "the game" of legal rules, Heat responds honestly that he'll be damned if he knows what game the Professor and his ilk are at. " 'I don't believe you know yourselves.' " In any event, he admonishes, " 'Give it up. You'll find we are too many for you' " (p. 83). To this he appends the dig (having just returned from Greenwich): " 'And anyway, you're not doing it well. You're always making a mess of it. Why, if the thieves didn't know their work better they would starve' " (p. 84). The Professor is ready with a comeback, but he leaves this chance run-in "sad-faced" and "miserable." Heat, by contrast, steps out briskly, full of purpose and the affirming consciousness that the population of the planet, the entire human race itself right "down to the very thieves and mendicants," are with him.

Heat remains, however, puzzled by revolutionaries. In his cognitive world, the carryings-on of the anarchists most resemble some kind of "disorderly conduct . . . without the human excuse of drunkenness." In any case, regarded as criminals, they "were distinctly no class—no class at all" (p. 84). On the one hand, they are not numerous and don't matter enough to constitute a separate category or classification; on the other, they don't have the social status of a class; they are not "classy," as a cracksman or swindler might be. Thieves, by contrast, are serious business; they belong to the realm of competitive sport, played under "perfectly comprehensible rules" (p. 85). But when it comes to dealing with anarchists, there are "no rules." He thinks of those he knows with "merciless contempt. . . . Not one of them had half the spunk of this or that burglar he had known. Not half—not one tenth" (p. 85). Spunk in this context, while denoting courage and energy, still carried the older popular meaning of semen or ejaculate. These anarchists are not real men: they have no balls.

Ossipon and the Professor meet once more, in the Professor's lodging, ten days later. Ossipon, utterly undone by the events and his role in them, has sought him out. The Professor's room is barren, starved in both its actual material emptiness and in the absence it asserts of provision for "every human need except mere bread." Even the dirty wall papers are poisonously colored an "arsenical green." The Perfect Anarchist has been down to the country to visit the Apostle Michaelis, his counterpart solitary, who is also living more or less on air. However, he looks "Angelic" on this diet and thrives on his idea of the future society as a hospital, with gardens and flowers, in which the strong will devote themselves to the nursing of the weak. This prospect is like nothing but arsenic to the Professor.

> "The weak! The source of all evil on this earth! . . . They are our sinister masters—the weak, the flabby, the silly . . . the faint of heart, and the slavish of mind. They have power. They are the multitude. Theirs is the kingdom of the earth. . . . the blind . . . the deaf and the dumb . . . the halt and the lame . . ." (p. 244).

This is the transfigured vision of the Gospels, the Utopia of Christian socialism, redemption brought down to earth. It is also in part the vision of William Morris, and in another part that of

H. G. Wells in *The Time Machine,* in which the enslaved have become the masters and feed on the former upper classes who have
degeneratively devolved into domestic cattle. And it is also the
nightmare vision of Friedrich Nietzsche:

> The French Revolution as the continuation of Christianity.
> Rousseau is the seducer: he again unfetters woman who is hence-
> forth represented . . . as suffering. Then the slaves and Mrs. Beecher-
> Stowe. Then the poor and the workers. Then the vice addicts and
> the sick—all this is moved into the foreground. . . . the most de-
> cided conviction that the lust to rule is the greatest vice; the perfect
> certainty that morality and disinterestedness are identical concepts
> and that the "happiness of all" is a goal worth striving for (i.e., the
> kingdom of heaven of Christ) . . . the kingdom of heaven of the
> poor in spirit has begun. . . . *

The Professor's own redemptive dream is " 'of a world like shambles, where the weak would be taken in hand for utter Extermination. . . . Exterminate, Exterminate! That is the only way of
progress. . . . First the great multitude of the weak must go, then the
only relatively strong. . . . Every taint, every vice, every prejudice,
every convention must meet its doom' " (p. 244). This voice has
been heard before in Conrad. It is Kurtz's conclusion scrawled
across the manuscript of his report on savage customs. It is, with all
due allowances conceded, the voice of such Social Darwinists as
the founder of eugenics, Francis Galton. It is the voice of
H. G. Wells, echoing Galton, in the final chapter of *Anticipations.*
It is the voice of Nietzsche in his worst moments. And it is one of
the powerful voices of the twentieth century that may be summed
up by the name of Hitler—which is to say that it is one of the voices
of "madness and despair" that reverberate throughout *The Secret
Agent* and support the claims to prophetic authenticity that have
been made on its behalf.

The Professor is, however, momentarily in high spirits. He taps
the bomb in the breast-pocket of his jacket and states "forcibly":

---

*Friedrich Nietzsche, *The Will to Power,* trans. Walter Kaufmann and R. J. Holling-
dale (New York: Random House, 1967), p. 58.

" 'And yet I *am* the force.' " He is indeed an ancestor of Darth Vader, as he is also himself a collateral descendant of the anti-type of Christ who descends in the apocalyptic conclusion of *The Dunciad*:

> Lo! thy dread Empire, CHAOS! is restored;
> Light dies before thy uncreating word:
> Thy hand, great Anarch! lets the curtain fall;
> And Universal Darkness buries All.

The Perfect Anarchist needles Ossipon on their way to the Silenus, and Ossipon needles him back. Ossipon is a continual and convenient object of the Professor's " 'amicable contempt. You couldn't kill a fly' " (p. 245). Not quite true, but close enough. And Ossipon in turn knows that the Professor has a secret weakness, that he has no time, not enough time to carry through his project of extermination, to annihilate the multitudes whose masses invariably cause him to subside into despondency. Although he can blow himself and, say, twenty others into eternity, that does not answer: " 'eternity is a damned hole. It's time that you need' " (p. 246). The Professor sententiously shoots back: " 'My device is: No God! No master[!]' " (p. 246), and Ossipon reminds him of how vain all that will be when he, the Professor, is on his deathbed.

The Professor puts Ossipon aside by saying " 'What's the good of thinking what will be!' " and proposes instead a Bakunin-like toast " 'To the destruction of what is.' " He does so "calmly" but relapses at once into his obsessive rumination.

> The thought of a mankind as numerous as the sands of the seashore,
> as indestructible, as difficult to handle, oppressed him. The sound
> of exploding bombs was lost in their immensity of passive grains
> without an echo (p. 246).

Mankind here takes on the majesty and impregnability of inorganic nature. This is the mankind of God's promise to Abraham: "I will multiply thy seed as the stars of the heaven, and as the sand which is upon the sea shore" (Genesis 22:17). These grains of sand, moreover, are not simply indestructible; they can also be as difficult to handle and control as grains of unstable, explosive powder. But in

their passive immensity they can also stifle the sound of his destructive bombs. Even more, they are the grains of sand in an hour-
glass, the sands of time itself—the time which the Professor's bomb
has not blown up and which is also running out on him.

In the meantime, Ossipon has been re-reading the newspaper
account of Winnie's suicide, visualizing Winnie's terrified face and
realizing that "behind that white mask there was struggling against
terror and despair a vigour of vitality, a love of life that could resist
the furious anguish which drives to murder and the fear . . . of the
gallows" (p. 248). It is this vitality and love that he has betrayed, deliberately and knowingly, and to his dumb confoundment it has
been his ruination. In broken bewilderment he asks the Professor,
" 'What do you know of madness and despair?' " The latter replies
"doctorally"—

> "There are no such things. All passion is lost now. The world is
> mediocre, limp, without force. And madness and despair are a force.
> And force is a crime in the eyes of the fools . . . who rule the roost.
> You are mediocre. Verloc . . . was mediocre. . . . Everybody is
> mediocre. Madness and despair! Give me that for a lever, and I'll
> move the world. Ossipon, you have my cordial scorn. . . . You have
> no force" (pp. 248–249).

The ironic accent of "doctorally" can be taken as either applying to
a physician delivering a diagnosis or to "a learned doctor" delivering a lecture. In either instance, the diagnosis is entropy: things are
running downhill. Ossipon and almost everyone else are limp,
without force. In this respect at least, the Professor agrees with Inspector Heat. And as for the force of madness and despair that have
been evacuated from the social world—well, beginning in 1914
and extending thereafter with no end in sight, that world would
find itself embroiled in a sufficiency of it.

"The incorruptible Professor" walks out leaving Ossipon alone
with his disintegrating consciousness. "This act of madness or
despair" keeps repeating itself in him like the automatic tunes of
the player piano or the recurring circles of Stevie's mad artwork. He
has literally been stricken impotent. Like Winnie, he is going to
drown himself, but for him it will be a drowning in alcohol. "I am

seriously ill," he mutters to himself "with scientific insight" (p. 250), which is to say with no insight at all, since his illness is of the soul. Ossipon walks "aimlessly" (p. 242), but the route that he has unconsciously pursued around London is circular, and at the same time his inevitable future lies in a straight line directly ahead of him. It will take place "in the gutter," where he, a specimen-to-be of alcoholic degeneracy, will carry a sandwich board and walk on "disregarded."

The incorruptible Professor, by contrast, has "no future." He does not need or want it, since he is a force. His thoughts caress images of ruin and devastation. He walks miserable, weak, shabby, insignificant—

> and terrible in the simplicity of his idea calling madness and despair to the regeneration of the world. Nobody looked at him. He passed on, unsuspected and deadly, like a pest in the street full of men (p. 250).

On one count he is mistaken. He has a great future ahead of him, but the distinctive shapes in which it would materialize were as yet unknown—to him and to others. This is no stand-off, no impasse. It is the form in which a novelist sends his imagination of disaster out into the world. It is an imagination of the social and cultural future grounded profoundly in a historical present and driven by deeply felt apprehension and foreboding. But it is also driven by his imaginative identification with the forces of dissatisfaction and distress and rebellion, with what, in the way of humanity, has brought them about.

Who, then, is the Professor? The researches of Norman Sherry and others have demonstrated that Conrad's wide reading in radical books and pamphlets (along with his being an immensely intelligent observer and hence vibrantly responsive to the significant life of his epoch) had characteristically stimulated his creative sense. He habitually so to speak "absorbed" relevant material from a wide range of sources and persons and then, in an internal process that was highly pressurized and entailed a great deal of what may be roughly described as creative brooding, brought forth such "material" transfigured, fused and annealed in singular dramatic syntheses. So one can find resonances of a host of passages from anarchist writings and revolutionary periodicals and journals (including Irish ones) in those passages of the text that foreground the Professor or his speech. For example, the Professor's "device," "No God! No master[!]" was the creation of Auguste Blanqui, the post-1848 Jacobin, and, as Sherry demonstrates, Conrad could have come across it in a number of places.

Conrad, in other words, fabricated imaginary characters and situations that were intended at the same time to embody particular social ideas and cultural attitudes and tendencies. His fiction accordingly has a certain unyielding referential and historical bearing. Although the characters in his narrative are inventions, they do nonetheless have prototypes, and are based in part on actual persons. In *The Secret Agent*, moreover, the central episode is founded on an historical, public event. As a result, questions that test the relations between Conrad's representations of persons and events, and the historical factualities that supplied Conrad's points of departure, claim a genuine pertinence. Although he is not writing history, he is basing his narrative on an imaginative interpretation of matters that occurred in the realm of "reality." He is neither reproducing nor reporting literal truth, but his narrative has to capture and attain to the general truth or inward and spiritual significance of the historical episode, of the characters involved in its generation and experience, and of the larger dramatic and moral tendencies that both bear witness to.

All this is salient to any reckoning of the remarkable character of the Professor. In my view he is also substantially derived from (or should one rather say inspired by) three or three-plus figures. The first is Bakunin himself, a founder of anarchism and its virtual symbol. Bakunin's mantra, "the passion for destruction is a creative passion, too," is more or less annexed by the Professor. Other characteristics of Bakunin, who was as much a propagandist as he was anything else, are in addition distributed between Michaelis and Yundt. At the time of Conrad's writing, Bakunin was also widely thought to be the author of the *Catechism of the Revolutionist*, a notorious document which he had purportedly written in collaboration with Sergei Nechaev, his one time junior side-kick and the original of Stepan Verkhovensky, the radical nihilist in Dostoevsky's *Demons*.* Here is how some passages from the *Catechism* run.

1. The revolutionary is a doomed man. He has no interests of his own, no affairs, no feelings, no attachments, no belongings, not even a name. Everything in him is absorbed by a single exclusive interest, a single thought, a single passion, the revolution.

2. . . . He is an implacable enemy of this world, and if he continues to live in it, that is only to destroy it more effectively.

3. . . . To this end . . . alone, he will study mechanics, physics, chemistry. . . .

5. . . . The revolutionary is a dedicated man, merciless toward the state and toward the whole of educated and privileged society.

6. Hard toward himself, he must be hard toward others also. . . . Night and day he must have but one thought, one aim— merciless destruction. . . .

7. . . . The revolutionary passion, which in him becomes a habitual state of mind, must at every moment be combined with cold calculation. . . .

13. . . . The revolutionary enters into the world of the state, of class, and of so-called culture, and lives in it only because he has faith in its speedy and total destruction. He is not a revolutionary if he feels pity for anything in this world.[†]

And so on. The Professor is nameless, he has one single aim, he is cold and pitiless, and he is the angel of destruction. What more?

He is also a Professor, Professor Nietzsche, yet another solitary and maker of explosives, intellectual bombs and an original human

---

*More recent researches have proposed a reversal in the attribution of authorship. It is now supposed that Nechaev wrote the Catechism with some help, perhaps, from Bakunin. It may be thought of as a collaboration.

†Walter Laqueur, ed., *Voices of Terror* (New York: Reed Press, 2004), pp. 71–75; Michael Confino, *Daughter of a Revolutionary* (London: Alcove Press, 1974), pp. 221–230; Franco Venturi, *Roots of Revolution* (London: Phoenix Press, 2001), pp. lxxix–lxxxiv.

Twenty-first-century readers may want to consult *The Master of Petersburg* (New York: Viking Press, 1994) by J. M. Coetzee. This novel is largely an effort to imagine a series of meetings between Dostoevsky and Nechaev that would have taken place shortly before Dostoevsky turned to the writing of *Demons*.

bomb himself.* Nietzsche's sense of his own superiority and his irrepressible distaste for the weak, the submissive, the Christian, the
egalitarian, and the mediocre democratic masses of men and
women are all fully present and accounted for in the Professor. As
is his scorn for the less assertive sentiments, his anticipations of a
European apocalypse, his prophetic agonizings, and his megalo-
maniacal spiritual seizures. ("Madness and despair! Give me that
for a lever, and I'll move the world.") His writings uniquely combine blinding clarity of negative critical insight into certain of the
major tendencies of European culture and society along with an
unbalanced, agitated, and finally explosive repudiation of virtually
everything else that was entailed along with them, such as any dis-
crimination among various kinds of progress. This mixture has
made for a matrix of critical complexity and intellectual contradiction that is in all likelihood unexampled and insurmountable. For
a novelist of Conrad's inveterate skepticism, such turbulence must
have seemed both a challenge and an opportunity.

Nietzsche figures, moreover, in still another dimension in *The
Secret Agent*. There is the maimed cab driver, with his macabre
and apocalyptic horse, who drives Winnie and Stevie and their
mother across London to the "charity cottage," a dwelling so "tiny"
that it seems to be a "place of training for the still more straitened
circumstances of the grave" (p. 134). This alcoholic figure with
"jovial purple cheeks" (p. 139) is likened by the narrator to Virgil's
Silenus. In Book VI of the *Eclogues*, Silenus, drunk and hungover
as usual, sings to "the innocent shepherds of Sicily" (p. 139). His
songs are about the creation and the gods; but they are also about
such mortals as Pasiphae, who fell in love with a bull and gave birth
to the monster Minotaur, and about Philomela, who, raped by her
brother-in-law Tereus, was avenged when Tereus was served a cannibal feast made of his son's own flesh. Silenus's music transforms
mourning sisters into "grieving poplars," and he sings as well of
Apollo, whose own lyrics moved the river Eurotas to command his

---

*In *Ecce Homo*, "Why I Am a Destiny," part 1, Nietzsche writes, "I am no man, I
am dynamite." Written in 1888, *Ecce Homo* was not published until 1908. Conrad
could not have read it before writing *The Secret Agent*. The point to be taken, however, is how precise a likeness he had struck off.

laurels to "learn them by heart."* Conrad's Silenus wheezes boozily to Stevie about "domestic matters and the affairs of men whose sufferings are great and immortality by no means assured" (p. 139). With his " 'missus and four kids at 'ome,' " this night cabby sits behind his poor horse until the small hours, " 'Cold and 'ungry. Looking for fares. Drunks' " (p. 139). Touchy, exasperated but resigned, he says in regard to his miserable horse, " 'I've got to take out what they will blooming well give me at the yard' " (p. 139). Virgil's Silenus belongs to a pastoral poetic, an already nostalgic imagination of a simpler world that no longer existed. Conrad's Silenus is displaced altogether into an urban universe and an anti-pastoral vision which can do no more than barely recollect that there was once a poetry that celebrated a lost pastoral innocence.

Silenus was the tutor and companion of Dionysus, and the lesson of which the cabman reminds Stevie begins with " 'This ain't an easy world.' " Stevie disjointedly recalls: "Bad!" then "Poor!" then "Poor brute; poor people," then "Shame!"

> That little word contained all his sense of indignation and horror at one sort of wretchedness having to feed upon the anguish of the other—at the poor cabman beating the poor horse in the name, as it were, of his poor kids at home. And Stevie knew what it was to be beaten (p. 143).

Finally Stevie puts together the fragments of this primary lesson: " 'Bad world for poor people' " (p. 143). Is this "the cosmic chaos" that his mad art of circles attempted inconceivably to represent (p. 44)? Perhaps. For as the maimed and limping Silenus slowly departs with his horse and cab, the narrator directs our attention to "the scrunched gravel of the drive crying out under the slowly turning wheels. . . . The plaint of the gravel travelled slowly all round the drive" (p. 141). This sound of agony gathers up in the first instance Stevie's mother's "wail of pain" as she thinks of her "heroic" abandonment of her son. It refers as well to the poetry and songs of Silenus and Orpheus and Apollo that could make stones and rivers

---

The Eclogues of Virgil, trans. David Ferry (New York: Farrar, Straus, and Giroux, 1999), pp. 45–51.

and trees tearfully lament and tell their woeful stories. And it looks back, finally, to the mute "majesty of inorganic nature, of matter that never dies" (p. 19), that poets and writers have from the outset interrogated in the hope of finding articulations of coherence and meaning.

Silenus was the tutor and companion of Dionysus, and Dionysus is the god of tragedy, of tragic suffering and destruction. He is the god who in the cycle of each year was ritually dismembered— torn asunder, as Stevie is at Greenwich. This Silenus is also, however, the wise satyr of Nietzsche's *The Birth of Tragedy*. Compelled by King Midas to say what is the best and most excellent thing for human beings, Silenus declares: "why do you force me to tell you the very thing which it would be most profitable for you *not* to hear? The very best thing is utterly beyond your reach, not to have been born, not to *be*, to be *nothing*. However, the second best thing for you is: to die soon."*

The last we see of Conrad's Silenus is his approaching a pub wherein he will no doubt refresh his satyr's wisdom. But there is still one more Silenus, the restaurant and beer hall at which Ossipon and the Professor meet and talk, a noted gathering place for anarchists. And as is appropriate to an institution so named, the Silenus is furnished with music—the player piano being a travesty technological equivalent of the trees and rocks and streams that archaic poets like Silenus and Orpheus enchanted into spontaneous lyrical expression. Not only is the Professor, on this account, a split-off derivation from Nietzsche himself, but he is also endowed with the destructive impetus and blindness of Dionysus (while Stevie is the separated victimized and suffering side of the tragic god). And the final personified element of Nietzsche's heroic mythological theory is there as well. In the devastated Comrade Ossipon, the narrator makes out the counterpart of Dionysus, Apollo himself: he "raised his bowed head, beloved of various humble women of these isles, Apollo-like in the sunniness of its bush of hair" (p. 248). Apollo, god of the sun and light of reason, patron of medicine and

---

*Friedrich Nietzsche, *The Birth of Tragedy*, ed. Raymond Geuss and Ronald Speirs (Cambridge: Cambridge University Press, 1999), pp. 22f.

poetry, is transmuted in Apollo–Ossipon, former medical student, writer, adherent of reason and science—transmuted, but also capsized and disintegrated. In the modern world, the Apollonian principle of individuation, of sculptural clarity and appearance, of structure and measure, goes down to defeat. Corrupted contemporary "reason" in the form of popular "science" is unhinged by its own unacknowledged irrationality and involuntary dishonesty. Ossipon will never make his appointment with another woman, "an elderly nursery governess putting her trust in an Apollo-like ambrosial head" (p. 249). That head is bowed and ready to receive the yoke.*

The Professor, however, remains unbowed and walks off. In the final pages, the narrator takes to calling him the "incorruptible Professor." There is only one singular "incorruptible" in the annals of modern political life, the imperishably named "incorruptible Robespierre." In Carlyle's *The French Revolution*, which Conrad had almost certainly read, he is also called the "seagreen Incorruptible."† And so in addition to copious material derived from well-known nihilists, anarchists, and terrorists, Conrad has incorporated into the Professor unmistakable references to the grandest of historical terrorists: to Robespierre, the remorseless symbolic figure who presided over an extended moment in the inception of modern extremist politics; and to Nietzsche, one of the earliest and certainly the greatest of modern intellectual terrorists. Part of the distinction of Conrad's imaginative conception as well as the staying power of the character of the Professor can be attributed to the

---

*That Apollo was also the name of Conrad's father—poet, translator, failed and defeated nationalist revolutionary—opens upon matters that cannot be entered on here.

†Some of the physical features of the Professor closely resemble those set down by Carlyle in his first description of Robespierre: among the six hundred Deputies at the "States-General," Robespierre appears as "the meanest . . . slight, ineffectual-looking, under thirty, in spectacles . . . complexion . . . the final shade of which may be the pale sea-green." See Thomas Carlyle, *The French Revolution* (1837), part 1, book 4, chapter 4, and passim. It may be noted that Robespierre's complexion turns up again in the wallpaper, "an expanse of arsenical green, soiled with indelible smudges here and there," that covers the otherwise bare walls of the Professor's rented room (p. 243).

extraordinary creative tact with which Conrad has summoned together these disparate features and qualities and fused them into a
radically innovative and coherent principle and character. For the
Professor is also the signal modern terrorist: destructive, implacable, fanatical, extreme, incorruptible, ideological, cold, intelligent,
irrational, intransigent and unpersuadable, suicidal and deadly.

As the Professor walks down the street and away from the reader,
we realize him one last time as demonic and terrible, an almost
invisible secret agent of some mortal infirmity. He incorporates that
aspect of Dionysus which bears upon the madness and despair that
are incorrigible elements of fatality in human social life and that are
projected for us mimetically in tragic drama, and in its descendant,
the modern novel. But he also walks down the street "averting his
eyes from the odious multitude of mankind" (p. 250). That multitude troubles and threatens him. It shadows forth, nonetheless,
what Nietzsche regarded as the paradoxical "metaphysical sol-
ace . . . which we derive from every true tragedy," namely, that "in
the ground of things, and despite all changing appearances, life is
indestructibly mighty and pleasurable." This powerful intimation
appears in "the chorus of satyrs, a chorus of natural beings whose
life goes on ineradicably behind and beyond all civilization, as it
were, and who remain eternally the same despite all the changes of
generations and in the history of nations."* These satyrs are pri-
mordial, infra-human creatures, untouched by the exalted dignity of
the principals of tragedy. They are like natural matter itself, "inorganic nature . . . that never dies" (p. 19). Like Stevie and Winnie's
mother, and even Winnie herself in the ferocity and perversity of
her passion for Stevie, as well as the drunken Silenus of a cabman,
they figure also in and as the multitude, grains of sand on the
seashore. The Professor cannot bring himself to look at them. They
are "mediocre" and inferior, but as the multitude they persist, and it
is to figures like them that Conrad attributes a good deal of whatever
positive human and moral life gets represented in this darkest of

---

*Nietzsche, *The Birth of Tragedy*, p. 39.

novels. In view of what was just over the horizon for twentieth-century Western civilization, it was not an implausible choice.

Steven Marcus is Professor of English and Comparative Literature and George Delacorte Professor in the Humanities at Columbia University and a specialist in nineteenth-century literature and culture. A fellow of both the American Academy of Arts and Sciences and the Academy of Literary Studies, he has received Fulbright, American Council of Learned Societies, Guggenheim, Center for Advanced Study in the Behavioral Sciences, Rockefeller, and Mellon grants. He is the author of more than 200 publications.

Note on
this Edition

The Secret Agent emerged in several stages from what Conrad originally conceived as a short story entitled "Verloc." Beginning this story in the early spring of 1906, Conrad soon came to enlarge upon it, and in the course of nine months he produced the six chapters that became the first version of the novel. This earlier version was completed in November of 1906, while the work was being serialized (October–December 1906) in *Ridgway's: A Militant Weekly for God and Country*, an American journal which called the novel *A Secret Agent* and advertised it, without Conrad's sanction, as "A Tale of Diplomatic Intrigue and Anarchist Treachery." Midway through the work's serialization, Conrad decided to revise and expand it for publication in book form, and, having arranged to have the volume published by Methuen in London, he proceeded with the changes in 1907. The first English edition of *The Secret Agent*, subtitled *A Simple Tale*, appeared under Methuen's imprint in September of 1907; shortly thereafter, it was published in America, using Methuen's proofs, by Harper's. The novel was subsequently republished in 1921 by William Heinemann in the English Collected Edition of Conrad's works. The present text follows this 1921 edition, as well as making alterations and emendations suggested by the notes to and the text of Bruce Harkness and S. W. Reid's scholarly edition of *The Secret Agent* (Cambridge: Cambridge University Press, 1990). The changes in question are as follows: "sincere" replaces "serious" (p. 7); "reclusion" replaces "seclusion" (p. 44); "right" has been amended to "left" (p. 61); "windows" has been amended to "window" (p. 151); "villeggiature" replaces "villeggiatura" (pp. 157 and 161); "in process of" replaces "in pass of" (p. 183); and "conscience" replaces "conception" (p. 228).

—Tatiana M. Holway and Steven Marcus

The original division of responsibilities for this edition assumed that I would undertake to write the Introduction, that Dr. Holway would provide the footnotes and endnotes for the text, and that additional, ancillary editorial material would emerge from our joint efforts. In fact, it became clear almost at once that no such watertight separation was possible. Dr. Holway has made both substantive and editorial suggestions, contributions, and corrections to my Introduction and its notes, and I have suggested changes and revisions to her notes and commentaries on the text. The undertaking, as a result, has turned out to be genuinely collaborative, and each of us is pleased to acknowledge the improvements attained by means of such a partnership.

—**Steven Marcus**

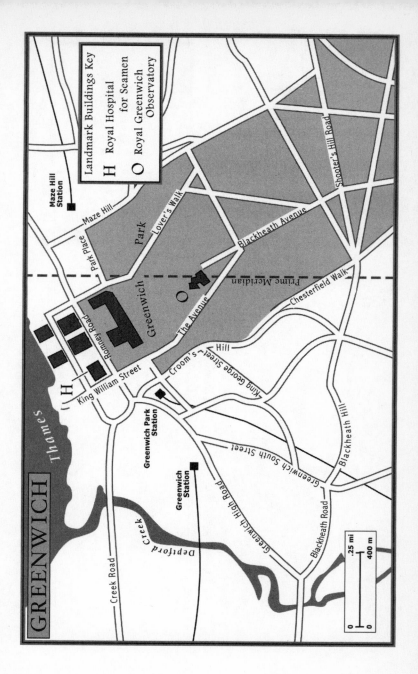

GREENWICH

Thames

Creek Road

Deptford Creek

Greenwich Station

Greenwich High Road

Blackheath Road

Greenwich South Street

.25 mi
0
400 m
0

Greenwich Park Station

King William Street

Croom's Hill

King George Street

Blackheath Hill

Chesterfield Walk

The Avenue

Blackheath Avenue

Shooter's Hill Road

Prime Meridian

Greenwich Park

Romney Road

Park Place

Maze Hill

Lover's Walk

Maze Hill Station

H

O

Landmark Buildings Key

H Royal Hospital
    for Seamen

O Royal Greenwich
    Observatory

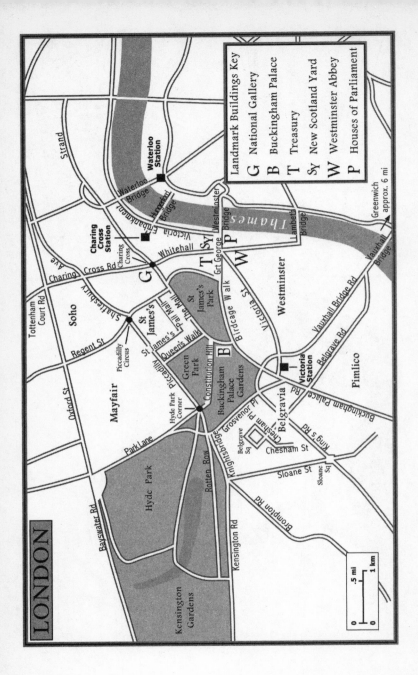

THE SECRET AGENT

A Simple Tale

TO

H. G. WELLS[1]

THE CHRONICLER OF MR. LEWISHAM'S LOVE
THE BIOGRAPHER OF KIPPS AND THE
HISTORIAN OF THE AGES TO COME
THIS SIMPLE TALE OF THE XIX CENTURY
IS AFFECTIONATELY OFFERED

Author's Note

The origin of *The Secret Agent*—subject, treatment, artistic purpose, and every other motive that may induce an author to take up his pen—can, I believe, be traced to a period of mental and emotional reaction.[1]

The actual facts are that I began this book impulsively and wrote it continuously.[2] When in due course it was bound and delivered to the public gaze I found myself reproved for having produced it at all. Some of the admonitions were severe, others had a sorrowful note. I have not got them textually before me, but I remember perfectly the general argument, which was very simple; and also my surprise at its nature. All this sounds a very old story now! And yet it is not such a long time ago. I must conclude that I had still preserved much of my pristine innocence in the year 1907. It seems to me now that even an artless person might have foreseen that some criticisms would be based on the ground of sordid surroundings and the moral squalor of the tale.

That of course is a serious objection. It was not universal. In fact it seems ungracious to remember so little reproof amongst so much intelligent and sympathetic appreciation;[3] and I trust that the readers of this Preface will not hasten to put it down to wounded vanity or a natural disposition to ingratitude. I suggest that a charitable heart could very well ascribe my choice to natural modesty. Yet it isn't exactly modesty that makes me select reproof for the illustration of my case. No, it isn't exactly modesty. I am not at all certain that I am modest; but those who have read so far through my work will credit me with enough decency, tact, savoir-faire, what you will, to prevent me from making a song for my own glory out of the words of other people. No! The true motive of my selection lies in quite a different trait. I have always had a propensity to justify my action. Not to defend. To justify. Not to insist that I was right, but simply to explain that there was no perverse intention, no secret scorn for the natural sensibilities of mankind at the bottom of my impulses.

3

It may be called an amiable weakness and dangerous only so far that it exposes one to the risk of becoming a bore. The world generally is not interested in the motives of any overt act, but in its consequences. Man may smile and smile,[4] but he is not an investigating animal. He loves the obvious. He shrinks from explanations. Yet I will go on with mine. It is obvious that I need not have written that book. I was under no necessity to deal with that subject—using the word subject both in the sense of the tale itself and in the larger one of a special manifestation in the life of mankind. This I fully admit. But the thought of elaborating mere ugliness in order to shock, or even simply to surprise my readers by a change of front, has never entered my head. In making this statement I expect to be believed, not only on the evidence of my general character, but also for the reason, which anybody can see, that the whole treatment of the tale, its inspiring indignation and underlying pity and contempt, prove my detachment from the squalor and sordidness which lie simply in the outward circumstances of the setting.

The inception of *The Secret Agent* followed immediately on a two years' period of intense absorption in the task of writing that remote novel, *Nostromo*, with its far-off Latin-American atmosphere and the profoundly personal *Mirror of the Sea*;[5] the first an intense creative effort on what I suppose will always remain my largest canvas, the second an unreserved attempt to unveil for a moment the profounder intimacies of the sea and the formative influences of nearly half my lifetime. It was a period too in which my sense of the truth of things was attended by a very intense imaginative and emotional readiness which, all genuine and faithful to facts as it was, yet made me feel (the task once done) as if I were left behind, aimless amongst mere husks of sensations and lost in a world of other, of inferior, values.

I don't know whether I really felt that I wanted a change—change in my imagination, in my vision, and in my mental attitude. I rather think that a change in the fundamental mood had already stolen over me unawares. I don't remember anything definite happening. With *The Mirror of the Sea* finished in the full consciousness that I had dealt honestly with myself and my readers in every line of that book, I gave myself up to a not unhappy pause.

Then, while I was yet standing still, as it were, and certainly not thinking of going out of my way to look for anything, the subject of *The Secret Agent*—I mean the tale—came to me in the shape of a few words uttered by a friend[6] in a casual conversation about anarchists or rather anarchist activities; how brought about I don't remember now.

I remember, however, remarking on the criminal futility of the whole thing, doctrine, action, mentality; and on the contemptible aspect of the half-crazy pose as of a brazen cheat exploiting the poignant miseries and passionate credulities of a mankind always so tragically eager for self-destruction. That was what made for me its philosophical pretences so unpardonable. Presently, passing to particular instances, we recalled the already old story of the attempt to blow up the Greenwich Observatory:[7] a blood-stained inanity of so fatuous a kind[8] that it was impossible to fathom its origin by any reasonable or even unreasonable process of thought. For perverse unreason has its own logical processes. But that thing could not be laid hold of mentally in any sort of way, so that one remained faced by the fact of a man blown to bits for nothing even most remotely resembling an idea, anarchistic or other. As to the outer wall of the Observatory, it did not show as much as the faintest crack.

I pointed all this out to my friend, who remained silent for a while, and then remarked in his characteristically casual and omniscient manner, "Oh, that fellow was half an idiot. His sister committed suicide afterwards."[9] These were absolutely the only words that passed between us; for extreme surprise at this unexpected piece of information kept me dumb for a moment, and he began at once to talk of something else. It never occurred to me later to ask how he arrived at his knowledge. I am sure that if he had seen once in his life the back of an anarchist that must have been the whole extent of his connection with the underworld. He was, however, a man who liked to talk with all sorts of people, and he may have gathered those illuminating facts at second or third hand, from a crossing-sweeper, from a retired police officer, from some vague man in his club, or even, perhaps, from a Minister of State met at some public or private reception.

Of the illuminating quality there could be no doubt whatever. One felt like a man walking out of a forest on to a plain—there was not much to see, but one had plenty of light. No, there was not much to see, and, frankly, for a considerable time I didn't even attempt to perceive anything. It was only the illuminating impression that remained. It remained satisfactory, but in a passive way. Then, about a week later, I came upon a book which as far as I know had never attained any prominence, the rather summary recollections of an Assistant Commissioner of Police,[10] an obviously able man with a strong religious strain in his character, who was appointed to his post on account of his special experience at the time of the dynamite outrages in London, away back in the eighties.[11] The book was fairly interesting, very discreet of course; and I have by now forgotten the bulk of its contents absolutely. It contained no revelations, it ran over the surface agreeably, and that was all. I won't even try to explain why I should have been arrested by a little passage of about ten lines, in which the author (I believe his name was Anderson) reproduced a short dialogue held in the Lobby of the House of Commons after some unexpected outrage, with the Secretary of State. I think it was Sir William Harcourt then.[12] He was very much irritated and the official was very apologetic. The phrase, amongst the three which passed between them, that struck me most was Sir W. Harcourt's angry sally: "All that's very well. But your idea of secrecy over there seems to consist of keeping the Home Secretary in the dark." Characteristic enough of Sir W. Harcourt's temper but not much in itself. There must have been, however, some sort of atmosphere in the whole incident, because all of a sudden I felt myself stimulated. And then ensued in my mind what a student of chemistry would best understand from the analogy of the addition of the tiniest little drop of the right kind, precipitating the process of crystallisation in a test tube containing some colourless solution.

It was at first for me a mental change, disturbing a quieted-down imagination, in which strange forms, sharp in outline but imperfectly apprehended, appeared and claimed attention as crystals will do by their bizarre and unexpected shapes. One fell to musing before the phenomenon — even of the past: of South America, a continent of crude sunshine and brutal revolutions, of the sea, the vast expanse of salt waters, the mirror of heaven's frowns and smiles, the reflector of the world's light. Then the vision of an enormous town presented itself, of a monstrous town more populous than some continents and in its man-made might as if indifferent to heaven's frowns and smiles; a cruel devourer of the world's light. There was room enough there to place any story, depth enough there for any passion, variety enough there for any setting, darkness enough to bury five millions of lives.

Irresistibly the town became the background for the ensuing period of deep and tentative meditations. Endless vistas opened before men in various directions. It would take years to find the right way! It seemed to take years! . . . Slowly the dawning conviction of Mrs. Verloc's maternal passion grew up to a flame between me and that background, tingeing it with its secret ardour and receiving from it in exchange some of its own hopeless colouring. At last the story of Winnie Verloc stood out complete from the days of her childhood to the end, unproportioned as yet, with everything still on the first plan, as it were; but ready now to be dealt with. All this took about three days.

This book is *that* story, reduced to manageable proportions, its whole course suggested and centred round the absurd cruelty of the Greenwich Park explosion. I had there a task I will not say arduous but of the most absorbing difficulty. But it had to be done. It was a necessity. The figures grouped about Mrs. Verloc and related directly or indirectly to her tragic suspicion that "life doesn't stand much looking into," are the outcome of that very necessity. Personally I have never had any doubt of the reality of Mrs. Verloc's story; but it had to be disengaged from its obscurity in that immense town, it had to be made credible, I don't mean so much as to her soul but as to her surroundings, not so much as to her psychology but as to her humanity. For the surroundings hints were not lacking. I had to fight hard to keep at arm's length the memories of my solitary and nocturnal walks all over London in my early days,[13] lest they should rush in and overwhelm each page of the story as these emerged one after another from a mood as sincere in feeling and thought as any in which I ever wrote a line. In that respect I really think that *The Secret Agent* is a perfectly genuine piece of work. Even the purely artistic purpose, that of applying an ironic method to a subject of that kind, was formulated with deliberation and in the earnest belief that ironic treatment alone would enable me to say all I felt I would have to say in scorn as well as in pity. It is one of the minor satisfactions of my writing life that having taken that resolve I did manage, it seems to me, to carry it right through to the end. As to the personages whom the absolute necessity of the case—Mrs. Verloc's case—brings out in front of the London background, from them too I obtained those little satisfactions which really count for so much against the mass of oppressive doubts that haunt so persistently every attempt at creative work. For instance, of Mr. Vladimir himself[14] (who was fair game for caricatural presentation) I was gratified to hear that an experienced man of the world had said "that Conrad must have been in touch with that sphere or else has an excellent intuition of things," because Mr. Vladimir was "not only possible in detail but quite right in essentials." Then a visitor from America informed me that all sorts of revolutionary refugees in New York[15] would have it that the book was written by somebody who knew a lot about them. This seems to me a very high compliment, considering that, as a matter of hard fact, I had seen even less of their kind than the omniscient friend who gave me the first suggestion for the novel. I have no doubt, however, that there had been moments during the writing of the book when I was an extreme revolutionist, I won't say more convinced than they, but certainly cherishing a more concentrated purpose than any of them had ever done in the whole course of his life. I don't say this to boast. I was simply attending to my business. In the matter of all my books I have always attended to my business. I have attended to it with complete self-surrender. And this statement too is not a boast. I could not have done otherwise. It would have bored me too much to make-believe.

The suggestions for certain personages of the tale, both law-abiding and lawless, came from various sources which, perhaps, here and there, some reader might have recognised. They are not very recondite. But I am not concerned here to legitimise any of those people, and even as to my general view of the moral reactions as between the criminal and the police all I will venture to say is that it seems to me to be at least arguable.

The twelve years that have elapsed since the publication of the book have not changed my attitude. I do not regret having written it. Lately, circumstances, which have nothing to do with the general tenor of this Preface, have compelled me to strip this tale of the literary robe[16] of indignant scorn it has cost me so much to fit on it decently, years ago. I have been forced, so to speak, to look upon its bare bones. I confess that it makes a grisly skeleton. But still I will submit that telling Winnie Verloc's story to its anarchistic end of utter desolation, madness, and despair, and telling it as I have told it here, I have not intended to commit a gratuitous outrage on the feelings of mankind.

J. C.
1920.

CHAPTER ONE

MR. VERLOC,[1] going out in the morning, left his shop nominally in charge of his brother-in-law. It could be done, because there was very little business at any time, and practically none at all before the evening. Mr. Verloc cared but little about his ostensible business. And, moreover, his wife was in charge of his brother-in-law.

The shop was small, and so was the house. It was one of those grimy brick houses which existed in large quantities before the era of reconstruction[2] dawned upon London. The shop was a square box of a place, with the front glazed in small panes. In the daytime the door remained closed; in the evening it stood discreetly but suspiciously ajar.

The window contained photographs of more or less undressed dancing girls; nondescript packages in wrappers like patent medicines; closed yellow paper envelopes, very flimsy, and marked two-and-six* in heavy black figures; a few numbers of ancient French comic publications[3] hung across a string as if to dry; a dingy blue china bowl, a casket of black wood, bottles of marking ink, and rubber stamps; a few books, with titles hinting at impropriety; a few apparently old copies of obscure newspapers, badly printed, with titles like *The Torch*, *The Gong*—rousing titles.[4] And the two gas-jets inside the panes were always turned low either for economy's sake or for the sake of the customers.

These customers were either very young men, who hung about the window for a time before slipping in suddenly; or men of a more mature age, but looking generally as if they were not in funds. Some of that last kind had the collars of their overcoats turned right up to their moustaches, and traces of mud on the bottom of their nether garments, which had the appearance of being much

---

*Two shillings and sixpence.

worn and not very valuable. And the legs inside them did not, as a general rule, seem of much account either. With their hands plunged deep in the side pockets of their coats, they dodged in sideways, one shoulder first, as if afraid to start the bell going.

The bell, hung on the door by means of a curved ribbon of steel, was difficult to circumvent. It was hopelessly cracked; but of an evening, at the slightest provocation, it clattered behind the customer with impudent virulence.

It clattered; and at that signal, through the dusty glass door behind the painted deal* counter, Mr. Verloc would issue hastily from the parlour at the back. His eyes were naturally heavy; he had an air of having wallowed, fully dressed, all day on an unmade bed. Another man would have felt such an appearance a distinct disadvantage. In a commercial transaction of the retail order much depends on the seller's engaging and amiable aspect. But Mr. Verloc knew his business, and remained undisturbed by any sort of æsthetic doubt about his appearance. With a firm, steady-eyed impudence, which seemed to hold back the threat of some abominable menace, he would proceed to sell over the counter some object looking obviously and scandalously not worth the money which passed in the transaction: a small cardboard box with apparently nothing inside, for instance, or one of those carefully closed yellow flimsy envelopes, or a soiled volume in paper covers with a promising title. Now and then it happened that one of the faded, yellow dancing girls would get sold to an amateur, as though she had been alive and young.

Sometimes it was Mrs. Verloc who would appear at the call of the cracked bell. Winnie Verloc was a young woman with a full bust, in a tight bodice, and with broad hips. Her hair was very tidy. Steady-eyed like her husband, she preserved an air of unfathomable indifference behind the rampart of the counter. Then the customer of comparatively tender years would get suddenly disconcerted at having to deal with a woman, and with rage in his heart would proffer a request for a bottle of marking ink, retail value sixpence (price in Verloc's shop one-and-sixpence),[5] which, once outside, he would drop stealthily into the gutter.

---

*Pine, fir, or other inexpensive wood.

The evening visitors—the men with collars turned up and soft hats rammed down—nodded familiarly to Mrs. Verloc, and with a muttered greeting, lifted up the flap at the end of the counter in order to pass into the back parlour, which gave access to a passage and to a steep flight of stairs. The door of the shop was the only means of entrance to the house in which Mr. Verloc carried on his business of a seller of shady wares, exercised his vocation of a protector of society, and cultivated his domestic virtues.[6] These last were pronounced. He was thoroughly domesticated. Neither his spiritual, nor his mental, nor his physical needs were of the kind to take him much abroad. He found at home the ease of his body and the peace of his conscience, together with Mrs. Verloc's wifely attentions and Mrs. Verloc's mother's deferential regard.

Winnie's mother was a stout, wheezy woman, with a large brown face. She wore a black wig under a white cap. Her swollen legs rendered her inactive. She considered herself to be of French descent, which might have been true; and after a good many years of married life with a licensed victualler* of the more common sort, she provided for the years of widowhood by letting furnished apartments for gentlemen near Vauxhall Bridge Road in a square once of some splendour and still included in the district of Belgravia.[7] This topographical fact was of some advantage in advertising her rooms; but the patrons of the worthy widow were not exactly of the fashionable kind. Such as they were, her daughter Winnie helped to look after them. Traces of the French descent which the widow boasted of were apparent in Winnie too. They were apparent in the extremely neat and artistic arrangement of her glossy dark hair. Winnie had also other charms: her youth; her full, rounded form; her clear complexion; the provocation of her unfathomable reserve, which never went so far as to prevent conversation, carried on on the lodgers' part with animation, and on hers with an equable amiability. It must be that Mr. Verloc was susceptible to these fascinations. Mr. Verloc was an intermittent patron. He came and went without any very apparent reason. He generally arrived in London (like the influenza) from the Continent, only he arrived unheralded by the Press;[8] and his visitations set in with great severity.

---

*Restaurant or tavern keeper licensed to sell alcohol.

He breakfasted in bed, and remained wallowing there with an air of quiet enjoyment till noon every day—and sometimes even to a later hour. But when he went out he seemed to experience a great difficulty in finding his way back to his temporary home in the Belgravian square. He left it late, and returned to it early—as early as three or four in the morning; and on waking up at ten addressed Winnie, bringing in the breakfast tray, with jocular, exhausted civility, in the hoarse, failing tones of a man who had been talking vehemently for many hours together. His prominent, heavy-lidded eyes rolled sideways amorously and languidly, the bedclothes were pulled up to his chin, and his dark smooth moustache covered his thick lips capable of much honeyed banter.

In Winnie's mother's opinion Mr. Verloc was a very nice gentleman. From her life's experience gathered in various "business houses" the good woman had taken into her retirement an ideal of gentlemanliness as exhibited by the patrons of private-saloon bars. Mr. Verloc approached that ideal; he attained it, in fact.

"Of course, we'll take over your furniture, mother," Winnie had remarked.

The lodging-house was to be given up. It seems it would not answer to carry it on. It would have been too much trouble for Mr. Verloc. It would not have been convenient for his other business. What his business was he did not say; but after his engagement to Winnie he took the trouble to get up before noon, and descending the basement stairs, make himself pleasant to Winnie's mother in the breakfast-room downstairs where she had her motionless being. He stroked the cat, poked the fire, had his lunch served to him there. He left its slightly stuffy cosiness with evident reluctance, but, all the same, remained out till the night was far advanced. He never offered to take Winnie to theatres, as such a nice gentleman ought to have done. His evenings were occupied. His work was in a way political, he told Winnie once. She would have, he warned her, to be very nice to his political friends. And with her straight, unfathomable glance she answered that she would be so, of course.

How much more he told her as to his occupation it was impossible for Winnie's mother to discover. The married couple took her over with the furniture. The mean aspect of the shop surprised her.

The change from the Belgravian square to the narrow street in Soho[9] affected her legs adversely. They became of an enormous size. On the other hand, she experienced a complete relief from material cares. Her son-in-law's heavy good nature inspired her with a sense of absolute safety. Her daughter's future was obviously assured, and even as to her son Stevie she need have no anxiety. She had not been able to conceal from herself that he was a terrible encumbrance, that poor Stevie. But in view of Winnie's fondness for her delicate brother, and of Mr. Verloc's kind and generous disposition, she felt that the poor boy was pretty safe in this rough world. And in her heart of hearts she was not perhaps displeased that the Verlocs had no children. As that circumstance seemed perfectly indifferent to Mr. Verloc, and as Winnie found an object of quasi-maternal affection in her brother, perhaps this was just as well for poor Stevie.

For he was difficult to dispose of, that boy. He was delicate and, in a frail way, good-looking too, except for the vacant droop of his lower lip. Under our excellent system of compulsory education[10] he had learned to read and write, notwithstanding the unfavourable aspect of the lower lip. But as errand-boy he did not turn out a great success. He forgot his messages; he was easily diverted from the straight path of duty by the attractions of stray cats and dogs, which he followed down narrow alleys into unsavoury courts; by the comedies of the streets, which he contemplated open-mouthed, to the detriment of his employer's interests; or by the dramas of fallen horses, whose pathos and violence induced him sometimes to shriek piercingly in a crowd, which disliked to be disturbed by sounds of distress in its quiet enjoyment of the national spectacle. When led away by a grave and protecting policeman, it would often become apparent that poor Stevie had forgotten his address — at least for a time. A brusque question caused him to stutter to the point of suffocation. When startled by anything perplexing he used to squint horribly. However, he never had any fits (which was encouraging); and before the natural outbursts of impatience on the part of his father he could always, in his childhood's days, run for protection behind the short skirts of his sister Winnie. On the other hand, he might have been suspected of hiding a fund of reckless naughtiness. When he had reached the age of fourteen, a friend of his late father, an agent for a foreign preserved-milk firm, having given him an opening as office-boy, he was discovered one foggy afternoon, in his chief's absence, busy letting off fireworks on the staircase. He touched off in quick succession a set of fierce rockets, angry catherine wheels,* loudly exploding squibs† —and the matter might have turned out very serious. An awful panic spread through the whole building. Wild-eyed, choking clerks stampeded through the passages full of smoke, silk hats and elderly business men could be seen rolling independently down the stairs. Stevie did not seem to derive any personal gratification from what he had done. His motives for this stroke of originality were difficult to discover. It was only later on that Winnie obtained from him a misty and confused confession. It seems that two other office-boys in the building had worked upon his feelings by tales of injustice and oppression till they had wrought his compassion to the pitch of that frenzy. But his father's friend, of course, dismissed him summarily as likely to ruin his business. After that altruistic exploit Stevie was put to help wash the dishes in the basement kitchen, and to black the boots of the gentlemen patronising the Belgravian mansion. There was obviously no future in such work. The gentlemen tipped him a shilling now and then. Mr. Verloc showed himself the most generous of lodgers. But altogether all that did not amount to much either in the way of gain or prospects; so that when Winnie announced her engagement to Mr. Verloc her mother could not help wondering, with a sigh and a glance towards the scullery,‡ what would become of poor Stephen now.

It appeared that Mr. Verloc was ready to take him over together with his wife's mother and with the furniture, which was the whole visible fortune of the family. Mr. Verloc gathered everything as it came to his broad, good-natured breast. The furniture was disposed to the best advantage all over the house, but Mrs. Verloc's mother was confined to two back rooms on the first floor. The luckless Stevie slept in one of them. By this time a growth of thin fluffy hair had come to blur, like a golden mist, the sharp line of his small lower

---

*Rotating fireworks.
†Firecrackers.
‡Area for washing dishes and performing other messy kitchen tasks.

jaw. He helped his sister with blind love and docility in her household duties. Mr. Verloc thought that some occupation would be good for him. His spare time he occupied by drawing circles with compass and pencil on a piece of paper. He applied himself to that pastime with great industry, with his elbows spread out and bowed low over the kitchen table. Through the open door of the parlour at the back of the shop Winnie, his sister, glanced at him from time to time with maternal vigilance.

CHAPTER TWO

SUCH was the house, the household, and the business Mr. Verloc left behind him on his way westward at the hour of half-past ten in the morning. It was unusually early for him; his whole person exhaled the charm of almost dewy freshness; he wore his blue cloth overcoat unbuttoned; his boots were shiny; his cheeks, freshly shaven, had a sort of gloss; and even his heavy-lidded eyes, refreshed by a night of peaceful slumber, sent out glances of comparative alertness. Through the park railings these glances beheld men and women riding in the Row,[1] couples can-tering past harmoniously, others advancing sedately at a walk, loi-tering groups of three or four, solitary horsemen looking unsociable, and solitary women followed at a long distance by a groom with a cockade* to his hat and a leather belt over his tight-fitting coat. Carriages went bowling by, mostly two-horse broughams,† with here and there a victoria‡ with the skin of some wild beast inside and a woman's face and hat emerging above the folded hood. And a peculiarly London sun—against which nothing could be said except that it looked bloodshot—glorified all this by its stare. It hung at a moderate elevation above Hyde Park Corner with an air of punctual and benign vigilance. The very pavement under Mr. Verloc's feet had an old-gold tinge in that diffused light, in which neither wall, nor tree, nor beast, nor man cast a shadow. Mr. Verloc was going westward through a town without shadows in an atmosphere of powdered old gold. There were red, coppery gleams on the roofs of houses, on the corners of walls, on the pan-els of carriages, on the very coats of the horses, and on the broad back of Mr. Verloc's overcoat, where they produced a dull effect of rustiness. But Mr. Verloc was not in the least conscious of having

---

*Ornament, such as a rosette, worn on a hat.
†Fashionable closed carriages.
‡Low, open carriage, seating one or two people; popular for ladies' outings.

got rusty. He surveyed through the park railings the evidences of the town's opulence and luxury with an approving eye. All these people had to be protected. Protection is the first necessity of opulence and luxury. They had to be protected; and their horses, carriages, houses, servants had to be protected; and the source of their wealth had to be protected in the heart of the city and the heart of the country; the whole social order favourable to their hygienic idleness had to be protected against the shallow enviousness of unhygienic labour.[2] It had to—and Mr. Verloc would have rubbed his hands with satisfaction had he not been constitutionally averse from every superfluous exertion. His idleness was not hygienic, but it suited him very well. He was in a manner devoted to it with a sort of inert fanaticism, or perhaps rather with a fanatical inertness. Born of industrious parents for a life of toil, he had embraced indolence from an impulse as profound, as inexplicable, and as imperious as the impulse which directs a man's preference for one particular woman in a given thousand. He was too lazy even for a mere demagogue, for a workman orator, for a leader of Labour. It was too much trouble. He required a more perfect form of ease; or it might have been that he was the victim of a philosophical unbelief in the effectiveness of every human effort. Such a form of indolence requires, implies, a certain amount of intelligence. Mr. Verloc was not devoid of intelligence—and at the notion of a menaced social order he would perhaps have winked to himself if there had not been an effort to make in that sign of scepticism. His big, prominent eyes were not well adapted to winking. They were rather of the sort that closes solemnly in slumber with majestic effect.

Undemonstrative and burly in a fat-pig style, Mr. Verloc, without either rubbing his hands with satisfaction or winking sceptically at his thoughts, proceeded on his way. He trod the pavement heavily with his shiny boots, and his general get-up was that of a well-to-do mechanic in business for himself. He might have been anything from a picture-frame maker to a locksmith; an employer of labour in a small way. But there was also about him an indescribable air which no mechanic could have acquired in the practice of his handicraft, however dishonestly exercised: the air common to men who live on the vices, the follies, or the baser fears of mankind; the air of moral nihilism common to keepers of gambling hells and disorderly houses; to private detectives and inquiry agents; to drink sellers and, I should say, to the sellers of invigorating electric belts and to the inventors of patent medicines.[3] But of that last I am not sure, not having carried my investigations so far into the depths. For all I know, the expression of these last may be perfectly diabolic. I shouldn't be surprised. What I want to affirm is that Mr. Verloc's expression was by no means diabolic.

Before reaching Knightsbridge, Mr. Verloc took a turn to the left out of the busy main thoroughfare, uproarious with the traffic of swaying omnibuses* and trotting vans, into the almost silent, swift flow of hansoms.† Under his hat, worn with a light backward tilt, his hair had been carefully brushed into respectful sleekness; for his business was with an Embassy. And Mr. Verloc, steady like a rock—a soft kind of rock—marched now along a street which could with every propriety be described as private. In its breadth, emptiness, and extent it had the majesty of inorganic nature, of matter that never dies. The only reminder of mortality was a doctor's brougham arrested in august solitude close to the curbstone. The polished knockers of the doors gleamed as far as the eye could reach, the clean windows shone with a dark opaque lustre. And all was still. But a milk cart rattled noisily across the distant perspective; a butcher boy, driving with the noble recklessness of a charioteer at Olympic Games,[4] dashed round the corner sitting high above a pair of red wheels. A guilty-looking cat issuing from under the stones ran for a while in front of Mr. Verloc, then dived into another basement; and a thick police constable, looking a stranger to every emotion, as if he, too, were part of inorganic nature, surging apparently out of a lamp-post, took not the slightest notice of Mr. Verloc. With a turn to the left Mr. Verloc pursued his way along a narrow street by the side of a yellow wall which, for some inscrutable reason, had No. 1 Chesham Square[5] written on it in black letters. Chesham Square was at least sixty yards away, and Mr. Verloc, cosmopolitan enough not to be deceived by London's topographical mysteries, held on steadily, without a sign

---

*Buses pulled by horses; used as mass transportation since the 1830s.
†Popular, small, two-wheeled carriages in which the driver sat in the back, thus permitting passengers to see where they were going.

of surprise or indignation. At last, with business-like persistency, he reached the Square, and made diagonally for the number 10. This belonged to an imposing carriage gate in a high, clean wall between two houses, of which one rationally enough bore the number 9 and the other was numbered 37; but the fact that this last belonged to Porthill Street, a street well known in the neighbourhood,[6] was proclaimed by an inscription placed above the ground-floor windows by whatever highly efficient authority is charged with the duty of keeping track of London's strayed houses.[7] Why powers are not asked of Parliament (a short Act would do) for compelling those edifices to return where they belong is one of the mysteries of municipal administration. Mr. Verloc did not trouble his head about it, his mission in life being the protection of the social mechanism, not its perfectionment or even its criticism.

It was so early that the porter of the Embassy issued hurriedly out of his lodge still struggling with the left sleeve of his livery coat. His waistcoat was red, and he wore knee-breeches, but his aspect was flustered. Mr. Verloc, aware of the rush on his flank, drove it off by simply holding out an envelope stamped with the arms of the Embassy, and passed on. He produced the same talisman also to the footman who opened the door, and stood back to let him enter the hall.

A clear fire burned in a tall fireplace, and an elderly man, standing with his back to it, in evening dress and with a chain round his neck, glanced up from the newspaper he was holding spread out in both hands before his calm and severe face. He didn't move; but another lackey, in brown trousers and claw-hammer coat* edged with thin yellow cord, approaching Mr. Verloc, listened to the murmur of his name, and turning round on his heel in silence, began to walk, without looking back once. Mr. Verloc, thus led along a ground-floor passage to the left of the great carpeted staircase, was suddenly motioned to enter a quite small room furnished with a heavy writing-table and a few chairs. The servant shut the door, and Mr. Verloc remained alone. He did not take a seat. With his hat

---

*Tailcoat.

and stick held in one hand he glanced about, passing his other podgy hand over his uncovered sleek head.

Another door opened noiselessly, and Mr. Verloc, immobilising his glance in that direction, saw at first only black clothes, the bald top of a head, and a drooping dark grey whisker on each side of a pair of wrinkled hands. The person who had entered was holding a batch of papers before his eyes and walked up to the table with a rather mincing step, turning the papers over the while. Privy Councillor Wurmt,[8] Chancelier d'Ambassade,* was rather short-sighted. This meritorious official, laying the papers on the table, disclosed a face of pasty complexion and of melancholy ugliness surrounded by a lot of fine, long dark grey hairs, barred heavily by thick and bushy eyebrows. He put on a black-framed pince-nez upon a blunt and shapeless nose, and seemed struck by Mr. Verloc's appearance. Under the enormous eyebrows his weak eyes blinked pathetically through the glasses.

He made no sign of greeting; neither did Mr. Verloc, who certainly knew his place; but a subtle change about the general outlines of his shoulders and back suggested a slight bending of Mr. Verloc's spine under the vast surface of his overcoat. The effect was of unobtrusive deference.

"I have here some of your reports," said the bureaucrat in an unexpectedly soft and weary voice, and pressing the tip of his forefinger on the papers with force. He paused; and Mr. Verloc, who had recognised his own handwriting very well, waited in an almost breathless silence. "We are not very satisfied with the attitude of the police here," the other continued, with every appearance of mental fatigue.

The shoulders of Mr. Verloc, without actually moving, suggested a shrug. And for the first time since he left his home that morning his lips opened.

"Every country has its police," he said philosophically. But as the official of the Embassy went on blinking at him steadily he felt constrained to add: "Allow me to observe that I have no means of action upon the police here."

---

*Chancellor of the embassy (French).

"What is desired," said the man of papers, "is the occurrence of something definite which should stimulate their vigilance. That is within your province—is it not so?"

Mr. Verloc made no answer except by a sigh, which escaped him involuntarily, for instantly he tried to give his face a cheerful expression. The official blinked doubtfully, as if affected by the dim light of the room. He repeated vaguely:

"The vigilance of the police—and the severity of the magistrates. The general leniency of the judicial procedure here, and the utter absence of all repressive measures, are a scandal to Europe. What is wished for just now is the accentuation of the unrest—of the fermentation which undoubtedly exists——"

"Undoubtedly, undoubtedly," broke in Mr. Verloc in a deep deferential bass of an oratorical quality, so utterly different from the tone in which he had spoken before that his interlocutor remained profoundly surprised. "It exists to a dangerous degree. My reports for the last twelve months make it sufficiently clear."

"Your reports for the last twelve months," State Councillor Wurmt began in his gentle and dispassionate tone, "have been read by me. I failed to discover why you wrote them at all."

A sad silence reigned for a time. Mr. Verloc seemed to have swallowed his tongue, and the other gazed at the papers on the table fixedly. At last he gave them a slight push.

"The state of affairs you expose there is assumed to exist as the first condition of your employment. What is required at present is not writing, but the bringing to light of a distinct, significant fact— I would almost say of an alarming fact."

"I need not say that all my endeavours shall be directed to that end," Mr. Verloc said, with convinced modulations in his conversational husky tone. But the sense of being blinked at watchfully behind the blind glitter of these eyeglasses on the other side of the table disconcerted him. He stopped short with a gesture of absolute devotion. The useful, hard-working, if obscure member of the Embassy had an air of being impressed by some newly born thought.

"You are very corpulent," he said.

This observation, really of a psychological nature, and advanced with the modest hesitation of an office-man more familiar with ink and paper than with the requirements of active life, stung

Mr. Verloc in the manner of a rude personal remark. He stepped back a pace.

"Eh? What were you pleased to say?" he exclaimed, with husky resentment.

The Chancelier d'Ambassade entrusted with the conduct of this interview seemed to find it too much for him.

"I think," he said, "that you had better see Mr. Vladimir. Yes, decidedly I think you ought to see Mr. Vladimir. Be good enough to wait here," he added, and went out with mincing steps.

At once Mr. Verloc passed his hand over his hair. A slight perspiration had broken out on his forehead. He let the air escape from his pursed-up lips like a man blowing at a spoonful of hot soup. But when the servant in brown appeared at the door silently, Mr. Verloc had not moved an inch from the place he had occupied throughout the interview. He had remained motionless, as if feeling himself surrounded by pitfalls.

He walked along a passage lighted by a lonely gas-jet, then up a flight of winding stairs, and through a glazed and cheerful corridor on the first floor. The footman threw open a door, and stood aside. The feet of Mr. Verloc felt a thick carpet. The room was large, with three windows; and a young man with a shaven, big face, sitting in a roomy arm-chair before a vast mahogany writing-table, said in French[9] to the Chancelier d'Ambassade, who was going out with the papers in his hand:

"You are quite right, *mon cher*.* He's fat—the animal."

Mr. Vladimir, First Secretary,[10] had a drawing-room reputation as an agreeable and entertaining man. He was something of a favourite in society. His wit consisted in discovering droll connections between incongruous ideas; and when talking in that strain he sat well forward on his seat, with his left hand raised, as if exhibiting his funny demonstrations between the thumb and forefinger, while his round and clean-shaven face wore an expression of merry perplexity.

But there was no trace of merriment or perplexity in the way he looked at Mr. Verloc. Lying far back in the deep arm-chair, with

---

*My dear (French).

squarely spread elbows, and throwing one leg over a thick knee, he had with his smooth and rosy countenance the air of a preternaturally thriving baby that will not stand nonsense from anybody.

"You understand French, I suppose?" he said.

Mr. Verloc stated huskily that he did. His whole vast bulk had a forward inclination. He stood on the carpet in the middle of the room, clutching his hat and stick in one hand; the other hung lifelessly by his side. He muttered unobtrusively somewhere deep down in his throat something about having done his military service in the French artillery. At once, with contemptuous perversity, Mr. Vladimir changed the language, and began to speak idiomatic English without the slightest trace of a foreign accent.

"Ah! Yes. Of course. Let's see. How much did you get for obtaining the design of the improved breech-block of their new field-gun?"

"Five years' rigorous confinement in a fortress," Mr. Verloc answered unexpectedly, but without any sign of feeling.

"You got off easily," was Mr. Vladimir's comment. "And, anyhow, it served you right for letting yourself get caught. What made you go in for that sort of thing—eh?"

Mr. Verloc's husky conversational voice was heard speaking of youth, of a fatal infatuation for an unworthy——

"Aha! *Cherchez la femme*,"* Mr. Vladimir deigned to interrupt, unbending, but without affability; there was, on the contrary, a touch of grimness in his condescension. "How long have you been employed by the Embassy here?" he asked.

"Ever since the time of the late Baron Stott-Wartenheim," Mr. Verloc answered in subdued tones, and protruding his lips sadly, in sign of sorrow for the deceased diplomat. The First Secretary observed this play of physiognomy steadily.

"Ah! ever since. . . . Well! What have you got to say for yourself?" he asked sharply.

Mr. Verloc answered with some surprise that he was not aware of having anything special to say. He had been summoned by a letter— And he plunged his hand busily into the side pocket of his overcoat,

---

*Literally, "Look for the woman" (French); figuratively, suggesting that a woman or an amatory entanglement will be found to be the source of the problem.

but before the mocking, cynical watchfulness of Mr. Vladimir concluded to leave it there.

"Bah!" said that latter. "What do you mean by getting out of condition like this? You haven't got even the physique of your profession. You—a member of a starving proletariat—never! You—a desperate socialist or anarchist—which is it?"

"Anarchist," stated Mr. Verloc in a deadened tone.

"Bosh!" went on Mr. Vladimir, without raising his voice. "You startled old Wurmt himself. You wouldn't deceive an idiot. They all are that, by-the-bye, but you seem to me simply impossible. So you began your connection with us by stealing the French gun designs. And you got yourself caught. That must have been very disagreeable to our Government. You don't seem to be very smart."

Mr. Verloc tried to exculpate himself huskily.

"As I've had occasion to observe before, a fatal infatuation for an unworthy——"

Mr. Vladimir raised a large white, plump hand.

"Ah yes. The unlucky attachment—of your youth. She got hold of the money, and then sold you to the police—eh?"

The doleful change in Mr. Verloc's physiognomy, the momentary drooping of his whole person, confessed that such was the regrettable case. Mr. Vladimir's hand clasped the ankle reposing on his knee. The sock was of dark blue silk.

"You see, that was not very clever of you. Perhaps you are too susceptible."

Mr. Verloc intimated in a throaty, veiled murmur that he was no longer young.

"Oh! That's a failing which age does not cure," Mr. Vladimir remarked, with sinister familiarity. "But no! You are too fat for that. You could not have come to look like this if you had been at all susceptible. I'll tell you what I think is the matter: you are a lazy fellow. How long have you been drawing pay from this Embassy?"

"Eleven years," was the answer, after a moment of sulky hesitation. "I've been charged with several missions to London while His Excellency Baron Stott-Wartenheim was still Ambassador in Paris. Then by His Excellency's instructions I settled down in London. I am English."

"You are! Are you? Eh?"

"A natural-born British subject," Mr. Verloc said stolidly. "But my father was French, and so——"

"Never mind explaining," interrupted the other. "I daresay you could have been legally a Marshal of France* and a Member of Parliament in England—and then, indeed, you would have been of some use to our Embassy."

This flight of fancy provoked something like a faint smile on Mr. Verloc's face. Mr. Vladimir retained an imperturbable gravity.

"But, as I've said, you are a lazy fellow; you don't use your opportunities. In the time of Baron Stott-Wartenheim we had a lot of soft-headed people running this Embassy. They caused fellows of your sort to form a false conception of the nature of a secret service fund. It is my business to correct this misapprehension by telling you what the secret service is not. It is not a philanthropic institution. I've had you called here on purpose to tell you this."

Mr. Vladimir observed the forced expression of bewilderment on Verloc's face, and smiled sarcastically.

"I see that you understand me perfectly. I daresay you are intelligent enough for your work. What we want now is activity—activity."

On repeating this last word Mr. Vladimir laid a long white forefinger on the edge of the desk. Every trace of huskiness disappeared from Verloc's voice. The nape of his gross neck became crimson above the velvet collar of his overcoat. His lips quivered before they came widely open.

"If you'll only be good enough to look up my record," he boomed out in his great, clear oratorical bass, "you'll see I gave a warning only three months ago, on the occasion of the Grand Duke Romuald's visit to Paris, which was telegraphed from here to the French police, and——"

"Tut, tut!" broke out Mr. Vladimir, with a frowning grimace. "The French police had no use for your warning. Don't roar like this. What the devil do you mean?"

With a note of proud humility Mr. Verloc apologised for forgetting himself. His voice, famous for years at open-air meetings and at workmen's assemblies in large halls, had contributed, he said, to

---

*A translation of *Maréchal de France*, a designation for the highest-ranking military officer of that country.

his reputation of a good and trustworthy comrade. It was, therefore, a part of his usefulness. It had inspired confidence in his principles. "I was always put up to speak by the leaders at a critical moment," Mr. Verloc declared, with obvious satisfaction. There was no uproar above which he could not make himself heard, he added; and suddenly he made a demonstration.

"Allow me," he said. With lowered forehead, without looking up, swiftly and ponderously he crossed the room to one of the French windows. As if giving way to an uncontrollable impulse, he opened it a little. Mr. Vladimir, jumping up amazed from the depths of the arm-chair, looked over his shoulder; and below, across the courtyard of the Embassy, well beyond the open gate, could be seen the broad back of a policeman watching idly the gorgeous perambulator of a wealthy baby being wheeled in state across the Square.

"Constable!" said Mr. Verloc, with no more effort than if he were whispering; and Mr. Vladimir burst into a laugh on seeing the policeman spin round as if prodded by a sharp instrument. Mr. Verloc shut the window quietly, and returned to the middle of the room.

"With a voice like that," he said, putting on the husky conversational pedal, "I was naturally trusted. And I knew what to say, too."

Mr. Vladimir, arranging his cravat,* observed him in the glass over the mantelpiece.

"I daresay you have the social revolutionary jargon by heart well enough," he said contemptuously. "*Vox et . . .*† You haven't ever studied Latin—have you?"

"No," growled Mr. Verloc. "You did not expect me to know it. I belong to the million. Who knows Latin? Only a few hundred imbeciles who aren't fit to take care of themselves."

For some thirty seconds longer Mr. Vladimir studied in the mirror the fleshy profile, the gross bulk, of the man behind him. And at the same time he had the advantage of seeing his own face, clean-shaved and round, rosy about the gills, and with the thin sensitive lips formed exactly for the utterance of those delicate

---

*A type of neck wear tied loosely in a bow.
†*Vox et prætera* (Latin): "a voice and nothing at all."

witticisms which had made him such a favourite in the very highest society. Then he turned, and advanced into the room with such determination that the very ends of his quaintly old-fashioned bow necktie seemed to bristle with unspeakable menaces. The movement was so swift and fierce that Mr. Verloc, casting an oblique glance, quailed inwardly.

"Aha! You dare be impudent," Mr. Vladimir began, with an amazingly guttural intonation not only utterly un-English, but absolutely un-European, and startling even to Mr. Verloc's experience of cosmopolitan slums. "You dare! Well, I am going to speak plain English to you. Voice won't do. We have no use for your voice. We don't want a voice. We want facts—startling facts—damn you!" he added, with a sort of ferocious discretion, right into Mr. Verloc's face.

"Don't you try to come over me with your hyperborean* manners," Mr. Verloc defended himself huskily, looking at the carpet. At this his interlocutor, smiling mockingly above the bristling bow of his necktie, switched the conversation into French.

"You give yourself for an *agent provocateur.*† The proper business of an *agent provocateur* is to provoke. As far as I can judge from your record kept here, you have done nothing to earn your money for the last three years."

"Nothing!" exclaimed Verloc, stirring not a limb, and not raising his eyes, but with the note of sincere feeling in his tone. "I have several times prevented what might have been——"

"There is a proverb in this country which says prevention is better than cure," interrupted Mr. Vladimir, throwing himself into the armchair. "It is stupid in a general way. There is no end to prevention. But it is characteristic. They dislike finality in this country. Don't you be too English. And in this particular instance, don't be absurd. The evil is already here. We don't want prevention—we want cure."

He paused, turned to the desk, and turning over some papers lying there, spoke in a changed business-like tone, without looking at Mr. Verloc.

---

*Literally, beyond the extreme north; figuratively, suggesting frigid; here, implying Russian and barbaric, as well.

†One employed to associate with suspected persons, feign sympathy with their cause, and incite them to take incriminating action (French).

"You know, of course, of the International Conference assembled in Milan?"[11]

Mr. Verloc intimated hoarsely that he was in the habit of reading the daily papers. To a further question his answer was that, of course, he understood what he read. At this Mr. Vladimir, smiling faintly at the documents he was still scanning one after another, murmured, "As long as it is not written in Latin, I suppose."

"Or Chinese," added Mr. Verloc stolidly.

"H'm. Some of your revolutionary friends' effusions are written in a *charabia** every bit as incomprehensible as Chinese——" Mr. Vladimir let fall disdainfully a grey sheet of printed matter. "What are all these leaflets headed F. P., with a hammer, pen, and torch crossed? What does it mean, this F. P.?"

Mr. Verloc approached the imposing writing-table.

"The Future of the Proletariat.[12] It's a society," he explained, standing ponderously by the side of the arm-chair, "not anarchist in principle, but open to all shades of revolutionary opinion."

"Are you in it?"

"One of the Vice-Presidents," Mr. Verloc breathed out heavily; and the First Secretary of the Embassy raised his head to look at him.

"Then you ought to be ashamed of yourself," he said incisively. "Isn't your society capable of anything else but printing this prophetic bosh in blunt type on this filthy paper—eh? Why don't you do something? Look here. I've this matter in hand now, and I tell you plainly that you will have to earn your money. The good old Stott-Wartenheim times are over. No work, no pay."

Mr. Verloc felt a queer sensation of faintness in his stout legs. He stepped back one pace, and blew his nose loudly.

He was, in truth, startled and alarmed. The rusty London sunshine struggling clear of the London mist shed a lukewarm brightness into the First Secretary's private room; and in the silence Mr. Verloc heard against a window-pane the faint buzzing of a fly—his first fly of the year—heralding better than any number of swallows the approach of spring. The useless fussing of that tiny

---

*Nonsense (French).

energetic organism affected unpleasantly this big man threatened in his indolence.

In the pause Mr. Vladimir formulated in his mind a series of disparaging remarks concerning Mr. Verloc's face and figure. The fellow was unexpectedly vulgar, heavy, and impudently unintelligent. He looked uncommonly like a master plumber[13] come to present his bill. The First Secretary of the Embassy, from his occasional excursions into the field of American humour, had formed a special notion of that class of mechanic as the embodiment of fraudulent laziness and incompetency.

This was then the famous and trusty secret agent, so secret that he was never designated otherwise but by the symbol Δ[14] in the late Baron Stott-Wartenheim's official, semi-official, and confidential correspondence; the celebrated agent Δ,[15] whose warnings had the power to change the schemes and the dates of royal, imperial, or grand ducal journeys, and sometimes caused them to be put off altogether! This fellow! And Mr. Vladimir indulged mentally in an enormous and derisive fit of merriment, partly at his own astonishment, which he judged naïve, but mostly at the expense of the universally regretted Baron Stott-Wartenheim. His late Excellency, whom the august favour of his Imperial master had imposed as Ambassador upon several reluctant Ministers of Foreign Affairs, had enjoyed in his lifetime a fame for an owlish, pessimistic gullibility. His Excellency had the social revolution on the brain. He imagined himself to be a diplomatist set apart by a special dispensation to watch the end of diplomacy, and pretty nearly the end of the world, in a horrid democratic upheaval. His prophetic and doleful dispatches had been for years the joke of Foreign Offices. He was said to have exclaimed on his deathbed (visited by his Imperial friend and master): "Unhappy Europe! Thou shalt perish by the moral insanity of thy children!" He was fated to be the victim of the first humbugging rascal that came along, thought Mr. Vladimir, smiling vaguely at Mr. Verloc.

"You ought to venerate the memory of Baron Stott-Wartenheim," he exclaimed suddenly.

The lowered physiognomy of Mr. Verloc expressed a sombre and weary annoyance.

"Permit me to observe to you," he said, "that I came here because I was summoned by a peremptory letter. I have been here only twice before in the last eleven years, and certainly never at eleven in the morning. It isn't very wise to call me up like this. There is just a chance of being seen. And that would be no joke for me."

Mr. Vladimir shrugged his shoulders.

"It would destroy my usefulness," continued the other hotly.

"That's your affair," murmured Mr. Vladimir, with soft brutality. "When you cease to be useful you shall cease to be employed. Yes. Right off. Cut short. You shall——" Mr. Vladimir, frowning, paused, at a loss for a sufficiently idiomatic expression, and instantly brightened up, with a grin of beautifully white teeth. "You shall be chucked," he brought out ferociously.

Once more Mr. Verloc had to react with all the force of his will against that sensation of faintness running down one's legs which once upon a time had inspired some poor devil with the felicitous expression: "My heart went down into my boots." Mr. Verloc, aware of the sensation, raised his head bravely.

Mr. Vladimir bore the look of heavy inquiry with perfect serenity.

"What we want is to administer a tonic to the Conference in Milan," he said airily. "Its deliberations upon international action for the suppression of political crime don't seem to get anywhere. England lags. This country is absurd with its sentimental regard for individual liberty. It's intolerable to think that all your friends have got only to come over to——"

"In that way I have them all under my eye," Mr. Verloc interrupted huskily.

"It would be much more to the point to have them all under lock and key. England must be brought into line. The imbecile bourgeoisie of this country make themselves the accomplices of the very people whose aim is to drive them out of their houses to starve in ditches. And they have the political power still, if they only had the sense to use it for their preservation. I suppose you agree that the middle classes are stupid?"

Mr. Verloc agreed hoarsely.

"They are."

"They have no imagination. They are blinded by an idiotic vanity. What they want just now is a jolly good scare. This is the psychological moment to set your friends to work. I have had you called here to develop to you my idea."

And Mr. Vladimir developed his idea from on high, with scorn and condescension, displaying at the same time an amount of ignorance as to the real aims, thoughts, and methods of the revolutionary world which filled the silent Mr. Verloc with inward consternation. He confounded causes with effects more than was excusable; the most distinguished propagandists with impulsive bomb-throwers; assumed organisation where in the nature of things it could not exist; spoke of the social revolutionary party one moment as of a perfectly disciplined army, where the word of chiefs was supreme, and at another as if it had been the loosest association of desperate brigands that ever camped in a mountain gorge. Once Mr. Verloc had opened his mouth for a protest, but the raising of a shapely, large white hand arrested him. Very soon he became too appalled to even try to protest. He listened in a stillness of dread which resembled the immobility of profound attention.

"A series of outrages," Mr. Vladimir continued calmly, "executed here in this country; not only *planned* here—that would not do—they would not mind. Your friends could set half the Continent on fire without influencing the public opinion here in favour of a universal repressive legislation. They will not look outside their backyard here."

Mr. Verloc cleared his throat, but his heart failed him, and he said nothing.

"These outrages need not be especially sanguinary," Mr. Vladimir went on, as if delivering a scientific lecture, "but they must be sufficiently startling—effective. Let them be directed against buildings, for instance. What is the fetish of the hour that all the bourgeoisie recognise—eh, Mr. Verloc?"

Mr. Verloc opened his hands and shrugged his shoulders slightly.

"You are too lazy to think," was Mr. Vladimir's comment upon that gesture. "Pay attention to what I say. The fetish of to-day is neither royalty nor religion. Therefore the palace and the church should be left alone. You understand what I mean, Mr. Verloc?"

The dismay and the scorn of Mr. Verloc found vent in an attempt at levity.

"Perfectly. But what of the Embassies? A series of attacks on the various Embassies," he began; but he could not withstand the cold, watchful stare of the First Secretary.

"You can be facetious, I see," the latter observed carelessly. "That's all right. It may enliven your oratory at socialistic congresses. But this room is no place for it. It would be infinitely safer for you to follow carefully what I am saying. As you are being called upon to furnish facts instead of cock-and-bull stories, you had better try to make your profit off what I am taking the trouble to explain to you. The sacrosanct fetish of to-day is science.[16] Why don't you get some of your friends to go for that wooden-faced panjandrum*—eh? Is it not part of these institutions which must be swept away before the F. P. comes along?"

Mr. Verloc said nothing. He was afraid to open his lips lest a groan should escape him.

"This is what you should try for. An attempt upon a crowned head or on a president is sensational enough in a way, but not so much as it used to be. It has entered into the general conception of the existence of all chiefs of state. It's almost conventional—especially since so many presidents have been assassinated.[17] Now let us take an outrage upon—say a church. Horrible enough at first sight, no doubt, and yet not so effective as a person of an ordinary mind might think. No matter how revolutionary and anarchist in inception, there would be fools enough to give such an outrage the character of a religious manifestation. And that would detract from the especial alarming significance we wish to give to the act. A murderous attempt on a restaurant or a theatre would suffer in the same way from the suggestion of non-political passion: the exasperation of a hungry man, an act of social revenge. All this is used up; it is no longer instructive as an object-lesson in revolutionary anarchism. Every newspaper has ready-made phrases to explain such manifestations away. I am about to give you the philosophy of bomb-throwing from my point of view; from the point of view you pretend to have been serving for the last eleven years. I will try not to talk above your head. The sensibilities of the class you are attacking are soon blunted. Property seems to them an indestructible thing. You can't count upon their emotions either of pity or fear[18] for very long. A bomb outrage to have any influence on public opinion now must go beyond

---

*Pompous personage, pretentious official (from the Grand Panjandrum, a figure in a nonsense story by the eighteenth-century satirical playwright Samuel Foote).

the intention of vengeance or terrorism. It must be purely destructive. It must be that, and only that, beyond the faintest suspicion of any other object. You anarchists should make it clear that you are perfectly determined to make a clean sweep of the whole social creation. But how to get that appallingly absurd notion into the heads of the middle classes so that there should be no mistake? That's the question. By directing your blows at something outside the ordinary passions of humanity is the answer. Of course, there is art. A bomb in the National Gallery[19] would make some noise. But it would not be serious enough. Art has never been their fetish. It's like breaking a few back windows in a man's house; whereas, if you want to make him really sit up, you must try at least to raise the roof. There would be some screaming, of course, but from whom? Artists—art critics and such like—people of no account. Nobody minds what they say. But there is learning—science. Any imbecile that has got an income believes in that. He does not know why, but he believes it matters somehow. It is the sacrosanct fetish. All the damned professors are Radicals at heart. Let them know that their great panjandrum has got to go too, to make room for the Future of the Proletariat. A howl from all these intellectual idiots is bound to help forward the labours of the Milan Conference. They will be writing to the papers. Their indignation would be above suspicion, no material interests being openly at stake, and it will alarm every selfishness of the class which should be impressed. They believe that in some mysterious way science is at the source of their material prosperity. They do. And the absurd ferocity of such a demonstration will affect them more profoundly than the mangling of a whole street—or theatre—full of their own kind. To that last they can always say: 'Oh! it's mere class hate.' But what is one to say to an act of destructive ferocity so absurd as to be incomprehensible, inexplicable, almost unthinkable; in fact, mad? Madness alone is truly terrifying, inasmuch as you cannot placate it either by threats, persuasion, or bribes. Moreover, I am a civilised man. I would never dream of directing you to organise a mere butchery, even if I expected the best results from it. But I wouldn't expect from a butchery the result I want. Murder is always with us. It is almost an institution. The demonstration must be against learning—science. But not every science will do. The attack must have all the shocking senselessness of gratuitous blasphemy.

Since bombs are your means of expression, it would be really telling if one could throw a bomb into pure mathematics. But that is impossible. I have been trying to educate you; I have expounded to you the higher philosophy of your usefulness, and suggested to you some serviceable arguments. The practical application of my teaching interests *you* mostly. But from the moment I have undertaken to interview you I have also given some attention to the practical aspect of the question. What do you think of having a go at astronomy?"

For some time already Mr. Verloc's immobility by the side of the arm-chair resembled a state of collapsed coma—a sort of passive insensibility interrupted by slight convulsive starts, such as may be observed in the domestic dog having a nightmare on the hearthrug. And it was in an uneasy doglike growl that he repeated the word:

"Astronomy."

He had not recovered thoroughly as yet from that state of bewilderment brought about by the effort to follow Mr. Vladimir's rapid incisive utterance. It had overcome his power of assimilation. It had made him angry. This anger was complicated by incredulity. And suddenly it dawned upon him that all this was an elaborate joke. Mr. Vladimir exhibited his white teeth in a smile, with dimples on his round, full face posed with a complacent inclination above the bristling bow of his necktie. The favourite of intelligent society women had assumed his drawing-room attitude accompanying the delivery of delicate witticisms. Sitting well forward, his white hand upraised, he seemed to hold delicately between his thumb and forefinger the subtlety of his suggestion.

"There could be nothing better. Such an outrage combines the greatest possible regard for humanity with the most alarming display of ferocious imbecility. I defy the ingenuity of journalists to persuade their public that any given member of the proletariat can have a personal grievance against astronomy. Starvation itself could hardly be dragged in there—eh? And there are other advantages. The whole civilised world has heard of Greenwich.[20] The very boot-blacks in the basement of Charing Cross Station know something of it. See?"

The features of Mr. Vladimir, so well known in the best society by their humorous urbanity, beamed with cynical self-satisfaction, which would have astonished the intelligent women his wit entertained so exquisitely. "Yes," he continued, with a contemptuous smile, "the blowing up of the first meridian is bound to raise a howl of execration."

"A difficult business," Mr. Verloc mumbled, feeling that this was the only safe thing to say.

"What is the matter? Haven't you the whole gang under your hand? The very pick of the basket? That old terrorist Yundt is here. I see him walking about Piccadilly[21] in his green havelock* almost every day. And Michaelis, the ticket-of-leave† apostle—you don't mean to say you don't know where he is? Because if you don't, I can tell you," Mr. Vladimir went on menacingly. "If you imagine that you are the only one on the secret fund list, you are mistaken."

This perfectly gratuitous suggestion caused Mr. Verloc to shuffle his feet slightly.

"And the whole Lausanne lot[22]—eh? Haven't they been flocking over here at the first hint of the Milan Conference? This is an absurd country."

"It will cost money," Mr. Verloc said, by a sort of instinct.

"That cock won't fight,"‡ Mr. Vladimir retorted, with an amazingly genuine English accent. "You'll get your screw§ every month, and no more till something happens. And if nothing happens very soon you won't get even that. What's your ostensible occupation? What are you supposed to live by?"

"I keep a shop," answered Mr. Verloc.

"A shop! What sort of shop?"

"Stationery, newspapers. My wife——"

"Your what?" interrupted Mr. Vladimir in his guttural Central Asian tones.

"My wife." Mr. Verloc raised his husky voice slightly. "I am married."

"That be damned for a yarn," exclaimed the other in unfeigned astonishment. "Married! And you a professed anarchist, too! What

---

*Usually, a covering attached to a hat to protect the neck; here, a cape attached to an overcoat.
†Paroled; in British usage, a colloquial term for "order of license," which allows a convict liberty, with some restrictions, before a sentence has expired.
‡Figurative expression for "That won't do."
§Wages.

is this confounded nonsense? But I suppose it's merely a manner of speaking. Anarchists don't marry. It's well known. They can't. It would be apostasy."

"My wife isn't one," Mr. Verloc mumbled sulkily. "Moreover, it's no concern of yours."

"Oh yes, it is," snapped Mr. Vladimir. "I am beginning to be convinced that you are not at all the man for the work you've been employed on. Why, you must have discredited yourself completely in your own world by your marriage. Couldn't you have managed without? This is your virtuous attachment—eh? What, with one sort of attachment and another you are doing away with your usefulness."

Mr. Verloc, puffing out his cheeks, let the air escape violently, and that was all. He had armed himself with patience. It was not to be tried much longer. The First Secretary became suddenly very curt, detached, final.

"You may go now," he said. "A dynamite outrage must be provoked. I give you a month. The sittings of the Conference are suspended. Before it reassembles again something must have happened here, or your connection with us ceases."

He changed the note once more with an unprincipled versatility.

"Think over my philosophy, Mr. — Mr. — Verloc," he said, with a sort of chaffing condescension, waving his hand towards the door. "Go for the first meridian. You don't know the middle classes as well as I do. Their sensibilities are jaded. The first meridian. Nothing better, and nothing easier, I should think."

He had got up, and with his thin sensitive lips twitching humorously, watched in the glass over the mantelpiece Mr. Verloc backing out of the room heavily, hat and stick in hand. The door closed.

The footman in trousers, appearing suddenly in the corridor, let Mr. Verloc another way out and through a small door in the corner of the courtyard. The porter standing at the gate ignored his exit completely; and Mr. Verloc retraced the path of his morning's pilgrimage as if in a dream—an angry dream. This detachment from the material world was so complete that, though the mortal envelope of Mr. Verloc had not hastened unduly along the streets, that part of him to which it would be unwarrantably rude to refuse immortality,

found itself at the shop door all at once, as if borne from west to east
on the wings of a great wind. He walked straight behind the counter,
and sat down on a wooden chair that stood there. No one appeared
to disturb his solitude. Stevie, put into a green baize* apron, was now
sweeping and dusting upstairs, intent and conscientious, as though
he were playing at it; and Mrs. Verloc, warned in the kitchen by the
clatter of the cracked bell, had merely come to the glazed door of the
parlour, and putting the curtain aside a little, had peered into the
dim shop. Seeing her husband sitting there shadowy and bulky, with
his hat tilted far back on his head, she had at once returned to her
stove. An hour or more later she took the green baize apron off her
brother Stevie, and instructed him to wash his hands and face in the
peremptory tone she had used in that connection for fifteen years or
so—ever since she had, in fact, ceased to attend to the boy's hands
and face herself. She spared presently a glance away from her dishing-up for the inspection of that face and those hands which Stevie,
approaching the kitchen table, offered for her approval with an air of
self-assurance hiding a perpetual residue of anxiety. Formerly the
anger of the father was the supremely effective sanction of these
rites, but Mr. Verloc's placidity in domestic life would have made
all mention of anger incredible—even to poor Stevie's nervousness.
The theory was that Mr. Verloc would have been inexpressibly
pained and shocked by any deficiency of cleanliness at mealtimes.
Winnie after the death of her father found considerable consolation
in the feeling that she need no longer tremble for poor Stevie. She
could not bear to see the boy hurt. It maddened her. As a little girl
she had often faced with blazing eyes the irascible licensed victualler
in defence of her brother. Nothing now in Mrs. Verloc's appearance
could lead one to suppose that she was capable of a passionate
demonstration.

She finished her dishing-up. The table was laid in the parlour.
Going to the foot of the stairs, she screamed out "Mother!" Then
opening the glazed door leading to the shop, she said quietly,
"Adolf!" Mr. Verloc had not changed his position; he had not apparently stirred a limb for an hour and a half. He got up heavily,

---

*Coarse woolen fabric.

and came to his dinner in his overcoat and with his hat on, without uttering a word. His silence in itself had nothing startlingly unusual in this household, hidden in the shades of the sordid street seldom touched by the sun, behind the dim shop with its wares of disreputable rubbish. Only that day Mr. Verloc's taciturnity was so obviously thoughtful that the two women were impressed by it. They sat silent themselves, keeping a watchful eye on poor Stevie, lest he should break out into one of his fits of loquacity. He faced Mr. Verloc across the table, and remained very good and quiet, staring vacantly. The endeavour to keep him from making himself objectionable in any way to the master of the house put no inconsiderable anxiety into these two women's lives. "That boy," as they alluded to him softly between themselves, had been a source of that sort of anxiety almost from the very day of his birth. The late licensed victualler's humiliation at having such a very peculiar boy for a son manifested itself by a propensity to brutal treatment; for he was a person of fine sensibilities, and his sufferings as a man and a father were perfectly genuine. Afterwards Stevie had to be kept from making himself a nuisance to the single gentlemen lodgers, who are themselves a queer lot, and are easily aggrieved. And there was always the anxiety of his mere existence to face. Visions of a workhouse infirmary for her child[23] had haunted the old woman in the basement breakfast-room of the decayed Belgravian house. "If you had not found such a good husband, my dear," she used to say to her daughter, "I don't know what would have become of that poor boy."

Mr. Verloc extended as much recognition to Stevie as a man not particularly fond of animals may give to his wife's beloved cat; and this recognition, benevolent and perfunctory, was essentially of the same quality. Both women admitted to themselves that not much more could be reasonably expected. It was enough to earn for Mr. Verloc the old woman's reverential gratitude. In the early days, made sceptical by the trials of friendless life, she used sometimes to ask anxiously: "You don't think, my dear, that Mr. Verloc is getting tired of seeing Stevie about?" To this Winnie replied habitually by a slight toss of her head. Once, however, she retorted, with a rather grim pertness: "He'll have to get tired of me first." A long silence ensued. The mother, with her feet propped up on a stool, seemed to be trying to get to the bottom of that answer, whose feminine profundity had struck her all of a heap. She had never really understood why Winnie had married Mr. Verloc. It was very sensible of her, and evidently had turned out for the best, but her girl might have naturally hoped to find somebody of a more suitable age. There had been a steady young fellow, only son of a butcher in the next street, helping his father in business, with whom Winnie had been walking out with obvious gusto. He was dependent on his father, it is true; but the business was good, and his prospects excellent. He took her girl to the theatre on several evenings. Then just as she began to dread to hear of their engagement (for what could she have done with that big house alone, with Stevie on her hands?), that romance came to an abrupt end, and Winnie went about looking very dull. But Mr. Verloc turning up providentially to occupy the first-floor front bedroom, there had been no more question of the young butcher. It was clearly providential.

CHAPTER THREE

ALL idealisation makes life poorer. To beautify it is to take away its character of complexity—it is to destroy it. ... Leave that to the moralists, my boy. History is made by men, but they do not make it in their heads. The ideas that are born in their consciousness play an insignificant part in the march of events. History is dominated and determined by the tool and the production—by the force of economic conditions. Capitalism has made socialism, and the laws made by capitalism for the protection of property are responsible for anarchism. No one can tell what form the social organisation may take in the future. Then why indulge in prophetic phantasies? At best they can only interpret the mind of the prophet, and can have no objective value. Leave that pastime to the moralists, my boy."

Michaelis, the ticket-of-leave apostle,[1] was speaking in an even voice, a voice that wheezed as if deadened and oppressed by the layer of fat on his chest. He had come out of a highly hygienic prison round like a tub, with an enormous stomach and distended cheeks of a pale, semi-transparent complexion, as though for fifteen years the servants of an outraged society had made a point of stuffing him with fattening foods in a damp and lightless cellar. And ever since he had never managed to get his weight down as much as an ounce.

It was said that for three seasons running a very wealthy old lady had sent him for a cure to Marienbad[2]—where he was about to share the public curiosity once with a crowned head—but the police on that occasion ordered him to leave within twelve hours. His martyrdom was continued by forbidding him all access to the healing waters. But he was resigned now.

With his elbow presenting no appearance of a joint, but more like a bend in a dummy's limb, thrown over the back of a chair, he leaned forward slightly over his short and enormous thighs to spit into the grate.

"Yes! I had the time to think things out a little," he added without emphasis. "Society has given me plenty of time for meditation."

On the other side of the fireplace, in the horsehair arm-chair where Mrs. Verloc's mother was generally privileged to sit, Karl Yundt[3] giggled grimly, with a faint black grimace of a toothless mouth. The terrorist, as he called himself, was old and bald, with a narrow, snow-white wisp of a goatee hanging limply from his chin. An extraordinary expression of underhand malevolence survived in his extinguished eyes. When he rose painfully the thrusting forward of a skinny groping hand deformed by gouty swellings* suggested the effort of a moribund murderer summoning all his remaining strength for a last stab. He leaned on a thick stick, which trembled under his other hand.

"I have always dreamed," he mouthed fiercely, "of a band of men absolute in their resolve to discard all scruples in the choice of means, strong enough to give themselves frankly the name of destroyers, and free from the taint of that resigned pessimism which rots the world. No pity for anything on earth, including themselves, and death enlisted for good and all in the service of humanity— that's what I would have liked to see."

His little bald head quivered, imparting a comical vibration to the wisp of white goatee. His enunciation would have been almost totally unintelligible to a stranger. His worn-out passion, resembling in its impotent fierceness the excitement of a senile sensualist, was badly served by a dried throat and toothless gums which seemed to catch the tip of his tongue. Mr. Verloc, established in the corner of the sofa at the other end of the room, emitted two hearty grunts of assent.

The old terrorist turned slowly his head on his skinny neck from side to side.

"And I could never get as many as three such men together. So much for your rotten pessimism," he snarled at Michaelis, who uncrossed his thick legs, similar to bolsters, and slid his feet abruptly under his chair in sign of exasperation.

---

*Inflammations of the joints traditionally associated with excessive consumption of meat and alcohol.

He a pessimist! Preposterous! He cried out that the charge was outrageous. He was so far from pessimism that he saw already the end of all private property coming along logically, unavoidably, by the mere development of its inherent viciousness. The possessors of property had not only to face the awakened proletariat, but they had also to fight amongst themselves. Yes. Struggle, warfare, was the condition of private ownership.[4] It was fatal. Ah! he did not depend upon emotional excitement to keep up his belief, no declamations, no anger, no visions of blood-red flags waving, or metaphorical lurid suns of vengeance rising above the horizon of a doomed society. Not he! Cold reason, he boasted, was the basis of his optimism. Yes, optimism——

His laborious wheezing stopped, then, after a gasp or two, he added:

"Don't you think that, if I had not been the optimist I am, I could not have found in fifteen years some means to cut my throat? And, in the last instance, there were always the walls of my cell to dash my head against."

The shortness of breath took all fire, all animation out of his voice; his great, pale cheeks hung like filled pouches, motionless, without a quiver; but in his blue eyes, narrowed as if peering, there was the same look of confident shrewdness, a little crazy in its fixity, they must have had while the indomitable optimist sat thinking at night in his cell. Before him, Karl Yundt remained standing, one wing of his faded greenish havelock thrown back cavalierly over his shoulder. Seated in front of the fireplace, Comrade Ossipon,[5] ex-medical student, the principal writer of the F. P. leaflets, stretched out his robust legs, keeping the soles of his boots turned up to the glow in the grate. A bush of crinkly yellow hair topped his red, freckled face, with a flattened nose and prominent mouth cast in the rough mould of the negro type. His almond-shaped eyes leered languidly over the high cheek-bones. He wore a grey flannel shirt, the loose ends of a black silk tie hung down the buttoned breast of his serge* coat; and his head resting on the back of his chair, his throat largely exposed, he raised to his lips a cigarette in a long wooden tube, puffing jets of smoke straight up at the ceiling.

---

*Durable twill fabric.

Michaelis pursued his idea—*the* idea of his solitary reclusion—the thought vouchsafed to his captivity and growing like a faith revealed in visions. He talked to himself, indifferent to the sympathy or hostility of his hearers, indifferent indeed to their presence, from the habit he had acquired of thinking aloud hopefully in the solitude of the four whitewashed walls of his cell, in the sepulchral silence of the great blind pile of bricks near a river, sinister and ugly like a colossal mortuary for the socially drowned.

He was no good in discussion, not because any amount of argument could shake his faith, but because the mere fact of hearing another voice disconcerted him painfully, confusing his thoughts at once—these thoughts that for so many years, in a mental solitude more barren than a waterless desert, no living voice had ever combated, commented, or approved.

No one interrupted him now, and he made again the confession of his faith, mastering him irresistible and complete like an act of grace: the secret of fate discovered in the material side of life; the economic condition of the world responsible for the past and shaping the future; the source of all history, of all ideas, guiding the mental development of mankind and the very impulses of their passion——

A harsh laugh from Comrade Ossipon cut the tirade dead short in a sudden faltering of the tongue and a bewildered unsteadiness of the apostle's mildly exalted eyes. He closed them slowly for a moment, as if to collect his routed thoughts. A silence fell; but what with the two gas-jets over the table and the glowing grate the little parlour behind Mr. Verloc's shop had become frightfully hot. Mr. Verloc, getting off the sofa with ponderous reluctance, opened the door leading into the kitchen to get more air, and thus disclosed the innocent Stevie, seated very good and quiet at a deal table, drawing circles, circles, circles; innumerable circles, concentric, eccentric; a coruscating whirl of circles that by their tangled multitude of repeated curves, uniformity of form, and confusion of intersecting lines suggested a rendering of cosmic chaos, the symbolism of a mad art attempting the inconceivable. The artist never turned his head; and in all his soul's application to the task his back quivered, his thin neck, sunk into a deep hollow at the base of the skull, seemed ready to snap.

Mr. Verloc, after a grunt of disapproving surprise, returned to the sofa. Alexander Ossipon got up, tall in his threadbare blue serge suit under the low ceiling, shook off the stiffness of long immobility, and strolled away into the kitchen (down two steps) to look over Stevie's shoulder. He came back, pronouncing oracularly: "Very good. Very characteristic, perfectly typical."

"What's very good?" grunted inquiringly Mr. Verloc, settled again in the corner of the sofa. The other explained his meaning negligently, with a shade of condescension and a toss of his head towards the kitchen:

"Typical of this form of degeneracy—these drawings, I mean."

"You would call that lad a degenerate, would you?" mumbled Mr. Verloc.

Comrade Alexander Ossipon—nicknamed the Doctor, ex-medical student without a degree; afterwards wandering lecturer to working-men's associations upon the socialistic aspects of hygiene; author of a popular quasi-medical study (in the form of a cheap pamphlet seized promptly by the police) entitled *The Corroding Vices of the Middle Classes*;[6] special delegate of the more or less mysterious Red Committee, together with Karl Yundt and Michaelis for the work of literary propaganda—turned upon the obscure familiar of at least two Embassies that glance of insufferable, hopelessly dense sufficiency which nothing but the frequentation of science can give to the dullness of common mortals.

"That's what he may be called scientifically. Very good type too, altogether, of that sort of degenerate. It's enough to glance at the lobes of his ears. If you read Lombroso[7]——"

Mr. Verloc, moody and spread largely on the sofa, continued to look down the row of his waistcoat buttons; but his cheeks became tinged by a faint blush. Of late even the merest derivative of the word science (a term in itself inoffensive and of indefinite meaning) had the curious power of evoking a definitely offensive mental vision of Mr. Vladimir, in his body as he lived, with an almost supernatural clearness. And this phenomenon, deserving justly to be classed amongst the marvels of science, induced in Mr. Verloc an emotional state of dread and exasperation tending to express itself in violent swearing. But he said nothing. It was Karl Yundt who was heard, implacable to his last breath:

"Lombroso is an ass."

Comrade Ossipon met the shock of this blasphemy by an awful, vacant stare. And the other, his extinguished eyes without gleams blackening the deep shadows under the great, bony forehead, mumbled, catching the tip of his tongue between his lips at every second word as though he were chewing it angrily:

"Did you ever see such an idiot? For him the criminal is the prisoner. Simple, is it not? What about those who shut him up there— forced him in there? Exactly. Forced him in there. And what is crime? Does he know that, this imbecile who has made his way in this world of gorged fools by looking at the ears and teeth of a lot of poor, luckless devils? Teeth and ears mark the criminal! Do they? And what about the law that marks him still better—the pretty branding instrument invented by the overfed to protect themselves against the hungry? Red-hot applications on their vile skins—hey? Can't you smell and hear from here the thick hide of the people burn and sizzle? That's how criminals are made for your Lombrosos to write their silly stuff about."

The knob of his stick and his legs shook together with passion, whilst the trunk, draped in the wings of the havelock, preserved his historic attitude of defiance. He seemed to sniff the tainted air of social cruelty, to strain his ear for its atrocious sounds. There was an extraordinary force of suggestion in this posturing. The all-but-moribund veteran of dynamite wars had been a great actor in his time—actor on platforms, in secret assemblies, in private interviews. The famous terrorist had never in his life raised personally as much as his little finger against the social edifice. He was no man of action; he was not even an orator of torrential eloquence, sweeping the masses along in the rushing noise and foam of a great enthusiasm. With a more subtle intention, he took the part of an insolent and venomous evoker of sinister impulses which lurk in the blind envy and exasperated vanity of ignorance, in the suffering and misery of poverty, in all the hopeful and noble illusions of righteous anger, pity, and revolt. The shadow of his evil gift clung to him yet like the smell of a deadly drug in an old vial of poison, emptied now, useless, ready to be thrown away upon the rubbish heap of things that had served their time.

Michaelis, the ticket-of-leave apostle, smiled vaguely with his glued lips; his pasty moon face drooped under the weight of melancholy assent. He had been a prisoner himself. His own skin had sizzled under the red-hot brand, he murmured softly. But Comrade Ossipon, nicknamed the Doctor, had got over the shock in time.

"You don't understand," he began disdainfully, but stopped short, intimidated by the dead blackness of the cavernous eyes in the face turned slowly towards him with a blind stare, as if guided only by the sound. He gave the discussion up, with a light shrug of the shoulders.

Stevie, accustomed to move about disregarded, had got up from the kitchen table, carrying off his drawing to bed with him. He had reached the parlour door in time to receive in full the shock of Karl Yundt's eloquent imagery. The sheet of paper covered with circles dropped out of his fingers, and he remained staring at the old terrorist, as if rooted suddenly to the spot by his morbid horror and dread of physical pain. Stevie knew very well that hot iron applied to one's skin hurt very much. His scared eyes blazed with indignation: it would hurt terribly. His mouth dropped open.

Michaelis by staring unwinkingly at the fire had regained that sentiment of isolation necessary for the continuity of his thought. His optimism had begun to flow from his lips. He saw Capitalism doomed in its cradle, born with the poison of the principle of competition in its system. The great capitalists devouring the little capitalists, concentrating the power and the tools of production in great masses, perfecting industrial processes, and in the madness of self-aggrandisement only preparing, organising, enriching, making ready the lawful inheritance of the suffering proletariat. Michaelis pronounced the great word "Patience"—and his clear blue glance, raised to the low ceiling of Mr. Verloc's parlour, had a character of seraphic trustfulness. In the doorway Stevie, calmed, seemed sunk in hebetude.*

Comrade Ossipon's face twitched with exasperation.

"Then it's no use doing anything—no use whatever."

"I don't say that," protested Michaelis gently. His vision of truth had grown so intense that the sound of a strange voice failed to rout it this time. He continued to look down at the red coals. Preparation for the future was necessary, and he was willing to admit that the great change would perhaps come in the upheaval of a revolution. But he argued that revolutionary propaganda was a delicate work of high conscience. It was the education of the masters of the

---

*Lethargy, dullness.

world. It should be as careful as the education given to kings. He would have it advance its tenets cautiously, even timidly, in our ignorance of the effect that may be produced by any given economic change upon the happiness, the morals, the intellect, the history of mankind. For history is made with tools, not with ideas; and everything is changed by economic conditions—art, philosophy, love, virtue—truth itself!

The coals in the grate settled down with a slight crash; and Michaelis, the hermit of visions in the desert of a penitentiary, got up impetuously. Round like a distended balloon, he opened his short, thick arms, as if in a pathetically hopeless attempt to embrace and hug to his breast a self-regenerated universe. He gasped with ardour.

"The future is as certain as the past—slavery, feudalism, individualism, collectivism. This is the statement of a law, not an empty prophecy."

The disdainful pout of Comrade Ossipon's thick lips accentuated the negro type of his face.

"Nonsense," he said calmly enough. "There is no law and no certainty. The teaching propaganda be hanged. What the people knows does not matter, were its knowledge ever so accurate. The only thing that matters to us is the emotional state of the masses. Without emotion there is no action."

He paused, then added with modest firmness:

"I am speaking now to you scientifically—scientifically——Eh? What did you say, Verloc?"

"Nothing," growled from the sofa Mr. Verloc, who, provoked by the abhorrent sound, had merely muttered a "Damn."

The venomous spluttering of the old terrorist without teeth was heard.

"Do you know how I would call the nature of the present economic conditions? I would call it cannibalistic. That's what it is! They are nourishing their greed on the quivering flesh and the warm blood of the people—nothing else."

Stevie swallowed the terrifying statement with an audible gulp, and at once, as though it had been swift poison, sank limply in a sitting posture on the steps of the kitchen door.

Michaelis gave no sign of having heard anything. His lips seemed glued together for good; not a quiver passed over his heavy cheeks. With troubled eyes he looked for his round, hard hat,* and put it on his round head. His round and obese body seemed to float low between the chairs under the sharp elbow of Karl Yundt. The old terrorist, raising an uncertain and clawlike hand, gave a swaggering tilt to a black felt sombrero shading the hollows and ridges of his wasted face. He got in motion slowly, striking the floor with his stick at every step. It was rather an affair to get him out of the house because, now and then, he would stop, as if to think, and did not offer to move again till impelled forward by Michaelis. The gentle apostle grasped his arm with brotherly care; and behind them, his hands in his pockets, the robust Ossipon yawned vaguely. A blue cap with a patent leather peak set well at the back of his yellow bush of hair gave him the aspect of a Norwegian sailor bored with the world after a thundering spree. Mr. Verloc saw his guests off the premises, attending them bareheaded, his heavy overcoat hanging open, his eyes on the ground.

He closed the door behind their backs with restrained violence, turned the key, shot the bolt. He was not satisfied with his friends. In the light of Mr. Vladimir's philosophy of bomb-throwing they appeared hopelessly futile. The part of Mr. Verloc in revolutionary politics having been to observe, he could not all at once, either in his own home or in larger assemblies, take the initiative of action. He had to be cautious. Moved by the just indignation of a man well over forty, menaced in what is dearest to him—his repose and his security—he asked himself scornfully what else could have been expected from such a lot, this Karl Yundt, this Michaelis—this Ossipon.

Pausing in his intention to turn off the gas burning in the middle of the shop, Mr. Verloc descended into the abyss of moral reflections. With the insight of a kindred temperament he pronounced his verdict. A lazy lot—this Karl Yundt, nursed by a blear-eyed old woman, a woman he had years ago enticed away from a friend, and afterwards had tried more than once to shake off into the gutter. Jolly lucky for Yundt that she had persisted in coming up time after time, or else there would have been no one now to help him out of the 'bus by the Green Park railings, where

---

*A bowler, a popular hat in late Victorian Britain.

that spectre took its constitutional crawl every fine morning. When that indomitable snarling old witch died the swaggering spectre would have to vanish too—there would be an end to fiery Karl Yundt. And Mr. Verloc's morality was offended also by the optimism of Michaelis, annexed by his wealthy old lady, who had taken lately to sending him to a cottage she had in the country. The ex-prisoner could moon about the shady lanes for days together in a delicious and humanitarian idleness. As to Ossipon, that beggar was sure to want for nothing as long as there were silly girls with savings-bank books in the world. And Mr. Verloc, temperamentally identical with his associates, drew fine distinctions in his mind on the strength of insignificant differences. He drew them with a certain complacency, because the instinct of conventional respectability was strong within him, being only overcome by his dislike of all kinds of recognised labour—a temperamental defect which he shared with a large proportion of revolutionary reformers of a given social state. For obviously one does not revolt against the advantages and opportunities of that state, but against the price which must be paid for the same in the coin of accepted morality, self-restraint, and toil. The majority of revolutionists are the enemies of discipline and fatigue mostly. There are natures, too, to whose sense of justice the price exacted looms up monstrously enormous, odious, oppressive, worrying, humiliating, extortionate, intolerable. Those are the fanatics. The remaining portion of social rebels is accounted for by vanity, the mother of all noble and vile illusions, the companion of poets, reformers, charlatans, prophets, and incendiaries.

Lost for a whole minute in the abyss of meditation, Mr. Verloc did not reach the depth of these abstract considerations. Perhaps he was not able. In any case he had not the time. He was pulled up painfully by the sudden recollection of Mr. Vladimir, another of his associates, whom in virtue of subtle moral affinities he was capable of judging correctly. He considered him as dangerous. A shade of envy crept into his thoughts. Loafing was all very well for these fellows, who knew not Mr. Vladimir, and had women to fall back upon; whereas he had a woman to provide for——

At this point, by a simple association of ideas, Mr. Verloc was brought face to face with the necessity of going to bed some time or other that evening. Then why not go now—at once? He sighed. The necessity was not so normally pleasurable as it ought to have been for a man of his age and temperament. He dreaded the demon of sleeplessness, which he felt had marked him for its own. He raised his arm, and turned off the flaring gas-jet above his head.

A bright band of light fell through the parlour door into the part of the shop behind the counter. It enabled Mr. Verloc to ascertain at a glance the number of silver coins in the till. These were but few; and for the first time since he opened his shop he took a commercial survey of its value. This survey was unfavourable. He had gone into trade for no commercial reasons. He had been guided in the selection of this peculiar line of business by an instinctive leaning towards shady transactions, where money is picked up easily. Moreover, it did not take him out of his own sphere—the sphere which is watched by the police. On the contrary, it gave him a publicly confessed standing in that sphere, and as Mr. Verloc had unconfessed relations which made him familiar with yet careless of the police, there was a distinct advantage in such a situation. But as a means of livelihood it was by itself insufficient.

He took the cash-box out of the drawer, and turning to leave the shop, became aware that Stevie was still downstairs.

What on earth is he doing there? Mr. Verloc asked himself. What's the meaning of these antics? He looked dubiously at his brother-in-law, but he did not ask him for information. Mr. Verloc's intercourse with Stevie was limited to the casual mutter of a morning, after breakfast, "My boots," and even that was more a communication at large of a need than a direct order or request. Mr. Verloc perceived with some surprise that he did not know really what to say to Stevie. He stood still in the middle of the parlour, and looked into the kitchen in silence. Nor yet did he know what would happen if he did say anything. And this appeared very queer to Mr. Verloc in view of the fact, borne upon him suddenly, that he had to provide for this fellow too. He had never given a moment's thought till then to that aspect of Stevie's existence.

Positively he did not know how to speak to the lad. He watched him gesticulating and murmuring in the kitchen. Stevie prowled round the table like an excited animal in a cage. A tentative "Hadn't you better go to bed now?" produced no effect whatever;

and Mr. Verloc, abandoning the stony contemplation of his brother-in-law's behaviour, crossed the parlour wearily, cash-box in hand. The cause of the general lassitude he felt while climbing the stairs being purely mental, he became alarmed by its inexplicable character. He hoped he was not sickening for anything.* He stopped on the dark landing to examine his sensations. But a slight and continuous sound of snoring pervading the obscurity interfered with their clearness. The sound came from his mother-in-law's room. Another one to provide for, he thought—and on this thought walked into the bedroom.

Mrs. Verloc had fallen asleep with the lamp (no gas was laid upstairs)[8] turned up full on the table by the side of the bed. The light thrown down by the shade fell dazzlingly on the white pillow sunk by the weight of her head reposing with closed eyes and dark hair done up in several plaits for the night. She woke up with the sound of her name in her ears, and saw her husband standing over her.

"Winnie! Winnie!"

At first she did not stir, lying very quiet and looking at the cash-box in Mr. Verloc's hand. But when she understood that her brother was "capering all over the place downstairs" she swung out in one sudden movement on to the edge of the bed. Her bare feet, as if poked through the bottom of an unadorned, sleeved calico sack, buttoned tightly at neck and wrists, felt over the rug for the slippers while she looked upward into her husband's face.

"I don't know how to manage him," Mr. Verloc explained peevishly. "Won't do to leave him downstairs alone with the lights."

She said nothing, glided across the room swiftly, and the door closed upon her white form.

Mr. Verloc deposited the cash-box on the night table, and began the operation of undressing by flinging his overcoat on to a distant chair. His coat and waistcoat followed. He walked about the room in his stockinged feet, and his burly figure, with the hands worrying nervously at his throat, passed and repassed across the long strip of looking-glass in the door of his wife's wardrobe. Then, after slipping his braces off his shoulders, he pulled up violently the venetian

---

*Becoming ill.

blind, and leaned his forehead against the cold window-pane—a fragile film of glass stretched between him and the enormity of cold, black, wet, muddy, inhospitable accumulation of bricks, slates, and stones, things in themselves unlovely and unfriendly to man.

Mr. Verloc felt the latent unfriendliness of all out of doors with a force approaching to positive bodily anguish. There is no occupation that fails a man more completely than that of a secret agent of police. It's like your horse suddenly falling dead under you in the midst of an uninhabited and thirsty plain. The comparison occurred to Mr. Verloc because he had sat astride various army horses in his time, and had now the sensation of an incipient fall. The prospect was as black as the window-pane against which he was leaning his forehead. And suddenly the face of Mr. Vladimir, clean-shaven and witty, appeared enhaloed in the glow of its rosy complexion like a sort of pink seal impressed on the fatal darkness.

This luminous and mutilated vision was so ghastly physically that Mr. Verloc started away from the window, letting down the venetian blind with a great rattle. Discomposed and speechless with the apprehension of more such visions, he beheld his wife re-enter the room and get into bed in a calm business-like manner which made him feel hopelessly lonely in the world. Mrs. Verloc expressed her surprise at seeing him up yet.

"I don't feel very well," he muttered, passing his hands over his moist brow.

"Giddiness?"

"Yes. Not at all well."

Mrs. Verloc, with all the placidity of an experienced wife, expressed a confident opinion as to the cause, and suggested the usual remedies; but her husband, rooted in the middle of the room, shook his lowered head sadly.

"You'll catch cold standing there," she observed.

Mr. Verloc made an effort, finished undressing, and got into bed. Down below in the quiet, narrow street measured footsteps approached the house, then died away unhurried and firm, as if the passer-by had started to pace out all eternity, from gas-lamp to gas-lamp in a night without end; and the drowsy ticking of the old clock on the landing became distinctly audible in the bedroom.

Mrs. Verloc, on her back, and staring at the ceiling, made a remark.

"Takings very small to-day."

Mr. Verloc, in the same position, cleared his throat as if for an important statement, but merely inquired:

"Did you turn off the gas downstairs?"

"Yes; I did," answered Mrs. Verloc conscientiously. "That poor boy is in a very excited state to-night," she murmured, after a pause which lasted for three ticks of the clock.

Mr. Verloc cared nothing for Stevie's excitement, but he felt horribly wakeful, and dreaded facing the darkness and silence that would follow the extinguishing of the lamp. This dread led him to make the remark that Stevie had disregarded his suggestion to go to bed. Mrs. Verloc, falling into the trap, started to demonstrate at length to her husband that this was not "impudence" of any sort, but simply "excitement." There was no young man of his age in London more willing and docile than Stevie, she affirmed; none more affectionate and ready to please, and even useful, as long as people did not upset his poor head. Mrs. Verloc, turning towards her recumbent husband, raised herself on her elbow, and hung over him in her anxiety that he should believe Stevie to be a useful member of the family. That ardour of protecting compassion, exalted morbidly in her childhood by the misery of another child, tinged her sallow cheeks with a faint dusky blush, made her big eyes gleam under the dark lids. Mrs. Verloc then looked younger; she looked as young as Winnie used to look, and much more animated than the Winnie of the Belgravian mansion days had ever allowed herself to appear to gentlemen lodgers. Mr. Verloc's anxieties had prevented him from attaching any sense to what his wife was saying. It was as if her voice were talking on the other side of a very thick wall. It was her aspect that recalled him to himself.

He appreciated this woman, and the sentiment of this appreciation, stirred by a display of something resembling emotion, only added another pang to his mental anguish. When her voice ceased he moved uneasily, and said:

"I haven't been feeling well for the last few days."

He might have meant this as an opening to a complete confidence; but Mrs. Verloc laid her head on the pillow again, and staring upward, went on:

"That boy hears too much of what is talked about here. If I had known they were coming to-night I would have seen to it that he went to bed at the same time I did. He was out of his mind with something he overheard about eating people's flesh and drinking blood. What's the good of talking like that?"

There was a note of indignant scorn in her voice. Mr. Verloc was fully responsive now.

"Ask Karl Yundt," he growled savagely.

Mrs. Verloc, with great decision, pronounced Karl Yundt "a disgusting old man." She declared openly her affection for Michaelis. Of the robust Ossipon, in whose presence she always felt uneasy behind an attitude of stony reserve, she said nothing whatever. And continuing to talk of that brother, who had been for so many years an object of care and fears:

"He isn't fit to hear what's said here. He believes it's all true. He knows no better. He gets into his passions over it."

Mr. Verloc made no comment.

"He glared at me, as if he didn't know who I was, when I went downstairs. His heart was going like a hammer. He can't help being excitable. I woke mother up, and asked her to sit with him till he went to sleep. It isn't his fault. He's no trouble when he's left alone."

Mr. Verloc made no comment.

"I wish he had never been to school," Mrs. Verloc began again brusquely. "He's always taking away those newspapers from the window to read. He gets a red face poring over them. We don't get rid of a dozen numbers in a month. They only take up room in the front window. And Mr. Ossipon brings every week a pile of these F. P. tracts to sell at a halfpenny each. I wouldn't give a halfpenny for the whole lot. It's silly reading—that's what it is. There's no sale for it. The other day Stevie got hold of one, and there was a story in it of a German soldier officer tearing half-off the ear of a recruit, and nothing was done to him for it. The brute! I couldn't do anything with Stevie that afternoon. The story was enough, too, to make one's blood boil. But what's the use of printing things like that? We aren't German slaves here, thank God. It's not our business—is it?"

Mr. Verloc made no reply.

"I had to take the carving knife from the boy," Mrs. Verloc continued, a little sleepily now. "He was shouting and stamping and sobbing. He can't stand the notion of any cruelty. He would have stuck that officer like a pig if he had seen him then. It's true, too! Some people don't deserve much mercy." Mrs. Verloc's voice ceased, and the expression of her motionless eyes became more and more contemplative and veiled during the long pause. "Comfortable, dear?" she asked in a faint, far-away voice. "Shall I put out the light now?"[9]

The dreary conviction that there was no sleep for him held Mr. Verloc mute and hopelessly inert in his fear of darkness. He made a great effort.

"Yes. Put it out," he said at last in a hollow tone.

CHAPTER FOUR

MOST of the thirty or so little tables covered by red cloths with a white design stood ranged at right angles to the deep brown wainscoting of the underground hall. Bronze chandeliers with many globes depended from the low, slightly vaulted ceiling, and the fresco paintings ran flat and dull all round the walls without windows, representing scenes of the chase and of outdoor revelry in mediæval costumes. Varlets* in green jerkins† brandished hunting knives and raised on high tankards of foaming beer.

"Unless I am very much mistaken, you are the man who would know the inside of this confounded affair," said the robust Ossipon, leaning over, his elbows far out on the table and his feet tucked back completely under his chair. His eyes stared with wild eagerness.

An upright semi-grand piano near the door, flanked by two palms in pots, executed suddenly all by itself a valse‡ tune with aggressive virtuosity. The din it raised was deafening. When it ceased, as abruptly as it had started, the bespectacled, dingy little man[1] who faced Ossipon behind a heavy glass mug full of beer emitted calmly what had the sound of a general proposition.

"In principle what one of us may or may not know as to any given fact can't be a matter for inquiry to the others."

"Certainly not," Comrade Ossipon agreed in a quiet undertone. "In principle."

With his big florid face held between his hands he continued to stare hard, while the dingy little man in spectacles coolly took a drink of beer and stood the glass mug back on the table. His flat,

---

*Attendants; also a term for a knave, rogue, or scoundrel, as well as for a person or a crowd of mean or low origins.
†Sleeveless jackets.
‡Waltz.

large ears departed widely from the sides of his skull, which looked frail enough for Ossipon to crush between thumb and forefinger; the dome of the forehead seemed to rest on the rim of the spectacles; the cheeks, of a greasy, unhealthy complexion, were merely smudged by the miserable poverty of a thin dark whisker. The lamentable inferiority of the whole physique was made ludicrous by the supremely self-confident bearing of the individual. His speech was curt, and he had a particularly impressive manner of keeping silent.

Ossipon spoke again from between his hands in a mutter.

"Have you been out much to-day?"

"No. I stayed in bed all the morning," answered the other. "Why?"

"Oh! Nothing," said Ossipon, gazing earnestly and quivering inwardly with the desire to find out something, but obviously intimidated by the little man's overwhelming air of unconcern. When talking with this comrade—which happened but rarely—the big Ossipon suffered from a sense of moral and even physical insignificance. However, he ventured another question. "Did you walk down here?"

"No; omnibus," the little man answered readily enough. He lived far away in Islington,[2] in a small house down a shabby street, littered with straw, and dirty paper, where out of school hours a troop of assorted children ran and squabbled with a shrill, joyless, rowdy clamour. His single back room, remarkable for having an extremely large cupboard, he rented furnished from two elderly spinsters, dressmakers in a humble way with a clientele of servant girls mostly. He had a heavy padlock put on the cupboard, but otherwise he was a model lodger, giving no trouble, and requiring practically no attendance. His oddities were that he insisted on being present when his room was being swept, and that when he went out he locked his door, and took the key away with him.

Ossipon had a vision of these round black-rimmed spectacles progressing along the streets on the top of an omnibus, their self-confident glitter falling here and there on the walls of houses, or lowered upon the heads of the unconscious stream of people on the pavements. The ghost of a sickly smile altered the set of Ossipon's thick lips at the thought of the walls nodding, of people running for their life at the sight of those spectacles. If they had only known! What a panic! He murmured interrogatively: "Been sitting long here?"

"An hour or more," answered the other negligently, and took a pull at the dark beer. All his movements—the way he grasped the mug, the act of drinking, the way he set the heavy glass down and folded his arms—had a firmness, an assured precision which made the big and muscular Ossipon, leaning forward with staring eyes and protruding lips, look the picture of eager indecision.

"An hour," he said. "Then it may be you haven't heard yet the news I've heard just now—in the street. Have you?"

The little man shook his head negatively the least bit. But as he gave no indication of curiosity Ossipon ventured to add that he had heard it just outside the place. A newspaper boy had yelled the thing under his very nose, and not being prepared for anything of that sort, he was very much startled and upset. He had to come in here with a dry mouth. "I never thought of finding you here," he added, murmuring steadily, with his elbows planted on the table.

"I come here sometimes," said the other, preserving his provoking coolness of demeanour.

"It's wonderful that you of all people should have heard nothing of it," the big Ossipon continued. His eyelids snapped nervously upon the shining eyes. "You of all people," he repeated tentatively. This obvious restraint argued an incredible and inexplicable timidity of the big fellow before the calm little man, who again lifted the glass mug, drank, and put it down with brusque and assured movements. And that was all.

Ossipon after waiting for something, word or sign, that did not come, made an effort to assume a sort of indifference.

"Do you," he said, deadening his voice still more, "give your stuff* to anybody who's up to asking you for it?"

"My absolute rule is never to refuse anybody—as long as I have a pinch by me," answered the little man with decision.

"That's a principle?" commented Ossipon.

"It's a principle."

"And you think it's sound?"

---

*Dynamite.

The large round spectacles, which gave a look of staring self-confidence to the sallow face, confronted Ossipon like sleepless, unwinking orbs flashing a cold fire.

"Perfectly. Always. Under every circumstance. What could stop me? Why should I not? Why should I think twice about it?"

Ossipon gasped, as it were, discreetly.

"Do you mean to say you would hand it over to a 'teck'* if one came to ask you for your wares?"

The other smiled faintly.

"Let them come and try it on, and you will see," he said. "They know me, but I know also every one of them. They won't come near me—not they."

His thin, livid lips snapped together firmly. Ossipon began to argue.

"But they could send some one—rig a plant on you. Don't you see? Get the stuff from you in that way, and then arrest you with the proof in their hands."

"Proof of what? Dealing in explosives without a licence perhaps." This was meant for a contemptuous jeer, though the expresssion of the thin, sickly face remained unchanged, and the utterance was negligent. "I don't think there's one of them anxious to make that arrest. I don't think they could get one of them to apply for a warrant. I mean one of the best. Not one."

"Why?" Ossipon asked.

"Because they know very well I take care never to part with the last handful of my wares. I've it always by me."[3] He touched the breast of his coat lightly. "In a thick glass flask," he added.

"So I have been told," said Ossipon, with a shade of wonder in his voice. "But I didn't know if——"

"They know," interrupted the little man crisply, leaning against the straight chair back, which rose higher than his fragile head. "I shall never be arrested. The game isn't good enough for any policeman of them all. To deal with a man like me you require sheer, naked, inglorious heroism."

---

*Detective.

Again his lips closed with a self-confident snap. Ossipon repressed a movement of impatience.

"Or recklessness—or simply ignorance," he retorted. "They've only to get somebody for the job who does not know you carry enough stuff in your pocket to blow yourself and everything within sixty yards of you to pieces."

"I never affirmed I could not be eliminated," rejoined the other. "But that wouldn't be an arrest. Moreover, it's not so easy as it looks."

"Bah!" Ossipon contradicted. "Don't be too sure of that. What's to prevent half a dozen of them jumping upon you from behind in the street? With your arms pinned to your sides you could do nothing—could you?"

"Yes; I could. I am seldom out in the streets after dark," said the little man impassively, "and never very late. I walk always with my left hand closed round the indiarubber ball which I have in my trouser pocket. The pressing of this ball actuates a detonator inside the flask I carry in my pocket. It's the principle of the pneumatic instantaneous shutter for a camera lens. The tube leads up—"

With a swift disclosing gesture he gave Ossipon a glimpse of an indiarubber tube, resembling a slender brown worm, issuing from the armhole of his waistcoat and plunging into the inner breast pocket of his jacket. His clothes, of a nondescript brown mixture, were threadbare and marked with stains, dusty in the folds, with ragged button-holes. "The detonator is partly mechanical, partly chemical," he explained, with casual condescension.

"It is instantaneous, of course?" murmured Ossipon, with a slight shudder.

"Far from it," confessed the other, with a reluctance which seemed to twist his mouth dolorously. "A full twenty seconds must elapse from the moment I press the ball till the explosion takes place."

"Phew!" whistled Ossipon, completely appalled. "Twenty seconds! Horrors! You mean to say that you could face that? I should go crazy——"

"Wouldn't matter if you did. Of course, it's the weak point of this special system, which is only for my own use. The worst is that the manner of exploding is always the weak point with us. I am trying to invent a detonator that would adjust itself to all conditions of action, and even to unexpected changes of conditions. A variable and yet perfectly precise mechanism. A really intelligent detonator."

"Twenty seconds," muttered Ossipon again. "Ough! And then——"

With a slight turn of the head the glitter of the spectacles seemed to gauge the size of the beer saloon in the basement of the renowned Silenus Restaurant.[4]

"Nobody in this room could hope to escape," was the verdict of that survey. "Nor yet this couple going up the stairs now."

The piano at the foot of the staircase clanged through a mazurka* with brazen impetuosity, as though a vulgar and impudent ghost were showing off. The keys sank and rose mysteriously. Then all became still. For a moment Ossipon imagined the over-lighted place changed into a dreadful black hole belching horrible fumes choked with ghastly rubbish of smashed brickwork and mutilated corpses. He had such a distinct perception of ruin and death that he shuddered again. The other observed, with an air of calm sufficiency:

"In the last instance it is character alone that makes for one's safety. There are very few people in the world whose character is as well established as mine."

"I wonder how you managed it," growled Ossipon.

"Force of personality," said the other, without raising his voice; and coming from the mouth of that obviously miserable organism the assertion caused the robust Ossipon to bite his lower lip. "Force of personality," he repeated, with ostentatious calm. "I have the means to make myself deadly, but that by itself, you understand, is absolutely nothing in the way of protection. What is effective is the belief those people have in my will to use the means. That's their impression. It is absolute. Therefore I am deadly."

"There are individuals of character amongst that lot too," muttered Ossipon ominously.

"Possibly. But it is a matter of degree obviously, since, for instance, I am not impressed by them. Therefore they are inferior. They cannot be otherwise. Their character is built upon conventional morality. It leans on the social order. Mine stands free from everything

---

*Music for a lively Polish folk dance.

artificial. They are bound in all sorts of conventions. They depend on life, which, in this connection, is a historical fact surrounded by all sorts of restraints and considerations, a complex organised fact open to attack at every point; whereas I depend on death, which knows no restraint and cannot be attacked. My superiority is evident."

"This is a transcendental way of putting it," said Ossipon, watching the cold glitter of the round spectacles. "I've heard Karl Yundt say much the same thing not very long ago."

"Karl Yundt," mumbled the other contemptuously, "the delegate of the International Red Committee, has been a posturing shadow all his life. There are three of you delegates, aren't there? I won't define the other two, as you are one of them. But what you say means nothing. You are the worthy delegates for revolutionary propaganda, but the trouble is not only that you are as unable to think independently as any respectable grocer or journalist of them all, but that you have no character whatever."

Ossipon could not restrain a start of indignation.

"But what do you want from us?" he exclaimed in a deadened voice. "What is it you are after yourself?"

"A perfect detonator," was the peremptory answer. "What are you making that face for? You see, you can't even bear the mention of something conclusive."

"I am not making a face," growled the annoyed Ossipon bearishly.

"You revolutionists," the other continued, with leisurely self-confidence, "are the slaves of the social convention, which is afraid of you; slaves of it as much as the very police that stand up in the defence of that convention. Clearly you are, since you want to revolutionise it. It governs your thought, of course, and your action too, and thus neither your thought nor your action can ever be conclusive." He paused, tranquil, with that air of close, endless silence, then almost immediately went on. "You are not a bit better than the forces arrayed against you—than the police, for instance. The other day I came suddenly upon Chief Inspector Heat at the corner of Tottenham Court Road. He looked at me very steadily. But I did not look at him. Why should I give him more than a glance? He was thinking of many things—of his superiors, of his reputation, of the law courts, of his salary, of newspapers—of a hundred things. But I was thinking of my perfect detonator only. He meant nothing to me. He was as insignificant as—I can't call to mind anything in-significant enough to compare him with—except Karl Yundt per-haps. Like to like. The terrorist and the policeman both come from the same basket. Revolution, legality—counter moves in the same game; forms of idleness at bottom identical. He plays his little game—so do you propagandists. But I don't play; I work fourteen hours a day, and go hungry sometimes. My experiments cost money now and again, and then I must do without food for a day or two. You're looking at my beer. Yes. I have had two glasses al-ready, and shall have another presently. This is a little holiday, and I celebrate it alone. Why not? I've the grit to work alone, quite alone, absolutely alone. I've worked alone for years."

Ossipon's face had turned dusky red.

"At the perfect detonator—eh?" he sneered, very low.

"Yes," retorted the other. "It is a good definition. You couldn't find anything half so precise to define the nature of your activity with all your committees and delegations. It is I who am the true propagandist."

"We won't discuss that point," said Ossipon, with an air of rising above personal considerations. "I am afraid I'll have to spoil your holiday for you, though. There's a man blown up in Greenwich Park this morning."

"How do you know?"

"They have been yelling the news in the streets since two o'clock. I bought the paper, and just ran in here. Then I saw you sitting at this table. I've got it in my pocket now."

He pulled the newspaper out. It was a good-sized rosy sheet,[5] as if flushed by the warmth of its own convictions, which were opti-mistic. He scanned the pages rapidly.

"Ah! Here it is. Bomb in Greenwich Park. There isn't much so far.[6] Half-past eleven. Foggy morning. Effects of explosion felt as far as Romney Road and Park Place. Enormous hole in the ground under a tree filled with smashed roots and broken branches. All round fragments of a man's body blown to pieces. That's all. The rest's mere newspaper gup.* No doubt a wicked attempt to blow up the Observatory, they say. H'm. That's hardly credible."

---

*Gossip.

He looked at the paper for a while longer in silence, then passed it to the other, who after gazing abstractly at the print laid it down without comment.

It was Ossipon who spoke first—still resentful.

"The fragments of only *one* man, you note. Ergo:* blew *himself* up. That spoils your day off for you—don't it? Were you expecting that sort of move? I hadn't the slightest idea—not the ghost of a notion of anything of the sort being planned to come off here—in this country. Under the present circumstances it's nothing short of criminal."

The little man lifted his thin black eyebrows with dispassionate scorn.

"Criminal! What is that? What *is* crime? What can be the meaning of such an assertion?"

"How am I to express myself? One must use the current words," said Ossipon impatiently. "The meaning of this assertion is that this business may affect our position very adversely in this country. Isn't that crime enough for you? I am convinced you have been giving away some of your stuff lately."

Ossipon stared hard. The other, without flinching, lowered and raised his head slowly.

"You have!" burst out the editor of the F. P. leaflets in an intense whisper. "No! And are you really handing it over at large like this, for the asking, to the first fool that comes along?"

"Just so! The condemned social order has not been built up on paper and ink, and I don't fancy that a combination of paper and ink will ever put an end to it, whatever you may think. Yes, I would give the stuff with both hands to every man, woman, or fool that likes to come along. I know what you are thinking about. But I am not taking my cue from the Red Committee. I would see you all hounded out of here, or arrested—or beheaded for that matter— without turning a hair. What happens to us as individuals is not of the least consequence."

He spoke carelessly, without heat, almost without feeling, and Ossipon, secretly much affected, tried to copy this detachment.

---

*Therefore (Latin).

"If the police here knew their business they would shoot you full of holes with revolvers, or else try to sandbag you from behind in broad daylight."

The little man seemed already to have considered that point of view in his dispassionate self-confident manner.

"Yes," he assented with the utmost readiness. "But for that they would have to face their own institutions. Do you see? That requires uncommon grit. Grit of a special kind."

Ossipon blinked.

"I fancy that's exactly what would happen to you if you were to set up your laboratory in the States. They don't stand on ceremony with their institutions there."

"I am not likely to go and see. Otherwise your remark is just," admitted the other. "They have more character over there, and their character is essentially anarchistic. Fertile ground for us, the States—very good ground. The great Republic has the root of the destructive matter in her. The collective temperament is lawless. Excellent. They may shoot us down, but——"

"You are too transcendental for me," growled Ossipon, with moody concern.

"Logical," protested the other. "There are several kinds of logic. This is the enlightened kind. America is all right. It is this country that is dangerous, with her idealistic conception of legality. The social spirit of this people is wrapped up in scrupulous prejudices, and that is fatal to our work. You talk of England being our only refuge! So much the worse. Capua!* What do we want with refuges? Here you talk, print, plot, and do nothing. I daresay it's very convenient for such Karl Yundts."

He shrugged his shoulders slightly, then added with the same leisurely assurance: "To break up the superstition and worship of legality should be our aim. Nothing would please me more than to see Inspector Heat and his likes take to shooting us down in broad daylight with the approval of the public. Half our battle would be won then; the disintegration of the old morality would have set in

---

*An opulent ancient Italian city, which served as a refuge for Hannibal (247–182 B.C.), the Carthaginian general who warred against Rome and whose own demise came soon after indulging in the luxuries of the city.

in its very temple.[7] That is what you ought to aim at. But you revolutionists will never understand that. You plan the future, you lose yourselves in reveries of economical systems derived from what is; whereas what's wanted is a clean sweep and a clear start for a new conception of life. That sort of future will take care of itself if you will only make room for it. Therefore I would shovel my stuff in heaps at the corners of the streets if I had enough for that; and as I haven't, I do my best by perfecting a really dependable detonator."

Ossipon, who had been mentally swimming in deep waters, seized upon the last word as if it were a saving plank.

"Yes. Your detonators. I shouldn't wonder if it weren't one of your detonators that made a clean sweep of the man in the park."

A shade of vexation darkened the determined sallow face confronting Ossipon.

"My difficulty consists precisely in experimenting practically with the various kinds. They must be tried after all. Besides——"

Ossipon interrupted.

"Who could that fellow be? I assure you that we in London had no knowledge—— Couldn't you describe the person you gave the stuff to?"

The other turned his spectacles upon Ossipon like a pair of searchlights.

"Describe him," he repeated slowly. "I don't think there can be the slightest objection now. I will describe him to you in one word—Verloc."

Ossipon, whom curiosity had lifted a few inches off his seat, dropped back, as if hit in the face.

"Verloc! Impossible."

The self-possessed little man nodded slightly once.

"Yes. He's the person. You can't say that in this case I was giving my stuff to the first fool that came along. He was a prominent member of the group as far as I understand."

"Yes," said Ossipon. "Prominent. No, not exactly. He was the centre for general intelligence, and usually received comrades coming over here. More useful than important. Man of no ideas. Years ago he used to speak at meetings—in France, I believe. Not very well, though. He was trusted by such men as Latorre, Moser, and all that old lot.[8] The only talent he showed really was his ability to elude the attentions of the police somehow. Here, for instance, he did not seem to be looked after very closely. He was regularly married, you know. I suppose it's with her money that he started that shop. Seemed to make it pay, too."

Ossipon paused abruptly, muttered to himself, "I wonder what that woman will do now?" and fell into thought.

The other waited with ostentatious indifference. His parentage was obscure, and he was generally known by his nickname of Professor. His title to that designation consisted in his having been once assistant demonstrator in chemistry at some technical institute. He quarrelled with the authorities upon a question of unfair treatment. Afterwards he obtained a post in the laboratory of a manufactory of dyes. There, too, he had been treated with revolting injustice. His struggles, his privations, his hard work to raise himself in the social scale, had filled him with such an exalted conviction of his merits that it was extremely difficult for the world to treat him with justice—the standard of that notion depending so much upon the patience of the individual. The Professor had genius, but lacked the great social virtue of resignation.

"Intellectually a nonentity," Ossipon pronounced aloud, abandoning suddenly the inward contemplation of Mrs. Verloc's bereaved person and business. "Quite an ordinary personality. You are wrong in not keeping more in touch with the comrades, Professor," he added in a reproving tone. "Did he say anything to you—give you some idea of his intentions? I hadn't seen him for a month. It seems impossible that he should be gone."

"He told me it was going to be a demonstration against a building," said the Professor. "I had to know that much to prepare the missile. I pointed out to him that I had hardly a sufficient quantity for a completely destructive result, but he pressed me very earnestly to do my best. As he wanted something that could be carried openly in the hand, I proposed to make use of an old one-gallon copal varnish* can I happened to have by me. He was pleased at the idea. It gave me some trouble, because I had to cut out the bottom first and solder it on again afterwards. When prepared for use, the can enclosed a wide-mouthed, well-corked jar of thick glass packed around

---

*Transparent varnish made from resin from tropical trees.

with some wet clay, and containing sixteen ounces of X2 green powder. The detonator was connected with the screw top of the can. It was ingenious—a combination of time and shock. I explained the system to him. It was a thin tube of tin enclosing a——"

Ossipon's attention had wandered.

"What do you think has happened?" he interrupted.

"Can't tell. Screwed the top on tight, which would make the connection, and then forgot the time. It was set for twenty minutes. On the other hand, the time contact being made, a sharp shock would bring about the explosion at once. He either ran the time too close, or simply let the thing fall. The contact was made all right— that's clear to me at any rate. The system's worked perfectly. And yet you would think that a common fool in a hurry would be much more likely to forget to make the contact altogether. I was worrying myself about that sort of failure mostly. But there are more kinds of fools than one can guard against. You can't expect a detonator to be absolutely fool-proof."

He beckoned to a waiter. Ossipon sat rigid, with the abstracted gaze of mental travail. After the man had gone away with the money he roused himself, with an air of profound dissatisfaction.

"It's extremely unpleasant for me," he mused. "Karl has been in bed with bronchitis for a week. There's an even chance that he will never get up again. Michaelis's luxuriating in the country somewhere. A fashionable publisher has offered him five hundred pounds for a book.[9] It will be a ghastly failure. He has lost the habit of consecutive thinking in prison, you know."

The Professor on his feet, now buttoning his coat, looked about him with perfect indifference.

"What are you going to do?" asked Ossipon wearily. He dreaded the blame of the Central Red Committee, a body which had no permanent place of abode, and of whose membership he was not exactly informed. If this affair eventuated in the stoppage of the modest subsidy allotted to the publication of the F. P. pamphlets, then indeed he would have to regret Verloc's inexplicable folly.

"Solidarity with the extremest form of action is one thing, and silly recklessness is another," he said, with a sort of moody brutality. "I don't know what came to Verloc. There's some mystery there. However, he's gone. You may take it as you like, but under the circumstances the only policy for the militant revolutionary group is to disclaim all connection with this damned freak of yours. How to make the disclaimer convincing enough is what bothers me."

The little man on his feet, buttoned up and ready to go, was no taller than the seated Ossipon. He levelled his spectacles at the latter's face point-blank.

"You might ask the police for a testimonial of good conduct. They know where every one of you slept last night. Perhaps if you asked them they would consent to publish some sort of official statement."

"No doubt they are aware well enough that we had nothing to do with this," mumbled Ossipon bitterly. "What they will say is another thing." He remained thoughtful, disregarding the short, owlish, shabby figure standing by his side. "I must lay hands on Michaelis at once, and get him to speak from his heart at one of our gatherings. The public has a sort of sentimental regard for that fellow. His name is known. And I am in touch with a few reporters in the big dailies. What he would say would be utter bosh, but he has a turn of talk that makes it go down all the same."

"Like treacle,"* interjected the Professor, rather low, keeping an impassive expression.

The perplexed Ossipon went on communing with himself half audibly, after the manner of a man reflecting in perfect solitude.

"Confounded ass! To leave such an imbecile business on my hands. And I don't even know if——"

He sat with compressed lips. The idea of going for news straight to the shop lacked charm. His notion was that Verloc's shop might have been turned already into a police trap. They will be bound to make some arrests, he thought, with something resembling virtuous indignation, for the even tenor of his revolutionary life was menaced by no fault of his. And yet unless he went there he ran the risk of remaining in ignorance of what perhaps it would be very material for him to know. Then he reflected that, if the man in the park had been so very much blown to pieces as the evening papers said, he could not have been identified. And if so, the police could

---

*Originally, a sweet medicinal compound; subsequently, also molasses.

have no special reason for watching Verloc's shop more closely than any other place known to be frequented by marked anarchists—no more reason, in fact, than for watching the doors of the Silenus. There would be a lot of watching all round, no matter where he went. Still——

"I wonder what I had better do now?" he muttered, taking counsel with himself.

A rasping voice at his elbow said, with sedate scorn:

"Fasten yourself upon the woman for all she's worth."

After uttering these words the Professor walked away from the table. Ossipon, whom that piece of insight had taken unawares, gave one ineffectual start, and remained still, with a helpless gaze, as though nailed fast to the seat of his chair. The lonely piano, without as much as a music-stool to help it, struck a few chords courageously, and beginning a selection of national airs, played him out at last to the tune of "The Blue-Bells of Scotland."[10] The painfully detached notes grew faint behind his back while he went slowly upstairs, across the hall, and into the street.

In front of the great doorway a dismal row of newspaper sellers standing clear of the pavement dealt out their wares from the gutter. It was a raw, gloomy day of the early spring; and the grimy sky, the mud of the streets, the rags of the dirty men, harmonised excellently with the eruption of the damp, rubbishy sheets of paper soiled with printer's ink. The posters, maculated* with filth, garnished like tapestry the sweep of the curbstone. The trade in afternoon papers was brisk, yet in comparison with the swift, constant march of foot traffic, the effect was of indifference, of a disregarded distribution. Ossipon looked hurriedly both ways before stepping out into the cross-currents, but the Professor was already out of sight.

---

*Blotched, besmirched.

CHAPTER FIVE

THE Professor had turned into a street to the left, and walked along, with his head carried rigidly erect, in a crowd whose every individual almost overtopped his stunted stature. It was vain to pretend to himself that he was not disappointed. But that was mere feeling; the stoicism of his thought could not be disturbed by this or any other failure. Next time, or the time after next, a telling stroke would be delivered—something really startling—a blow fit to open the first crack in the imposing front of the great edifice of legal conceptions sheltering the atrocious injustice of society. Of humble origin, and with an appearance really so mean as to stand in the way of his considerable natural abilities, his imagination had been fired early by the tales of men rising from the depths of poverty to positions of authority and affluence. The extreme, almost ascetic purity of his thought, combined with an astounding ignorance of worldly conditions, had set before him a goal of power and prestige to be attained without the medium of arts, graces, tact, wealth—by sheer weight of merit alone. On that view he considered himself entitled to undisputed success. His father, a delicate dark enthusiast with a sloping forehead, had been an itinerant and rousing preacher of some obscure but rigid Christian sect—a man supremely confident in the privileges of his righteousness. In the son, individualist by temperament, once the science of colleges had replaced thoroughly the faith of conventicles,* this moral attitude translated itself into a frenzied puritanism of ambition. He nursed it as something secularly holy. To see it thwarted opened his eyes to the true nature of the world, whose morality was artificial, corrupt, and blasphemous. The way of even the most justifiable revolutions is prepared by personal impulses disguised into creeds. The Professor's indignation found in itself a final cause that absolved him from the sin of turning to destruction as the agent of his ambition.

---

*Secretive religious meetings.

To destroy public faith in legality was the imperfect formula of his pedantic fanaticism; but the subconscious conviction that the framework of an established social order cannot be effectually shattered except by some form of collective or individual violence was precise and correct. He was a moral agent—that was settled in his mind. By exercising his agency with ruthless defiance he procured for himself the appearances of power and personal prestige. That was undeniable to his vengeful bitterness. It pacified its unrest; and in their own way the most ardent of revolutionaries are perhaps doing no more but seeking for peace in common with the rest of mankind—the peace of soothed vanity, of satisfied appetites, or perhaps of appeased conscience.

Lost in the crowd, miserable and undersized, he meditated confidently on his power, keeping his hand in the left pocket of his trousers, grasping lightly the indiarubber ball, the supreme guarantee of his sinister freedom; but after a while he became disagreeably affected by the sight of the roadway thronged with vehicles and of the pavement crowded with men and women. He was in a long, straight street, peopled by a mere fraction of an immense multitude; but all round him, on and on, even to the limits of the horizon hidden by the enormous piles of bricks, he felt the mass of mankind mighty in its numbers. They swarmed numerous like locusts, industrious like ants, thoughtless like a natural force, pushing on blind and orderly and absorbed, impervious to sentiment, to logic, to terror too, perhaps.

That was the form of doubt he feared most. Impervious to fear! Often while walking abroad, when he happened also to come out of himself, he had such moments of dreadful and sane mistrust of mankind. What if nothing could move them? Such moments come to all men whose ambition aims at a direct grasp upon humanity—to artists, politicians, thinkers, reformers, or saints. A despicable emotional state this, against which solitude fortifies a superior character; and with severe exultation the Professor thought of the refuge of his room, with its padlocked cupboard, lost in a wilderness of poor houses, the hermitage of the perfect anarchist. In order to reach sooner the point where he could take his omnibus, he turned brusquely out of the populous street into a narrow and dusky alley paved with flagstones. On one side the low brick houses had in their dusty windows the sightless, moribund look of incurable decay—empty shells awaiting demolition. From the other side life had not departed wholly as yet. Facing the only gas-lamp yawned the cavern of a second-hand furniture dealer, where, deep in the gloom of a sort of narrow avenue winding through a bizarre forest of wardrobes, with an undergrowth tangle of table legs, a tall pier-glass* glimmered like a pool of water in a wood. An unhappy, homeless couch, accompanied by two unrelated chairs, stood in the open. The only human being making use of the alley besides the Professor, coming stalwart and erect from the opposite direction, checked his swinging pace suddenly.

"Hullo!" he said, and stood a little on one side watchfully.

The Professor had already stopped, with a ready half turn which brought his shoulders very near the other wall. His right hand fell lightly on the back of the outcast couch, the left remained purposefully plunged deep in the trousers pocket, and the roundness of the heavy-rimmed spectacles imparted an owlish character to his moody, unperturbed face.

It was like a meeting in a side corridor of a mansion full of life.[1] The stalwart man was buttoned up in a dark overcoat, and carried an umbrella. His hat, tilted back, uncovered a good deal of forehead, which appeared very white in the dusk. In the dark patches of the orbits the eyeballs glimmered piercingly. Long, drooping moustaches, the colour of ripe corn, framed with their points the square block of his shaved chin.

"I am not looking for you," he said curtly.

The Professor did not stir an inch. The blended noises of the enormous town sank down to an inarticulate low murmur. Chief Inspector Heat of the Special Crimes Department[2] changed his tone.

"Not in a hurry to get home?" he asked, with mocking simplicity.

The unwholesome-looking little moral agent of destruction exulted silently in the possession of personal prestige, keeping in check this man armed with the defensive mandate of a menaced society. More fortunate than Caligula, who wished that the Roman Senate had only one head for the better satisfaction of his cruel lust,[†] he beheld in that one man all the forces he had set at defiance: the force

---

*Mirror.

[†]Notoriously sadistic, the Roman Emperor Gaius Caligula (reigned A.D. 37–41) is reputed to have said, "I wish the Roman people had only one neck."

of law, property, oppression, and injustice. He beheld all his enemies, and fearlessly confronted them all in a supreme satisfaction of his vanity. They stood perplexed before him as if before a dreadful portent. He gloated inwardly over the chance of this meeting affirming his superiority over all the multitude of mankind.[3]

It was in reality a chance meeting. Chief Inspector Heat had had a disagreeably busy day since his department received the first telegram from Greenwich a little before eleven in the morning. First of all, the fact of the outrage being attempted less than a week after he had assured a high official that no outbreak of anarchist activity was to be apprehended was sufficiently annoying. If he ever thought himself safe in making a statement, it was then. He had made that statement with infinite satisfaction to himself, because it was clear that the high official desired greatly to hear that very thing. He had affirmed that nothing of the sort could even be thought of without the department being aware of it within twenty-four hours; and he had spoken thus in his consciousness of being the great expert of his department. He had gone even so far as to utter words which true wisdom would have kept back. But Chief Inspector Heat was not very wise—at least not truly so. True wisdom, which is not certain of anything in this world of contradictions, would have prevented him from attaining his present position. It would have alarmed his superiors, and done away with his chances of promotion. His promotion had been very rapid.

"There isn't one of them, sir, that we couldn't lay our hands on at any time of night and day. We know what each of them is doing hour by hour," he had declared. And the high official had deigned to smile. This was so obviously the right thing to say for an officer of Chief Inspector Heat's reputation that it was perfectly delightful. The high official believed the declaration, which chimed in with his idea of the fitness of things. His wisdom was of an official kind, or else he might have reflected upon a matter not of theory but of experience, that in the close-woven stuff of relations between conspirator and police there occur unexpected solutions of continuity, sudden holes in space and time. A given anarchist may be watched inch by inch and minute by minute, but a moment always comes when somehow all sight and touch of him are lost for a few hours, during which something (generally an explosion) more or less deplorable does happen. But the high official, carried away by his sense of the fitness of things, had smiled, and now the recollection of that smile was very annoying to Chief Inspector Heat, principal expert in anarchist procedure.

This was not the only circumstance whose recollection depressed the usual serenity of the eminent specialist. There was another, dating back only to that very morning. The thought that when called urgently to his Assistant Commissioner's private room he had been unable to conceal his astonishment was distinctly vexing. His instinct of a successful man had taught him long ago that, as a general rule, a reputation is built on manner as much as on achievement. And he felt that his manner when confronted with the telegram had not been impressive. He had opened his eyes widely, and had exclaimed "Impossible!" exposing himself thereby to the unanswerable retort of a finger-tip laid forcibly on the telegram which the Assistant Commissioner, after reading it aloud, had flung on the desk. To be crushed, as it were, under the tip of a forefinger was an unpleasant experience. Very damaging, too! Furthermore, Chief Inspector Heat was conscious of not having mended matters by allowing himself to express a conviction.

"One thing I can tell you at once: none of our lot had anything to do with this."

He was strong in his integrity of a good detective, but he saw now that an impenetrably attentive reserve towards this incident would have served his reputation better. On the other hand, he admitted to himself that it was difficult to preserve one's reputation if rank outsiders were going to take a hand in the business. Outsiders are the bane of the police as of other professions. The tone of the Assistant Commissioner's remarks had been sour enough to set one's teeth on edge.

And since breakfast Chief Inspector Heat had not managed to get anything to eat.

Starting immediately to begin his investigation on the spot, he had swallowed a good deal of raw, unwholesome fog in the park. Then he had walked over to the hospital;[4] and when the investigation in Greenwich was concluded at last he had lost his inclination for food. Not accustomed, as the doctors are, to examine closely the mangled remains of human beings, he had been shocked by the sight disclosed to his view when a waterproof sheet had been lifted off a table in a certain apartment of the hospital.

Another waterproof sheet was spread over that table in the manner of a tablecloth, with the corners turned up over a sort of mound—a heap of rags, scorched and bloodstained, half concealing what might have been an accumulation of raw material for a cannibal feast. It required considerable firmness of mind not to recoil before that sight. Chief Inspector Heat, an efficient officer of his department, stood his ground, but for a whole minute he did not advance. A local constable in uniform cast a sidelong glance, and said, with stolid simplicity:

"He's all there. Every bit of him. It was a job."

He had been the first man on the spot after the explosion. He mentioned the fact again. He had seen something like a heavy flash of lightning in the fog. At that time he was standing at the door of the King William Street Lodge talking to the keeper. The concussion* made him tingle all over. He ran between the trees towards the Observatory. "As fast as my legs would carry me," he repeated twice.

Chief Inspector Heat, bending forward over the table in a gingerly and horrified manner, let him run on. The hospital porter and another man turned down the corners of the cloth, and stepped aside. The Chief Inspector's eyes searched the gruesome detail of that heap of mixed things, which seemed to have been collected in shambles and rag shops.

"You used a shovel," he remarked, observing a sprinkling of small gravel, tiny brown bits of bark, and particles of splintered wood as fine as needles.

"Had to in one place," said the stolid constable. "I sent a keeper to fetch a spade. When he heard me scraping the ground with it he leaned his forehead against a tree, and was as sick as a dog."

The Chief Inspector, stooping guardedly over the table, fought down the unpleasant sensation in his throat. The shattering violence of destruction which had made of that body a heap of nameless fragments affected his feelings with a sense of ruthless cruelty,

---

*Effect of a blast.

though his reason told him the effect must have been as swift as a flash of lightning. The man, whoever he was, had died instantaneously; and yet it seemed impossible to believe that a human body could have reached that state of disintegration without passing through the pangs of inconceivable agony. No physiologist, and still less of a metaphysician, Chief Inspector Heat rose by the force of sympathy, which is a form of fear, above the vulgar conception of time. Instantaneous! He remembered all he had ever read in popular publications of long and terrifying dreams dreamed in the instant of waking; of the whole past life lived with frightful intensity by a drowning man as his doomed head bobs up, streaming, for the last time. The inexplicable mysteries of conscious existence beset Chief Inspector Heat till he evolved a horrible notion that ages of atrocious pain and mental torture could be contained between two successive winks of an eye. And meantime the Chief Inspector went on peering at the table with a calm face and the slightly anxious attention of an indigent customer bending over what may be called the by-products of a butcher's shop with a view to an inexpensive Sunday dinner. All the time his trained faculties of an excellent investigator, who scorns no chance of information, followed the self-satisfied, disjointed loquacity of the constable.

"A fair-haired fellow," the last observed in a placid tone, and paused. "The old woman who spoke to the sergeant noticed a fair-haired fellow coming out of Maze Hill Station." He paused. "And he was a fair-haired fellow. She noticed two men coming out of the station after the up train* had gone on," he continued slowly. "She couldn't tell if they were together. She took no particular notice of the big one, but the other was a fair, slight chap, carrying a tin varnish can in one hand." The constable ceased.

"Know the woman?" muttered the Chief Inspector, with his eyes fixed on the table, and a vague notion in his mind of an inquest to be held presently upon a person likely to remain for ever unknown.

"Yes. She's housekeeper to a retired publican,† and attends the chapel in Park Place sometimes," the constable uttered weightily, and paused, with another oblique glance at the table. Then suddenly:

---

*Train traveling to London from the country.
†Pub keeper.

"Well, here he is—all of him I could see. Fair. Slight—slight enough. Look at that foot there. I picked up the legs first, one after another. He was that scattered you didn't know where to begin."

The constable paused; the least flicker of an innocent self-laudatory smile invested his round face with an infantile expression.

"Stumbled," he announced positively. "I stumbled once myself, and pitched on my head too, while running up. Them roots do stick out all about the place. Stumbled against the root of a tree and fell, and that thing he was carrying must have gone off right under his chest, I expect."

The echo of the words "Person unknown" repeating itself in his inner consciousness bothered the Chief Inspector considerably. He would have liked to trace this affair back to its mysterious origin for his own information. He was professionally curious. Before the public he would have liked to vindicate the efficiency of his department by establishing the identity of that man. He was a loyal servant. That, however, appeared impossible. The first term of the problem was unreadable—lacked all suggestion but that of atrocious cruelty.

Overcoming his physical repugnance, Chief Inspector Heat stretched out his hand without conviction for the salving of his conscience, and took up the least soiled of the rags. It was a narrow strip of velvet with a larger triangular piece of dark blue cloth hanging from it. He held it up to his eyes; and the police constable spoke.

"Velvet collar. Funny the old woman should have noticed the velvet collar. Dark blue overcoat with a velvet collar, she has told us. He was the chap she saw, and no mistake. And here he is all complete, velvet collar and all. I don't think I missed a single piece as big as a postage stamp."

At this point the trained faculties of the Chief Inspector ceased to hear the voice of the constable. He moved to one of the windows for better light. His face, averted from the room, expressed a startled intense interest while he examined closely the triangular piece of broadcloth. By a sudden jerk he detached it, and only after stuffing it into his pocket turned round to the room, and flung the velvet collar back on the table.

"Cover up," he directed the attendants curtly, without another look, and, saluted by the constable, carried off his spoil hastily.

A convenient train whirled him up to town, alone and pondering deeply, in a third-class compartment. That singed piece of cloth was incredibly valuable, and he could not defend himself from aston-ishment at the casual manner it had come into his possession. It was as if Fate had thrust that clue into his hands. And after the manner of the average man, whose ambition is to command events, he began to mistrust such a gratuitous and accidental success—just because it seemed forced upon him. The practical value of success depends not a little on the way you look at it. But Fate looks at nothing. It has no discretion. He no longer considered it eminently desirable all round to establish publicly the identity of the man who had blown himself up that morning with such horrible completeness. But he was not certain of the view his department would take. A depart-ment is to those it employs a complex personality with ideas and even fads of its own. It depends on the loyal devotion of its servants, and the devoted loyalty of trusted servants is associated with a cer-tain amount of affectionate contempt, which keeps it sweet, as it were. By a benevolent provision of Nature no man is a hero to his valet,[5] or else the heroes would have to brush their own clothes. Likewise no department appears perfectly wise to the intimacy of its workers. A department does not know so much as some of its ser-vants. Being a dispassionate organism, it can never be perfectly in-formed. It would not be good for its efficiency to know too much. Chief Inspector Heat got out of the train in a state of thoughtfulness entirely untainted with disloyalty, but not quite free of that jealous mistrust which so often springs on the ground of perfect devotion, whether to women or to institutions.

It was in this mental disposition, physically very empty, but still nauseated by what he had seen, that he had come upon the Professor. Under these conditions which make for irascibility in a sound, normal man, this meeting was specially unwelcome to Chief Inspector Heat. He had not been thinking of the Professor; he had not been thinking of any individual anarchist at all. The complexion of that case had somehow forced upon him the general idea of the absurdity of things human, which in the abstract is sufficiently annoying to an unphilo-sophical temperament, and in concrete instances becomes exasperat-ing beyond endurance. At the beginning of his career Chief Inspector Heat had been concerned with the more energetic forms of thieving.

He had gained his spurs in that sphere, and naturally enough had kept for it, after his promotion to another department, a feeling not very far removed from affection. Thieving was not a sheer absurdity. It was a form of human industry, perverse indeed, but still an industry exercised in an industrious world; it was work undertaken for the same reason as the work in potteries, in coal mines, in fields, in tool-grinding shops. It was labour, whose practical difference from the other forms of labour consisted in the nature of its risk, which did not lie in ankylosis,* or lead poisoning, or fire-damp,† or gritty dust, but in what may be briefly defined in its own special phraseology as "Seven years' hard."‡ Chief Inspector Heat was, of course, not insensible to the gravity of moral differences. But neither were the thieves he had been looking after. They submitted to the severe sanctions of a morality familiar to Chief Inspector Heat with a certain resignation. They were his fellow-citizens gone wrong because of imperfect education, Chief Inspector Heat believed; but allowing for that difference, he could understand the mind of a burglar, because, as a matter of fact, the mind and the instincts of a burglar are of the same kind as the mind and the instincts of a police officer. Both recognise the same conventions, and have a working knowledge of each other's methods and of the routine of their respective trades. They understand each other, which is advantageous to both, and establishes a sort of amenity in their relations. Products of the same machine, one classed as useful and the other as noxious, they take the machine for granted in different ways, but with a seriousness essentially the same. The mind of Chief Inspector Heat was inaccessible to ideas of revolt. But his thieves were not rebels. His bodily vigour, his cool inflexible manner, his courage and his fairness, had secured for him much respect and some adulation in the sphere of his early successes. He had felt himself revered and admired. And Chief Inspector Heat, arrested within six paces of the anarchist nicknamed the Professor, gave a thought of regret to the world of thieves—sane, without morbid ideals, working by routine, respectful of constituted authorities, free from all taint of hate and despair.

---

*Stiffening of the joints.
†Combustible mine gas.
‡Sentence of seven years' hard labor.

After paying this tribute to what is normal in the constitution of society (for the idea of thieving appeared to his instinct as normal as the idea of property), Chief Inspector Heat felt very angry with himself for having stopped, for having spoken, for having taken that way at all on the ground of it being a short cut from the station to the headquarters. And he spoke again in his big authoritative voice, which, being moderated, had a threatening character.

"You are not wanted, I tell you," he repeated.

The anarchist did not stir. An inward laugh of derision uncovered not only his teeth but his gums as well, shook him all over, without the slightest sound. Chief Inspector Heat was led to add, against his better judgment:

"Not yet. When I want you I shall know where to find you."

Those were perfectly proper words, within the tradition and suitable to his character of a police officer addressing one of his special flock. But the reception they got departed from tradition and propriety. It was outrageous. The stunted, weakly figure before him spoke at last.

"I've no doubt the papers would give you an obituary notice then. You know best what that would be worth to you. I should think you can imagine easily the sort of stuff that would be printed. But you may be exposed to the unpleasantness of being buried together with me, though I suppose your friends would make an effort to sort us out as much as possible."

With all his healthy contempt for the spirit dictating such speeches, the atrocious allusiveness of the words had its effect on Chief Inspector Heat. He had too much insight, and too much exact information as well, to dismiss them as rot. The dusk of this narrow lane took on a sinister tint from the dark, frail little figure, its back to the wall, and speaking with a weak, self-confident voice. To the vigorous, tenacious vitality of the Chief Inspector, the physical wretchedness of that being, so obviously not fit to live, was ominous; for it seemed to him that if he had the misfortune to be such a miserable object he would not have cared how soon he died. Life had such a strong hold upon him that a fresh wave of nausea broke out in slight perspiration upon his brow. The murmur of town life, the subdued rumble of wheels in the two invisible streets to the right and left, came through the curve of the sordid lane to his ears with a precious familiarity and an appealing sweetness. He was human. But Chief Inspector Heat was also a man, and he could not let such words pass.

"All this is good to frighten children with," he said. "I'll have you yet."

It was very well said, without scorn, with an almost austere quietness.

"Doubtless," was the answer; "but there's no time like the present, believe me. For a man of real convictions this is a fine opportunity of self-sacrifice. You may not find another so favourable, so humane. There isn't even a cat near us, and these condemned old houses would make a good heap of bricks where you stand. You'll never get me at so little cost to life and property, which you are paid to protect."

"You don't know who you're speaking to," said Chief Inspector Heat firmly. "If I were to lay my hands on you now I would be no better than yourself."

"Ah! The game!"

"You may be sure our side will win in the end. It may yet be necessary to make people believe that some of you ought to be shot at sight like mad dogs. Then that will be the game. But I'll be damned if I know what yours is. I don't believe you know yourselves. You'll never get anything by it."

"Meantime, it's you who get something from it—so far. And you get it easily, too. I won't speak of your salary, but haven't you made your name simply by not understanding what we are after?"

"What are you after, then?" asked Chief Inspector Heat, with scornful haste, like a man in a hurry who perceives he is wasting his time.

The perfect anarchist answered by a smile which did not part his thin colourless lips; and the celebrated Chief Inspector felt a sense of superiority which induced him to raise a warning finger.

"Give it up—whatever it is," he said in an admonishing tone, but not so kindly as if he were condescending to give good advice to a cracksman of repute. "Give it up. You'll find we are too many for you."

The fixed smile on the Professor's lips wavered, as if the mocking spirit within had lost its assurance. Chief Inspector Heat went on:

"Don't you believe me—eh? Well, you've only got to look about you. We are. And anyway, you're not doing it well. You're always making a mess of it. Why, if the thieves didn't know their work better they would starve."

The hint of an invincible multitude behind that man's back roused a sombre indignation in the breast of the Professor. He smiled no longer his enigmatic and mocking smile. The resisting power of numbers, the unattackable stolidity of a great multitude, was the haunting fear of his sinister loneliness. His lips trembled for some time before he managed to say in a strangled voice:

"I am doing my work better than you're doing yours."

"That'll do now," interrupted Chief Inspector Heat hurriedly; and the Professor laughed right out this time. While still laughing he moved on; but he did not laugh long. It was a sad-faced, miserable little man who emerged from the narrow passage into the bustle of the broad thoroughfare. He walked with the nerveless gait of a tramp going on, still going on, indifferent to rain or sun in a sinister detachment from the aspects of sky and earth. Chief Inspector Heat, on the other hand, after watching him for a while, stepped out with the purposeful briskness of a man disregarding indeed the inclemencies of the weather, but conscious of having an authorised mission on this earth and the moral support of his kind. All the inhabitants of the immense town, the population of the whole country, and even the teeming millions struggling upon the planet, were with him—down to the very thieves and mendicants. Yes, the thieves themselves were sure to be with him in his present work. The consciousness of universal support in his general activity heartened him to grapple with the particular problem.

The problem immediately before the Chief Inspector was that of managing the Assistant Commissioner of his department, his immediate superior. This is the perennial problem of trusty and loyal servants; anarchism gave it its particular complexion, but nothing more. Truth to say, Chief Inspector Heat thought but little of anarchism. He did not attach undue importance to it, and could never bring himself to consider it seriously. It had more the character of disorderly conduct; disorderly without the human excuse of drunkenness, which at any rate implies good feeling and an amiable leaning towards festivity. As criminals, anarchists were distinctly no class—no class at all. And recalling the Professor, Chief Inspector Heat, without checking his swinging pace, muttered through his teeth:

"Lunatic."

Catching thieves was another matter altogether. It had that quality of seriousness belonging to every form of open sport where the best man wins under perfectly comprehensible rules. There were no rules for dealing with anarchists. And that was distasteful to the Chief Inspector. It was all foolishness, but that foolishness excited the public mind, affected persons in high places, and touched upon international relations. A hard, merciless contempt settled rigidly on the Chief Inspector's face as he walked on. His mind ran over all the anarchists of his flock. Not one of them had half the spunk of this or that burglar he had known. Not half—not one-tenth.

At headquarters the Chief Inspector was admitted at once to the Assistant Commissioner's private room. He found him, pen in hand, bent over a great table bestrewn with papers, as if worshipping an enormous double inkstand of bronze and crystal. Speaking tubes* resembling snakes were tied by the heads to the back of the Assistant Commissioner's wooden armchair, and their gaping mouths seemed ready to bite his elbows. And in this attitude he raised only his eyes, whose lids were darker than his face and very much creased. The reports had come in: every anarchist had been exactly accounted for.

After saying this he lowered his eyes, signed rapidly two single sheets of paper, and only then laid down his pen, and sat well back, directing an inquiring gaze at his renowned subordinate. The Chief Inspector stood it well, deferential but inscrutable.

"I daresay you were right," said the Assistant Commissioner, "in telling me at first that the London anarchists had nothing to do with this. I quite appreciate the excellent watch kept on them by your men. On the other hand, this, for the public, does not amount to more than a confession of ignorance."

The Assistant Commissioner's delivery was leisurely, as it were cautious. His thought seemed to rest poised on a word before

---

*Used for communication within a building.

passing to another, as though words had been the stepping-stones
for his intellect picking its way across the waters of error. "Unless
you have brought something useful from Greenwich," he added.

The Chief Inspector began at once the account of his investigation in a clear, matter-of-fact manner. His superior, turning his chair
a little, and crossing his thin legs, leaned sideways on his elbow, with
one hand shading his eyes. His listening attitude had a sort of angular and sorrowful grace. Gleams as of highly burnished silver
played on the sides of his ebony black head when he inclined it
slowly at the end.

Chief Inspector Heat waited with the appearance of turning over
in his mind all he had just said, but, as a matter of fact, considering
the advisability of saying something more. The Assistant Commissioner cut his hesitation short.

"You believe there were two men?" he asked, without uncover-
ing his eyes.

The Chief Inspector thought it more than probable. In his opinion, the two men had parted from each other within a hundred yards
from the Observatory walls. He explained also how the other man
could have got out of the park speedily without being observed. The
fog, though not very dense, was in his favour. He seemed to have es-
corted the other to the spot, and then to have left him there to do the
job single-handed. Taking the time those two were seen coming out
of Maze Hill Station by the old woman, and the time when the explosion was heard, the Chief Inspector thought that the other man
might have been actually at the Greenwich Park Station, ready to
catch the next train up, at the moment his comrade was destroying
himself so thoroughly.

"Very thoroughly—eh?" murmured the Assistant Commissioner
from under the shadow of his hand.

The Chief Inspector in a few vigorous words described the aspect of the remains. "The coroner's jury will have a treat," he added
grimly.

The Assistant Commissioner uncovered his eyes.

"We shall have nothing to tell them," he remarked languidly.

He looked up, and for a time watched the markedly noncommittal attitude of his Chief Inspector. His nature was one that
is not easily accessible to illusions. He knew that a department is at

the mercy of its subordinate officers, who have their own conceptions of loyalty. His career had begun in a tropical colony. He had liked his work there. It was police work. He had been very successful in tracking and breaking up certain nefarious secret societies amongst the natives. Then he took his long leave, and got married rather impulsively. It was a good match from a worldly point of view, but his wife formed an unfavourable opinion of the colonial climate on hearsay evidence. On the other hand, she had influential connections. It was an excellent match. But he did not like the work he had to do now. He felt himself dependent on too many subordinates and too many masters. The near presence of that strange emotional phenomenon called public opinion weighed upon his spirits, and alarmed him by its irrational nature. No doubt that from ignorance he exaggerated to himself its power for good and evil—especially for evil; and the rough east winds of the English spring (which agreed with his wife) augmented his general mistrust of men's motives and of the efficiency of their organisation. The futility of office work especially appalled him on those days so trying to his sensitive liver.

He got up, unfolding himself to his full height, and with a heaviness of step remarkable in so slender a man, moved across the room to the window. The panes streamed with rain, and the short street he looked down into lay wet and empty, as if swept clear suddenly by a great flood. It was a very trying day, choked in raw fog to begin with, and now drowned in cold rain. The flickering, blurred flames of gas-lamps seemed to be dissolving in a watery atmosphere. And the lofty pretensions of a mankind oppressed by the miserable indignities of the weather appeared as a colossal and hopeless vanity deserving of scorn, wonder, and compassion.

"Horrible, horrible!" thought the Assistant Commissioner to himself, with his face near the window-pane. "We have been having this sort of thing now for ten days; no, a fortnight—a fortnight." He ceased to think completely for a time. That utter stillness of his brain lasted about three seconds. Then he said perfunctorily: "You have set inquiries on foot for tracing that other man up and down the line?"

He had no doubt that everything needful had been done. Chief Inspector Heat knew, of course, thoroughly the business of man-hunting.

And these were the routine steps, too, that would be taken as a matter of course by the merest beginner. A few inquiries amongst the ticket collectors and the porters of the two small railway stations would give additional details as to the appearance of the two men; the inspection of the collected tickets would show at once where they came from that morning. It was elementary, and could not have been neglected. Accordingly the Chief Inspector answered that all this had been done directly the old woman had come forward with her deposition. And he mentioned the name of a station. "That's where they came from, sir," he went on. "The porter who took the tickets at Maze Hill remembers two chaps answering to the description passing the barrier. They seemed to him two respectable working men of a superior sort—sign painters or house decorators. The big man got out of a third-class compartment backward, with a bright tin can in his hand. On the platform he gave it to carry to the fair young fellow who followed him. All this agrees exactly with what the old woman told the police sergeant in Greenwich."

The Assistant Commissioner, still with his face turned to the window, expressed his doubt as to these two men having had anything to do with the outrage. All this theory rested upon the utterances of an old charwoman who had been nearly knocked down by a man in a hurry. Not a very substantial authority indeed, unless on the ground of sudden inspiration, which was hardly tenable.

"Frankly now, could she have been really inspired?" he queried, with grave irony, keeping his back to the room, as if entranced by the contemplation of the town's colossal forms half lost in the night. He did not even look round when he heard the mutter of the word "Providential" from the principal subordinate of his department, whose name, printed sometimes in the papers, was familiar to the great public as that of one of its zealous and hard-working protectors. Chief Inspector Heat raised his voice a little.

"Strips and bits of bright tin were quite visible to me," he said. "That's a pretty good corroboration."

"And these men came from that little country station," the Assistant Commissioner mused aloud, wondering. He was told that such was the name on two tickets out of three given up out of that

train at Maze Hill. The third person who got out was a hawker*
from Gravesend[6] well known to the porters. The Chief Inspector
imparted that information in a tone of finality with some ill-
humour, as loyal servants will do in the consciousness of their
fidelity and with the sense of the value of their loyal exertions. And
still the Assistant Commissioner did not turn away from the darkness outside, as vast as a sea.

"Two foreign anarchists coming from that place," he said, apparently to the window-pane. "It's rather unaccountable."

"Yes, sir. But it would be still more unaccountable if that Michaelis
weren't staying in a cottage in the neighbourhood."

At the sound of that name, falling unexpectedly into this annoying affair, the Assistant Commissioner dismissed brusquely the vague
remembrance of his daily whist[†] party at his club. It was the most
comforting habit of his life, in a mainly successful display of his skill
without the assistance of any subordinate. He entered his club to play
from five to seven, before going home to dinner, forgetting for those
two hours whatever was distasteful in his life, as though the game
were a beneficent drug for allaying the pangs of moral discontent.
His partners were the gloomily humorous editor of a celebrated magazine; a silent, elderly barrister[‡] with malicious little eyes; and a highly
martial, simple-minded old colonel with nervous brown hands. They
were his club acquaintances merely. He never met them elsewhere
except at the card-table. But they all seemed to approach the game
in the spirit of co-sufferers, as if it were indeed a drug against the
secret ills of existence; and every day as the sun declined over
the countless roofs of the town, a mellow, pleasurable impatience, resembling the impulse of a sure and profound friendship, lightened
his professional labours. And now this pleasurable sensation went out
of him with something resembling a physical shock, and was replaced by a special kind of interest in his work of social protection—
an improper sort of interest, which may be defined best as a sudden
and alert mistrust of the weapon in his hand.

---

*Salesman.

†A card game that was especially popular in the nineteenth century; a forerunner
to bridge.

‡A lawyer who argues cases before the higher courts of Britain.

CHAPTER SIX

THE lady patroness[1] of Michaelis, the ticket-of-leave apostle of humanitarian hopes, was one of the most influential and distinguished connections of the Assistant Commissioner's wife, whom she called Annie, and treated still rather as a not very wise and utterly inexperienced young girl. But she had consented to accept him on a friendly footing, which was by no means the case with all of his wife's influential connections. Married young and splendidly at some remote epoch of the past, she had had for a time a close view of great affairs and even of some great men. She herself was a great lady. Old now in the number of her years, she had that sort of exceptional temperament which defies time with scornful disregard, as if it were a rather vulgar convention submitted to by the mass of inferior mankind. Many other conventions easier to set aside, alas! failed to obtain her recognition, also on temperamental grounds— either because they bored her, or else because they stood in the way of her scorns and sympathies. Admiration was a sentiment unknown to her (it was one of the secret griefs of her most noble husband against her)—first, as always more or less tainted with mediocrity, and next, as being in a way an admission of inferiority. And both were frankly inconceivable to her nature. To be fearlessly outspoken in her opinions came easily to her, since she judged solely from the standpoint of her social position. She was equally untrammelled in her actions; and as her tactfulness proceeded from genuine humanity, her bodily vigour remained remarkable and her superiority was serene and cordial, three generations had admired her infinitely, and the last she was likely to see had pronounced her a wonderful woman. Meantime intelligent, with a sort of lofty simplicity, and curious at heart, but not like many women merely of social gossip, she amused her age by attracting within her ken through the power of her great, almost historical, social prestige everything that rose above the dead level of mankind, lawfully or unlawfully, by position, wit, audacity, fortune or misfortune. Royal highnesses, artists, men of science,

young statesmen, and charlatans of all ages and conditions, who, un-
substantial and light, bobbing up like corks, show best the direction
of the surface currents, had been welcomed in that house, listened
to, penetrated, understood, appraised, for her own edification. In her
own words, she liked to watch what the world was coming to. And as
she had a practical mind her judgment of men and things, though
based on special prejudices, was seldom totally wrong, and almost
never wrong-headed. Her drawing-room was probably the only place
in the wide world where an Assistant Commissioner of Police could
meet a convict liberated on a ticket-of-leave on other than professional and official ground. Who had brought Michaelis there one afternoon the Assistant Commissioner did not remember very well. He
had a notion it must have been a certain Member of Parliament of
illustrious parentage and unconventional sympathies, which were
the standing joke of the comic papers. The notabilities and even the
simple notorieties of the day brought each other freely to that temple
of an old woman's not ignoble curiosity. You never could guess whom
you were likely to come upon being received in semi-privacy within
the faded blue silk and gilt-frame screen, making a cosy nook for a
couch and a few arm-chairs in the great drawing-room, with its hum
of voices and the groups of people seated or standing in the light of
six tall windows.

Michaelis had been the object of a revulsion of popular sentiment, the same sentiment which years ago had applauded the ferocity of the life sentence passed upon him for complicity in a
rather mad attempt to rescue some prisoners from a police van.[2]
The plan of the conspirators had been to shoot down the horses and
overpower the escort. Unfortunately, one of the police constables
got shot too. He left a wife and three small children, and the death
of that man aroused through the length and breadth of a realm for
whose defence, welfare, and glory men die every day as a matter of
duty, an outburst of furious indignation, of a raging implacable pity
for the victim. Three ring-leaders got hanged. Michaelis, young
and slim, locksmith by trade, and great frequenter of evening
schools, did not even know that anybody had been killed, his part
with a few others being to force open the door at the back of the
special conveyance. When arrested he had a bunch of skeleton
keys in one pocket, a heavy chisel in another, and a short crowbar

in his hand: neither more nor less than a burglar. But no burglar would have received such a heavy sentence. The death of the constable had made him miserable at heart, but the failure of the plot also. He did not conceal either of these sentiments from his empanelled countrymen,* and that sort of compunction appeared shockingly imperfect to the crammed court. The judge on passing sentence commented feelingly upon the depravity and callousness of the young prisoner.

That made the groundless fame of his condemnation; the fame of his release was made for him on no better grounds by people who wished to exploit the sentimental aspect of his imprisonment either for purposes of their own or for no intelligible purpose. He let them do so in the innocence of his heart and the simplicity of his mind. Nothing that happened to him individually had any importance. He was like those saintly men whose personality is lost in the contemplation of their faith. His ideas were not in the nature of convictions. They were inaccessible to reasoning. They formed in all their contradictions and obscurities an invincible and humanitarian creed, which he confessed rather than preached, with an obstinate gentleness, a smile of pacific assurance on his lips, and his candid blue eyes cast down because the sight of faces troubled his inspiration developed in solitude. In that characteristic attitude, pathetic in his grotesque and incurable obesity which he had to drag like a galley-slave's bullet† to the end of his days, the Assistant Commissioner of Police beheld the ticket-of-leave apostle filling a privileged arm-chair within the screen.‡ He sat there by the head of the old lady's couch, mild-voiced and quiet, with no more self-consciousness than a very small child, and with something of a child's charm—the appealing charm of trustfulness. Confident of the future, whose secret ways had been revealed to him within the four walls of a well-known penitentiary, he had no reason to look with suspicion upon anybody. If he could not give the great and curious lady a very definite idea as to what the world was coming

---

*Jurors.
†Prisoner's ball and chain.
‡Partition shielding an area from heat or draft as well as from public view.

to, he had managed without effort to impress her by his unembittered faith, by the sterling quality of his optimism.

A certain simplicity of thought is common to serene souls at both ends of the social scale. The great lady was simple in her own way. His views and beliefs had nothing in them to shock or startle her, since she judged them from the standpoint of her lofty position. Indeed, her sympathies were easily accessible to a man of that sort. She was not an exploiting capitalist herself; she was, as it were, above the play of economic conditions. And she had a great capacity of pity for the more obvious forms of common human miseries, precisely because she was such a complete stranger to them that she had to translate her conception into terms of mental suffering before she could grasp the notion of their cruelty. The Assistant Commissioner remembered very well the conversation between these two. He had listened in silence. It was something as exciting in a way, and even touching in its foredoomed futility, as the efforts at moral intercourse between the inhabitants of remote planets. But this grotesque incarnation of humanitarian passion appealed somehow to one's imagination. At last Michaelis rose, and taking the great lady's extended hand, shook it, retained it for a moment in his great cushioned palm with unembarrassed friendliness, and turned upon the semi-private nook of the drawing-room his back, vast and square, and as if distended under the short tweed jacket. Glancing about in serene benevolence, he waddled along to the distant door between the knots of other visitors. The murmur of conversations paused on his passage. He smiled innocently at a tall, brilliant girl, whose eyes met his accidentally, and went out unconscious of the glances following him across the room. Michaelis's first appearance in the world was a success—a success of esteem* unmarred by a single murmur of derision. The interrupted conversations were resumed in their proper tone, grave or light. Only a well-set-up, long-limbed, active-looking man of forty talking with two ladies near a window remarked aloud, with an unexpected depth of feeling: "Eighteen stone,† I should say, and not five foot six. Poor fellow! It's terrible—terrible."

---

*A worthy or notable accomplishment (from the French expression *succès d'estime*).

†Over 250 pounds (a stone is a British unit of measure equal to 14 pounds).

The lady of the house, gazing absently at the Assistant Commissioner, left alone with her on the private side of the screen, seemed to be rearranging her mental impressions behind the thoughtful immobility of her handsome old face. Men with grey moustaches and full, healthy, vaguely smiling countenances approached, circling round the screen; two mature women with a matronly air of gracious resolution; a clean-shaved individual with sunken cheeks, and dangling a gold-mounted eyeglass on a broad black ribbon with an old-world, dandified effect. A silence deferential, but full of reserves, reigned for a moment, and then the great lady exclaimed, not with resentment, but with a sort of protesting indignation:

"And that officially is supposed to be a revolutionist! What nonsense." She looked hard at the Assistant Commissioner, who murmured apologetically:

"Not a dangerous one perhaps."

"Not dangerous—I should think not, indeed. He is a mere believer. It's the temperament of a saint," declared the great lady in a firm tone. "And they kept him shut up for twenty years. One shudders at the stupidity of it. And now they have let him out everybody belonging to him is gone away somewhere or dead. His parents are dead; the girl he was to marry has died while he was in prison; he has lost the skill necessary for his manual occupation. He told me all this himself with the sweetest patience, but then, he said, he had had plenty of time to think out things for himself. A pretty compensation! If that's the stuff revolutionists are made of some of us may well go on our knees to them," she continued in a slightly bantering voice, while the banal society smiles hardened on the worldly faces turned towards her with conventional deference. "The poor creature is obviously no longer in a position to take care of himself. Somebody will have to look after him a little."

"He should be recommended to follow a treatment of some sort," the soldierly voice of the active-looking man was heard advising earnestly from a distance. He was in the pink of condition for his age, and even the texture of his long frock-coat had a character of elastic soundness, as if it were a living tissue. "The man is virtually a cripple," he added with unmistakable feeling.

Other voices, as if glad of the opening, murmured hasty compassion. "Quite startling," "Monstrous," "Most painful to see." The lank man, with the eyeglass on a broad ribbon, pronounced mincingly the word "Grotesque," whose justness was appreciated by those standing near him. They smiled at each other.

The Assistant Commissioner had expressed no opinion either then or later, his position making it impossible for him to ventilate any independent view of a ticket-of-leave convict. But, in truth, he shared the view of his wife's friend and patron that Michaelis was a humanitarian sentimentalist, a little mad, but upon the whole incapable of hurting a fly intentionally. So when that name cropped up suddenly in this vexing bomb affair he realised all the danger of it for the ticket-of-leave apostle, and his mind reverted at once to the old lady's well-established infatuation. Her arbitrary kindness would not brook patiently any interference with Michaelis's freedom. It was a deep, calm, convinced infatuation. She had not only felt him to be inoffensive, but she had said so, which last by a confusion of her absolutist mind became a sort of incontrovertible demonstration. It was as if the monstrosity of the man, with his candid infant's eyes and a fat angelic smile, had fascinated her. She had come to believe almost his theory of the future, since it was not repugnant to her prejudices. She disliked the new element of plutocracy in the social compound, and industrialism as a method of human development appeared to her singularly repulsive in its mechanical and unfeeling character. The humanitarian hopes of the mild Michaelis tended not towards utter destruction, but merely towards the complete economic ruin of the system. And she did not really see where was the moral harm of it. It would do away with all the multitude of the "parvenus,"* whom she disliked and mistrusted, not because they had arrived anywhere (she denied that), but because of their profound unintelligence of the world, which was the primary cause of the crudity of their perceptions and the aridity of their hearts. With the annihilation of all capital they would vanish too; but universal ruin (providing it was universal, as it was revealed to Michaelis) would leave the social values untouched. The disappearance of the last piece of money could not affect people of position. She could not conceive how it could

---

*Those who have newly come into wealth; social upstarts (French).

affect her position, for instance. She had developed these discoveries to the Assistant Commissioner with all the serene fearlessness of an old woman who had escaped the blight of indifference. He had made for himself the rule to receive everything of that sort in a silence which he took care from policy and inclination not to make offensive. He had an affection for the aged disciple of Michaelis, a complex sentiment depending a little on her prestige, on her personality, but most of all on the instinct of flattered gratitude. He felt himself really liked in her house. She was kindness personified. And she was practically wise too, after the manner of experienced women. She made his married life much easier than it would have been without her generously full recognition of his rights as Annie's husband. Her influence upon his wife, a woman devoured by all sorts of small selfishnesses, small envies, small jealousies, was excellent. Unfortunately, both her kindness and her wisdom were of unreasonable complexion, distinctly feminine, and difficult to deal with. She remained a perfect woman all along her full tale of years, and not as some of them do become—a sort of slippery, pestilential old man in petticoats. And it was as of a woman that he thought of her—the specially choice incarnation of the feminine, wherein is recruited the tender, ingenuous, and fierce bodyguard for all sorts of men who talk under the influence of an emotion, true or fraudulent; for preachers, seers, prophets, or reformers.

Appreciating the distinguished and good friend of his wife, and himself, in that way, the Assistant Commissioner became alarmed at the convict Michaelis' possible fate. Once arrested on suspicion of being in some way, however remote, a party to this outrage, the man could hardly escape being sent back to finish his sentence at least. And that would kill him; he would never come out alive. The Assistant Commissioner made a reflection extremely unbecoming his official position without being really creditable to his humanity.

"If the fellow is laid hold of again," he thought, "she will never forgive me."

The frankness of such a secretly outspoken thought could not go without some derisive self-criticism. No man engaged in a work he does not like can preserve many saving illusions about himself. The distaste, the absence of glamour, extend from the occupation to the personality. It is only when our appointed activities seem by a lucky accident to obey the particular earnestness of our temperament that we can taste the comfort of complete self-deception. The Assistant Commissioner did not like his work at home. The police work he had been engaged on in a distant part of the globe had the saving character of an irregular sort of warfare, or at least the risk and excitement of open-air sport. His real abilities, which were mainly of an administrative order, were combined with an adventurous disposition. Chained to a desk in the thick of four millions of men, he considered himself the victim of ironic fate—the same, no doubt, which had brought about his marriage with a woman exceptionally sensitive in the matter of colonial climate, besides other limitations testifying to the delicacy of her nature—and her tastes. Though he judged his alarm sardonically he did not dismiss the improper thought from his mind. The instinct of self-preservation was strong within him. On the contrary, he repeated it mentally with profane emphasis and a fuller precision: "Damn it! If that infernal Heat has his way the fellow'll die in prison smothered in his fat, and she'll never forgive me."

His black, narrow figure, with the white band of the collar under the silvery gleams on the close-cropped hair at the back of the head, remained motionless. The silence had lasted such a long time that Chief Inspector Heat ventured to clear his throat. This noise produced its effect. The zealous and intelligent officer was asked by his superior, whose back remained turned to him immovably:

"You connect Michaelis with this affair?"

Chief Inspector Heat was very positive, but cautious.

"Well, sir," he said, "we have enough to go upon. A man like that has no business to be at large, anyhow."

"You will want some conclusive evidence," came the observation in a murmur.

Chief Inspector Heat raised his eyebrows at the black, narrow back, which remained obstinately presented to his intelligence and his zeal.

"There will be no difficulty in getting up sufficient evidence against *him*," he said, with virtuous complacency. "You may trust me for that, sir," he added, quite unnecessarily, out of the fullness of his heart; for it seemed to him an excellent thing to have that man in hand to be thrown down to the public should it think fit to roar with any special indignation in this case. It was impossible to say yet whether it would roar or not. That in the last instance depended, of course, on the newspaper press. But in any case, Chief Inspector Heat, purveyor of prisons by trade, and a man of legal instincts, did logically believe that incarceration was the proper fate for every declared enemy of the law. In the strength of that conviction he committed a fault of tact. He allowed himself a little conceited laugh, and repeated:

"Trust me for that, sir."

This was too much for the forced calmness under which the Assistant Commissioner had for upwards of eighteen months concealed his irritation with the system and the subordinates of his office. A square peg forced into a round hole, he had felt like a daily outrage that long-established smooth roundness into which a man of less sharply angular shape would have fitted himself, with voluptuous acquiescence, after a shrug or two. What he resented most was just the necessity of taking so much on trust. At the little laugh of Chief Inspector Heat's he spun swiftly on his heels, as if whirled away from the window-pane by an electric shock. He caught on the latter's face not only the complacency proper to the occasion lurking under the moustache, but the vestiges of experimental watchfulness in the round eyes, which had been, no doubt, fastened on his back, and now met his glance for a second before the intent character of their stare had the time to change to a merely startled appearance.

The Assistant Commissioner of Police[3] had really some qualifications for his post. Suddenly his suspicion was awakened. It is but fair to say that his suspicions of the police methods (unless the police happened to be a semi-military body organised by himself) was not difficult to arouse. If it ever slumbered from sheer weariness, it was but lightly; and his appreciation of Chief Inspector Heat's zeal and ability, moderate in itself, excluded all notion of moral confidence. "He's up to something," he exclaimed mentally, and at once became angry. Crossing over to his desk with headlong strides, he sat down violently. "Here I am stuck in a litter of paper," he reflected, with unreasonable resentment, "supposed to hold all the threads in my hands, and yet I can but hold what is put in my hand, and nothing else. And they can fasten the other ends of the threads where they please."

He raised his head, and turned towards his subordinate a long, meagre face with the accentuated features of an energetic Don Quixote.*

"Now what is it you've got up your sleeve?"

The other stared. He stared without winking in a perfect immobility of his round eyes, as he was used to stare at the various members of the criminal class when, after being duly cautioned, they made their statements in the tones of injured innocence, or false simplicity, or sullen resignation. But behind that professional and stony fixity there was some surprise too, for in such a tone, combining nicely the note of contempt and impatience, Chief Inspector Heat, the right-hand man of the department, was not used to be addressed. He began in a procrastinating manner, like a man taken unawares by a new and unexpected experience.

"What I've got against that man Michaelis you mean, sir?"

The Assistant Commissioner watched the bullet head;[4] the points of that Norse rover's moustache, falling below the line of the heavy jaw; the whole full and pale physiognomy,† whose determined character was marred by too much flesh; at the cunning wrinkles radiating from the outer corners of the eyes—and in that purposeful contemplation of the valuable and trusted officer he drew a conviction so sudden that it moved him like an inspiration.

"I have reason to think that when you came into this room," he said in measured tones, "it was not Michaelis who was in your mind; not principally—perhaps not at all."

"You have reason to think, sir?" muttered Chief Inspector Heat, with every appearance of astonishment, which up to a certain point was genuine enough. He had discovered in this affair a delicate and perplexing side, forcing upon the discoverer a certain amount of insincerity—that sort of insincerity which, under the names of skill, prudence, discretion, turns up at one point or another in most human affairs. He felt at the moment like a tight-rope artist might feel if suddenly, in the middle of the performance, the manager of the music hall were to rush out of the proper managerial seclusion and begin to

---

*Hence, extremely gaunt, like the hero of Miguel de Cervantes's *Don Quixote* (1605, 1615).

†Facial features, as taken to be expressive of an individual's character.

shake the rope. Indignation, the sense of moral insecurity engendered by such a treacherous proceeding, joined to the immediate apprehension of a broken neck, would, in the colloquial phrase, put him in a state. And there would be also some scandalised concern for his art too, since a man must identify himself with something more tangible than his own personality, and establish his pride somewhere, either in his social position, or in the quality of the work he is obliged to do, or simply in the superiority of the idleness he may be fortunate enough to enjoy.

"Yes," said the Assistant Commissioner; "I have. I do not mean to say that you have not thought of Michaelis at all. But you are giving the fact you've mentioned a prominence which strikes me as not quite candid, Inspector Heat. If that is really the track of discovery, why haven't you followed it up at once, either personally or by sending one of your men to that village?"

"Do you think, sir, I have failed in my duty there?" the Chief Inspector asked, in a tone which he sought to make simply reflective. Forced unexpectedly to concentrate his faculties upon the task of preserving his balance, he had seized upon that point, and exposed himself to a rebuke; for the Assistant Commissioner, frowning slightly, observed that this was a very improper remark to make.

"But since you've made it," he continued coldly, "I'll tell you that this is not my meaning."

He paused, with a straight glance of his sunken eyes which was a full equivalent of the unspoken termination "and you know it." The head of the so-called Special Crimes Department, debarred by his position from going out of doors personally in quest of secrets locked up in guilty breasts, had a propensity to exercise his considerable gifts for the detection of incriminating truth upon his own subordinates. That peculiar instinct could hardly be called a weakness. It was natural. He was a born detective. It had unconsciously governed his choice of a career, and if it ever failed him in life it was perhaps in the one exceptional circumstance of his marriage — which was also natural. It fed, since it could not roam abroad, upon the human material which was brought to it in its official seclusion. We can never cease to be ourselves.

His elbow on the desk, his thin legs crossed, and nursing his cheek in the palm of his meagre hand, the Assistant Commissioner in charge of the Special Crimes branch was getting hold of the case with growing interest. His Chief Inspector, if not an absolutely worthy foeman of his penetration, was at any rate the most worthy of all within his reach. A mistrust of established reputations was strictly in character with the Assistant Commissioner's ability as detector. His memory evoked a certain old fat and wealthy native chief in the distant colony whom it was a tradition for the successive Colonial Governors to trust and make much of as a firm friend and supporter of the order and legality established by white men; whereas, when examined sceptically, he was found out to be principally his own good friend, and nobody else's. Not precisely a traitor, but still a man of many dangerous reservations in his fidelity, caused by a due regard for his own advantage, comfort, and safety. A fellow of some innocence in his native duplicity, but none the less dangerous. He took some finding out. He was physically a big man, too, and (allowing for the difference of colour, of course) Chief Inspector Heat's appearance recalled him to the memory of the superior. It was not the eyes nor yet the lips exactly. It was bizarre. But does not Alfred Wallace relate in his famous book on the Malay Archipelago[5] how, amongst the Aru Islanders, he discovered in an old and naked savage with a sooty skin a peculiar resemblance to a dear friend at home?

For the first time since he took up his appointment the Assistant Commissioner felt as if he were going to do some real work for his salary. And that was a pleasurable sensation. "I'll turn him inside out like an old glove," thought the Assistant Commissioner, with his eyes resting pensively upon Chief Inspector Heat.

"No, that was not my thought," he began again. "There is no doubt about you knowing your business—no doubt at all; and that's precisely why I——" He stopped short, and changing his tone: "What could you bring up against Michaelis of a definite nature? I mean apart from the fact that the two men under suspicion—you're certain there were two of them—came last from a railway station within three miles of the village where Michaelis is living now."

"This by itself is enough for us to go upon, sir, with that sort of man," said the Chief Inspector, with returning composure. The slight approving movement of the Assistant Commissioner's head went far to pacify the resentful astonishment of the renowned officer. For Chief Inspector Heat was a kind man, an excellent husband, a devoted father; and the public and departmental confidence he enjoyed acting favourably upon an amiable nature, disposed him to feel friendly towards the successive Assistant Commissioners he had seen pass through that very room. There had been three in his time. The first one, a soldierly, abrupt, red-faced person, with white eyebrows and an explosive temper, could be managed with a silken thread. He left on reaching the age limit. The second, a perfect gentleman, knowing his own and everybody else's place to a nicety, on resigning to take up a higher appointment out of England got decorated for (really) Inspector Heat's services. To work with him had been a pride and a pleasure. The third, a bit of a dark horse from the first, was at the end of eighteen months something of a dark horse still to the department. Upon the whole, Chief Inspector Heat believed him to be in the main harmless — odd-looking, but harmless. He was speaking now, and the Chief Inspector listened with outward deference (which means nothing, being a matter of duty) and inwardly with benevolent toleration.

"Michaelis reported himself before leaving London for the country?"

"Yes, sir; he did."

"And what may he be doing there?" continued the Assistant Commissioner, who was perfectly informed on that point. Fitted with painful tightness into an old wooden arm-chair, before a worm-eaten oak table in an upstairs room of a four-roomed cottage with a roof of moss-grown tiles, Michaelis was writing night and day in a shaky, slanting hand that "Autobiography of a Prisoner" which was to be like a Book of Revelation in the history of mankind.[6] The conditions of confined space, seclusion, and solitude in a small four-roomed cottage were favourable to his inspiration. It was like being in prison, except that one was never disturbed for the odious purpose of taking exercise according to the tyrannical regulations of his old home in the penitentiary. He could not tell whether the sun still shone on the earth or not. The perspiration of the literary labour dropped from his brow. A delightful enthusiasm urged him on. It was the liberation of his inner life, the letting out of his soul into the wide world. And the zeal of his guileless vanity (first awakened by the offer of five hundred pounds from a publisher) seemed something predestined and holy.

"It would be, of course, most desirable to be informed exactly," insisted the Assistant Commissioner uncandidly.

Chief Inspector Heat, conscious of renewed irritation at this display of scrupulousness, said that the county police had been notified from the first of Michaelis' arrival, and that a full report could be obtained in a few hours. A wire to the superintendent——

Thus he spoke, rather slowly, while his mind seemed already to be weighing the consequences. A slight knitting of the brow was the outward sign of this. But he was interrupted by a question.

"You've sent that wire already?"

"No, sir," he answered, as if surprised.

The Assistant Commissioner uncrossed his legs suddenly. The briskness of that movement contrasted with the casual way in which he threw out a suggestion.

"Would you think that Michaelis had anything to do with the preparation of that bomb, for instance?"

The Chief Inspector assumed a reflective manner.

"I wouldn't say so. There's no necessity to say anything at present. He associates with men who are classed as dangerous. He was made a delegate of the Red Committee less than a year after his release on licence. A sort of compliment, I suppose."

And the Chief Inspector laughed a little angrily, a little scornfully. With a man of that sort scrupulousness was a misplaced and even an illegal sentiment. The celebrity bestowed upon Michaelis on his release two years ago by some emotional journalists in want of special copy had rankled ever since in his breast. It was perfectly legal to arrest that man on the barest suspicion. It was legal and expedient on the face of it. His two former chiefs would have seen the point at once; whereas this one, without saying either yes or no, sat there, as if lost in a dream. Moreover, besides being legal and expedient, the arrest of Michaelis solved a little personal difficulty which worried Chief Inspector Heat somewhat. This difficulty had its bearing upon his reputation, upon his comfort, and even upon the efficient performance of his duties. For, if Michaelis no doubt knew something about this outrage, the Chief Inspector was fairly certain that he did not know too much. This was just as well. He knew much less—the Chief Inspector was positive—than certain other individuals he had in his mind, but whose arrest seemed to him inexpedient, besides being a more complicated matter, on account of the rules of the game. The rules of the game did not protect so much Michaelis, who was an ex-convict. It would be stupid not to take advantage of legal facilities, and the journalists who had written him up with emotional gush would be ready to write him down with emotional indignation.

This prospect, viewed with confidence, had the attraction of a personal triumph for Chief Inspector Heat. And deep down in his blameless bosom of an average married citizen, almost unconscious but potent nevertheless, the dislike of being compelled by events to meddle with the desperate ferocity of the Professor had its say. This dislike had been strengthened by the chance meeting in the lane. The encounter did not leave behind with Chief Inspector Heat that satisfactory sense of superiority the members of the police force get from the unofficial but intimate side of their intercourse with the criminal classes, by which the vanity of power is soothed, and the vulgar love of domination over our fellow-creatures is flattered as worthily as it deserves.

The perfect anarchist was not recognised as a fellow-creature by Chief Inspector Heat. He was impossible—a mad dog to be left alone. Not that the Chief Inspector was afraid of him; on the contrary, he meant to have him some day. But not yet; he meant to get hold of him in his own time, properly and effectively according to the rules of the game. The present was not the right time for attempting that feat, not the right time for many reasons, personal and of public service. This being the strong feeling of Inspector Heat, it appeared to him just and proper that this affair should be shunted off its obscure and inconvenient track, leading goodness knows where, into a quiet (and lawful) siding called Michaelis. And he repeated, as if reconsidering the suggestion conscientiously:

"The bomb. No, I would not say that exactly. We may never find that out. But it's clear that he is connected with this in some way, which we can find out without much trouble."

His countenance had that look of grave, overbearing indifference once well known and much dreaded by the better sort of thieves. Chief Inspector Heat, though what is called a man, was not a smiling animal. But his inward state was that of satisfaction at the passively receptive attitude of the Assistant Commissioner, who murmured gently:

"And you really think that the investigation should be made in that direction?"

"I do, sir."

"Quite convinced?"

"I am, sir. That's the true line for us to take."

The Assistant Commissioner withdrew the support of his hand from his reclining head with a suddenness that, considering his languid attitude, seemed to menace his whole person with collapse. But, on the contrary, he sat up, extremely alert, behind the great writing-table on which his hand had fallen with the sound of a sharp blow.

"What I want to know is, what put it out of your head till now?"

"Put it out of my head?" repeated the Chief Inspector very slowly.

"Yes. Till you were called into this room—you know."

The Chief Inspector felt as if the air between his clothing and his skin had become unpleasantly hot. It was the sensation of an unprecedented and incredible experience.

"Of course," he said, exaggerating the deliberation of his utterance to the utmost limits of possibility, "if there is a reason, of which I know nothing, for not interfering with the convict Michaelis, perhaps it's just as well I didn't start the county police after him."

This took such a long time to say that the unflagging attention of the Assistant Commissioner seemed a wonderful feat of endurance. His retort came without delay.

"No reason whatever that I know of. Come, Chief Inspector, this finessing with me is highly improper on your part—highly improper. And it's also unfair, you know. You shouldn't leave me to puzzle things out for myself like this. Really, I am surprised."

He paused, then added smoothly: "I need scarcely tell you that this conversation is altogether unofficial."

These words were far from pacifying the Chief Inspector. The indignation of a betrayed tight-rope performer was strong within him. In his pride of a trusted servant he was affected by the assurance that the rope was not shaken for the purpose of breaking his neck, as by an exhibition of impudence. As if anybody were afraid!

Assistant Commissioners come and go, but a valuable Chief Inspector is not an ephemeral office phenomenon. He was not afraid of getting a broken neck. To have his performance spoiled was more than enough to account for the glow of honest indignation. And as thought is no respecter of persons, the thought of Chief Inspector Heat took a threatening and prophetic shape. "You, my boy," he said to himself, keeping his round and habitually roving eyes fastened upon the Assistant Commissioner's face—"you, my boy, you don't know your place, and your place won't know you very long either, I bet."

As if in provoking answer to that thought, something like the ghost of an amiable smile passed on the lips of the Assistant Commissioner. His manner was easy and business-like while he persisted in administering another shake to the tight rope.

"Let us come now to what you have discovered on the spot, Chief Inspector," he said.

"A fool and his job are soon parted,"[7] went on the train of prophetic thought in Chief Inspector Heat's head. But it was immediately followed by the reflection that a higher official, even when "fired out" (this was the precise image), has still the time as he flies through the door to launch a nasty kick at the shin-bones of a subordinate. Without softening very much the basilisk* nature of his stare, he said impassively:

"We are coming to that part of my investigation, sir."

"That's right. Well, what have you brought away from it?"

The Chief Inspector, who had made up his mind to jump off the rope, came to the ground with gloomy frankness.

"I've brought away an address," he said, pulling out of his pocket without haste a singed rag of dark blue cloth. "This belongs to the overcoat the fellow who got himself blown to pieces was wearing. Of course, the overcoat may not have been his, and may even have been stolen. But that's not at all probable if you look at this."

The Chief Inspector, stepping up to the table, smoothed out carefully the rag of blue cloth. He had picked it up from the repulsive heap in the mortuary, because a tailor's name is found

---

* Baleful, malignant (from the basilisk, a fabled reptile with a fatal glance).

sometimes under the collar. It is not often of much use, but still——
He only half expected to find anything useful, but certainly he did
not expect to find—not under the collar at all, but stitched carefully
on the underside of the lapel—a square piece of calico with an address written on it in marking-ink.

The Chief Inspector removed his smoothing hand.

"I carried it off with me without anybody taking notice," he said.
"I thought it best. It can always be produced if required."

The Assistant Commissioner, rising a little in his chair, pulled
the cloth over to his side of the table. He sat looking at it in silence.
Only the number 32 and the name of Brett Street[8] were written in
marking-ink on a piece of calico slightly larger than an ordinary cigarette paper. He was genuinely surprised.

"Can't understand why he should have gone about labelled like
this," he said, looking up at Chief Inspector Heat. "It's a most extraordinary thing."

"I met once in the smoking-room of an hotel an old gentleman
who went about with his name and address sewn on in all his coats
in case of an accident or sudden illness," said the Chief Inspector.
"He professed to be eighty-four years old, but he didn't look his age.
He told me he was also afraid of losing his memory suddenly, like
those people he had been reading of in the papers."

A question from the Assistant Commissioner, who wanted to
know what was No. 32 Brett Street, interrupted that reminiscence
abruptly. The Chief Inspector, driven down to the ground by unfair artifices, had elected to walk the path of unreserved openness.
If he believed firmly that to know too much was not good for the
department, the judicious holding back of knowledge was as far as
his loyalty dared to go for the good of the service. If the Assistant
Commissioner wanted to mismanage this affair nothing, of course,
could prevent him. But, on his own part, he now saw no reason for
a display of alacrity. So he answered concisely:

"It's a shop, sir."

The Assistant Commissioner, with his eyes lowered on the rag of
blue cloth, waited for more information. As that did not come he
proceeded to obtain it by a series of questions propounded with gentle patience. Thus he acquired an idea of the nature of Mr. Verloc's
commerce, of his personal appearance, and heard at last his name.

In a pause the Assistant Commissioner raised his eyes, and discovered some animation on the Chief Inspector's face. They looked at each other in silence.

"Of course," said the latter, "the department has no record of that man."

"Did any of my predecessors have any knowledge of what you have told me now?" asked the Assistant Commissioner, putting his elbows on the table and raising his joined hands before his face, as if about to offer prayer, only that his eyes had not a pious expression.

"No, sir; certainly not. What would have been the object? That sort of man could never be produced publicly to any good purpose. It was sufficient for me to know who he was, and to make use of him in a way that could be used publicly."

"And do you think that sort of private knowledge consistent with the official position you occupy?"

"Perfectly, sir. I think it's quite proper. I will take the liberty to tell you, sir, that it makes me what I am—and I am looked upon as a man who knows his work. It's a private affair of my own. A personal friend of mine in the French police gave me the hint that the fellow was an Embassy spy. Private friendship, private information, private use of it—that's how I look upon it."

The Assistant Commissioner after remarking to himself that the mental state of the renowned Chief Inspector seemed to affect the outline of his lower jaw, as if the lively sense of his high professional distinction had been located in that part of his anatomy, dismissed the point for the moment with a calm "I see." Then leaning his cheek on his joined hands:

"Well then—speaking privately if you like—how long have you been in private touch with this Embassy spy?"

To this inquiry the private answer of the Chief Inspector, so private that it was never shaped into audible words, was:

"Long before you were even thought of for your place here."

The so-to-speak public utterance was much more precise:

"I saw him for the first time in my life a little more than seven years ago, when two Imperial Highnesses and the Imperial Chancellor were on a visit here. I was put in charge of all the arrangements for looking after them. Baron Stott-Wartenheim was Ambassador then. He was a very nervous old gentleman. One evening, three days before the Guildhall Banquet,[9] he sent word that he wanted to see me for a moment. I was downstairs, and the carriages were at the door to take the Imperial Highnesses and the Chancellor to the Opera. I went up at once. I found the Baron walking up and down his bedroom in a pitiable state of distress, squeezing his hands together. He assured me he had the fullest confidence in our police and in my abilities, but he had there a man just come over from Paris whose information could be trusted implicitly. He wanted me to hear what that man had to say. He took me at once into a dressing-room next door, where I saw a big fellow in a heavy overcoat sitting all alone on a chair, and holding his hat and stick in one hand. The Baron said to him in French, 'Speak, my friend.' The light in that room was not very good. I talked with him for some five minutes perhaps. He certainly gave me a piece of very startling news. Then the Baron took me aside nervously to praise him up to me, and when I turned round again I discovered that the fellow had vanished like a ghost. Got up and sneaked out down some back stairs, I suppose. There was no time to run after him, as I had to hurry off after the Ambassador down the great staircase, and see the party started safe for the Opera. However, I acted upon the information that very night. Whether it was perfectly correct or not, it did look serious enough. Very likely it saved us from an ugly trouble on the day of the Imperial visit to the city.

"Some time later, a month or so after my promotion to Chief Inspector, my attention was attracted to a big burly man I thought I had seen somewhere before, coming out in a hurry from a jeweller's shop in the Strand. I went after him, as it was on my way towards Charing Cross, and there seeing one of our detectives across the road, I beckoned him over, and pointed out the fellow to him, with instructions to watch his movements for a couple of days, and then report to me. No later than next afternoon my man turned up to tell me that the fellow had married his landlady's daughter at a registrar's office that very day at 11.30 a.m., and had gone off with her to Margate for a week.[10] Our man had seen the luggage being put on the cab. There were some old Paris labels on one of the bags. Somehow I couldn't get the fellow out of my head, and the very next time I had to go to Paris on service I spoke about him to that friend of mine in the Paris police. My friend said: 'From what you tell me I think you must mean a rather well-known hanger-on and emissary of the Revolutionary Red Committee. He says he is an Englishman by birth. We have an idea that he has been for a good few years now a secret agent of one of the foreign Embassies in London.' This woke up my memory completely. He was the vanishing fellow I saw sitting on a chair in Baron Stott-Wartenheim's bedroom. I told my friend that he was quite right. The fellow was a secret agent to my certain knowledge. Afterwards my friend took the trouble to ferret out the complete record of that man for me. I thought I had better know all there was to know; but I don't suppose you want to hear his history now, sir?"

The Assistant Commissioner shook his supported head. "The history of your relations with that useful personage is the only thing that matters just now," he said, closing slowly his weary, deep-set eyes, and then opening them swiftly with a greatly refreshed glance.

"There's nothing official about them," said the Chief Inspector bitterly. "I went into his shop one evening, told him who I was, and reminded him of our first meeting. He didn't as much as twitch an eyebrow. He said that he was married and settled now, and that all he wanted was not to be interfered with in his little business. I took it upon myself to promise him that as long as he didn't go in for anything obviously outrageous he would be left alone by the police. That was worth something to him, because a word from us to the Custom-House people would have been enough to get some of these packages he gets from Paris and Brussels opened in Dover,[11] with confiscation to follow for certain, and perhaps a prosecution as well at the end of it."

"That's a very precarious trade," murmured the Assistant Commissioner. "Why did he go in for that?"

The Chief Inspector raised scornful eyebrows dispassionately.

"Most likely got a connection—friends on the Continent—amongst people who deal in such wares. They would be just the sort he would consort with. He's a lazy dog, too—like the rest of them."

"What do you get from him in exchange for your protection?"

The Chief Inspector was not inclined to enlarge on the value of Mr. Verloc's services.

"He would not be much good to anybody but myself. One has got to know a good deal beforehand to make use of a man like that. I can understand the sort of hint he can give. And when I want a hint he can generally furnish it to me."

The Chief Inspector lost himself suddenly in a discreet reflective mood; and the Assistant Commissioner repressed a smile at the fleeting thought that the reputation of Chief Inspector Heat might possibly have been made in a great part by the Secret Agent Verloc.

"In a more general way of being of use, all our men of the Special Crimes section on duty at Charing Cross and Victoria [12] have orders to take careful notice of anybody they may see with him. He meets the new arrivals frequently, and afterwards keeps track of them. He seems to have been told off* for that sort of duty. When I want an address in a hurry, I can always get it from him. Of course, I know how to manage our relations. I haven't seen him to speak to three times in the last two years. I drop him a line, unsigned, and he answers me in the same way at my private address."

From time to time the Assistant Commissioner gave an almost imperceptible nod. The Chief Inspector added that he did not suppose Mr. Verloc to be deep in the confidence of the prominent members of the Revolutionary International Council, but that he was generally trusted, of that there could be no doubt. "Whenever I've had reason to think there was something in the wind," he concluded, "I've always found he could tell me something worth knowing."

The Assistant Commissioner made a significant remark.

"He failed you this time."

"Neither had I wind of anything in any other way," retorted Chief Inspector Heat. "I asked him nothing, so he could tell me nothing. He isn't one of our men. It isn't as if he were in our pay."

"No," muttered the Assistant Commissioner. "He's a spy in the pay of a foreign government. We could never confess to him."

---

*Appointed.

"I must do my work in my own way," declared the Chief Inspector. "When it comes to that I would deal with the devil himself, and take the consequences. There are things not fit for everybody to know."

"Your idea of secrecy seems to consist in keeping the chief of your department in the dark. That's stretching it perhaps a little too far, isn't it? He lives over his shop?"

"Who—Verloc? Oh yes. He lives over his shop. The wife's mother, I fancy, lives with them."

"Is the house watched?"

"Oh dear, no. It wouldn't do. Certain people who come there are watched. My opinion is that he knows nothing of this affair."

"How do you account for this?" The Assistant Commissioner nodded at the cloth rag lying before him on the table.

"I don't account for it at all, sir. It's simply unaccountable. It can't be explained by what I know." The Chief Inspector made those admissions with the frankness of a man whose reputation is established as if on a rock, "At any rate not at this present moment. I think that the man who had most to do with it will turn out to be Michaelis."

"You do?"

"Yes, sir; because I can answer for all the others."

"What about that other man supposed to have escaped from the park?"

"I should think he's far away by this time," opined the Chief Inspector.

The Assistant Commissioner looked hard at him, and rose suddenly, as though having made up his mind to some course of action. As a matter of fact, he had that very moment succumbed to a fascinating temptation. The Chief Inspector heard himself dismissed with instructions to meet his superior early next morning for further consultation upon the case. He listened with an impenetrable face, and walked out of the room with measured steps.

Whatever might have been the plans of the Assistant Commissioner they had nothing to do with that desk work, which was the bane of his existence because of its confined nature and apparent lack of reality. It could not have had, or else the general air of alacrity that came upon the Assistant Commissioner would have been inexplicable. As soon as he was left alone he looked for his hat impulsively, and put it on his head. Having done that, he sat down again to reconsider the whole matter. But as his mind was already made up, this did not take long. And before Chief Inspector Heat had gone very far on the way home, he also left the building.

CHAPTER SEVEN

T HE Assistant Commissioner walked along a short and narrow street like a wet, muddy ditch, then crossing a very broad thoroughfare entered a public edifice, and sought speech with a young private secretary (unpaid) of a great personage.

This fair, smooth-faced young man, whose symmetrically arranged hair gave him the air of a large and neat schoolboy, met the Assistant Commissioner's request with a doubtful look, and spoke with bated breath.

"Would he see you? I don't know about that. He has walked over from the House an hour ago to talk with the permanent Under-Secretary, and now he's ready to walk back again. He might have sent for him; but he does it for the sake of a little exercise, I suppose. It's all the exercise he can find time for while this session lasts. I don't complain; I rather enjoy these little strolls. He leans on my arm, and doesn't open his lips. But, I say, he's very tired, and—well—not in the sweetest of tempers just now."

"It's in connection with that Greenwich affair."

"Oh! I say! He's very bitter against you people. But I will go and see, if you insist."

"Do. That's a good fellow," said the Assistant Commissioner.

The unpaid secretary admired this pluck. Composing for himself an innocent face, he opened a door, and went in with the assurance of a nice and privileged child. And presently he reappeared, with a nod to the Assistant Commissioner, who, passing through the same door left open for him, found himself with the great Personage in a large room.

Vast in bulk and stature, with a long white face, which, broadened at the base by a big double chin, appeared egg-shaped in the fringe of thin greyish whisker, the great Personage[1] seemed an expanding man. Unfortunate from a tailoring point of view, the cross-folds in the middle of a buttoned black coat added to the impression, as if the fastenings of the garment were tried to the utmost. From the head, set upward on a thick neck, the eyes, with puffy lower lids, stared with a haughty droop on each side of a hooked aggressive nose, nobly salient in the vast pale circumference of the face. A shiny silk hat and a pair of worn gloves lying ready on the end of a long table looked expanded too, enormous.

He stood on the hearthrug in big, roomy boots, and uttered no word of greeting.

"I would like to know if this is the beginning of another dynamite campaign," he asked at once in a deep, very smooth voice. "Don't go into details. I have no time for that."

The Assistant Commissioner's figure before this big and rustic Presence had the frail slenderness of a reed addressing an oak. And indeed the unbroken record of that man's descent surpassed in the number of centuries the age of the oldest oak in the country.

"No. As far as one can be positive about anything, I can assure you that it is not."

"Yes. But your idea of assurances over there," said the great man with a contemptuous wave of his hand towards a window giving on the broad thoroughfare, "seems to consist mainly in making the Secretary of State look a fool. I have been told positively in this very room less than a month ago that nothing of the sort was even possible."

The Assistant Commissioner glanced in the direction of the window calmly.

"You will allow me to remark, Sir Ethelred, that so far I have had no opportunity to give you assurances of any kind."

The haughty droop of the eyes was focused now upon the Assistant Commissioner.

"True," confessed the deep, smooth voice. "I sent for Heat. You are still rather a novice in your new berth. And how are you getting on over there?"

"I believe I am learning something every day."

"Of course, of course. I hope you will get on."

"Thank you, Sir Ethelred. I've learned something to-day, and even within the last hour or so. There is much in this affair of a kind that does not meet the eye in a usual anarchist outrage, even if one looked into it as deep as can be. That's why I am here."

The great man put his arms akimbo, the backs of his big hands resting on his hips.

"Very well. Go on. Only no details, pray. Spare me the details."

"You shall not be troubled with them, Sir Ethelred," the Assistant Commissioner began, with a calm and untroubled assurance. While he was speaking the hands on the face of the clock behind the great man's back—a heavy, glistening affair of massive scrolls in the same dark marble as the mantelpiece, and with a ghostly, evanescent tick—had moved through the space of seven minutes. He spoke with a studious fidelity to a parenthetical manner, into which every little fact—that is, every detail—fitted with delightful ease. Not a murmur nor even a movement hinted at interruption. The great Personage might have been the statue of one of his own princely ancestors stripped of a crusader's war harness, and put into an ill-fitting frock-coat. The Assistant Commissioner felt as though he were at liberty to talk for an hour. But he kept his head, and at the end of the time mentioned above he broke off with a sudden conclusion, which, reproducing the opening statement, pleasantly surprised Sir Ethelred by its apparent swiftness and force.

"The kind of thing which meets us under the surface of this affair, otherwise without gravity, is unusual—in this precise form at least—and requires special treatment."

The tone of Sir Ethelred was deepened, full of conviction.

"I should think so—involving the Ambassador of a foreign power!"

"Oh! The Ambassador!" protested the other, erect and slender, allowing himself a mere half-smile. "It would be stupid of me to advance anything of the kind. And it is absolutely unnecessary, because if I am right in my surmises, whether ambassador or hall porter, it's a mere detail."

Sir Ethelred opened a wide mouth, like a cavern, into which the hooked nose seemed anxious to peer; there came from it a subdued rolling sound, as from a distant organ with the scornful indignation stop.

"No! These people are too impossible. What do they mean by importing their methods of Crim-Tartary here? A Turk would have more decency."*

---

*That is, utterly barbaric, according to popular prejudice.

"You forget, Sir Ethelred, that, strictly speaking, we know nothing positively—as yet."

"No! But how would you define it? Shortly."

"Barefaced audacity amounting to childishness of a peculiar sort."

"We can't put up with the innocence of nasty little children," said the great and expanded Personage, expanding a little more, as it were. The haughty drooping glance struck crushingly the carpet at the Assistant Commissioner's feet. "They'll have to get a hard rap on the knuckles over this affair. We must be in a position to—— What is your general idea, stated shortly? No need to go into details."

"No, Sir Ethelred. In principle, I should lay it down that the existence of secret agents should not be tolerated, as tending to augment the positive dangers of the evil against which they are used. That the spy will fabricate his information is a mere commonplace. But in the sphere of political and revolutionary action, relying partly on violence, the professional spy has every facility to fabricate the very facts themselves, and will spread the double evil of emulation in one direction, and of panic, hasty legislation, unreflecting hate, on the other. However, this is an imperfect world——"

The deep-voiced Presence on the hearthrug, motionless, with big elbows stuck out, said hastily:

"Be lucid, please."

"Yes, Sir Ethelred—— An imperfect world. Therefore directly the character of this affair suggested itself to me, I thought it should be dealt with with special secrecy, and ventured to come over here."

"That's right," approved the great Personage, glancing down complacently over his double chin. "I am glad there's somebody over at your shop who thinks that the Secretary of State may be trusted now and then."

The Assistant Commissioner had an amused smile.

"I was really thinking that it might be better at this stage for Heat to be replaced by——"

"What! Heat? An ass—eh?" exclaimed the great man, with distinct animosity.

"Not at all. Pray, Sir Ethelred, don't put that unjust interpretation on my remarks."

"Then what? Too clever by half?"

"Neither—at least not as a rule. All the grounds of my surmises I have from him. The only thing I've discovered by myself is that he has been making use of that man privately. Who could blame him? He's an old police hand. He told me virtually that he must have tools to work with. It occurred to me that this tool should be surrendered to the Special Crimes division as a whole, instead of remaining the private property of Chief Inspector Heat. I extend my conception of our departmental duties to the suppression of the secret agent. But Chief Inspector Heat is an old departmental hand. He would accuse me of perverting its morality and attacking its efficiency. He would define it bitterly as protection extended to the criminal class of revolutionists. It would mean just that to him."

"Yes. But what do you mean?"

"I mean to say, first, that there's but poor comfort in being able to declare that any given act of violence—damaging property or destroying life—is not the work of anarchism at all, but of something else altogether—some species of authorised scoundrelism. This, I fancy, is much more frequent than we suppose. Next, it's obvious that the existence of these people in the pay of foreign governments destroys in a measure the efficiency of our supervision. A spy of that sort can afford to be more reckless than the most reckless of conspirators. His occupation is free from all restraint. He's without as much faith as is necessary for complete negation, and without that much law as is implied in lawlessness. Thirdly, the existence of these spies amongst the revolutionary groups, which we are reproached for harbouring here, does away with all certitude. You have received a reassuring statement from Chief Inspector Heat some time ago. It was by no means groundless—and yet this episode happens. I call it an episode, because this affair, I make bold to say, is episodic; it is no part of any general scheme, however wild. The very peculiarities which surprise and perplex Chief Inspector Heat establish its character in my eyes. I am keeping clear of details, Sir Ethelred."

The Personage on the hearthrug had been listening with profound attention.

"Just so. Be as concise as you can."

The Assistant Commissioner intimated by an earnest deferential gesture that he was anxious to be concise.

"There is a peculiar stupidity and feebleness in the conduct of this affair which gives me excellent hopes of getting behind it, and finding there something else than an individual freak of fanaticism. For it is a planned thing, undoubtedly. The actual perpetrator seems to have been led by the hand to the spot, and then abandoned hurriedly to his own devices. The inference is that he was imported from abroad for the purpose of committing this outrage. At the same time one is forced to the conclusion that he did not know enough English to ask his way, unless one were to accept the fantastic theory that he was a deaf mute. I wonder now— But this is idle. He has destroyed himself by an accident, obviously. Not an extraordinary accident. But an extraordinary little fact remains: the address on his clothing, discovered by the merest accident, too. It is an incredible little fact, so incredible that the explanation which will account for it is bound to touch the bottom of this affair. Instead of instructing Heat to go on with this case, my intention is to seek this explanation personally—by myself, I mean—where it may be picked up. That is in a certain shop in Brett Street, and on the lips of a certain secret agent, once upon a time the confidential and trusted spy of the late Baron Stott-Wartenheim, Ambassador of a Great Power to the Court of St. James."[2]

The Assistant Commissioner paused, then added: "Those fellows are a perfect pest." In order to raise his drooping glance to the speaker's face, the Personage on the hearthrug had gradually tilted his head farther back, which gave him an aspect of extraordinary haughtiness.

"Why not leave it to Heat?"

"Because he is an old departmental hand. They have their own morality. My line of inquiry would appear to him an awful perversion of duty. For him the plain duty is to fasten the guilt upon as many prominent anarchists as he can on some slight indications he had picked up in the course of his investigation on the spot; whereas I, he would say, am bent upon vindicating their innocence. I am trying to be as lucid as I can in presenting this obscure matter to you without details."

"He would, would he?" muttered the proud head of Sir Ethelred from its lofty elevation.

"I am afraid so—with an indignation and disgust of which you or I can have no idea. He's an excellent servant. We must not put an undue strain on his loyalty. That's always a mistake. Besides, I want a free hand—a freer hand than it would be perhaps advisable to give Chief Inspector Heat. I haven't the slightest wish to spare this man Verloc. He will, I imagine, be extremely startled to find his connection with this affair, whatever it may be, brought home to him so quickly. Frightening him will not be very difficult. But our true objective lies behind him somewhere. I want your authority to give him such assurances of personal safety as I may think proper."

"Certainly," said the Personage on the hearthrug. "Find out as much as you can; find it out in your own way."

"I must set about it without loss of time, this very evening," said the Assistant Commissioner.

Sir Ethelred shifted one hand under his coat tails, and tilting back his head, looked at him steadily.

"We'll have a late sitting to-night," he said. "Come to the House* with your discoveries if we are not gone home. I'll warn Toodles[3] to look out for you. He'll take you into my room."

The numerous family and the wide connections of the youthful-looking private secretary cherished for him the hope of an austere and exalted destiny. Meantime the social sphere he adorned in his hours of idleness chose to pet him under the above nickname. And Sir Ethelred, hearing it on the lips of his wife and girls every day (mostly at breakfast-time), had conferred upon it the dignity of unsmiling adoption.

The Assistant Commissioner was surprised and gratified extremely.

"I shall certainly bring my discoveries to the House on the chance of you having the time to——"

"I won't have the time," interrupted the great Personage. "But I will see you. I haven't the time now—— And you are going yourself?"

"Yes, Sir Ethelred. I think it the best way."

The Personage had tilted his head so far back that, in order to keep the Assistant Commissioner under his observation, he had to nearly close his eyes.

---

*The House of Commons.

"H'm. Ha! And how do you propose—— Will you assume a disguise?"

"Hardly a disguise! I'll change my clothes, of course."

"Of course," repeated the great man, with a sort of absentminded loftiness. He turned his big head slowly, and over his shoulder gave a haughty oblique stare to the ponderous marble timepiece with the sly, feeble tick. The gilt hands had taken the opportunity to steal through no less than five and twenty minutes behind his back.

The Assistant Commissioner, who could not see them, grew a little nervous in the interval. But the great man presented to him a calm and undismayed face.

"Very well," he said, and paused, as if in deliberate contempt of the official clock. "But what first put you in motion in this direction?"

"I have been always of opinion——" began the Assistant Commissioner.

"Ah! Yes. Opinion. That's of course. But the immediate motive?"

"What shall I say, Sir Ethelred? A new man's antagonism to old methods. A desire to know something at first hand. Some impatience. It's my old work, but the harness is different. It has been chafing me a little in one or two tender places."

"I hope you'll get on over there," said the great man kindly, extending his hand, soft to the touch, but broad and powerful like the hand of a glorified farmer. The Assistant Commissioner shook it, and withdrew.

In the outer room Toodles, who had been waiting perched on the edge of a table, advanced to meet him, subduing his natural buoyancy.

"Well? Satisfactory?" he asked, with airy importance.

"Perfectly. You've earned my undying gratitude," answered the Assistant Commissioner, whose long face looked wooden in contrast with the peculiar character of the other's gravity, which seemed perpetually ready to break into ripples and chuckles.

"That's all right. But seriously, you can't imagine how irritated he is by the attacks on his Bill for the Nationalisation of Fisheries. They call it the beginning of social revolution. Of course, it is a revolutionary measure. But these fellows have no decency. The personal attacks——"

"I read the papers," remarked the Assistant Commissioner.

"Odious? Eh? And you have no notion what a mass of work he has got to get through every day. He does it all himself. Seems unable to trust any one with these Fisheries."

"And yet he's given a whole half-hour to the consideration of my very small sprat,"* interjected the Assistant Commissioner.

"Small! Is it? I'm glad to hear that. But it's a pity you didn't keep away, then. This fight takes it out of him frightfully. The man's getting exhausted. I feel it by the way he leans on my arm as we walk over. And, I say, is he safe in the streets? Mullins has been marching his men up here this afternoon. There's a constable stuck by every lamp-post, and every second person we meet between this and Palace Yard[4] is an obvious 'tec.' It will get on his nerves presently. I say, these foreign scoundrels aren't likely to throw something at him—are they? It would be a national calamity. The country can't spare him."

"Not to mention yourself. He leans on your arm," suggested the Assistant Commissioner soberly. "You would both go."

"It would be an easy way for a young man to go down into history! Not so many British Ministers have been assassinated[5] as to make it a minor incident. But seriously now——"

"I am afraid that if you want to go down into history you'll have to do something for it. Seriously, there's no danger whatever for both of you but from overwork."

The sympathetic Toodles welcomed this opening for a chuckle.

"The Fisheries won't kill me. I am used to late hours," he declared, with ingenuous levity. But, feeling an instant compunction, he began to assume an air of statesman-like moodiness, as one draws on a glove. "His massive intellect will stand any amount of work. It's his nerves that I am afraid of. The reactionary gang, with that abusive brute Cheeseman at their head, insult him every night."

"If he will insist on beginning a revolution!" murmured the Assistant Commissioner.

---

*Insignificant matter or person (from the name for a type of small fish).

"The time has come, and he is the only man great enough for the work," protested the revolutionary Toodles, flaring up under the calm, speculative gaze of the Assistant Commissioner. Somewhere in a corridor a distant bell tinkled urgently, and with devoted vigilance the young man pricked up his ears at the sound. "He's ready to go now," he exclaimed in a whisper, snatched up his hat, and vanished from the room.

The Assistant Commissioner went out by another door in a less elastic manner. Again he crossed the wide thoroughfare, walked along a narrow street, and re-entered hastily his own departmental buildings.[6] He kept up this accelerated pace to the door of his private room. Before he had closed it fairly his eyes sought his desk. He stood still for a moment, then walked up, looked all round on the floor, sat down in his chair, rang a bell, and waited.

"Chief Inspector Heat gone yet?"

"Yes, sir. Went away half an hour ago."

He nodded. "That will do." And sitting still, with his hat pushed off his forehead, he thought that it was just like Heat's confounded cheek to carry off quietly the only piece of material evidence. But he thought this without animosity. Old and valued servants will take liberties. The piece of overcoat with the address sewn on was certainly not a thing to leave about. Dismissing from his mind this manifestation of Chief Inspector Heat's mistrust, he wrote and dispatched a note to his wife, charging her to make his apologies to Michaelis's great lady, with whom they were engaged to dine that evening.

The short jacket and the low, round hat he assumed in a sort of curtained alcove containing a washstand, a row of wooden pegs and a shelf, brought out wonderfully the length of his grave, brown face. He stepped back into the full light of the room, looking like the vision of a cool, reflective Don Quixote, with the sunken eyes of a dark enthusiast and a very deliberate manner. He left the scene of his daily labours quickly like an unobtrusive shadow. His descent into the street was like the descent into a slimy aquarium from which the water had been run off. A murky, gloomy dampness enveloped him. The walls of the houses were wet, the mud of the roadway glistened with an effect of phosphorescence, and when he emerged into the Strand out of a narrow street by the side of

Charing Cross Station the genius of the locality* assimilated him.
He might have been but one more of the queer foreign fish that can
be seen of an evening about there flitting round the dark corners.

He came to a stand on the very edge of the pavement, and
waited. His exercised eyes had made out in the confused movements of lights and shadows thronging the roadway the crawling
approach of a hansom. He gave no sign; but when the low step gliding along the curbstone came to his feet he dodged in skilfully in
front of the big turning wheel, and spoke up through the little trap-
door almost before the man gazing supinely ahead from his perch
was aware of having been boarded by a fare.

It was not a long drive. It ended by signal abruptly, nowhere in
particular, between two lamp-posts before a large drapery establishment—a long range of shops already lapped up in sheets of cor-
rugated iron for the night. Tendering a coin through the trap-door
the fare slipped out and away, leaving an effect of uncanny, eccentric ghostliness upon the driver's mind. But the size of the coin was
satisfactory to his touch, and his education not being literary, he
remained untroubled by the fear of finding it presently turned to a
dead leaf in his pocket. Raised above the world of fares by the nature of his calling, he contemplated their actions with a limited interest. The sharp pulling of his horse right round expressed his
philosophy.

Meantime the Assistant Commissioner was already giving his
order to a waiter in a little Italian restaurant round the corner—one
of those traps for the hungry, long and narrow, baited with a perspective of mirrors and white napery; without air, but with an atmosphere
of their own—an atmosphere of fraudulent cookery mocking an abject mankind in the most pressing of its miserable necessities. In this
immoral atmosphere the Assistant Commissioner, reflecting upon his
enterprise, seemed to lose some more of his identity. He had a sense
of loneliness, of evil freedom. It was rather pleasant. When, after paying for his short meal, he stood up and waited for his change, he saw
himself in the sheet of glass, and was struck by his foreign appearance.
He contemplated his own image with a melancholy and inquisitive

---

*The pervading spirit of a place (from the Latin *genius loci*).

gaze, then by sudden inspiration raised the collar of his jacket. This arrangement appeared to him commendable, and he completed it by giving an upward twist to the ends of his black moustache. He was satisfied by the subtle modification of his personal aspect caused by these small changes. "That'll do very well," he thought. "I'll get a little wet, a little splashed——"

He became aware of the waiter at his elbow and of a small pile of silver coins on the edge of the table before him. The waiter kept one eye on it, while his other eye followed the long back of a tall, not very young girl, who passed up to a distant table looking perfectly sightless and altogether unapproachable. She seemed to be an habitual customer.

On going out the Assistant Commissioner made to himself the observation that the patrons of the place had lost in the frequentation of fraudulent cookery all their national and private characteristics. And this was strange, since the Italian restaurant is such a peculiarly British institution.[7] But these people were as denationalised as the dishes set before them with every circumstance of unstamped respectability. Neither was their personality stamped in any way, professionally, socially, or racially. They seemed created for the Italian restaurant, unless the Italian restaurant had been perchance created for them. But that last hypothesis was unthinkable, since one could not place them anywhere outside those special establishments. One never met these enigmatical persons elsewhere. It was impossible to form a precise idea what occupations they followed by day and where they went to bed at night. And he himself had become unplaced. It would have been impossible for anybody to guess his occupation. As to going to bed, there was a doubt even in his own mind. Not indeed in regard to his domicile itself, but very much so in respect of the time when he would be able to return there. A pleasurable feeling of independence possessed him when he heard the glass doors swing to behind his back with a sort of imperfect baffled thud. He advanced at once into an immensity of greasy slime and damp plaster interspersed with lamps, and enveloped, oppressed, penetrated, choked, and suffocated by the blackness of a wet London night, which is composed of soot and drops of water.

Brett Street was not very far away. It branched off, narrow, from the side of an open triangular space surrounded by dark and mysterious houses, temples of petty commerce emptied of traders for the night. Only a fruiterer's stall at the corner made a violent blaze of light and colour. Beyond all was black, and the few people passing in that direction vanished at one stride beyond the glowing heaps of oranges and lemons. No footsteps echoed. They would never be heard of again. The adventurous head of the Special Crimes Department watched these disappearances from a distance with an interested eye. He felt light-hearted, as though he had been ambushed all alone in a jungle many thousands of miles away from departmental desks and official inkstands. This joyousness and dispersion of thought before a task of some importance seems to prove that this world of ours is not such a very serious affair after all. For the Assistant Commissioner was not constitutionally inclined to levity.

The policeman on the beat projected his sombre and moving form against the luminous glory of oranges and lemons, and entered Brett Street without haste. The Assistant Commissioner, as though he were a member of the criminal classes, lingered out of sight, awaiting his return. But this constable seemed to be lost for ever to the force. He never returned: must have gone out at the other end of Brett Street.

The Assistant Commissioner, reaching this conclusion, entered the street in his turn, and came upon a large van arrested in front of the dimly lit window-panes of a carters' eating-house.* The man was refreshing himself inside, and the horses, their big heads lowered to the ground, fed out of nose-bags steadily. Farther on, on the opposite side of the street, another suspect patch of dim light issued from Mr. Verloc's shop front, hung with papers, heaving with vague piles of cardboard boxes and the shapes of books. The Assistant Commissioner stood observing it across the roadway. There could be no mistake. By the side of the front window, encumbered by the shadows of nondescript things, the door, standing ajar, let escape on the pavement a narrow, clear streak of gaslight within.

Behind the Assistant Commissioner the van and horses, merged into one mass, seemed something alive—a square-backed black monster blocking half the street, with sudden iron-shod stampings,

---

*Place where drivers of carts or wagons ate.

fierce jingles, and heavy, blowing sighs. The harshly festive, ill-omened glare of a large and prosperous public-house faced the other end of Brett Street across a wide road. This barrier of blazing lights, opposing the shadows gathered about the humble abode of Mr. Verloc's domestic happiness, seemed to drive the obscurity of the street back upon itself, make it more sullen, brooding, and sinister.

CHAPTER EIGHT

HAVING infused by persistent importunities some sort of heat into the chilly interest of several licensed victuallers (the acquaintances once upon a time of her late unlucky husband), Mrs. Verloc's mother had at last secured her admission to certain almshouses founded by a wealthy innkeeper for the destitute widows of the trade.[1]

This end, conceived in the astuteness of her uneasy heart, the old woman had pursued with secrecy and determination. That was the time when her daughter Winnie could not help passing a remark to Mr. Verloc that "Mother has been spending half-crowns and five shillings almost every day this last week[2] in cab fares." But the remark was not made grudgingly. Winnie respected her mother's infirmities. She was only a little surprised at this sudden mania for locomotion. Mr. Verloc, who was sufficiently magnificent in his way, had grunted the remark impatiently aside as interfering with his meditations. These were frequent, deep, and prolonged; they bore upon a matter more important than five shillings — distinctly more important, and beyond all comparison more difficult to consider in all its aspects with philosophical serenity.

Her objects attained in astute secrecy, the heroic old woman had made a clean breast of it to Mrs. Verloc. Her soul was triumphant and her heart tremulous. Inwardly she quaked, because she dreaded and admired the calm, self-contained character of her daughter Winnie, whose displeasure was made redoubtable by a diversity of dreadful silences. But she did not allow her inward apprehensions to rob her of the advantage of venerable placidity conferred upon her outward person by her triple chin, the floating ampleness of her ancient form, and the impotent condition of her legs.

The shock of the information was so unexpected that Mrs. Verloc, against her usual practice when addressed, interrupted the domestic occupation she was engaged upon. It was the dusting of the furniture in the parlour behind the shop. She turned her head towards her mother.

"Whatever did you want to do that for?" she exclaimed, in scandalised astonishment.

The shock must have been severe to make her depart from that distant and uninquiring acceptance of facts which was her force and her safeguard in life.

"Weren't you made comfortable enough here?"

She had lapsed into these inquiries, but next moment she saved the consistency of her conduct by resuming her dusting, while the old woman sat scared and dumb under her dingy white cap and lustreless dark wig.

Winnie finished the chair, and ran the duster along the mahogany at the back of the horse-hair sofa on which Mr. Verloc loved to take his ease in hat and overcoat. She was intent on her work, but presently she permitted herself another question.

"How in the world did you manage it, mother?"

As not affecting the inwardness of things, which it was Mrs. Verloc's principle to ignore, this curiosity was excusable. It bore merely on the methods. The old woman welcomed it eagerly as bringing forward something that could be talked about with much sincerity.

She favoured her daughter by an exhaustive answer, full of names and enriched by side comments upon the ravages of time as observed in the alteration of human countenances. The names were principally the names of licensed victuallers—"poor daddy's friends, my dear." She enlarged with special appreciation on the kindness and condescension of a large brewer, a Baronet* and an M.P.,† the Chairman of the Governors of the Charity.[3] She expressed herself thus warmly because she had been allowed to interview by appointment his private secretary—"a very polite gentleman, all in black, with a gentle, sad voice, but so very, very thin and quiet. He was like a shadow, my dear."

Winnie, prolonging her dusting operations till the tale was told to the end, walked out of the parlour into the kitchen (down two steps) in her usual manner, without the slightest comment.

---

*Lowest hereditary rank in Britain.
†Member of Parliament.

Shedding a few tears in sign of rejoicing at her daughter's man-suetude* in this terrible affair, Mrs. Verloc's mother gave play to her astuteness in the direction of her furniture, because it was her own; and sometimes she wished it hadn't been. Heroism is all very well, but there are circumstances when the disposal of a few tables and chairs, brass bedsteads, and so on, may be big with remote and disastrous consequences. She required a few pieces herself, the Foundation which, after many importunities, had gathered her to its charitable breast, giving nothing but bare planks and cheaply papered bricks to the objects of its solicitude. The delicacy guiding her choice to the least valuable and most dilapidated articles passed unacknowledged, because Winnie's philosophy consisted in not taking notice of the inside of facts; she assumed that mother took what suited her best. As to Mr. Verloc, his intense meditation, like a sort of Chinese wall,† isolated him completely from the phenomena of this world of vain effort and illusory appearances.

Her selection made, the disposal of the rest became a perplexing question in a particular way. She was leaving it in Brett Street, of course. But she had two children. Winnie was provided for by her sensible union with that excellent husband, Mr. Verloc. Stevie was destitute—and a little peculiar. His position had to be considered before the claims of legal justice and even the promptings of partiality. The possession of the furniture would not be in any sense a provision. He ought to have it—the poor boy. But to give it to him would be like tampering with his position of complete dependence. It was a sort of claim which she feared to weaken. Moreover, the susceptibilities of Mr. Verloc would perhaps not brook being beholden to his brother-in-law for the chairs he sat on. In a long experience of gentlemen lodgers, Mrs. Verloc's mother had acquired a dismal but resigned notion of the fantastic side of human nature. What if Mr. Verloc suddenly took it into his head to tell Stevie to take his blessed sticks‡ somewhere out of that? A division, on the

---

*Meekness, submission.
†Hence, entirely sequestered, as the Chinese were believed to be behind the Great Wall of China, a vast fortification built to protect the country against invasion from the north and west.
‡Furniture.

other hand, however carefully made, might give some cause of offence to Winnie. No. Stevie must remain destitute and dependent. And at the moment of leaving Brett Street she had said to her daughter: "No use waiting till I am dead, is there? Everything I leave here is altogether your own now, my dear."

Winnie, with her hat on, silent behind her mother's back, went on arranging the collar of the old woman's cloak. She got her handbag, an umbrella, with an impassive face. The time had come for the expenditure of the sum of three-and-sixpence on what might well be supposed the last cab drive of Mrs. Verloc's mother's life. They went out at the shop door.

The conveyance awaiting them would have illustrated the proverb that "truth can be more cruel than caricature," if such a proverb existed.[4] Crawling behind an infirm horse, a metropolitan hackney carriage* drew up on wobbly wheels and with a maimed driver on the box. This last peculiarity caused some embarrassment. Catching sight of a hooked iron contrivance protruding from the left sleeve of the man's coat, Mrs. Verloc's mother lost suddenly the heroic courage of these days. She really couldn't trust herself. "What do you think, Winnie?" She hung back. The passionate expostulations of the big-faced cabman seemed to be squeezed out of a blocked throat. Leaning over from his box, he whispered with mysterious indignation. What was the matter now? Was it possible to treat a man so? His enormous and unwashed countenance flamed red in the muddy stretch of the street. Was it likely they would have given him a licence, he inquired desperately, if——

The police constable of the locality quieted him by a friendly glance; then addressing himself to the two women without marked consideration, said:

"He's been driving a cab for twenty years. I never knew him to have an accident."

"Accident!" shouted the driver in a scornful whisper.

The policeman's testimony settled it. The modest assemblage of seven people, mostly under age, dispersed. Winnie followed her mother into the cab. Stevie climbed on the box. His vacant mouth

---

*Coach for hire.

and distressed eyes depicted the state of his mind in regard to the transactions which were taking place. In the narrow streets the progress of the journey was made sensible to those within by the near fronts of the houses gliding past slowly and shakily, with a great rattle and jingling of glass, as if about to collapse behind the cab; and the infirm horse, with the harness hung over his sharp backbone flapping very loose about his thighs, appeared to be dancing mincingly on his toes with infinite patience. Later on, in the wider space of Whitehall,[5] all visual evidences of motion became imperceptible. The rattle and jingle of glass went on indefinitely in front of the long Treasury building—and time itself seemed to stand still.

At last Winnie observed: "This isn't a very good horse."

Her eyes gleamed in the shadow of the cab straight ahead, immovable. On the box, Stevie shut his vacant mouth first, in order to ejaculate earnestly: "Don't."

The driver, holding high the reins twisted around the hook, took no notice. Perhaps he had not heard. Stevie's breast heaved.

"Don't whip."

The man turned slowly his bloated and sodden face of many colours bristling with white hairs. His little red eyes glistened with moisture. His big lips had a violet tint. They remained closed. With the dirty back of his whip-hand he rubbed the stubble sprouting on his enormous chin.

"You mustn't," stammered out Stevie violently. "It hurts."[6]

"Mustn't whip?" queried the other in a thoughtful whisper, and immediately whipped. He did this, not because his soul was cruel and his heart evil, but because he had to earn his fare. And for a time the walls of St. Stephen's,[7] with its towers and pinnacles, contemplated in immobility and silence a cab that jingled. It rolled too, however. But on the bridge[8] there was a commotion. Stevie suddenly proceeded to get down from the box. There were shouts on the pavement, people ran forward, the driver pulled up, whispering curses of indignation and astonishment. Winnie lowered the window, and put her head out, white as a ghost. In the depths of the cab, her mother was exclaiming, in tones of anguish: "Is that boy hurt? Is that boy hurt?"

Stevie was not hurt, he had not even fallen, but excitement as usual had robbed him of the power of connected speech. He could

do no more than stammer at the window: "Too heavy. Too heavy."
Winnie put out her hand on to his shoulder.

"Stevie! Get up on the box directly, and don't try to get down
again."

"No. No. Walk. Must walk."

In trying to state the nature of that necessity he stammered himself into utter incoherence. No physical impossibility stood in the
way of his whim. Stevie could have managed easily to keep pace
with the infirm, dancing horse without getting out of breath. But
his sister withheld her consent decisively. "The idea! Who ever
heard of such a thing! Run after a cab!" Her mother, frightened
and helpless in the depths of the conveyance, entreated:

"Oh, don't let him, Winnie. He'll get lost. Don't let him."

"Certainly not. What next! Mr. Verloc will be sorry to hear of
this nonsense, Stevie—I can tell you. He won't be happy at all."

The idea of Mr. Verloc's grief and unhappiness acting as usual
powerfully upon Stevie's fundamentally docile disposition, he
abandoned all resistance, and climbed up again on the box, with a
face of despair.

The cabby turned at him his enormous and inflamed countenance truculently. "Don't you go for trying this silly game again,
young fellow."

After delivering himself thus in a stern whisper, strained almost
to extinction, he drove on, ruminating solemnly. To his mind the incident remained somewhat obscure. But his intellect, though it had
lost its pristine vivacity in the benumbing years of sedentary exposure to the weather, lacked not independence or sanity. Gravely he
dismissed the hypothesis of Stevie being a drunken young nipper.*

Inside the cab the spell of silence, in which the two women had
endured shoulder to shoulder the jolting, rattling, and jingling of
the journey, had been broken by Stevie's outbreak. Winnie raised
her voice.

"You've done what you wanted, mother. You'll have only yourself to thank for it if you aren't happy afterwards. And I don't think
you'll be. That I don't. Weren't you comfortable enough in the

---

*Small boy; also a name for a pickpocket.

house? Whatever people'll think of us—you throwing yourself like this on a Charity!"

"My dear," screamed the old woman earnestly above the noise, "you've been the best of daughters to me. As to Mr. Verloc— there——"

Words failing her on the subject of Mr. Verloc's excellence, she turned her old tearful eyes to the roof of the cab. Then she averted her head on the pretence of looking out of the window, as if to judge of their progress. It was insignificant, and went on close to the curbstone. Night, the early dirty night, the sinister, noisy, hopeless, and rowdy night of South London, had overtaken her on her last cab drive. In the gas-light of the low-fronted shops her big cheeks glowed with an orange hue under a black and mauve bonnet.

Mrs. Verloc's mother's complexion had become yellow by the effect of age and from a natural predisposition to biliousness,* favoured by the trials of a difficult and worried existence, first as wife, then as widow. It was a complexion that under the influence of a blush would take on an orange tint. And this woman, modest indeed but hardened in the fires of adversity, of an age, moreover, when blushes are not expected, had positively blushed before her daughter. In the privacy of a four-wheeler, on her way to a charity cottage (one of a row) which by the exiguity† of its dimensions and the simplicity of its accommodation might well have been devised in kindness as a place of training for the still more straitened circumstances of the grave, she was forced to hide from her own child a blush of remorse and shame.

Whatever people will think? She knew very well what they did think, the people Winnie had in her mind—the old friends of her husband, and others too, whose interest she had solicited with such flattering success. She had not known before what a good beggar she could be. But she guessed very well what inference was drawn from her application. On account of that shrinking delicacy, which exists side by side with aggressive brutality in masculine nature, the inquiries into her circumstances had not been pushed very far. She had checked them by a visible compression of the lips and some

---

*Peevishness, irascibility (traditionally associated with a diseased liver).
†Scantiness.

display of an emotion determined to be eloquently silent. And the men would become suddenly incurious, after the manner of their kind. She congratulated herself more than once on having nothing to do with women, who being naturally more callous and avid of details, would have been anxious to be exactly informed by what sort of unkind conduct her daughter and son-in-law had driven her to that sad extremity. It was only before the secretary of the great brewer M.P. and Chairman of the Charity, who, acting for his principal, felt bound to be conscientiously inquisitive as to the real circumstances of the applicant, that she had burst into tears outright and aloud, as a cornered woman will weep. The thin and polite gentleman, after contemplating her with an air of being "struck all of a heap," abandoned his position under the cover of soothing remarks. She must not distress herself. The deed of the Charity did not absolutely specify "childless widows." In fact, it did not by any means disqualify her. But the discretion of the Committee must be an informed discretion. One could understand very well her unwillingness to be a burden, etc. etc. Thereupon, to his profound disappointment, Mrs. Verloc's mother wept some more with an augmented vehemence.

The tears of that large female in a dark, dusty wig, and ancient silk dress festooned with dingy white cotton lace, were the tears of genuine distress. She had wept because she was heroic and unscrupulous and full of love for both her children. Girls frequently get sacrificed to the welfare of the boys. In this case she was sacrificing Winnie. By the suppression of truth she was slandering her. Of course, Winnie was independent, and need not care for the opinion of people that she would never see, and who would never see her; whereas poor Stevie had nothing in the world he could call his own except his mother's heroism and unscrupulousness.

The first sense of security following on Winnie's marriage wore off in time (for nothing lasts), and Mrs. Verloc's mother, in the seclusion of the back bedroom, had recalled the teaching of that experience which the world impresses upon a widowed woman. But she had recalled it without vain bitterness; her store of resignation amounted almost to dignity. She reflected stoically that everything decays, wears out, in this world; that the way of kindness should be made easy to the well disposed; that her daughter Winnie was a most

devoted sister, and a very self-confident wife indeed. As regards Winnie's sisterly devotion, her stoicism flinched. She excepted that sentiment from the rule of decay affecting all things human and some
things divine. She could not help it; not to do so would have frightened her too much. But in considering the conditions of her daughter's married state, she rejected firmly all flattering illusions. She took
the cold and reasonable view that the less strain put on Mr. Verloc's
kindness the longer its effects were likely to last. That excellent
man loved his wife, of course, but he would, no doubt, prefer to
keep as few of her relations as was consistent with the proper display
of that sentiment. It would be better if its whole effect were concentrated on poor Stevie. And the heroic old woman resolved on
going away from her children as an act of devotion and as a move of
deep policy.

The "virtue" of this policy consisted in this (Mrs. Verloc's mother
was subtle in her way), that Stevie's moral claim would be strengthened. The poor boy—a good, useful boy, if a little peculiar—had
not a sufficient standing. He had been taken over with his mother,
somewhat in the same way as the furniture of the Belgravian mansion had been taken over, as if on the ground of belonging to her exclusively. What will happen, she asked herself (for Mrs. Verloc's
mother was in a measure imaginative), when I die? And when she
asked herself that question it was with dread. It was also terrible to
think that she would not then have the means of knowing what happened to the poor boy. But by making him over to his sister, by going
thus away, she gave him the advantage of a directly dependent position. This was the more subtle sanction of Mrs. Verloc's mother's
heroism and unscrupulousness. Her act of abandonment was really
an arrangement for settling her son permanently in life. Other people made material sacrifices for such an object, she in that way. It
was the only way. Moreover, she would be able to see how it worked.
Ill or well, she would avoid the horrible incertitude on her deathbed. But it was hard, hard, cruelly hard.

The cab rattled, jingled, jolted; in fact, the last was quite extraordinary. By its disproportionate violence and magnitude it obliterated
every sensation of onward movement; and the effect was of being
shaken in a stationary apparatus like a mediaeval device for the punishment of crime, or some very new-fangled invention for the cure

of a sluggish liver. It was extremely distressing; and the raising of
Mrs. Verloc's mother's voice sounded like a wail of pain.

"I know, my dear, you'll come to see me as often as you can
spare the time. Won't you?"

"Of course," answered Winnie shortly, staring straight before her.
And the cab jolted in front of a steamy, greasy shop in a blaze of
gas and in the smell of fried fish.

The old woman raised a wail again.

"And, my dear, I must see that poor boy every Sunday. He won't
mind spending the day with his old mother——"

Winnie screamed out stolidly:

"Mind! I should think not. That poor boy will miss you something cruel. I wish you had thought a little of that, mother."

Not think of it! The heroic woman swallowed a playful and inconvenient object like a billiard ball, which had tried to jump out
of her throat. Winnie sat mute for a while, pouting at the front of
the cab, then snapped out, which was an unusual tone with her:

"I expect I'll have a job with him at first, he'll be that restless——"

"Whatever you do, don't let him worry your husband, my dear."

Thus they discussed on familiar lines the bearings of a new situation. And the cab jolted. Mrs. Verloc's mother expressed some
misgivings. Could Stevie be trusted to come all that way alone?
Winnie maintained that he was much less "absent-minded" now.
They agreed as to that. It could not be denied. Much less—
hardly at all. They shouted at each other in the jingle with comparative cheerfulness. But suddenly the maternal anxiety broke
out afresh. There were two omnibuses to take, and a short walk
between. It was too difficult! The old woman gave way to grief
and consternation.

Winnie stared forward.

"Don't you upset yourself like this, mother. You must see him,
of course."

"No, my dear. I'll try not to."

She mopped her streaming eyes.

"But you can't spare the time to come with him, and if he should
forget himself and lose his way and somebody spoke to him sharply,
his name and address may slip his memory, and he'll remain lost for
days and days——"

The vision of a workhouse infirmary for poor Stevie—if only during inquiries—wrung her heart. For she was a proud woman. Winnie's stare had grown hard, intent, inventive.

"I can't bring him to you myself every week," she cried. "But don't you worry, mother. I'll see to it that he don't get lost for long."

They felt a peculiar bump; a vision of brick pillars lingered before the rattling windows of the cab; a sudden cessation of atrocious jolting and uproarious jingling dazed the two women. What had happened? They sat motionless and scared in the profound stillness till the door came open, and a rough, strained whispering was heard:

" 'Ere you are!"

A range of gabled little houses, each with one dim yellow window, on the ground floor, surrounded the dark open space of a grass plot planted with shrubs and railed off from the patchwork of lights and shadows in the wide road, resounding with the dull rumble of traffic. Before the door of one of these tiny houses—one without a light in the little downstairs window—the cab had come to a standstill. Mrs. Verloc's mother got out first, backwards, with a key in her hand. Winnie lingered on the flagstone path to pay the cabman. Stevie, after helping to carry inside a lot of small parcels, came out and stood under the light of a gas-lamp belonging to the Charity. The cabman looked at the pieces of silver, which, appearing very minute in his big, grimy palm, symbolised the insignificant results which reward the ambitious courage and toil of a mankind whose day is short on this earth of evil.

He had been paid decently—four one-shilling pieces—and he contemplated them in perfect stillness, as if they had been the surprising terms of a melancholy problem. The slow transfer of that treasure to an inner pocket demanded much laborious groping in the depths of decayed clothing. His form was squat and without flexibility. Stevie, slender, his shoulders a little up, and his hands thrust deep in the side pockets of his warm overcoat, stood at the edge of the path, pouting.

The cabman, pausing in his deliberate movements, seemed struck by some misty recollection.

"Oh! 'Ere you are, young fellow," he whispered. "You'll know him again—won't you?"

Stevie was staring at the horse, whose hind quarters appeared unduly elevated by the effect of emaciation. The little stiff tail seemed to have been fitted in for a heartless joke; and at the other end the thin, flat neck, like a plank covered with old horse-hide, drooped to the ground under the weight of an enormous bony head. The ears hung at different angles, negligently; and the macabre figure of that mute dweller on the earth steamed straight up from ribs and back-bone in the muggy stillness of the air.

The cabman struck lightly Stevie's breast with the iron hook pro-truding from a ragged, greasy sleeve.

"Look 'ere, young feller. 'Ow'd *you* like to sit behind this 'oss up to two o'clock in the morning p'r'aps?"

Stevie looked vacantly into the fierce little eyes with red-edged lids.

"He ain't lame," pursued the other, whispering with energy. "He ain't got no sore places on 'im. 'Ere he is. 'Ow would *you* like——"

His strained, extinct voice invested his utterance with a charac-ter of vehement secrecy. Stevie's vacant gaze was changing slowly into dread.

"You may well look! Till three and four o'clock in the morning. Cold and 'ungry. Looking for fares. Drunks."

His jovial purple cheeks bristled with white hairs; and like Virgil's Silenus, who, his face smeared with the juice of berries, discoursed of Olympian gods to the innocent shepherds of Sicily,[9] he talked to Stevie of domestic matters and the affairs of men whose sufferings are great and immortality by no means assured.

"I am a night cabby, I am," he whispered, with a sort of boastful exasperation. "I've got to take out what they will blooming well give me at the yard. I've got my missus and four kids at 'ome."

The monstrous nature of that declaration of paternity seemed to strike the world dumb. A silence reigned, during which the flanks of the old horse, the steed of apocalyptic misery,[10] smoked upwards in the light of the charitable gas-lamp.

The cabman grunted, then added in his mysterious whisper:

"This ain't an easy world."

Stevie's face had been twitching for some time, and at last his feelings burst out in their usual concise form.

"Bad! Bad!"

His gaze remained fixed on the ribs of the horse, self-conscious and sombre, as though he were afraid to look about him at the badness of the world. And his slenderness, his rosy lips and pale, clear complexion, gave him the aspect of a delicate boy, notwithstanding the fluffy growth of golden hair on his cheeks. He pouted in a scared way like a child. The cabman, short and broad, eyed him with his fierce little eyes that seemed to smart in a clear and corroding liquid.

" 'Ard on 'osses, but dam' sight 'arder on poor chaps like me," he wheezed just audibly.

"Poor! Poor!" stammered out Stevie, pushing his hands deeper into his pockets with convulsive sympathy. He could say nothing; for the tenderness to all pain and all misery, the desire to make the horse happy and the cabman happy, had reached the point of a bizarre longing to take them to bed with him. And that, he knew, was impossible. For Stevie was not mad. It was, as it were, a symbolic longing; and at the same time it was very distinct, because springing from experience, the mother of wisdom. Thus when as a child he cowered in a dark corner scared, wretched, sore, and miserable with the black, black misery of the soul, his sister Winnie used to come along and carry him off to bed with her, as into a heaven of consoling peace. Stevie, though apt to forget mere facts, such as his name and address for instance, had a faithful memory of sensations. To be taken into a bed of compassion was the supreme remedy, with the only one disadvantage of being difficult of application on a large scale. And looking at the cabman, Stevie perceived this clearly, because he was reasonable.

The cabman went on with his leisurely preparations as if Stevie had not existed. He made as if to hoist himself on the box, but at the last moment from some obscure motive, perhaps merely from disgust with carriage exercise, desisted. He approached instead the motionless partner of his labours, and stooping to seize the bridle, lifted up the big weary head to the height of his shoulder with one effort of his right arm, like a feat of strength.

"Come on," he whispered secretly.

Limping, he led the cab away. There was an air of austerity in this departure, the scrunched gravel of the drive crying out under the slowly turning wheels, the horse's lean thighs moving with ascetic deliberation away from the light into the obscurity of the open space bordered dimly by the pointed roofs and the feebly shining windows of the little almshouses. The plaint* of the gravel travelled slowly all round the drive. Between the lamps of the charitable gateway the slow cortège† reappeared, lighted up for a moment, the short, thick man limping busily, with the horse's head held aloft in his fist, the lank animal walking in stiff and forlorn dignity, the dark, low box on wheels rolling behind comically with an air of waddling. They turned to the left. There was a pub down the street, within fifty yards of the gate.

Stevie, left alone beside the private lamp-post of the Charity, his hands thrust deep into his pockets, glared with vacant sulkiness. At the bottom of his pockets his incapable weak hands were clenched hard into a pair of angry fists. In the face of anything which affected directly or indirectly his morbid dread of pain, Stevie ended by turning vicious. A magnanimous indignation swelled his frail chest to bursting, and caused his candid eyes to squint. Supremely wise in knowing his own powerlessness, Stevie was not wise enough to restrain his passions. The tenderness of his universal charity had two phases as indissolubly joined and connected as the reverse and obverse sides of a medal. The anguish of immoderate compassion was succeeded by the pain of an innocent but pitiless rage. Those two states expressing themselves outwardly by the same signs of futile bodily agitation, his sister Winnie soothed his excitement without ever fathoming its twofold character. Mrs. Verloc wasted no portion of this transient life in seeking for fundamental information. This is a sort of economy having all the appearances and some of the advantages of prudence. Obviously it may be good for one not to know too much. And such a view accords very well with constitutional indolence.

On that evening on which it may be said that Mrs. Verloc's mother having parted for good from her children had also departed this life, Winnie Verloc did not investigate her brother's psychology. The poor boy was excited, of course. After once more assuring the old woman on the threshold that she would know how to guard

---

*Lament.
†Retinue, train of attendants.

against the risk of Stevie losing himself for very long on his pilgrimages of filial piety, she took her brother's arm to walk away. Stevie did not even mutter to himself, but with the special sense of sisterly devotion developed in her earliest infancy, she felt that the boy was very much excited indeed. Holding tight to his arm, under the appearance of leaning on it, she thought of some words suitable to the occasion.

"Now, Stevie, you must look well after me at the crossings, and get first into the 'bus, like a good brother."

This appeal to manly protection was received by Stevie with his usual docility. It flattered him. He raised his head and threw out his chest.

"Don't be nervous, Winnie. Mustn't be nervous! 'Bus all right," he answered in a brusque, slurring stammer partaking of the timorousness of a child and the resolution of a man. He advanced fearlessly with the woman on his arm, but his lower lip dropped. Nevertheless, on the pavement of the squalid and wide thoroughfare, whose poverty in all the amenities of life stood foolishly exposed by a mad profusion of gas-lights, their resemblance to each other was so pronounced as to strike the casual passers-by.

Before the doors of the public-house at the corner where the profusion of gas-light reached the height of positive wickedness, a four-wheeled cab standing by the curbstone, with no one on the box, seemed cast out into the gutter on account of irremediable decay. Mrs. Verloc recognised the conveyance. Its aspect was so profoundly lamentable, with such a perfection of grotesque misery and weirdness of macabre detail, as if it were the Cab of Death itself, that Mrs. Verloc, with that ready compassion of a woman for a horse (when she is not sitting behind him), exclaimed vaguely:

"Poor brute!"

Hanging back suddenly, Stevie inflicted an arresting jerk upon his sister.

"Poor! Poor!" he ejaculated appreciatively. "Cabman poor too. He told me himself."

The contemplation of the infirm and lonely steed overcame him. Jostled, but obstinate, he would remain there, trying to express the view newly opened to his sympathies of the human and equine misery in close association. But it was very difficult. "Poor brute; poor people!" was all he could repeat. It did not seem forcible enough, and he came to a stop with an angry splutter: "Shame!" Stevie was not a master of phrases, and perhaps for that very reason his thoughts lacked clearness and precision. But he felt with greater completeness and some profundity. That little word contained all his sense of indignation and horror at one sort of wretchedness having to feed upon the anguish of the other—at the poor cabman beating the poor horse in the name, as it were, of his poor kids at home. And Stevie knew what it was to be beaten. He knew it from experience. It was a bad world. Bad! Bad!

Mrs. Verloc, his only sister, guardian, and protector, could not pretend to such depths of insight. Moreover, she had not experienced the magic of the cabman's eloquence. She was in the dark as to the inwardness of the word "Shame." And she said placidly:

"Come along, Stevie. You can't help that."

The docile Stevie went along; but now he went along without pride, shamblingly, and muttering half words, and even words that would have been whole if they had not been made up of halves that did not belong to each other. It was as though he had been trying to fit all the words he could remember to his sentiments in order to get some sort of corresponding idea. And, as a matter of fact, he got it at last. He hung back to utter it at once.

"Bad world for poor people."

Directly he had expressed that thought he became aware that it was familiar to him already in all its consequences. This circumstance strengthened his conviction immensely, but also augmented his indignation. Somebody, he felt, ought to be punished for it—punished with great severity. Being no sceptic, but a moral creature, he was in a manner at the mercy of his righteous passions.

"Beastly!" he added concisely.

It was clear to Mrs. Verloc that he was greatly excited.

"Nobody can help that," she said. "Do come along. Is that the way you're taking care of me?"

Stevie mended his pace obediently. He prided himself on being a good brother. His morality, which was very complete, demanded that from him. Yet he was pained at the information imparted by his sister Winnie—who was good. Nobody could help that! He came along gloomily, but presently he brightened up. Like the rest of mankind, perplexed by the mystery of the universe, he had his moments of consoling trust in the organised powers of the earth.

"Police," he suggested confidently.

"The police aren't for that," observed Mrs. Verloc cursorily, hurrying on her way.

Stevie's face lengthened considerably. He was thinking. The more intense his thinking the slacker was the droop of his lower jaw. And it was with an aspect of hopeless vacancy that he gave up his intellectual enterprise.

"Not for that?" he mumbled, resigned but surprised. "Not for that?" He had formed for himself an ideal conception of the metropolitan police as a sort of benevolent institution for the suppression of evil. The notion of benevolence especially was very closely associated with his sense of the power of the men in blue. He had liked all police constables tenderly, with a guileless trustfulness. And he was pained. He was irritated, too, by a suspicion of duplicity in the members of the force. For Stevie was frank and as open as the day himself. What did they mean by pretending then? Unlike his sister, who put her trust in face values, he wished to go to the bottom of the matter. He carried on his inquiry by means of an angry challenge.

"What for are they then, Winn? What are they for? Tell me."

Winnie disliked controversy. But fearing most a fit of black depression consequent on Stevie missing his mother very much at first, she did not altogether decline the discussion. Guiltless of all irony, she answered yet in a form which was not perhaps unnatural in the wife of Mr. Verloc, Delegate of the Central Red Committee, personal friend of certain anarchists, and a votary of social revolution.

"Don't you know what the police are for, Stevie? They are there so that them as have nothing shouldn't take anything away from them who have."[11]

She avoided using the verb "to steal" because it always made her brother uncomfortable. For Stevie was delicately honest. Certain simple principles had been instilled into him so anxiously (on account of his "queerness") that the mere names of certain transgressions filled him with horror. He had been always easily impressed by speeches. He was impressed and startled now, and his intelligence was very alert.

"What?" he asked at once anxiously. "Not even if they were hungry? Mustn't they?"

The two had paused in their walk.

"Not if they were ever so," said Mrs. Verloc, with the equanimity of a person untroubled by the problem of the distribution of wealth, and exploring the perspective of the roadway for an omnibus of the right colour. "Certainly not. But what's the use of talking about all that? You aren't ever hungry."

She cast a swift glance at the boy, like a young man, by her side. She saw him amiable, attractive, affectionate, and only a little, a very little, peculiar. And she could not see him otherwise, for he was connected with what there was of the salt of passion in her tasteless life[12] —the passion of indignation, of courage, of pity, and even of self-sacrifice. She did not add: "And you aren't likely ever to be as long as I live." But she might very well have done so, since she had taken effectual steps to that end. Mr. Verloc was a very good husband. It was her honest impression that nobody could help liking the boy. She cried out suddenly:

"Quick, Stevie. Stop that green 'bus."

And Stevie, tremulous and important with his sister Winnie on his arm, flung up the other high above his head at the approaching 'bus, with complete success.

An hour afterwards Mr. Verloc raised his eyes from a newspaper he was reading, or at any rate looking at, behind the counter, and in the expiring clatter of the door bell beheld Winnie, his wife, enter and cross the shop on her way upstairs, followed by Stevie, his brother-in-law. The sight of his wife was agreeable to Mr. Verloc. It was his idiosyncrasy. The figure of his brother-in-law remained imperceptible to him because of the morose thoughtfulness that lately had fallen like a veil between Mr. Verloc and the appearances of the world of senses. He looked after his wife fixedly, without a word, as though she had been a phantom. His voice for home use was husky and placid, but now it was heard not at all. It was not heard at supper, to which he was called by his wife in the usual brief manner: "Adolf." He sat down to consume it without conviction, wearing his hat pushed far back on his head. It was not devotion to an outdoor life, but the frequentation of foreign cafés which was responsible for that habit, investing with a character of unceremonious impermanency Mr. Verloc's steady fidelity to his own fireside. Twice at the clatter of the cracked bell he arose without a word, disappeared into the shop, and came back silently. During these absences Mrs. Verloc, becoming acutely aware of the vacant place at her right hand, missed her mother very much, and stared stonily; while Stevie, from the same reason, kept on shuffling his feet, as though the floor under the table was uncomfortably hot. When Mr. Verloc returned to sit in his place, like the very embodiment of silence, the character of Mrs. Verloc's stare underwent a subtle change, and Stevie ceased to fidget with his feet, because of his great and awed regard for his sister's husband. He directed at him glances of respectful compassion. Mr. Verloc was sorry. His sister Winnie had impressed upon him (in the omnibus) that Mr. Verloc would be found at home in a state of sorrow, and must not be worried. His father's anger, the irritability of gentlemen lodgers, and Mr. Verloc's predisposition to immoderate grief, had been the main sanctions of Stevie's self-restraint. Of these sentiments, all easily provoked, but not always easy to understand, the last had the greatest moral efficiency—because Mr. Verloc was *good*. His mother and his sister had established that ethical fact on an unshakable foundation. They had established, erected, consecrated it behind Mr. Verloc's back, for reasons that had nothing to do with abstract morality. And Mr. Verloc was not aware of it. It is but bare justice to him to say that he had no notion of appearing good to Stevie. Yet so it was. He was even the only man so qualified in Stevie's knowledge, because the gentlemen lodgers had been too transient and too remote to have anything very distinct about them but perhaps their boots; and as regards the disciplinary measures of his father, the desolation of his mother and sister shrank from setting up a theory of goodness before the victim. It would have been too cruel. And it was even possible that Stevie would not have believed them. As far as Mr. Verloc was concerned, nothing could stand in the way of Stevie's belief. Mr. Verloc was obviously yet mysteriously *good*. And the grief of a good man is august.

Stevie gave glances of reverential compassion to his brother-in-law. Mr. Verloc was sorry. The brother of Winnie had never before felt himself in such close communion with the mystery of that man's goodness. It was an understandable sorrow. And Stevie himself was sorry. He was very sorry. The same sort of sorrow. And his attention being drawn to this unpleasant state, Stevie shuffled his feet. His feelings were habitually manifested by the agitation of his limbs.

"Keep your feet quiet, dear," said Mrs. Verloc, with authority and tenderness; then turning towards her husband in an indifferent voice, the masterly achievement of instinctive tact: "Are you going out to-night?" she asked.

The mere suggestion seemed repugnant to Mr. Verloc. He shook his head moodily, and then sat still with downcast eyes, looking at the piece of cheese on his plate for a whole minute. At the end of that time he got up, and went out—went right out in the clatter of the shop-door bell. He acted thus inconsistently, not from any desire to make himself unpleasant, but because of an unconquerable restlessness. It was no earthly good going out. He could not find anywhere in London what he wanted. But he went out. He led a cortège of dismal thoughts along dark streets, through lighted streets, in and out of two flash bars,* as if in a half-hearted attempt to make a night of it, and finally back again to his menaced home, where he sat down fatigued behind the counter, and they crowded urgently round him, like a pack of hungry black hounds.[13] After locking up the house and putting out the gas he took them upstairs with him—a dreadful escort for a man going to bed. His wife had preceded him some time before, and with her ample form defined vaguely under the counterpane† her head on the pillow, and a hand under the cheek, offered to his distraction the view of early drowsiness arguing the possession of an equable soul. Her big eyes stared wide open, inert and dark against the snowy whiteness of the linen. She did not move.

She had an equable soul. She felt profoundly that things do not stand much looking into.[14] She made her force and her wisdom of that instinct. But the taciturnity of Mr. Verloc had been lying heavily upon her for a good many days. It was, as a matter of fact, affecting her nerves. Recumbent and motionless, she said placidly:

"You'll catch cold walking about in your socks like this."

This speech, becoming the solicitude of the wife and the prudence of the woman, took Mr. Verloc unawares. He had left his boots downstairs, but he had forgotten to put on his slippers, and he had

---

*Pubs frequented by criminals and riffraff.
†Quilt or coverlet.

been turning about the bedroom on noiseless pads like a bear in a cage. At the sound of his wife's voice he stopped and stared at her with a somnambulistic, expressionless gaze so long that Mrs. Verloc moved her limbs slightly under the bedclothes. But she did not move her black head sunk in the white pillow, one hand under her cheek and the big, dark, unwinking eyes.

Under her husband's expressionless stare, and remembering her mother's empty room across the landing, she felt an acute pang of loneliness. She had never been parted from her mother before. They had stood by each other. She felt that they had, and she said to herself that now mother was gone—gone for good. Mrs. Verloc had no illusions. Stevie remained, however. And she said:

"Mother's done what she wanted to do. There's no sense in it that I can see. I'm sure she couldn't have thought you had enough of her. It's perfectly wicked, leaving us like that."

Mr. Verloc was not a well-read person; his range of allusive phrases was limited, but there was a peculiar aptness in circumstances which made him think of rats leaving a doomed ship. He very nearly said so. He had grown suspicious and embittered. Could it be that the old woman had such an excellent nose? But the unreasonableness of such a suspicion was patent, and Mr. Verloc held his tongue. Not altogether, however. He muttered heavily:

"Perhaps it's just as well."

He began to undress. Mrs. Verloc kept very still, perfectly still, with her eyes fixed in a dreamy, quiet stare. And her heart for the fraction of a second seemed to stand still too. That night she was "not quite herself," as the saying is, and it was borne upon her with some force that a simple sentence may hold several diverse meanings—mostly disagreeable. *How* was it just as well? And why? But she did not allow herself to fall into the idleness of barren speculation. She was rather confirmed in her belief that things did not stand being looked into. Practical and subtle in her way, she brought Stevie to the front without loss of time, because in her the singleness of purpose had the unerring nature and the force of an instinct.

"What I am going to do to cheer up that boy for the first few days I'm sure I don't know. He'll be worrying himself from morning till night before he gets used to mother being away. And he's such a good boy. I couldn't do without him."

Mr. Verloc went on divesting himself of his clothing with the unnoticing inward concentration of a man undressing in the solitude of a vast and hopeless desert. For thus inhospitably did this fair earth, our common inheritance, present itself to the mental vision of Mr. Verloc. All was so still without and within that the lonely ticking of the clock on the landing stole into the room as if for the sake of company.

Mr. Verloc, getting into bed on his own side, remained prone and mute behind Mrs. Verloc's back. His thick arms rested abandoned on the outside of the counterpane like dropped weapons, like discarded tools. At that moment he was within a hairbreadth of making a clean breast of it all to his wife. The moment seemed propitious. Looking out of the corners of his eyes, he saw her ample shoulders draped in white, the back of her head, with the hair done for the night in three plaits tied up with black tapes at the ends. And he forbore. Mr. Verloc loved his wife as a wife should be loved— that is, maritally, with the regard one has for one's chief possession. This head arranged for the night, those ample shoulders, had an aspect of familiar sacredness—the sacredness of domestic peace. She moved not, massive and shapeless like a recumbent statue in the rough; he remembered her wide-open eyes looking into the empty room. She was mysterious, with the mysteriousness of living beings. The far-famed secret agent Δ of the late Baron Stott-Wartenheim's alarmist dispatches was not the man to break into such mysteries. He was easily intimidated. And he was also indolent, with the indolence which is so often the secret of good nature. He forbore touching that mystery out of love, timidity, and indolence. There would be always time enough. For several minutes he bore his sufferings silently in the drowsy silence of the room. And then he disturbed it by a resolute declaration.

"I am going on the Continent to-morrow."

His wife might have fallen asleep already. He could not tell. As a matter of fact, Mrs. Verloc had heard him. Her eyes remained very wide open, and she lay very still, confirmed in her instinctive conviction that things don't bear looking into very much. And yet it was nothing very unusual for Mr. Verloc to take such a trip. He renewed his stock from Paris and Brussels. Often he went over to make his purchases personally. A little select connection of amateurs was

forming around the shop in Brett Street, a secret connection eminently proper for any business undertaken by Mr. Verloc, who, by a
mystic accord of temperament and necessity, had been set apart to
be a secret agent all his life.

He waited for a while, then added: "I'll be away a week or perhaps a fortnight. Get Mrs. Neale to come for the day."

Mrs. Neale was the charwoman* of Brett Street. Victim of her
marriage with a debauched joiner,† she was oppressed by the needs
of many infant children. Red-armed, and aproned in coarse sacking
up to the arm-pits, she exhaled the anguish of the poor in a breath
of soap-suds and rum, in the uproar of scrubbing, in the clatter of tin
pails.

Mrs. Verloc, full of deep purpose, spoke in the tone of the shal-
lowest indifference.

"There is no need to have the woman here all day. I shall do very
well with Stevie."

She let the lonely clock on the landing count off fifteen ticks
into the abyss of eternity, and asked:

"Shall I put the light out?"

Mr. Verloc snapped at his wife huskily.

"Put it out."

CHAPTER NINE

M R. VERLOC, returning from the Continent at the end of ten days, brought back a mind evidently unrefreshed by the wonders of foreign travel and a countenance unlighted by the joys of home-coming. He entered in the clatter of the shop bell with an air of sombre and vexed exhaustion. His bag in hand, his head lowered, he strode straight behind the counter, and let himself fall into the chair, as though he had tramped all the way from Dover. It was early morning. Stevie, dusting various objects displayed in the front window, turned to gape at him with reverence and awe.

"Here!" said Mr. Verloc, giving a slight kick to the Gladstone bag* on the floor; and Stevie flung himself upon it, seized it, bore it off with triumphant devotion. He was so prompt that Mr. Verloc was distinctly surprised.

Already at the clatter of the shop bell Mrs. Neale, blackleading† the parlour grate, had looked through the door, and rising from her knees had gone, aproned, and grimy with everlasting toil, to tell Mrs. Verloc in the kitchen that "there was the master come back."

Winnie came no farther than the inner shop door.

"You'll want some breakfast," she said from a distance.

Mr. Verloc moved his hands slightly, as if overcome by an impossible suggestion. But once enticed into the parlour he did not reject the food set before him. He ate as if in a public place, his hat pushed off his forehead, the skirts of his heavy overcoat hanging in a triangle on each side of the chair. And across the length of the table covered with brown oilcloth, Winnie, his wife, talked evenly at him the wifely talk, as artfully adapted, no doubt, to the circumstances of this return as the talk of Penelope to the return of the

---

*Small traveling bag, named after the Liberal prime minister William Gladstone (1809–1898).
†Polishing with blacklead, the name for a type of graphite.

wandering Odysseus. Mrs. Verloc, however, had done no weaving
during her husband's absence.[1] But she had had all the upstairs
rooms cleaned thoroughly, had sold some wares, had seen
Mr. Michaelis several times. He had told her the last time that he
was going to live in a cottage in the country,[2] somewhere on the
London, Chatham, and Dover line. Karl Yundt had come too,
once, led under the arm by that "wicked old housekeeper of his."
He was "a disgusting old man." Of Comrade Ossipon, whom she
had received curtly, entrenched behind the counter with a stony
face and a far-away gaze, she said nothing, her mental reference to
the robust anarchist being marked by a short pause, with the
faintest possible blush. And bringing in her brother Stevie as soon
as she could into the current of domestic events, she mentioned
that the boy had moped a good deal.

"It's all along of mother leaving us like this."

Mr. Verloc neither said "Damn!" nor yet "Stevie be hanged!"
And Mrs. Verloc, not let into the secret of his thoughts, failed to
appreciate the generosity of this restraint.

"It isn't that he doesn't work as well as ever," she continued.
"He's been making himself very useful. You'd think he couldn't do
enough for us."

Mr. Verloc directed a casual and somnolent glance at Stevie,
who sat on his right, delicate, pale-faced, his rosy mouth open vacantly. It was not a critical glance. It had no intention. And if
Mr. Verloc thought for a moment that his wife's brother looked uncommonly useless, it was only a dull and fleeting thought, devoid
of that force and durability which enables sometimes a thought to
move the world. Leaning back, Mr. Verloc uncovered his head.
Before his extended arm could put down the hat Stevie pounced
upon it, and bore it off reverently into the kitchen. And again
Mr. Verloc was surprised.

"You could do anything with that boy, Adolf," Mrs. Verloc said,
with her best air of inflexible calmness. "He would go through fire
for you. He——"

She paused attentive, her ear turned towards the door of the
kitchen.

There Mrs. Neale was scrubbing the floor. At Stevie's appearance she groaned lamentably, having observed that he could be
induced easily to bestow for the benefit of her infant children the

shilling his sister Winnie presented him with from time to time. On all fours amongst the puddles, wet and begrimed, like a sort of amphibious and domestic animal living in ash-bins and dirty water, she uttered the usual exordium: "It's all very well for you, kept doing nothing like a gentleman." And she followed it with the everlasting plaint of the poor, pathetically mendacious, miserably authenticated by the horrible breath of cheap rum and soap-suds. She scrubbed hard, snuffling all the time, and talking volubly. And she was sincere. And on each side of her thin red nose her bleared, misty eyes swam in tears, because she felt really the want of some sort of stimulant in the morning.

In the parlour Mrs. Verloc observed, with knowledge:

"There's Mrs. Neale at it again with her harrowing tales about her little children. They can't be all so little as she makes them out, Some of them must be big enough by now to try to do something for themselves. It only makes Stevie angry."

These words were confirmed by a thud as of a fist striking the kitchen table. In the normal evolution of his sympathy Stevie had become angry on discovering that he had no shilling in his pocket. In his inability to relieve at once Mrs. Neale's "little uns' " privations he felt that somebody should be made to suffer for it. Mrs. Verloc rose, and went into the kitchen to "stop that nonsense." And she did it firmly but gently. She was well aware that directly Mrs. Neale received her money she went round the corner to drink ardent spirits in a mean and musty public-house—the unavoidable station on the *via dolorosa** of her life. Mrs. Verloc's comment upon this practice had an unexpected profundity, as coming from a person disinclined to look under the surface of things. "Of course, what is she to do to keep up? If I were like Mrs. Neale I expect I wouldn't act any different."

In the afternoon of the same day, as Mr. Verloc, coming with a start out of the last of a long series of dozes before the parlour fire, declared his intention of going out for a walk, Winnie said from the shop:

"I wish you would take that boy out with you, Adolf."

For the third time that day Mr. Verloc was surprised. He stared stupidly at his wife. She continued in her steady manner. The

---

*Sorrowing way (Latin); alluding to the path Christ reputedly took through Jerusalem on the way to the Crucifixion, as well as to the stations of the cross, which represent this journey in a church.

boy, whenever he was not doing anything, moped in the house. It made her uneasy; it made her nervous, she confessed. And that from the calm Winnie sounded like exaggeration. But, in truth, Stevie moped in the striking fashion of an unhappy domestic animal. He would go up on the dark landing, to sit on the floor at the foot of the tall clock, with his knees drawn up and his head in his hands. To come upon his pallid face, with its big eyes gleaming in the dusk, was discomposing; to think of him up there was uncomfortable.

Mr. Verloc got used to the startling novelty of the idea. He was fond of his wife as a man should be—that is, generously. But a weighty objection presented itself to his mind, and he formulated it.

"He'll lose sight of me perhaps, and get lost in the street," he said.

Mrs. Verloc shook her head competently.

"He won't. You don't know him. That boy just worships you. But if you should miss him——"

Mrs. Verloc paused for a moment, but only for a moment.

"You just go on, and have your walk out. Don't worry. He'll be all right. He's sure to turn up safe here before very long."

This optimism procured for Mr. Verloc his fourth surprise of the day.

"Is he?" he grunted doubtfully. But perhaps his brother-in-law was not such an idiot as he looked. His wife would know best. He turned away his heavy eyes, saying huskily: "Well, let him come along then," and relapsed into the clutches of black care, that perhaps prefers to sit behind a horseman,[3] but knows also how to tread close on the heels of people not sufficiently well off to keep horses—like Mr. Verloc, for instance.

Winnie, at the shop door, did not see this fatal attendant upon Mr. Verloc's walks. She watched the two figures down the squalid street, one tall and burly, the other slight and short, with a thin neck, and the peaked shoulders raised slightly under the large semi-transparent ears. The material of their overcoats was the same, their hats were black and round in shape. Inspired by the similarity of wearing apparel, Mrs. Verloc gave rein to her fancy.

"Might be father and son," she said to herself. She thought also that Mr. Verloc was as much of a father as poor Stevie ever had in his life. She was aware also that it was her work. And with peaceful pride she congratulated herself on a certain resolution she had taken a few years before. It had cost her some effort, and even a few tears.

She congratulated herself still more on observing in the course of days that Mr. Verloc seemed to be taking kindly to Stevie's companionship. Now, when ready to go out for his walk, Mr. Verloc called aloud to the boy, in the spirit, no doubt, in which a man invites the attendance of the household dog, though, of course, in a different manner. In the house Mr. Verloc could be detected staring curiously at Stevie a good deal. His own demeanour had changed. Taciturn still, he was not so listless. Mrs. Verloc thought that he was rather jumpy at times. It might have been regarded as an improvement. As to Stevie, he moped no longer at the foot of the clock, but muttered to himself in corners instead in a threatening tone. When asked "What is it you're saying, Stevie?" he merely opened his mouth, and squinted at his sister. At odd times he clenched his fists without apparent cause, and when discovered in solitude would be scowling at the wall, with the sheet of paper and the pencil given him for drawing circles lying blank and idle on the kitchen table. This was a change, but it was no improvement. Mrs. Verloc, including all these vagaries under the general definition of "excitement," began to fear that Stevie was hearing more than was good for him of her husband's conversations with his friends. During his "walks" Mr. Verloc, of course, met and conversed with various persons. It could hardly be otherwise. His walks were an integral part of his outdoor activities, which his wife had never looked deeply into. Mrs. Verloc felt that the position was delicate, but she faced it with the same impenetrable calmness which impressed and even astonished the customers of the shop, and made the other visitors keep their distance a little wonderingly. No! she feared that there were things not good for Stevie to hear of, she told her husband. It only excited the poor boy, because he could not help them being so. Nobody could.

It was in the shop. Mr. Verloc made no comment. He made no retort, and yet the retort was obvious. But he refrained from pointing out to his wife that the idea of making Stevie the companion of his walks was her own, and nobody else's. At that moment, to an impartial observer, Mr. Verloc would have appeared more than human in his magnanimity. He took down a small cardboard box from a shelf, peeped in to see that the contents were all right, and put it down gently on the counter. Not till that was done did he break the silence, to the effect that most likely Stevie would profit greatly by being sent out of town for a while; only he supposed his wife could not get on without him.

"Could not get on without him?" repeated Mrs. Verloc slowly. "I couldn't get on without him if it were for his good! The idea! Of course, I can get on without him. But there's nowhere for him to go."

Mr. Verloc got out some brown paper and a ball of string; and meanwhile he muttered that Michaelis was living in a little cottage in the country. Michaelis wouldn't mind giving Stevie a room to sleep in. There were no visitors and no talk there. Michaelis was writing a book.

Mrs. Verloc declared her affection for Michaelis; mentioned her abhorrence of Karl Yundt, "nasty old man"; and of Ossipon she said nothing. As to Stevie, he could be no other than very pleased. Mr. Michaelis was always so nice and kind to him. He seemed to like the boy. Well, the boy was a good boy.

"You, too, seem to have grown quite fond of him of late," she added, after a pause, with her inflexible assurance.

Mr. Verloc tying up the cardboard box into a parcel for the post, broke the string by an injudicious jerk, and muttered several swearwords confidentially to himself. Then raising his tone to the usual husky mutter, he announced his willingness to take Stevie into the country himself, and leave him all safe with Michaelis.

He carried out this scheme on the very next day. Stevie offered no objection. He seemed rather eager, in a bewildered sort of way. He turned his candid gaze inquisitively to Mr. Verloc's heavy countenance at frequent intervals, especially when his sister was not looking at him. His expression was proud, apprehensive, and concentrated, like that of a small child entrusted for the first time with a box of matches and the permission to strike a light. But Mrs. Verloc, gratified by her brother's docility, recommended him not to dirty his clothes unduly in the country. At this Stevie gave his sister, guardian, and protector a look, which for the first time in his life seemed to lack the quality of perfect childlike trustfulness. It was haughtily gloomy. Mrs, Verloc smiled.

"Goodness me! You needn't be offended. You know you do get yourself very untidy when you get a chance, Stevie."

Mr. Verloc was already gone some way down the street.

Thus in consequence of her mother's heroic proceedings, and of her brother's absence on this villeggiature,* Mrs. Verloc found herself oftener than usual all alone, not only in the shop, but in the house. For Mr. Verloc had to take his walks. She was alone longer than usual on the day of the attempted bomb outrage in Greenwich Park, because Mr. Verloc went out very early that morning, and did not come back till nearly dusk. She did not mind being alone. She had no desire to go out. The weather was too bad, and the shop was cosier than the streets. Sitting behind the counter with some sewing, she did not raise her eyes from her work when Mr. Verloc entered in the aggressive clatter of the bell. She had recognised his step on the pavement outside.

She did not raise her eyes, but as Mr. Verloc, silent, and with his hat rammed down upon his forehead, made straight for the parlour door, she said serenely:

"What a wretched day. You've been perhaps to see Stevie?"

"No! I haven't," said Mr. Verloc softly, and slammed the glazed parlour door behind him with unexpected energy.

For some time Mrs. Verloc remained quiescent, with her work dropped in her lap, before she put it away under the counter and got up to light the gas. This done, she went into the parlour on her way to the kitchen. Mr. Verloc would want his tea presently. Confident of the power of her charms, Winnie did not expect from her husband in the daily intercourse of their married life a ceremonious amenity of address and courtliness of manner; vain and antiquated forms at best, probably never very exactly observed, discarded nowadays even in the highest spheres, and always foreign to the standards of her class. She did not look for courtesies from him. But he was a good husband, and she had a loyal respect for his rights.

Mrs. Verloc would have gone through the parlour and on to her domestic duties in the kitchen with the perfect serenity of a woman sure of the power of her charms. But a slight, very slight, and rapid rattling sound grew upon her hearing. Bizarre and incomprehensible,

---

*Residence or holiday in the country (from the French *villéggiature*).

it arrested Mrs. Verloc's attention. Then, as its character became plain to the ear, she stopped short, amazed and concerned. Striking a match on the box she held in her hand, she turned on and lighted, above the parlour table, one of the two gas-burners, which, being defective, first whistled as if astonished, and then went on purring comfortably like a cat.

Mr. Verloc, against his usual practice, had thrown off his overcoat. It was lying on the sofa. His hat, which he must also have thrown off, rested overturned under the edge of the sofa. He had dragged a chair in front of the fireplace, and his feet planted inside the fender,* his head held between his hands, he was hanging low over the glowing grate. His teeth rattled with an ungovernable violence, causing his whole enormous back to tremble at the same rate. Mrs. Verloc was startled.

"You've been getting wet," she said.

"Not very," Mr. Verloc managed to falter out, in a profound shudder. By a great effort he suppressed the rattling of his teeth.

"I'll have you laid up on my hands," she said, with genuine uneasiness.

"I don't think so," remarked Mr. Verloc, snuffling huskily.

He had certainly contrived somehow to catch an abominable cold between seven in the morning and five in the afternoon. Mrs. Verloc looked at his bowed back.

"Where have you been to-day?" she asked.

"Nowhere," answered Mr. Verloc in a low, choked nasal tone. His attitude suggested aggrieved sulks or a severe headache. The insufficiency and uncandidness of his answer became painfully apparent in the dead silence of the room. He snuffled apologetically, and added: "I've been to the bank."

Mrs. Verloc became attentive.

"You have!" she said dispassionately. "What for?"

Mr. Verloc mumbled, with his nose over the grate, and with marked unwillingness.

"Draw the money out!"

"What do you mean? All of it?"

---

*Border in front of a fireplace grate, used to prevent sparks or coals from spilling out onto the floor.

"Yes. All of it."

Mrs. Verloc spread out with care the scanty tablecloth, got two knives and two forks out of the table-drawer, and suddenly stopped in her methodical proceedings.

"What did you do that for?"

"May want it soon," snuffled vaguely Mr. Verloc, who was coming to the end of his calculated indiscretions.

"I don't know what you mean," remarked his wife in a tone perfectly casual, but standing stock-still between the table and the cupboard.

"You know you can trust me," Mr. Verloc remarked to the grate, with hoarse feeling.

Mrs. Verloc turned slowly towards the cupboard, saying with deliberation:

"Oh yes. I can trust you."

And she went on with her methodical proceedings. She laid two plates, got the bread, the butter, going to and fro quietly between the table and the cupboard in the peace and silence of her home. On the point of taking out the jam, she reflected practically: "He will be feeling hungry, having been away all day," and she returned to the cupboard once more to get the cold beef. She set it under the purring gas-jet, and with a passing glance at her motionless husband hugging the fire, she went (down two steps) into the kitchen. It was only when coming back, carving knife and fork in hand, that she spoke again.

"If I hadn't trusted you I wouldn't have married you."

Bowed under the overmantel,* Mr. Verloc, holding his head in both hands, seemed to have gone to sleep. Winnie made the tea, and called out in an undertone:

"Adolf."

Mr. Verloc got up at once, and staggered a little before he sat down at the table. His wife examining the sharp edge. of the carving knife, placed it on the dish, and called his attention to the cold beef. He remained insensible to the suggestion, with his chin on his breast.

"You should feed your cold," Mrs. Verloc said dogmatically.

---

*Ornamental work over a fireplace mantel.

He looked up, and shook his head. His eyes were bloodshot and his face red. His fingers had ruffled his hair into a dissipated untidiness. Altogether he had a disreputable aspect, expressive of the discomfort, the irritation, and the gloom following a heavy debauch. But Mr. Verloc was not a debauched man. In his conduct he was respectable. His appearance might have been the effect of a feverish cold. He drank three cups of tea, but abstained from food entirely. He recoiled from it with sombre aversion when urged by Mrs. Verloc, who said at last:

"Aren't your feet wet? You had better put on your slippers. You aren't going out any more this evening."

Mr. Verloc intimated by morose grunts and signs that his feet were not wet, and that anyhow he did not care. The proposal as to slippers was disregarded as beneath his notice. But the question of going out in the evening received an unexpected development. It was not of going out in the evening that Mr. Verloc was thinking. His thoughts embraced a vaster scheme. From moody and incomplete phrases it became apparent that Mr. Verloc had been considering the expediency of emigrating. It was not very clear whether he had in his mind France or California.

The utter unexpectedness, improbability, and inconceivableness of such an event robbed this vague declaration of all its effect. Mrs. Verloc, as placidly as if her husband had been threatening her with the end of the world, said:

"The idea!"

Mr. Verloc declared himself sick and tired of everything, and besides—— She interrupted him:

"You've a bad cold."

It was indeed obvious that Mr. Verloc was not in his usual state, physically and even mentally. A sombre irresolution held him silent for a while. Then he murmured a few ominous generalities on the theme of necessity.

"Will have to?" repeated Winnie, sitting calmly back, with folded arms, opposite her husband. "I should like to know who's to make you. You ain't a slave. No one need be a slave in this country—and don't you make yourself one." She paused, and with invincible and steady candour: "The business isn't so bad," she went on. "You've a comfortable home."

She glanced all round the parlour, from the corner cupboard to the good fire in the grate. Ensconced cosily behind the shop of doubtful wares, with the mysteriously dim window, and its door suspiciously ajar in the obscure and narrow street, it was in all essentials of domestic propriety and domestic comfort a respectable home. Her devoted affection missed out of it her brother Stevie, now enjoying a damp villeggiature in the Kentish lanes under the care of Mr. Michaelis. She missed him poignantly, with all the force of her protecting passion. This was the boy's home too—the roof, the cupboard, the stoked grate. On this thought Mrs. Verloc rose, and walking to the other end of the table, said in the fullness of her heart:

"And you are not tired of me."

Mr. Verloc made no sound. Winnie leaned on his shoulder from behind, and pressed her lips to his forehead. Thus she lingered. Not a whisper reached them from the outside world. The sound of footsteps on the pavement died out in the discreet dimness of the shop. Only the gas-jet above the table went on purring equably in the brooding silence of the parlour.

During the contact of that unexpected and lingering kiss Mr. Verloc, gripping with both hands the edges of his chair, preserved a hieratic* immobility. When the pressure was removed he let go the chair, rose, and went to stand before the fireplace. He turned no longer his back to the room. With his features swollen, and an air of being drugged, he followed his wife's movements with his eyes.

Mrs. Verloc went about serenely, clearing up the table. Her tranquil voice commented the idea thrown out in a reasonable and domestic tone. It wouldn't stand examination. She condemned it from every point of view. But her only real concern was Stevie's welfare. He appeared to her thought in that connection as sufficiently "peculiar" not to be taken rashly abroad. And that was all. But talking round that vital point, she approached absolute vehemence in her delivery. Meanwhile, with brusque movements, she arrayed herself in an apron for the washing up of cups. And as if

---

*Dignified, solemn, priestly.

excited by the sound of her uncontradicted voice, she went so far as to say in a tone almost tart:

"If you go abroad you'll have to go without me."

"You know I wouldn't," said Mr. Verloc huskily, and the unresonant voice of his private life trembled with an enigmatical emotion.

Already Mrs. Verloc was regretting her words. They had sounded more unkind than she meant them to be. They had also the unwisdom of unnecessary things. In fact, she had not meant them at all. It was a sort of phrase that is suggested by the demon of perverse inspiration. But she knew a way to make it as if it had not been.

She turned her head over her shoulder and gave that man planted heavily in front of the fireplace a glance, half-arch, half-cruel, out of her large eyes—a glance of which the Winnie of the Belgravian mansion days would have been incapable, because of her respectability and her ignorance. But the man was her husband now, and she was no longer ignorant. She kept it on him for a whole second, with her grave face motionless like a mask, while she said playfully:

"You couldn't. You would miss me too much."

Mr. Verloc started forward.

"Exactly," he said in a louder tone, throwing his arms out and making a step towards her. Something wild and doubtful in his expression made it appear uncertain whether he meant to strangle or to embrace his wife. But Mrs. Verloc's attention was called away from that manifestation by the clatter of the shop bell.

"Shop, Adolf. You go."

He stopped, his arms came down slowly.

"You go," repeated Mrs. Verloc. "I've got my apron on."

Mr. Verloc obeyed woodenly, stony-eyed, and like an automaton whose face had been painted red. And this resemblance to a mechanical figure went so far that he had an automaton's absurd air of being aware of the machinery inside of him.

He closed the parlour door, and Mrs. Verloc, moving briskly, carried the tray into the kitchen. She washed the cups and some other things before she stopped in her work to listen. No sound reached her. The customer was a long time in the shop. It was a customer, because if he had not been Mr. Verloc would have taken him inside. Undoing the strings of her apron with a jerk, she threw it on a chair, and walked back to the parlour slowly.

At that precise moment Mr. Verloc entered from the shop.

He had gone in red. He came out a strange papery white. His face, losing its drugged, feverish stupor, had in that short time acquired a bewildered and harassed expression. He walked straight to the sofa, and stood looking down at his overcoat lying there, as though he were afraid to touch it.

"What's the matter?" asked Mrs. Verloc in a subdued voice. Through the door left ajar she could see that the customer was not gone yet.

"I find I'll have to go out this evening," said Mr. Verloc. He did not attempt to pick up his outer garment.

Without a word Winnie made for the shop, and shutting the door after her, walked in behind the counter. She did not look overtly at the customer till she had established herself comfortably on the chair. But by that time she had noted that he was tall and thin, and wore his moustaches twisted up. In fact, he gave the sharp points a twist just then. His long, bony face rose out of a turned-up collar. He was a little splashed, a little wet. A dark man, with the ridges of the cheek-bone well defined under the slightly hollow temple. A complete stranger. Not a customer either.

Mrs. Verloc looked at him placidly.

"You came over from the Continent?" she said after a time.

The long, thin stranger, without exactly looking at Mrs. Verloc, answered only by a faint and peculiar smile.

Mrs. Verloc's steady, incurious gaze rested on him.

"You understand English, don't you?"

"Oh yes. I understand English."

There was nothing foreign in his accent, except that he seemed in his slow enunciation to be taking pains with it. And Mrs. Verloc, in her varied experience, had come to the conclusion that some foreigners could speak better English than the natives. She said, looking at the door of the parlour fixedly:

"You don't think perhaps of staying in England for good?"

The stranger gave her again a silent smile. He had a kindly mouth and probing eyes. And he shook his head a little sadly, it seemed.

"My husband will see you through all right. Meantime for a few days you couldn't do better than take lodgings with Mr. Giugliani. Continental Hotel it's called.[4] Private. It's quiet. My husband will take you there."

"A good idea," said the thin, dark man, whose glance had hardened suddenly.

"You knew Mr. Verloc before—didn't you? Perhaps in France?"

"I have heard of him," admitted the visitor in his slow, painstaking tone, which yet had a certain curtness of intention.

There was a pause. Then he spoke again, in a far less elaborate manner.

"Your husband has not gone out to wait for me in the street by chance?"

"In the street!" repeated Mrs. Verloc, surprised. "He couldn't. There's no other door to the house."

For a moment she sat impassive, then left her seat to go and peep through the glazed door. Suddenly she opened it, and disappeared into the parlour.

Mr. Verloc had done no more than put on his overcoat. But why he should remain afterwards leaning over the table propped up on his two arms as though he were feeling giddy or sick, she could not understand. "Adolf," she called out half aloud; and when he had raised himself:

"Do you know that man?" she asked rapidly.

"I've heard of him," whispered uneasily Mr. Verloc, darting a wild glance at the door.

Mrs. Verloc's fine incurious eyes lighted up with a flash of abhorrence.

"One of Karl Yundt's friends, beastly old man."

"No! No!" protested Mr. Verloc, busy fishing for his hat. But when he got it from under the sofa he held it as if he did not know the use of a hat.

"Well—he's waiting for you," said Mrs. Verloc at last. "I say, Adolf, he ain't one of them Embassy people you have been bothered with of late?"

"Bothered with Embassy people," repeated Mr. Verloc, with a heavy start of surprise and fear. "Who's been talking to you of the Embassy people?"

"Yourself."

"I! I! Talked of the Embassy to you!"

Mr. Verloc seemed scared and bewildered beyond measure. His wife explained:

"You've been talking a little in your sleep of late, Adolf."

"What—what did I say? What do you know?"

"Nothing much. It seemed mostly nonsense. Enough to let me guess that something worried you."

Mr. Verloc rammed his hat on his head. A crimson flood of anger ran over his face.

"Nonsense—eh? The Embassy people! I would cut their hearts out one after another. But let them look out. I've got a tongue in my head."

He fumed, pacing up and down between the table and the sofa, his open overcoat catching against the angles. The red flood of anger ebbed out, and left his face all white, with quivering nostrils. Mrs. Verloc, for the purposes of practical existence, put down these appearances to the cold.

"Well," she said, "get rid of the man, whoever he is, as soon as you can, and come back home to me. You want looking after for a day or two."

Mr. Verloc calmed down, and, with resolution imprinted on his pale face, had already opened the door, when his wife called him back in a whisper:

"Adolf! Adolf!" He came back startled. "What about that money you drew out?" she asked. "You've got it in your pocket? Hadn't you better——"

Mr. Verloc gazed stupidly into the palm of his wife's extended hand for some time before he slapped his brow.

"Money! Yes! Yes! I didn't know what you meant."

He drew out of his breast pocket a new pigskin pocket-book. Mrs. Verloc received it without another word, and stood still till the bell, clattering after Mr. Verloc and Mr. Verloc's visitor, had quieted down. Only then she peeped in at the amount, drawing the notes out for the purpose. After this inspection she looked round thoughtfully, with an air of mistrust in the silence and solitude of the house. This abode of her married life appeared to her as lonely and unsafe as though it had been situated in the midst of a forest.

No receptacle she could think of amongst the solid heavy furniture seemed other but flimsy and particularly tempting to her conception of a housebreaker. It was an ideal conception, endowed with sublime faculties and a miraculous insight. The till was not to be thought of. It was the first spot a thief would make for. Mrs. Verloc unfastening hastily a couple of hooks, slipped the pocket-book under the bodice of her dress. Having thus disposed of her husband's capital, she was rather glad to hear the clatter of the door bell, announcing an arrival. Assuming the fixed, unabashed stare and the stony expression reserved for the casual customer, she walked in behind the counter.

A man standing in the middle of the shop was inspecting it with a swift, cool, all-round glance. His eyes ran over the walls, took in the ceiling, noted the floor—all in a moment. The points of a long fair moustache fell below the line of the jaw. He smiled the smile of an old if distant acquaintance, and Mrs. Verloc remembered having seen him before. Not a customer. She softened her "customer stare" to mere indifference, and faced him across the counter.

He approached, on his side, confidentially, but not too markedly so.

"Husband at home, Mrs. Verloc?" he asked in an easy, full tone.

"No. He's gone out."

"I am sorry for that. I've called to get from him a little private information."

This was the exact truth. Chief Inspector Heat had been all the way home, and had even gone so far as to think of getting into his slippers, since practically he was, he told himself, chucked out of that case. He indulged in some scornful and in a few angry thoughts, and found the occupation so unsatisfactory that he resolved to seek relief out of doors. Nothing prevented him paying a friendly call to Mr. Verloc, casually as it were. It was in the character of a private citizen that walking out privately he made use of his customary conveyances. Their general direction was towards Mr. Verloc's home. Chief Inspector Heat respected his own private character so consistently that he took especial pains to avoid all the police constables on point and patrol duty in the vicinity of Brett Street. This precaution was much more necessary for a man of his standing than for an obscure Assistant Commissioner. Private Citizen Heat entered the street, manoeuvring in a way which in a member of the criminal classes would have been stigmatised as slinking. The piece of cloth picked up in Greenwich was in his pocket. Not that he had the slightest intention of producing it in his private capacity. On the contrary, he wanted to know just what Mr. Verloc would be disposed to say voluntarily. He hoped Mr. Verloc's talk would be of a nature to incriminate Michaelis. It was a conscientiously professional hope in the main, but not without its moral value. For Chief Inspector Heat was a servant of justice. Finding Mr. Verloc from home, he felt disappointed.

"I would wait for him a little if I were sure he wouldn't be long," he said.

Mrs. Verloc volunteered no assurance of any kind.

"The information I need is quite private," he repeated. "You understand what I mean? I wonder if you could give me a notion where he's gone to?"

Mrs. Verloc shook her head.

"Can't say."

She turned away to range some boxes on the shelves behind the counter. Chief Inspector Heat looked at her thoughtfully for a time.

"I suppose you know who I am?" he said.

Mrs. Verloc glanced over her shoulder. Chief Inspector Heat was amazed at her coolness.

"Come! You know I am in the police," he said sharply.

"I don't trouble my head much about it," Mrs. Verloc remarked, returning to the ranging of her boxes.

"My name is Heat. Chief Inspector Heat of the Special Crimes section."

Mrs. Verloc adjusted nicely in its place a small cardboard box, and turning round, faced him again, heavy-eyed, with idle hands hanging down. A silence reigned for a time.

"So your husband went out a quarter of an hour ago! And he didn't say when he would be back?"

"He didn't go out alone," Mrs. Verloc let fall negligently.

"A friend?"

Mrs. Verloc touched the back of her hair. It was in perfect order.

"A stranger who called."

"I see. What sort of man was that stranger? Would you mind telling me?"

Mrs. Verloc did not mind. And when Chief Inspector Heat heard of a man dark, thin, with a long face and turned-up moustaches, he gave signs of perturbation, and exclaimed:

"Dash me if I didn't think so! He hasn't lost any time."

He was intensely disgusted in the secrecy of his heart at the unofficial conduct of his immediate chief. But he was not quixotic.* He lost all desire to await Mr. Verloc's return. What they had gone out for he did not know, but he imagined it possible that they would return together. The case is not followed properly, it's being tampered with, he thought bitterly.

"I am afraid I haven't time to wait for your husband," he said.

Mrs. Verloc received this declaration listlessly. Her detachment had impressed Chief Inspector Heat all along. At this precise moment it whetted his curiosity. Chief Inspector Heat hung in the wind, swayed by his passions like the most private of citizens.

"I think," he said, looking at her steadily, "that you could give me a pretty good notion of what's going on if you liked."

Forcing her fine, inert eyes to return his gaze, Mrs. Verloc murmured:

"Going on! What *is* going on?"

"Why, the affair I came to talk about a little with your husband."

That day Mrs. Verloc had glanced at a morning paper as usual. But she had not stirred out of doors. The newsboys never invaded Brett Street. It was not a street for their business. And the echo of their cries, drifting along the populous thoroughfares, expired between the dirty brick walls without reaching the threshold of the shop. Her husband had not brought an evening paper home. At any rate she had not seen it. Mrs. Verloc knew nothing whatever of any affair. And she said so, with a genuine note of wonder in her quiet voice.

Chief Inspector Heat did not believe for a moment in so much ignorance. Curtly, without amiability, he stated the bare fact.

Mrs. Verloc turned away her eyes.

"I call it silly," she pronounced slowly. She paused. "We ain't downtrodden slaves here."

---

*Fanciful, unrealistic.

The Chief Inspector waited watchfully. Nothing more came.
"And your husband didn't mention anything to you when he
came home?"

Mrs. Verloc simply turned her face from right to left in sign of
negation. A languid, baffling silence reigned in the shop. Chief Inspector Heat felt provoked beyond endurance.

"There was another small matter," he began in a detached tone,
"which I wanted to speak to your husband about. There came into
our hands a—a—what we believe is—a stolen overcoat."

Mrs. Verloc, with her mind specially aware of thieves that evening,
touched lightly the bosom of her dress.

"We have lost no overcoat," she said calmly.

"That's funny," continued Private Citizen Heat. "I see you keep
a lot of marking-ink here——"

He took up a small bottle, and looked at it against the gas-jet in
the middle of the shop.

"Purple—isn't it?" he remarked, setting it down again. "As I said,
it's strange. Because the overcoat has got a label sewn on the inside
with your address written in marking-ink."

Mrs. Verloc leaned over the counter with a low exclamation.

"That's my brother's, then."

"Where's your brother? Can I see him?" asked the Chief Inspector briskly. Mrs. Verloc leaned a little more over the counter.

"No. He isn't here. I wrote that label myself."

"Where's your brother now?"

"He's been away living with—a friend—in the country."

"The overcoat comes from the country. And what's the name of
the friend?"

"Michaelis," confessed Mrs. Verloc in an awed whisper.

The Chief Inspector let out a whistle. His eyes snapped.

"Just so. Capital. And your brother now, what's he like—a sturdy,
darkish chap—eh?"

"Oh no," exclaimed Mrs. Verloc fervently. "That must be the
thief. Stevie's slight and fair."

"Good," said the Chief Inspector in an approving tone. And
while Mrs. Verloc, wavering between alarm and wonder, stared at
him, he sought for information. Why have the address sewn like

this inside the coat? And he heard that the mangled remains he had inspected that morning with extreme repugnance were those of a youth, nervous, absent-minded, peculiar, and also that the woman who was speaking to him had had the charge of that boy since he was a baby.

"Easily excitable?" he suggested.

"Oh yes. He is. But how did he come to lose his coat——"

Chief Inspector Heat suddenly pulled out a pink newspaper he had bought less than half an hour ago. He was interested in horses. Forced by his calling into an attitude of doubt and suspicion towards his fellow-citizens, Chief Inspector Heat relieved the instinct of credulity implanted in the human breast by putting unbounded faith in the sporting prophets of that particular evening publication. Dropping the extra special on to the counter, he plunged his hand again into his pocket, and pulling out the piece of cloth Fate had presented him with out of a heap of things that seemed to have been collected in shambles and rag shops, he offered it to Mrs. Verloc for inspection.

"I suppose you recognise this?"

She took it mechanically in both her hands. Her eyes seemed to grow bigger as she looked.

"Yes," she whispered, then raised her head, and staggered backward a little.

"Whatever is it torn out like this for?"

The Chief Inspector snatched across the counter the cloth out of her hands, and she sat heavily on the chair. He thought: identification's perfect. And in that moment he had a glimpse into the whole amazing truth. Verloc was the "other man."

"Mrs. Verloc," he said, "it strikes me that you know more of this bomb affair than even you yourself are aware of."

Mrs. Verloc sat still, amazed, lost in boundless astonishment. What was the connection? And she became so rigid all over that she was not able to turn her head at the clatter of the bell, which caused the private investigator Heat to spin round on his heel. Mr. Verloc had shut the door, and for a moment the two men looked at each other.

Mr. Verloc, without looking at his wife, walked up to the Chief Inspector, who was relieved to see him return alone.

"You here!" muttered Mr. Verloc heavily. "Who are you after?"

"No one," said Chief Inspector Heat in a low tone. "Look here, I would like a word or two with you."

Mr. Verloc, still pale, had brought an air of resolution with him. Still he didn't look at his wife. He said:

"Come in here, then." And he led the way into the parlour.

The door was hardly shut when Mrs. Verloc, jumping up from the chair, ran to it as if to fling it open, but instead of doing so fell on her knees, with her ear to the keyhole. The two men must have stopped directly they were through, because she heard plainly the Chief Inspector's voice, though she could not see his finger pressed against her husband's breast emphatically.

"You are the other man, Verloc. Two men were seen entering the park."

And the voice of Mr. Verloc said:

"Well, take me now. What's to prevent you? You have the right."

"Oh no! I know too well whom you have been giving yourself away to. He'll have to manage this little affair all by himself. But don't you make a mistake, it's I who found you out."

Then she heard only muttering. Inspector Heat must have been showing to Mr. Verloc the piece of Stevie's overcoat, because Stevie's sister, guardian, and protector heard her husband a little louder.

"I never noticed that she had hit upon that dodge."

Again for a time Mrs. Verloc heard nothing but murmurs, whose mysteriousness was less nightmarish to her brain than the horrible suggestions of shaped words. Then Chief Inspector Heat, on the other side of the door, raised his voice.

"You must have been mad."

And Mr. Verloc's voice answered, with a sort of gloomy fury:

"I have been mad for a month or more, but I am not mad now. It's all over. It shall all come out of my head, and hang the consequences."

There was a silence, and then Private Citizen Heat murmured:

"What's coming out?"

"Everything," exclaimed the voice of Mr. Verloc, and then sank very low.

After a while it rose again.

"You have known me for several years now, and you've found me useful, too. You know I was a straight man. Yes, straight."

This appeal to an old acquaintance must have been extremely distasteful to the Chief Inspector.

His voice took on a warning note.

"Don't you trust so much to what you have been promised. If I were you I would clear out. I don't think we will run after you."

Mr. Verloc was heard to laugh a little.

"Oh yes; you hope the others will get rid of me for you—don't you? No, no; you don't shake me off now. I have been a straight man to those people too long, and now everything must come out."

"Let it come out, then," the indifferent voice of Chief Inspector Heat assented. "But tell me now, how did you get away?"

"I was making for Chesterfield Walk," Mrs. Verloc heard her husband's voice, "when I heard the bang. I started running then. Fog. I saw no one till I was past the end of George Street. Don't think I met any one till then."

"So easy as that!" marvelled the voice of Chief Inspector Heat. "The bang startled you, eh?"

"Yes; it came too soon," confessed the gloomy, husky voice of Mr. Verloc.

Mrs. Verloc pressed her ear to the keyhole; her lips were blue, her hands cold as ice, and her pale face, in which the two eyes seemed like two black holes, felt to her as if it were enveloped in flames.

On the other side of the door the voices sank very low. She caught words now and then, sometimes in her husband's voice, sometimes in the smooth tones of the Chief Inspector. She heard this last say:

"We believe he stumbled against the root of a tree."

There was a husky, voluble murmur, which lasted for some time, and then the Chief Inspector, as if answering some inquiry, spoke emphatically:

"Of course. Blown to small bits: limbs, gravel, clothing, bones, splinters—all mixed up together. I tell you they had to fetch a shovel to gather him up with."

Mrs. Verloc sprang up suddenly from her crouching position, and stopping her ears, reeled to and fro between the counter and the shelves on the wall towards the chair. Her crazed eyes noted the sporting sheet left by the Chief Inspector, and as she knocked herself against the counter she snatched it up, fell into the chair, tore the optimistic, rosy sheet right across in trying to open it, then flung it on the floor. On the other side of the door, Chief Inspector Heat was saying to Mr. Verloc, the secret agent:

"So your defence will be practically a full confession?"

"It will. I am going to tell the whole story."

"You won't be believed as much as you fancy you will."

And the Chief Inspector remained thoughtful. The turn this affair was taking meant the disclosure of many things—the laying waste of fields of knowledge, which, cultivated by a capable man, had a distinct value for the individual and for the society. It was sorry, sorry meddling. It would leave Michaelis unscathed; it would drag to light the Professor's home industry; disorganise the whole system of supervision; make no end of a row in the papers, which, from that point of view, appeared to him by a sudden illumination as invariably written by fools for the reading of imbeciles. Mentally he agreed with the words Mr. Verloc let fall at last in answer to his last remark.

"Perhaps not. But it will upset many things. I have been a straight man, and I shall keep straight in this——"

"If they let you," said the Chief Inspector cynically. "You will be preached to, no doubt, before they put you into the dock. And in the end you may yet get let in for a sentence that will surprise you. I wouldn't trust too much the gentleman who's been talking to you."

Mr. Verloc listened, frowning.

"My advice to you is to clear out while you may. I have no instructions. There are some of them," continued Chief Inspector Heat, laying a peculiar stress on the word "them," "who think you are already out of the world."

"Indeed!" Mr. Verloc was moved to say. Though since his return from Greenwich he had spent most of his time sitting in the taproom˚ of an obscure little public-house, he could hardly have hoped for such favourable news.

˚Room in an inn or tavern where commoners and laborers were served.

"That's the impression about you." The Chief Inspector nodded at him. "Vanish. Clear out."

"Where to?" snarled Mr. Verloc. He raised his head, and gazing at the closed door of the parlour, muttered feelingly: "I only wish you would take me away to-night. I would go quietly."

"I daresay," assented sardonically the Chief Inspector, following the direction of his glance.

The brow of Mr. Verloc broke into slight moisture. He lowered his husky voice confidentially before the unmoved Chief Inspector.

"The lad was half-witted, irresponsible. Any court would have seen that at once. Only fit for the asylum. And that was the worst that would've happened to him if——"

The Chief Inspector, his hand on the door handle, whispered into Mr. Verloc's face.

"He may've been half-witted, but you must have been crazy. What drove you off your head like this?"

Mr. Verloc, thinking of Mr. Vladimir, did not hesitate in the choice of words.

"A hyperborean swine," he hissed forcibly. "A what you might call a—a gentleman."

The Chief Inspector, steady-eyed, nodded briefly his comprehension, and opened the door. Mrs. Verloc, behind the counter, might have heard but did not see his departure, pursued by the aggressive clatter of the bell. She sat at her post of duty behind the counter. She sat rigidly erect in the chair with two dirty pink pieces of paper lying spread at her feet. The palms of her hands were pressed convulsively to her face, with the tips of the fingers contracted against the forehead, as though the skin had been a mask which she was ready to tear off violently. The perfect immobility of her pose expressed the agitation of rage and despair, all the potential violence of tragic passions, better than any shallow display of shrieks, with the beating of a distracted head against the walls, could have done. Chief Inspector Heat, crossing the shop at his busy, swinging pace, gave her only a cursory glance. And when the cracked bell ceased to tremble on its curved ribbon of steel nothing stirred near Mrs. Verloc, as if her attitude had the locking power of a spell. Even the butterfly-shaped gas-flames posed on the ends of the suspended T-bracket burned without a quiver. In that shop of shady wares fitted with deal shelves painted a dull brown, which seemed to devour the sheen of the light, the gold circlet of the wedding ring on Mrs. Verloc's left hand glittered exceedingly with the untarnished glory of a piece from some splendid treasure of jewels, dropped in a dust-bin.

CHAPTER TEN

THE Assistant Commissioner, driven rapidly in a hansom from the neighbourhood of Soho in the direction of Westminster, got out at the very centre of the Empire on which the sun never sets.[1] Some stalwart constables, who did not seem particularly impressed by the duty of watching the august spot, saluted him. Penetrating through a portal by no means lofty into the precincts of the House which is *the* House *par excellence* in the minds of many millions of men, he was met at last by the volatile and revolutionary Toodles.

That neat and nice young man concealed his astonishment at the early appearance of the Assistant Commissioner, whom he had been told to look out for some time about midnight. His turning up so early he concluded to be the sign that things, whatever they were, had gone wrong. With an extremely ready sympathy, which in nice youngsters goes often with a joyous temperament, he felt sorry for the Great Presence he called "The Chief," and also for the Assistant Commissioner, whose face appeared to him more ominously wooden than ever before, and quite wonderfully long. "What a queer, foreign-looking chap he is," he thought to himself, smiling from a distance with friendly buoyancy. And directly they came together he began to talk with the kind intention of burying the awkwardness of failure under a heap of words. It looked as if the great assault threatened for that night were going to fizzle out. An inferior henchman of "that brute Cheeseman" was up boring mercilessly a very thin House with some shamelessly cooked statistics. He, Toodles, hoped he would bore them into a count-out* every minute. But then he might be only marking time to let that guzzling

---

*Procedure for determining whether there were enough members of parliament present to vote on an issue. If there were not at least forty in the House of Commons, the meeting would be adjourned.

Cheeseman dine at his leisure. Anyway, the Chief could not be persuaded to go home.

"He will see you at once, I think. He's sitting all alone in his room thinking of all the fishes of the sea,"[2] concluded Toodles airily. "Come along."

Notwithstanding the kindness of his disposition, the young private secretary (unpaid) was accessible to the common failings of humanity. He did not wish to harrow the feelings of the Assistant Commissioner, who looked to him uncommonly like a man who has made a mess of his job. But his curiosity was too strong to be restrained by mere compassion. He could not help, as they went along, to throw over his shoulder lightly:

"And your sprat?"

"Got him," answered the Assistant Commissioner with a concision which did not mean to be repellent in the least.

"Good. You've no idea how these great men dislike to be disappointed in small things."

After this profound observation the experienced Toodles seemed to reflect. At any rate he said nothing for quite two seconds. Then:

"I'm glad. But—I say—is it really such a very small thing as you make it out?"

"Do you know what may be done with a sprat?" the Assistant Commissioner asked in his turn.

"He's sometimes put into a sardine box," chuckled Toodles, whose erudition on the subject of the fishing industry was fresh and, in comparison with his ignorance of all other industrial matters, immense. "There are sardine canneries on the Spanish coast which——"

The Assistant Commissioner interrupted the apprentice statesman:

"Yes. Yes. But a sprat is also thrown away sometimes in order to catch a whale."[3]

"A whale. Phew!" exclaimed Toodles, with bated breath. "You're after a whale, then?"

"Not exactly. What I am after is more like a dog-fish. You don't know perhaps what a dog-fish* is like?"

---

*A type of shark.

"Yes, I do. We're buried in special books up to our necks—whole shelves full of them—with plates. . . . It's a noxious, rascally-looking, altogether detestable beast, with a sort of smooth face and moustaches."

"Described to a T," commended the Assistant Commissioner. "Only mine is clean-shaven altogether. You've seen him. It's a witty fish."

"I have seen him!" said Toodles incredulously.

"I can't conceive where I could have seen him."

"At the Explorers',[4] I should say," dropped the Assistant Commissioner calmly. At the name of that extremely exclusive club Toodles looked scared, and stopped short.

"Nonsense," he protested, but in an awe-struck tone. "What do you mean? A member?"

"Honorary," muttered the Assistant Commissioner through his teeth.

"Heavens!"

Toodles looked so thunderstruck that the Assistant Commissioner smiled faintly.

"That's between ourselves strictly," he said.

"That's the beastliest thing I've ever heard in my life," declared Toodles feebly, as if astonishment had robbed him of all his buoyant strength in a second.

The Assistant Commissioner gave him an unsmiling glance. Till they came to the door of the great man's room, Toodles preserved a scandalised and solemn silence, as though he were offended with the Assistant Commissioner for exposing such an unsavoury and disturbing fact. It revolutionised his idea of the Explorers' Club's extreme selectness, of its social purity. Toodles was revolutionary only in politics; his social beliefs and personal feelings he wished to preserve unchanged through all the years allotted to him on this earth, which, upon the whole, he believed to be a nice place to live on.

He stood aside.

"Go in without knocking," he said.

Shades of green silk fitted low over all the lights imparted to the room something of a forest's deep gloom. The haughty eyes were physically the great man's weak point. This point was wrapped up in secrecy. When an opportunity offered, he rested them conscientiously. The Assistant Commissioner entering saw at first only a big pale hand supporting a big head, and concealing the upper part of a big pale face. An open dispatch-box stood on the writing-table near a few oblong sheets of paper and a scattered handful of quill pens. There was absolutely nothing else on the large flat surface except a little bronze statuette draped in a toga, mysteriously watchful in its shadowy immobility. The Assistant Commissioner, invited to take a chair, sat down. In the dim light, the salient points of his personality, the long face, the black hair, his lankness, made him look more foreign than ever.

The great man manifested no surprise, no eagerness, no sentiment whatever. The attitude in which he rested his menaced eyes was profoundly meditative. He did not alter it the least bit. But his tone was not dreamy.

"Well! What is it that you've found out already? You came upon something unexpected on the first step."

"Not exactly unexpected, Sir Ethelred. What I mainly came upon was a psychological state."

The Great Presence made a slight movement.

"You must be lucid, please."

"Yes, Sir Ethelred. You know no doubt that most criminals at some time or other feel an irresistible need of confessing—of making a clean breast of it to somebody—to anybody. And they do it often to the police. In that Verloc whom Heat wished so much to screen I've found a man in that particular psychological state. The man, figuratively speaking, flung himself on my breast. It was enough on my part to whisper to him who I was and to add, 'I know that you are at the bottom of this affair.' It must have seemed miraculous to him that we should know already, but he took it all in the stride. The wonderfulness of it never checked him for a moment. There remained for me only to put to him the two questions: Who put you up to it? and Who was the man who did it? He answered the first with remarkable emphasis. As to the second question, I gather that the fellow with the bomb was his brother-in-law—quite a lad—a weak-minded creature. . . . It is rather a curious affair—too long, perhaps, to state fully just now."

"What then have you learned?" asked the great man.

"First, I've learned that the ex-convict Michaelis had nothing to do with it, though indeed the lad had been living with him temporarily in the country up to eight o'clock this morning. It is more than likely that Michaelis knows nothing of it to this moment."

"You are positive as to that?" asked the great man.

"Quite certain, Sir Ethelred. This fellow Verloc went there this morning, and took away the lad on the pretence of going out for a walk in the lanes. As it was not the first time that he did this, Michaelis could not have the slightest suspicion of anything unusual. For the rest, Sir Ethelred, the indignation of this man Verloc had left nothing in doubt—nothing whatever. He had been driven out of his mind almost by an extraordinary performance, which for you or me it would be difficult to take as seriously meant, but which produced a great impression obviously on him."

The Assistant Commissioner then imparted briefly to the great man, who sat still, resting his eyes under the screen of his hand, Mr. Verloc's appreciation of Mr. Vladimir's proceedings and character. The Assistant Commissioner did not seem to refuse it a certain amount of competency. But the Great Personage remarked:

"All this seems very fantastic."

"Doesn't it? One would think a ferocious joke. But our man took it seriously, it appears. He felt himself threatened. In his time, you know, he was in direct communication with old Stott-Wartenheim himself, and had come to regard his services as indispensable. It was an extremely rude awakening. I imagine that he lost his head. He became angry and frightened. Upon my word, my impression is that he thought these Embassy people quite capable not only of throwing him out, but of giving him away, too, in some manner or other——"

"How long were you with him?" interrupted the Presence from behind his big hand.

"Some forty minutes, Sir Ethelred, in a house of bad repute called the Continental Hotel, closeted in a room which, by-the-bye, I took for the night. I found him under the influence of that reaction which follows the effort of crime. The man cannot be defined as a hardened criminal. It is obvious that he did not plan the death of that wretched lad—his brother-in-law. That was a shock to him—I could see that. Perhaps he is a man of strong sensibilities.

Perhaps he was even fond of the lad—who knows? He might have hoped that the fellow would get clear away; in which case it would have been almost impossible to bring this thing home to any one. At any rate, he risked consciously nothing more than arrest for him."

The Assistant Commissioner paused in his speculations to reflect for a moment.

"Though how, in that last case, he could hope to have his own share in the business concealed is more than I can tell," he continued, in his ignorance of poor Stevie's devotion to Mr. Verloc (who was *good*), and of his truly peculiar dumbness, which in the old affair of fireworks on the stairs had for many years resisted entreaties, coaxing, anger, and other means of investigation used by his beloved sister. For Stevie was loyal. . . . "No, I can't imagine. It's possible that he never thought of that at all. It sounds an extravagant way of putting it, Sir Ethelred, but his state of dismay suggested to me an impulsive man who, after committing suicide with the notion that it would end all his troubles, had discovered that it did nothing of the kind."

The Assistant Commissioner gave this definition in an apologetic voice. But in truth there is a sort of lucidity proper to extravagant language, and the great man was not offended. A slight jerky movement of the big body half lost in the gloom of the green silk shades, of the big head leaning on the big hand, accompanied an intermittent stifled but powerful sound. The great man had laughed.

"What have you done with him?"

The Assistant Commissioner answered very readily:

"As he seemed very anxious to get back to his wife in the shop I let him go, Sir Ethelred."

"You did? But the fellow will disappear."

"Pardon me. I don't think so. Where could he go to? Moreover, you must remember that he has got to think of the danger from his comrades too. He's there at his post. How could he explain leaving it? But even if there were no obstacles to his freedom of action he would do nothing. At present he hasn't enough moral energy to take a resolution of any sort. Permit me also to point out that if I had detained him we would have been committed to a course of action on which I wished to know your precise intentions first."

The Great Personage rose heavily, an imposing shadowy form in the greenish gloom of the room.

"I'll see the Attorney-General to-night, and will send for you to-morrow morning. Is there anything more you wish to tell me now?"

The Assistant Commissioner had stood up also, slender and flexible.

"I think not, Sir Ethelred, unless I were to enter into details which——"

"No. No details, please."

The great shadowy form seemed to shrink away as if in physical dread of details; then came forward, expanded, enormous, and weighty, offering a large hand. "And you say that this man has got a wife?"

"Yes, Sir Ethelred," said the Assistant Commissioner, pressing deferentially the extended hand. "A genuine wife and a genuinely, respectably, marital relation. He told me that after his interview at the Embassy he would have thrown everything up, would have tried to sell his shop, and leave the country, only he felt certain that his wife would not even hear of going abroad. Nothing could be more characteristic of the respectable bond than that," went on, with a touch of grimness, the Assistant Commissioner, whose own wife, too, had refused to hear of going abroad. "Yes, a genuine wife. And the victim was a genuine brother-in-law. From a certain point of view we are here in the presence of a domestic drama."

The Assistant Commissioner laughed a little; but the great man's thoughts seemed to have wandered far away, perhaps to the questions of his country's domestic policy, the battle-ground of his crusading valour against the paynim* Cheeseman. The Assistant Commissioner withdrew quietly, unnoticed, as if already forgotten.

He had his own crusading instincts. This affair, which, in one way or another, disgusted Chief Inspector Heat, seemed to him a providentially given starting-point for a crusade. He had it much at heart to begin. He walked slowly home, meditating that enterprise on the way, and thinking over Mr. Verloc's psychology in a composite mood of repugnance and satisfaction. He walked all the way

---

*Pagan, infidel.

home. Finding the drawing-room dark, he went upstairs, and spent some time between the bedroom and the dressing-room, changing his clothes, going to and fro with the air of a thoughtful somnambulist. But he shook it off before going out again to join his wife at the house of the great lady patroness of Michaelis.

He knew he would be welcomed there. On entering the smaller of the two drawing-rooms he saw his wife in a small group near the piano. A youngish composer in pass of becoming famous was discoursing from a music stool to two thick men whose backs looked old, and three slender women whose backs looked young. Behind the screen the great lady had only two persons with her: a man and a woman, who sat side by side on arm-chairs at the foot of her couch. She extended her hand to the Assistant Commissioner.

"I never hoped to see you here to-night. Annie told me——"

"Yes. I had no idea myself that my work would be over so soon."

The Assistant Commissioner added in a low tone, "I am glad to tell you that Michaelis is altogether clear of this——"

The patroness of the ex-convict received this assurance indignantly.

"Why? Were your people stupid enough to connect him with——"

"Not stupid," interrupted the Assistant Commissioner, contradicting deferentially. "Clever enough—quite clever enough for that."

A silence fell. The man at the foot of the couch had stopped speaking to the lady, and looked on with a faint smile.

"I don't know whether you ever met before," said the great lady.

Mr. Vladimir and the Assistant Commissioner, introduced, acknowledged each other's existence with punctilious and guarded courtesy.

"He's been frightening me," declared suddenly the lady who sat by the side of Mr. Vladimir, with an inclination of the head towards that gentleman. The Assistant Commissioner knew the lady.

"You do not look frightened," he pronounced, after surveying her conscientiously with his tired and equable gaze. He was thinking meantime to himself that in this house one met everybody sooner or later. Mr. Vladimir's rosy countenance was wreathed in smiles, because he was witty, but his eyes remained serious, like the eyes of a convinced man.

"Well, he tried to at least," amended the lady.

"Force of habit perhaps," said the Assistant Commissioner, moved by an irresistible inspiration.

"He has been threatening society with all sorts of horrors," continued the lady, whose enunciation was caressing and slow, "apropos of this explosion in Greenwich Park. It appears we all ought to quake in our shoes at what's coming if those people are not suppressed all over the world. I had no idea this was such a grave affair."

Mr. Vladimir, affecting not to listen, leaned towards the couch, talking amiably in subdued tones, but he heard the Assistant Commissioner say:

"I've no doubt that Mr. Vladimir has a very precise notion of the true importance of this affair."

Mr. Vladimir asked himself what that confounded and intrusive policeman was driving at. Descended from generations victimised by the instruments of an arbitrary power, he was racially, nationally, and individually afraid of the police. It was an inherited weakness, altogether independent of his judgment, of his reason, of his experience. He was born to it. But that sentiment, which resembled the irrational horror some people have of cats, did not stand in the way of his immense contempt for the English police. He finished the sentence addressed to the great lady, and turned slightly in his chair.

"You mean that we have a great experience of these people. Yes; indeed, we suffer greatly from their activity, while you"— Mr. Vladimir hesitated for a moment, in smiling perplexity— "while you suffer their presence gladly in your midst," he finished, displaying a dimple on each clean-shaven cheek. Then he added more gravely: "I may even say—because you do."

When Mr. Vladimir ceased speaking the Assistant Commissioner lowered his glance, and the conversation dropped. Almost immediately afterwards Mr. Vladimir took leave. Directly his back was turned on the couch the Assistant Commissioner rose too.

"I thought you were going to stay and take Annie home," said the lady patroness of Michaelis.

"I find that I've yet a little work to do to-night."

"In connection——?"

"Well, yes—in a way."

"Tell me, what is it really—this horror?"

"It's difficult to say what it is, but it may yet be a *cause célèbre*,"* said the Assistant Commissioner.

He left the drawing-room hurriedly, and found Mr. Vladimir still in the hall, wrapping up his throat carefully in a large silk handkerchief. Behind him a footman waited, holding his overcoat. Another stood ready to open the door. The Assistant Commissioner was duly helped into his coat, and let out at once. After descending the front steps he stopped, as if to consider the way he should take. On seeing this through the door held open, Mr. Vladimir lingered in the hall to get out a cigar and asked for a light. It was furnished to him by an elderly man out of livery with an air of calm solicitude. But the match went out; the footman then closed the door, and Mr. Vladimir lighted his large Havana with leisurely care. When at last he got out of the house, he saw with disgust the "confounded policeman" still standing on the pavement.

"Can he be waiting for me?" thought Mr. Vladimir, looking up and down for some signs of a hansom. He saw none. A couple of carriages waited by the curbstone, their lamps blazing steadily, the horses standing perfectly still, as if carved in stone, the coachmen sitting motionless under the big fur capes, without as much as a quiver stirring the white thongs of their big whips. Mr. Vladimir walked on, and the "confounded policeman" fell into step at his elbow. He said nothing. At the end of the fourth stride Mr. Vladimir felt infuriated and uneasy. This could not last.

"Rotten weather," he growled savagely.

"Mild," said the Assistant Commissioner without passion. He remained silent for a little while. "We've got hold of a man called Verloc," he announced casually.

Mr. Vladimir did not stumble, did not stagger back, did not change his stride. But he could not prevent himself from exclaiming: "What?" The Assistant Commissioner did not repeat his statement. "You know him," he went on in the same tone.

Mr. Vladimir stopped, and became guttural.

"What makes you say that?"

---

*Celebrated or notorious case (French).

"I don't. It's Verloc who says that."

"A lying dog of some sort," said Mr. Vladimir in somewhat Oriental phraseology. But in his heart he was almost awed by the miraculous cleverness of the English police. The change of his opinion on the subject was so violent that it made him for the moment feel slightly sick. He threw away his cigar, and moved on.

"What pleased me most in this affair," the Assistant went on, talking slowly, "is that it makes such an excellent starting-point for a piece of work which I've felt must be taken in hand—that is, the clearing out of this country of all the foreign political spies, police, and that sort of—of—dogs. In my opinion they are a ghastly nuisance; also an element of danger. But we can't very well seek them out individually. The only way is to make their employment unpleasant to their employers. The thing's becoming indecent. And dangerous, too, for us here."

Mr. Vladimir stopped again for a moment.

"What do you mean?"

"The prosecution of this Verloc will demonstrate to the public both the danger and the indecency."

"Nobody will believe what a man of that sort says," said Mr. Vladimir contemptuously.

"The wealth and precision of detail will carry conviction to the great mass of the public," advanced the Assistant Commissioner gently.

"So that is seriously what you mean to do?"

"We've got the man; we have no choice."

"You will be only feeding up the lying spirit of these revolutionary scoundrels," Mr. Vladimir protested. "What do you want to make a scandal for?—from morality—or what?"

Mr. Vladimir's anxiety was obvious. The Assistant Commissioner having ascertained in this way that there must be some truth in the summary statements of Mr. Verloc, said indifferently:

"There's a practical side too. We have really enough to do to look after the genuine article. You can't say we are not effective. But we don't intend to let ourselves be bothered by shams under any pretext whatever."

Mr. Vladimir's tone became lofty.

"For my part, I can't share your view. It is selfish. My sentiments for my own country cannot be doubted; but I've always felt that we ought to be good Europeans besides—I mean governments and men."

"Yes," said the Assistant Commissioner simply. "Only you look at Europe from its other end. But," he went on in a good-natured tone, "the foreign governments cannot complain of the inefficiency of our police. Look at this outrage; a case specially difficult to trace inasmuch as it was a sham. In less than twelve hours we have established the identity of a man literally blown to shreds, have found the organiser of the attempt, and have had a glimpse of the inciter behind him. And we could have gone further; only we stopped at the limits of our territory."

"So this instructive crime was planned abroad?" Mr. Vladimir said quickly. "You admit it was planned abroad?"

"Theoretically. Theoretically only on foreign territory; abroad only by a fiction," said the Assistant Commissioner, alluding to the character of Embassies, which are supposed to be part and parcel of the country to which they belong. "But that's a detail. I talked to you of this business because it's your government that grumbles most at our police. You see that we are not so bad. I wanted particularly to tell you of our success."

"I'm sure I'm very grateful," muttered Mr. Vladimir through his teeth.

"We can put our finger on every anarchist here," went on the Assistant Commissioner, as though he were quoting Chief Inspector Heat. "All that's wanted now is to do away with the *agent provocateur* to make everything safe."

Mr. Vladimir held up his hand to a passing hansom.

"You're not going in here?" remarked the Assistant Commissioner, looking at a building of noble proportions and hospitable aspect, with the light of a great hall falling through its glass doors on a broad flight of steps.

But Mr. Vladimir, sitting, stony-eyed, inside the hansom, drove off without a word.

The Assistant Commissioner himself did not turn into the noble building. It was the Explorers' Club. The thought passed through his mind that Mr. Vladimir, honorary member, would not be seen very often there in the future. He looked at his watch. It was only half-past ten. He had had a very full evening.

CHAPTER ELEVEN

AFTER Chief Inspector Heat had left him Mr. Verloc moved about the parlour. From time to time he eyed his wife through the open door. "She knows all about it now," he thought to himself with commiseration for her sorrow and with some satisfaction as regarded himself. Mr. Verloc's soul, if lacking greatness perhaps, was capable of tender sentiments. The prospect of having to break the news to her had put him into a fever. Chief Inspector Heat had relieved him of the task. That was good as far as it went. It remained for him now to face her grief.

Mr. Verloc had never expected to have to face it on account of death, whose catastrophic character cannot be argued away by sophisticated reasoning or persuasive eloquence. Mr. Verloc never meant Stevie to perish with such abrupt violence. He did not mean him to perish at all. Stevie dead was a much greater nuisance than ever he had been when alive. Mr. Verloc had augured a favourable issue to his enterprise, basing himself not on Stevie's intelligence, which sometimes plays queer tricks with a man, but on the blind docility and on the blind devotion of the boy. Though not much of a psychologist, Mr. Verloc had gauged the depth of Stevie's fanaticism. He dared cherish the hope of Stevie walking away from the walls of the Observatory as he had been instructed to do, taking the way shown to him several times previously, and rejoining his brother-in-law, the wise and good Mr. Verloc, outside the precincts of the park. Fifteen minutes ought to have been enough for the veriest fool to deposit the engine and walk away. And the Professor had guaranteed more than fifteen minutes. But Stevie had stumbled within five minutes of being left to himself. And Mr. Verloc was shaken morally to pieces. He had foreseen everything but that. He had foreseen Stevie distracted and lost—sought for—found in some police station or provincial workhouse in the end. He had foreseen Stevie arrested, and was not afraid, because Mr. Verloc had a great opinion of Stevie's loyalty, which had been carefully indoctrinated with the necessity of silence in the course of many walks. Like a peripatetic philosopher, Mr. Verloc, strolling along the streets of London, had modified Stevie's view of the police by conversations full of subtle reasonings. Never had a sage a more attentive and admiring disciple. The submission and worship were so apparent that Mr. Verloc had come to feel something like a liking for the boy. In any case, he had not foreseen the swift bringing home of his connection. That his wife should hit upon the precaution of sewing the boy's address inside his overcoat was the last thing Mr. Verloc would have thought of. One can't think of everything. That was what she meant when she said that he need not worry if he lost Stevie during their walks. She had assured him that the boy would turn up all right. Well, he had turned up with a vengeance!

"Well, well," muttered Mr. Verloc in his wonder. What did she mean by it? Spare him the trouble of keeping an anxious eye on Stevie? Most likely she had meant well. Only she ought to have told him of the precaution she had taken.

Mr. Verloc walked behind the counter of the shop. His intention was not to overwhelm his wife with bitter reproaches. Mr. Verloc felt no bitterness. The unexpected march of events had converted him to the doctrine of fatalism. Nothing could be helped now. He said:

"I didn't mean any harm to come to the boy."

Mrs. Verloc shuddered at the sound of her husband's voice. She did not uncover her face. The trusted secret agent of the late Baron Stott-Wartenheim looked at her for a time with a heavy, persistent, undiscerning glance. The torn evening paper was lying at her feet. It could not have told her much. Mr. Verloc felt the need of talking to his wife.

"It's that damned Heat—eh?" he said. "He upset you. He's a brute, blurting it out like this to a woman. I made myself ill thinking how to break it to you. I sat for hours in the little parlour of the Cheshire Cheese[1] thinking over the best way. You understand I never meant any harm to come to that boy."

Mr. Verloc, the Secret Agent, was speaking the truth. It was his marital affection that had received the greatest shock from the premature explosion. He added:

"I didn't feel particularly gay sitting there and thinking of you."

He observed another slight shudder of his wife, which affected his sensibility. As she persisted in hiding her face in her hands, he thought he had better leave her alone for a while. On this delicate impulse Mr. Verloc withdrew into the parlour again, where the gas-jet purred like a contented cat. Mrs. Verloc's wifely forethought had left the cold beef on the table with carving knife and fork and half a loaf of bread for Mr. Verloc's supper. He noticed all these things now for the first time, and cutting himself a piece of bread and meat, began to eat.

His appetite did not proceed from callousness. Mr. Verloc had not eaten any breakfast that day. He had left his home fasting. Not being an energetic man, he found his resolution in nervous excitement, which seemed to hold him mainly by the throat. He could not have swallowed anything solid. Michaelis' cottage was as destitute of provisions as the cell of a prisoner. The ticket-of-leave apostle lived on a little milk and crusts of stale bread. Moreover, when Mr. Verloc arrived he had already gone upstairs after his frugal meal. Absorbed in the toil and delight of literary composition, he had not even answered Mr. Verloc's shout up the little staircase.

"I am taking this young fellow home for a day or two."

And, in truth, Mr. Verloc did not wait for an answer, but had marched out of the cottage at once, followed by the obedient Stevie.

Now that all action was over, and his fate taken out of his hands with unexpected swiftness, Mr. Verloc felt terribly empty physically. He carved the meat, cut the bread, and devoured his supper standing by the table, and now and then casting a glance towards his wife. Her prolonged immobility disturbed the comfort of his refection. He walked again into the shop, and came up very close to her. This sorrow with a veiled face made Mr. Verloc uneasy. He expected, of course, his wife to be very much upset, but he wanted her to pull herself together. He needed all her assistance and all her loyalty in these new conjunctures his fatalism had already accepted.

"Can't be helped," he said in a tone of gloomy sympathy. "Come, Winnie, we've got to think of to-morrow. You'll want all your wits about you after I am taken away."

He paused. Mrs. Verloc's breast heaved convulsively. This was not reassuring to Mr. Verloc, in whose view the newly created situation required from the two people most concerned in it calmness, decision, and other qualities incompatible with the mental disorder of passionate sorrow. Mr. Verloc was a humane man; he had come home prepared to allow every latitude to his wife's affection for her brother. Only he did not understand either the nature or the whole extent of that sentiment. And in this he was excusable, since it was impossible for him to understand it without ceasing to be himself. He was startled and disappointed, and his speech conveyed it by a certain roughness of tone.

"You might look at a fellow," he observed after waiting a while.

As if forced through the hands covering Mrs. Verloc's face the answer came, deadened, almost pitiful.

"I don't want to look at you as long as I live."

"Eh? What?" Mr. Verloc was merely startled by the superficial and literal meaning of this declaration. It was obviously unreasonable, the mere cry of exaggerated grief. He threw over it the mantle of his marital indulgence. The mind of Mr. Verloc lacked profundity. Under the mistaken impression that the value of individuals consists in what they are in themselves, he could not possibly comprehend the value of Stevie in the eyes of Mrs. Verloc. She was taking it confoundedly hard he thought to himself. It was all the fault of that damned Heat. What did he want to upset the woman for? But she mustn't be allowed, for her own good, to carry on so till she got quite beside herself.

"Look here! You can't sit like this in the shop," he said with affected severity, in which there was some real annoyance; for urgent practical matters must be talked over if they had to sit up all night. "Somebody might come in at any minute," he added, and waited again. No effect was produced, and the idea of the finality of death occurred to Mr. Verloc during the pause. He changed his tone. "Come. This won't bring him back," he said gently, feeling ready to take her in his arms and press her to his breast, where impatience and compassion dwelt side by side. But except for a short shudder Mrs. Verloc remained apparently unaffected by the force of that terrible truism. It was Mr. Verloc himself who was moved. He was moved in his simplicity to urge moderation by asserting the claims of his own personality.

"Do be reasonable, Winnie. What would it have been if you had lost me!"

He had vaguely expected to hear her cry out. But she did not budge. She leaned back a little, quieted down to a complete unreadable stillness. Mr. Verloc's heart began to beat faster with exasperation and something resembling alarm. He laid his hand on her shoulder, saying:

"Don't be a fool, Winnie."

She gave no sign. It was impossible to talk to any purpose with a woman whose face one cannot see. Mr. Verloc caught hold of his wife's wrists. But her hands seemed glued fast. She swayed forward bodily to his tug, and nearly went off the chair. Startled to feel her so helplessly limp, he was trying to put her back on the chair when she stiffened suddenly all over, tore herself out of his hands, ran out of the shop, across the parlour, and into the kitchen. This was very swift. He had just a glimpse of her face and that much of her eyes that he knew she had not looked at him.

It all had the appearance of a struggle for the possession of a chair, because Mr. Verloc instantly took his wife's place in it. Mr. Verloc did not cover his face with his hands, but a sombre thoughtfulness veiled his features. A term of imprisonment could not be avoided. He did not wish now to avoid it. A prison was a place as safe from certain unlawful vengeances as the grave, with this advantage, that in a prison there is room for hope. What he saw before him was a term of imprisonment, an early release, and then life abroad somewhere, such as he had contemplated already, in case of failure. Well, it was a failure, if not exactly the sort of failure he had feared. It had been so near success that he could have positively terrified Mr. Vladimir out of his ferocious scoffing with this proof of occult efficiency. So at least it seemed now to Mr. Verloc. His prestige with the Embassy would have been immense if—if his wife had not had the unlucky notion of sewing on the address inside Stevie's overcoat. Mr. Verloc, who was no fool, had soon perceived the extraordinary character of the influence he had over Stevie, though he did not understand exactly its origin—the doctrine of his supreme wisdom and goodness inculcated by two anxious women. In all the eventualities he had foreseen Mr. Verloc had calculated with correct insight on Stevie's instinctive loyalty and blind discretion. The eventuality he had not foreseen had appalled him as a humane man and a fond husband. From every other point of view it was rather advantageous. Nothing can equal the everlasting discretion of death. Mr. Verloc, sitting perplexed and frightened in the small parlour of the Cheshire Cheese, could not help acknowledging that to himself, because his sensibility did not stand in the way of his judgment. Stevie's violent disintegration, however disturbing to think about, only assured the success; for, of course, the knocking down of a wall was not the aim of Mr. Vladimir's menaces, but the production of a moral effect. With much trouble and distress on Mr. Verloc's part the effect might be said to have been produced. When, however, most unexpectedly, it came home to roost in Brett Street, Mr. Verloc, who had been struggling like a man in a nightmare for the preservation of his position, accepted the blow in the spirit of a convinced fatalist. The position was gone through no one's fault really. A small, tiny fact had done it. It was like slipping on a bit of orange peel in the dark and breaking your leg.

Mr. Verloc drew a weary breath. He nourished no resentment against his wife. He thought: She will have to look after the shop while they keep me locked up. After thinking also how cruelly she would miss Stevie at first, he felt greatly concerned about her health and spirits. How would she stand her solitude—absolutely alone in that house? It would not do for her to break down while he was locked up? What would become of the shop then? The shop was an asset. Though Mr. Verloc's fatalism accepted his undoing as a secret agent, he had no mind to be utterly ruined, mostly, it must be owned, from regard for his wife.

Silent, and out of his line of sight in the kitchen, she frightened him. If only she had had her mother with her. But that silly old woman—— An angry dismay possessed Mr. Verloc. He must talk with his wife. He could tell her certainly that a man does get desperate under certain circumstances. But he did not go incontinently to impart to her that information. First of all, it was clear to him that this evening was no time for business. He got up to close the street door and put the gas out in the shop.

Having thus assured a solitude around his hearth-stone, Mr. Verloc walked into the parlour and glanced down into the kitchen. Mrs. Verloc was sitting in the place where poor Stevie usually established himself of an evening with paper and pencil for the pastime of drawing these coruscations of innumerable circles suggesting chaos and eternity. Her arms were folded on the table, and her head was lying on her arms. Mr. Verloc contemplated her back and the arrangement of her hair for a time, then walked away from the kitchen door. Mrs. Verloc's philosophical, almost disdainful incuriosity, the foundation of their accord in domestic life, made it extremely difficult to get into contact with her now this tragic necessity had arisen. Mr. Verloc felt this difficulty acutely. He turned around the table in the parlour with his usual air of a large animal in a cage.

Curiosity being one of the forms of self-revelation, a systematically incurious person remains always partly mysterious. Every time he passed near the door Mr. Verloc glanced at his wife uneasily. It was not that he was afraid of her. Mr. Verloc imagined himself loved by that woman. But she had not accustomed him to make confidences. And the confidence he had to make was of a profound psychological order. How with his want of practice could he tell her what he himself felt but vaguely: that there are conspiracies of fatal destiny, that a notion grows in a mind sometimes till it acquires an outward existence, an independent power of its own, and even a suggestive voice? He could not inform her that a man may be haunted by a fat, witty, clean-shaven face till the wildest expedient to get rid of it appears a child of wisdom.

On this mental reference to a First Secretary of a great Embassy, Mr. Verloc stopped in the doorway, and looking down into the kitchen with an angry face and clenched fists addressed his wife.

"You don't know what a brute I had to deal with."

He started off to make another perambulation of the table; then when he had come to the door again he stopped, glaring in from the height of two steps.

"A silly, jeering, dangerous brute, with no more sense than— After all these years! A man like me! And I have been playing my head* at that game. You didn't know. Quite right, too. What was the good of telling you that I stood the risk of having a knife stuck into me any time these seven years we've been married? I am not a chap to worry a woman that's fond of me. You had no business to know."

---

*Risking my neck (from the French expression *jouer sa tête*, used in gambling).

Mr. Verloc took another turn round the parlour, fuming.

"A venomous beast," he began again from the doorway. "Drive me out into a ditch to starve for a joke. I could see he thought it was a damned good joke. A man like me! Look here! Some of the highest in the world got to thank me for walking on their two legs to this day. That's the man you've got married to, my girl!"

He perceived that his wife had sat up. Mrs. Verloc's arms remained lying stretched on the table. Mr. Verloc watched her back as if he could read there the effect of his words.

"There isn't a murdering plot for the last eleven years that I hadn't my finger in at the risk of my life. There's scores of these revolutionists I've sent off, with their bombs in their blamed pockets, to get themselves caught on the frontier. The old Baron knew what I was worth to his country. And here suddenly a swine comes along—an ignorant, overbearing swine."

Mr. Verloc, stepping slowly down two steps, entered the kitchen, took a tumbler off the dresser, and holding it in his hand, approached the sink, without looking at his wife.

"It wasn't the old Baron who would have had the wicked folly of getting me to call on him at eleven in the morning. There are two or three in this town that, if they had seen me going in, would have made no bones about knocking me on the head sooner or later. It was a silly, murderous trick to expose for nothing a man—like me."

Mr. Verloc, turning on the tap above the sink, poured three glasses of water, one after another, down his throat to quench the fires of his indignation. Mr. Vladimir's conduct was like a hot brand which set his internal economy in a blaze. He could not get over the disloyalty of it. This man, who would not work at the usual hard tasks which society sets to its humbler members, had exercised his secret industry with an indefatigable devotion. There was in Mr. Verloc a fund of loyalty. He had been loyal to his employers, to the cause of social stability—and to his affections too—as became apparent when, after standing the tumbler in the sink, he turned about, saying:

"If I hadn't thought of you I would have taken the bullying brute by the throat and rammed his head into the fireplace. I'd have been more than a match for that pink-faced, smooth-shaved——"

Mr. Verloc neglected to finish the sentence, as if there could be no doubt of the terminal word. For the first time in his life he was taking that incurious woman into his confidence. The singularity of the event, the force and importance of the personal feelings aroused in the course of this confession, drove Stevie's fate clean out of Mr. Verloc's mind. The boy's stuttering existence of fears and indignations, together with the violence of his end, had passed out of Mr. Verloc's mental sight for a time. For that reason, when he looked up he was startled by the inappropriate character of his wife's stare. It was not a wild stare, and it was not inattentive, but its attention was peculiar and not satisfactory, inasmuch that it seemed concentrated upon some point beyond Mr. Verloc's person. The impression was so strong that Mr. Verloc glanced over his shoulder. There was nothing behind him: there was just the whitewashed wall. The excellent husband of Winnie Verloc saw no writing on the wall.[2] He turned to his wife again, repeating, with some emphasis:

"I would have taken him by the throat. As true as I stand here, if I hadn't thought of you then I would have half choked the life out of the brute before I let him get up. And don't you think he would have been anxious to call the police—either. He wouldn't have dared. You understand why—don't you?"

He blinked at his wife knowingly.

"No," said Mrs. Verloc in an unresonant voice, and without looking at him at all. "What are you talking about?"

A great discouragement, the result of fatigue, came upon Mr. Verloc. He had had a very full day, and his nerves had been tried to the utmost. After a month of maddening worry, ending in an unexpected catastrophe, the storm-tossed spirit of Mr. Verloc longed for repose. His career as a secret agent had come to an end in a way no one could have foreseen; only now, perhaps, he could manage to get a night's sleep at last. But looking at his wife, he doubted it. She was taking it very hard—not at all like herself, he thought. He made an effort to speak.

"You'll have to pull yourself together, my girl," he said sympathetically. "What's done can't be undone."[3]

Mrs. Verloc gave a slight start, though not a muscle of her white face moved in the least. Mr. Verloc, who was not looking at her, continued ponderously:

"You go to bed now. What you want is a good cry."

This opinion had nothing to recommend it but the general consent of mankind. It is universally understood that, as if it were nothing more substantial than vapour floating in the sky, every emotion of a woman is bound to end in a shower. And it is very probable that had Stevie died in his bed under her despairing gaze, in her protecting arms, Mrs. Verloc's grief would have found relief in a flood of bitter and pure tears. Mrs. Verloc, in common with other human beings, was provided with a fund of unconscious resignation sufficient to meet the normal manifestation of human destiny. Without "troubling her head about it," she was aware that it "did not stand looking into very much." But the lamentable circumstances of Stevie's end, which to Mr. Verloc's mind had only an episodic character, as part of a greater disaster, dried her tears at their very source. It was the effect of a white-hot iron drawn across her eyes; at the same time her heart, hardened and chilled into a lump of ice, kept her body in an inward shudder, set her features into a frozen contemplative immobility addressed to a whitewashed wall with no writing on it. The exigencies of Mrs. Verloc's temperament, which, when stripped of its philosophical reserve, was maternal and violent, forced her to roll a series of thoughts in her motionless head. These thoughts were rather imagined than expressed. Mrs. Verloc was a woman of singularly few words, either for public or private use. With the rage and dismay of a betrayed woman, she reviewed the tenor of her life in visions concerned mostly with Stevie's difficult existence from its earliest days. It was a life of single purpose and of a noble unity of inspiration, like those rare lives that have left their mark on the thoughts and feelings of mankind. But the visions of Mrs. Verloc lacked nobility and magnificence. She saw herself putting the boy to bed by the light of a single candle on the deserted top floor of a "business house," dark under the roof and scintillating exceedingly with lights and cut glass at the level of the street like a fairy palace. That meretricious splendour was the only one to be met in Mrs. Verloc's visions. She remembered brushing the boy's hair and tying his pinafores* — herself in a pinafore still; the consolations administered to a small and badly scared creature by another creature nearly as small but not quite so badly scared;

---

*Aprons fastened to children's clothes to prevent them from becoming dirty.

she had the vision of the blows intercepted (often with her own head), of a door held desperately shut against a man's rage (not for very long), of a poker flung once (not very far), which stilled that particular storm into the dumb and awful silence which follows a thunder-clap. And all these scenes of violence came and went accompanied by the unrefined noise of deep vociferations proceeding from a man wounded in his paternal pride, declaring himself obviously accursed since one of his kids was a "slobbering idjut and the other a wicked she-devil." It was of her that this had been said many years ago.

Mrs. Verloc heard the words again in a ghostly fashion, and then the dreary shadow of the Belgravian mansion descended upon her shoulders. It was a crushing memory, an exhausting vision of count-less breakfast trays carried up and down innumerable stairs, of end-less haggling over pence, of the endless drudgery of sweeping, dusting, cleaning, from basement to attics; while the impotent mother, staggering on swollen legs, cooked in a grimy kitchen, and poor Stevie, the unconscious presiding genius of all their toil, blacked the gentlemen's boots in the scullery. But this vision had a breath of a hot London summer in it, and for a central figure a young man wearing his Sunday best, with a straw hat on his dark head and a wooden pipe in his mouth. Affectionate and jolly, he was a fascinating companion for a voyage down the sparkling stream of life; only his boat was very small. There was room in it for a girl-partner at the oar, but no accommodation for passengers. He was allowed to drift away from the threshold of the Belgravian man-sion while Winnie averted her tearful eyes. He was not a lodger. The lodger was Mr. Verloc, indolent, and keeping late hours, sleep-ily jocular of a morning from under his bedclothes, but with gleams of infatuation in his heavy-lidded eyes, and always with some money in his pockets. There was no sparkle of any kind on the lazy stream of his life. It flowed through secret places. But his barque seemed a roomy craft, and his taciturn magnanimity accepted as a matter of course the presence of passengers.

Mrs. Verloc pursued the visions of seven years' security for Ste-vie, loyally paid for on her part; of security growing into confi-dence, into a domestic feeling, stagnant and deep like a placid pool, whose guarded surface hardly shuddered on the occasional passage of Comrade Ossipon, the robust anarchist with shamelessly

inviting eyes, whose glance had a corrupt clearness sufficient to en-
lighten any woman not absolutely imbecile.

A few seconds only had elapsed since the last word had been uttered aloud in the kitchen, and Mrs. Verloc was staring already at
the vision of an episode not more than a fortnight old. With eyes
whose pupils were extremely dilated she stared at the vision of her
husband and poor Stevie walking up Brett Street side by side away
from the shop. It was the last scene of an existence created by Mrs.
Verloc's genius; an existence foreign to all grace and charm, without beauty and almost without decency, but admirable in the continuity of feeling and tenacity of purpose. And this last vision had
such plastic relief, such nearness of form, such a fidelity of suggestive detail, that it wrung from Mrs. Verloc an anguished and faint
murmur, reproducing the supreme illusion of her life, an appalled
murmur that died out on her blanched lips.

"Might have been father and son."

Mr. Verloc stopped, and raised a careworn face. "Eh? What did
you say?" he asked. Receiving no reply, he resumed his sinister
tramping. Then with a menacing flourish of a thick, fleshy fist, he
burst out:

"Yes. The Embassy people. A pretty lot, ain't they? Before a
week's out I'll make some of them wish themselves twenty feet underground. Eh? What?"

He glanced sideways, with his head down. Mrs. Verloc gazed at
the whitewashed wall. A blank wall—perfectly blank. A blankness to
run at and dash your head against. Mrs. Verloc remained immovably seated. She kept still as the population of half the globe would
keep still in astonishment and despair, were the sun suddenly put
out in the summer sky by the perfidy of a trusted providence.

"The Embassy," Mr. Verloc began again, after a preliminary grimace which bared his teeth wolfishly. "I wish I could get loose in
there with a cudgel for half an hour. I would keep on hitting till
there wasn't a single unbroken bone left amongst the whole lot. But
never mind; I'll teach them yet what it means trying to throw out
a man like me to rot in the streets. I've a tongue in my head. All
the world shall know what I've done for them. I am not afraid. I
don't care. Everything'll come out. Every damned thing. Let them
look out!"

In these terms did Mr. Verloc declare his thirst for revenge. It was a very appropriate revenge. It was in harmony with the promptings of Mr. Verloc's genius. It had also the advantage of being within the range of his powers and of adjusting itself easily to the practice of his life, which had consisted precisely in betraying the secret and unlawful proceedings of his fellow-men. Anarchists or diplomats were all one to him. Mr. Verloc was temperamentally no respecter of persons. His scorn was equally distributed over the whole field of his operations. But as a member of a revolutionary proletariat—which he undoubtedly was—he nourished a rather inimical sentiment against social distinction.

"Nothing on earth can stop me now," he added, and paused, looking fixedly at his wife, who was looking fixedly at a blank wall.

The silence in the kitchen was prolonged, and Mr. Verloc felt disappointed. He had expected his wife to say something. But Mrs. Verloc's lips, composed in their usual form, preserved a statuesque immobility like the rest of her face. And Mr. Verloc was disappointed. Yet the occasion did not, he recognised, demand speech from her. She was a woman of very few words. For reasons involved in the very foundation of his psychology, Mr. Verloc was inclined to put his trust in any woman who had given herself to him. Therefore he trusted his wife. Their accord was perfect, but it was not precise. It was a tacit accord, congenial to Mrs. Verloc's incuriosity and to Mr. Verloc's habits of mind, which were indolent and secret. They refrained from going to the bottom of facts and motives.

This reserve, expressing, in a way, their profound confidence in each other, introduced at the same time a certain element of vagueness into their intimacy. No system of conjugal relations is perfect. Mr. Verloc presumed that his wife had understood him, but he would have been glad to hear her say what she thought at the moment. It would have been a comfort.

There were several reasons why this comfort was denied him. There was a physical obstacle: Mrs. Verloc had not sufficient command over her voice. She did not see any alternative between screaming and silence, and instinctively she chose the silence. Winnie Verloc was temperamentally a silent person. And there was the paralysing atrocity of the thought which occupied her. Her cheeks were blanched, her lips ashy, her immobility amazing. And she thought without looking at Mr. Verloc: "This man took the boy away to murder him. He took the boy away from his home to murder him. He took the boy away from me to murder him!"

Mrs. Verloc's whole being was racked by that inconclusive and maddening thought. It was in her veins, in her bones, in the roots of her hair. Mentally she assumed the Biblical attitude of mourning—the covered face, the rent garments; the sound of wailing and lamentation filled her head. But her teeth were violently clenched, and her tearless eyes were hot with rage, because she was not a submissive creature. The protection she had extended over her brother had been in its origin of a fierce and indignant complexion. She had to love him with a militant love. She had battled for him—even against herself. His loss had the bitterness of defeat, with the anguish of a baffled passion. It was not an ordinary stroke of death. Moreover, it was not death that took Stevie from her. It was Mr. Verloc who took him away. She had seen him. She had watched him, without raising a hand, take the boy away. And she had let him go, like—like a fool—a blind fool. Then after he had murdered the boy he came home to her. Just came home like any other man would come home to his wife. . . .

Through her set teeth Mrs. Verloc muttered at the wall:

"And I thought he had caught a cold."

Mr. Verloc heard these words and appropriated them.

"It was nothing," he said moodily. "I was upset. I was upset on your account."

Mrs. Verloc, turning her head slowly, transferred her stare from the wall to her husband's person. Mr. Verloc, with the tips of his fingers between his lips, was looking on the ground.

"Can't be helped," he mumbled, letting his hand fall. "You must pull yourself together. You'll want all your wits about you. It is you who brought the police about our ears. Never mind; I won't say anything more about it," continued Mr. Verloc magnanimously. "You couldn't know."

"I couldn't," breathed out Mrs. Verloc. It was as if a corpse had spoken. Mr. Verloc took up the thread of his discourse.

"I don't blame you. I'll make them sit up. Once under lock and key it will be safe enough for me to talk—you understand. You must reckon on me being two years away from you," he continued, in a tone of sincere concern. "It will be easier for you than for me. You'll have something to do, while I—— Look here, Winnie, what you must do is to keep this business going for two years. You know enough for that. You've a good head on you. I'll send you word when it's time to go about trying to sell. You'll have to be extra careful. The comrades will be keeping an eye on you all the time. You'll have to be as artful as you know how, and as close as the grave. No one must know what you are going to do. I have no mind to get a knock on the head or a stab in the back directly I am let out."

Thus spoke Mr. Verloc, applying his mind with ingenuity and forethought to the problems of the future. His voice was sombre, because he had a correct sentiment of the situation. Everything which he did not wish to happen had come to pass. The future had become precarious. His judgment, perhaps, had been momentarily obscured by his dread of Mr. Vladimir's truculent folly. A man somewhat over forty may be excusably thrown into considerable disorder by the prospect of losing his employment, especially if the man is a secret agent of political police, dwelling secure in the consciousness of his high value and in the esteem of high personages. He was excusable.

Now the thing had ended in a crash. Mr. Verloc was cool; but he was not cheerful. A secret agent who throws his secrecy to the winds from desire of vengeance, and flaunts his achievements before the public eye, becomes the mark for desperate and bloodthirsty indignations. Without unduly exaggerating the danger, Mr. Verloc tried to bring it clearly before his wife's mind. He repeated that he had no intention to let the revolutionists do away with him.

He looked straight into his wife's eyes. The enlarged pupils of the woman received his stare into their unfathomable depths.

"I am too fond of you for that," he said, with a little nervous laugh.

A faint flush coloured Mrs. Verloc's ghastly and motionless face. Having done with the visions of the past, she had not only heard, but had also understood the words uttered by her husband. By their extreme disaccord with her mental condition these words produced on her a slightly suffocating effect. Mrs. Verloc's mental condition had the merit of simplicity; but it was not sound. It was governed too much by a fixed idea. Every nook and cranny of her brain was filled with the thought that this man, with whom she had lived without distaste for seven years, had taken the "poor boy" away from her in order to kill him—the man to whom she had grown accustomed in body and mind; the man whom she had trusted, took the boy away to kill him! In its form, in its substance, in its effect, which was universal, altering even the aspect. of inanimate things, it was a thought to sit still and marvel at for ever and ever. Mrs. Verloc sat still. And across that thought (not across the kitchen) the form of Mr. Verloc went to and fro, familiarly in hat and overcoat, stamping with his boots upon her brain. He was probably talking too; but Mrs. Verloc's thought for the most part covered the voice.

Now and then, however, the voice would make itself heard. Several connected words emerged at times. Their purport was generally hopeful. On each of these occasions Mrs. Verloc's dilated pupils, losing their far-off fixity, followed her husband's movements with the effect of black care and impenetrable attention. Well informed upon all matters relating to his secret calling, Mr. Verloc augured well for the success of his plans and combinations. He really believed that it would be upon the whole easy for him to escape the knife of infuriated revolutionists. He had exaggerated the strength of their fury and the length of their arm (for professional purposes) too often to have many illusions one way or the other. For to exaggerate with judgment one must begin by measuring with nicety. He knew also how much virtue and how much infamy is forgotten in two years—two long years. His first really confidential discourse to his wife was optimistic from conviction. He also thought it good policy to display all the assurance he could muster. It would put heart into the poor woman. On his liberation, which, harmonising with the whole tenor of his life, would be secret, of course, they would vanish together without loss of time. As to covering up the tracks, he begged his wife to trust him for that. He knew how it was to be done so that the devil himself——

He waved his hand. He seemed to boast. He wished only to put heart into her. It was a benevolent intention, but Mr. Verloc had the misfortune not to be in accord with his audience.

The self-confident tone grew upon Mrs. Verloc's ear, which let most of the words go by; for what were words to her now? What could words do to her for good or evil in the face of her fixed idea? Her black glance followed that man who was asserting his impunity—the man who had taken poor Stevie from home to kill him somewhere. Mrs. Verloc could not remember exactly where, but her heart began to beat very perceptibly.

Mr. Verloc, in a soft and conjugal tone, was now expressing his firm belief that there were yet a good few years of quiet life before them both. He did not go into the question of means. A quiet life it must be, and, as it were, nestling in the shade, concealed among men whose flesh is grass; modest, like the life of violets.[4] The words used by Mr. Verloc were: "Lie low for a bit." And far from England, of course. It was not clear whether Mr. Verloc had in his mind Spain or South America; but at any rate somewhere abroad.

This last word, falling into Mrs. Verloc's ear, produced a definite impression. This man was talking of going abroad. The impression was completely disconnected; and such is the force of mental habit that Mrs. Verloc at once and automatically asked herself: "And what of Stevie?"

It was a sort of forgetfulness; but instantly she became aware that there was no longer any occasion for anxiety on that score. There would never be any occasion any more. The poor boy had been taken out and killed. The poor boy was dead.

This shaking piece of forgetfulness stimulated Mrs. Verloc's intelligence. She began to perceive certain consequences which would have surprised Mr. Verloc. There was no need for her now to stay there, in that kitchen, in that house, with that man—since the boy was gone for ever. No need whatever. And on that Mrs. Verloc rose as if raised by a spring. But neither could she see what there was to keep her in the world at all. And this inability arrested her. Mr. Verloc watched her with marital solicitude.

"You're looking more like yourself," he said uneasily. Something peculiar in the blackness of his wife's eyes disturbed his optimism. At that precise moment Mrs. Verloc began to look upon herself as released from all earthly ties. She had her freedom. Her contract with existence, as represented by that man standing over there, was at an end. She was a free woman. Had this view become in some way perceptible to Mr. Verloc he would have been extremely shocked. In his affairs of the heart Mr. Verloc had been always carelessly generous, yet always with no other idea than that of being loved for himself. Upon this matter, his ethical notions being in agreement with his vanity, he was completely incorrigible. That this should be so in the case of his virtuous and legal connection he was perfectly certain. He had grown older, fatter, heavier, in the belief that he lacked no fascination for being loved for his own sake. When he saw Mrs. Verloc starting to walk out of the kitchen without a word he was disappointed.

"Where are you going to?" he called out rather sharply. "Upstairs?"

Mrs. Verloc in the doorway turned at the voice. An instinct of prudence born of fear, the excessive fear of being approached and touched by that man, induced her to nod at him slightly (from the height of two steps), with a stir of the lips which the conjugal optimism of Mr. Verloc took for a wan and uncertain smile.

"That's right," he encouraged her gruffly. "Rest and quiet's what you want. Go on. It won't be long before I am with you."

Mrs. Verloc, the free woman who had had really no idea where she was going to, obeyed the suggestion with rigid steadiness.

Mr. Verloc watched her. She disappeared up the stairs. He was disappointed. There was that within him which would have been more satisfied if she had been moved to throw herself upon his breast. But he was generous and indulgent. Winnie was always undemonstrative and silent. Neither was Mr. Verloc himself prodigal of endearments and words as a rule. But this was not an ordinary evening. It was an occasion when a man wants to be fortified by open proofs of sympathy and affection. Mr. Verloc sighed, and put out the gas in the kitchen. Mr. Verloc's sympathy with his wife was genuine and intense. It almost brought tears into his eyes as he stood in the parlour reflecting on the loneliness hanging over her head. In this mood Mr. Verloc missed Stevie very much out of a difficult world. He thought mournfully of his end. If only that lad had not stupidly destroyed himself!

The sensation of unappeasable hunger, not unknown after the strain of a hazardous enterprise to adventurers of tougher fibre than Mr. Verloc, overcame him again. The piece of roast beef, laid out in the likeness of funereal baked meats[5] for Stevie's obsequies, offered itself largely to his notice. And Mr. Verloc again partook. He partook ravenously, without restraint and decency, cutting thick slices with the sharp carving knife, and swallowing them without bread. In the course of that refection it occurred to Mr. Verloc that he was not hearing his wife move about the bedroom as he should have done. The thought of finding her, perhaps, sitting on the bed in the dark not only cut Mr. Verloc's appetite, but also took from him the inclination to follow her upstairs just yet. Laying down the carving knife, Mr. Verloc listened with careworn attention.

He was comforted by hearing her move at last. She walked suddenly across the room, and threw the window up. After a period of stillness up there, during which he figured her to himself with her head out, he heard the sash being lowered slowly. Then she made a few steps, and sat down. Every resonance of his house was familiar to Mr. Verloc, who was thoroughly domesticated. When next he heard his wife's footsteps overhead he knew, as well as if he had seen her doing it, that she had been putting on her walking shoes. Mr. Verloc wriggled his shoulders slightly at this ominous symptom, and moving away from the table, stood with his back to the fireplace, his head on one side, and gnawing perplexedly at the tips of his fingers. He kept track of her movements by the sound. She walked here and there violently, with abrupt stoppages, now before the chest of drawers, then in front of the wardrobe. An immense load of weariness, the harvest of a day of shocks and surprises, weighed Mr. Verloc's energies to the ground.

He did not raise his eyes till he heard his wife descending the stairs. It was as he had guessed. She was dressed for going out.

Mrs. Verloc was a free woman. She had thrown open the window of the bedroom either with the intention of screaming "Murder! Help!" or of throwing herself out. For she did not exactly know what use to make of her freedom. Her personality seemed to have been torn into two pieces, whose mental operations did not adjust themselves very well to each other. The street, silent and deserted from end to end, repelled her by taking sides with that man who was so certain of his impunity. She was afraid to shout lest no one should come. Obviously no one would come. Her instinct of self-preservation recoiled from the depth of the fall into that sort of slimy, deep trench. Mrs. Verloc closed the window, and dressed herself to go out into the street by another way. She was a free woman. She had dressed herself thoroughly, down to the tying of a black veil over her face. As she appeared before him in the light of the parlour, Mr. Verloc observed that she had even her little hand-bag hanging from her left wrist. . . . Flying off to her mother, of course.

The thought that women were wearisome creatures after all presented itself to his fatigued brain. But he was too generous to harbour it for more than an instant. This man, hurt cruelly in his vanity, remained magnanimous in his conduct, allowing himself no satisfaction of a bitter smile or of a contemptuous gesture. With true greatness of soul, he only glanced at the wooden clock on the wall, and said in a perfectly calm but forcible manner:

"Five-and-twenty minutes past eight, Winnie. There's no sense in going over there so late. You will never manage to get back to-night."

Before his extended hand Mrs. Verloc had stopped short. He added heavily: "Your mother will be gone to bed before you get there. This is the sort of news that can wait."

Nothing was further from Mrs. Verloc's thoughts than going to her mother. She recoiled at the mere idea, and feeling a chair behind her, she obeyed the suggestion of the touch, and sat down. Her intention had been simply to get outside the door for ever. And if this feeling was correct, its mental form took an unrefined shape corresponding to her origin and station. "I would rather walk the streets all the days of my life," she thought. But this creature, whose moral nature had been subjected to a shock of which, in the physical order, the most violent earthquake of history could only be a faint and languid rendering, was at the mercy of mere trifles, of casual contacts. She sat down. With her hat and veil she had the air of a visitor, of having looked in on Mr. Verloc for a moment. Her instant docility encouraged him, whilst her aspect of only temporary and silent acquiescence provoked him a little.

"Let me tell you, Winnie," he said with authority, "that your place is here this evening. Hang it all! you brought the damned police high and low about my ears. I don't blame you—but it's your doing all the same. You'd better take this confounded hat off. I can't let you go out, old girl," he added in a softened voice.

Mrs. Verloc's mind got hold of that declaration with morbid tenacity. The man who had taken Stevie out from under her very

eyes to murder him in a locality whose name was at the moment
not present to her memory would not allow her to go out. Of course
he wouldn't. Now he had murdered Stevie he would never let her
go. He would want to keep her for nothing. And on this characteristic reasoning, having all the force of insane logic, Mrs. Verloc's
disconnected wits went to work practically. She could slip by him,
open the door, run out. But he would dash out after her, seize her
round the body, drag her back into the shop. She could scratch,
kick, and bite—and stab too; but for stabbing she wanted a knife.
Mrs. Verloc sat still under her black veil, in her own house, like a
masked and mysterious visitor of impenetrable intentions.

Mr. Verloc's magnanimity was not more than human. She had
exasperated him at last.

"Can't you say something? You have your own dodges for vexing
a man. Oh yes! I know your deaf-and-dumb trick. I've seen you at
it before today. But just now it won't do. And to begin with, take
this damned thing off. One can't tell whether one is talking to a
dummy or to a live woman."

He advanced, and stretching out his hand, dragged the veil off,
unmasking a still, unreadable face, against which his nervous exasperation was shattered like a glass bubble flung against a rock.
"That's better," he said, to cover his momentary uneasiness, and re-
treated back to his old station by the mantelpiece. It never entered
his head that his wife could give him up. He felt a little ashamed of
himself, for he was fond and generous. What could he do? Everything had been said already. He protested vehemently.

"By Heavens! You know that I hunted high and low. I ran the
risk of giving myself away to find somebody for that accursed job.
And I tell you again I couldn't find any one crazy enough or hungry enough. What do you take me for—a murderer, or what? The
boy is gone. Do you think I wanted him to blow himself up? He's
gone. His troubles are over. Ours are just going to begin, I tell you,
precisely because he did blow himself up. I don't blame you. But
just try to understand that it was a pure accident; as much an accident as if he had been run over by a 'bus while crossing the street."

His generosity was not infinite, because he was a human
being—and not a monster, as Mrs. Verloc believed him to be. He
paused, and a snarl lifting his moustaches above a gleam of white

teeth gave him the expression of a reflective beast, not very dangerous—a slow beast with a sleek head, gloomier than a seal, and with a husky voice.

"And when it comes to that, it's as much your doing as mine. That's so. You may glare as much as you like. I know what you can do in that way. Strike me dead if I ever would have thought of the lad for that purpose. It was you who kept on shoving him in my way when I was half distracted with the worry of keeping the lot of us out of trouble. What the devil made you? One would think you were doing it on purpose. And I am damned if I know that you didn't. There's no saying how much of what's going on you have got hold of on the sly with your infernal don't-care-a-damn way of looking nowhere in particular, and saying nothing at all. . . ."

His husky domestic voice ceased for a while. Mrs. Verloc made no reply. Before that silence he felt ashamed of what he had said. But as often happens to peaceful men in domestic tiffs, being ashamed he pushed another point.

"You have a devilish way of holding your tongue sometimes," he began again, without raising his voice. "Enough to make some men go mad. It's lucky for you that I am not so easily put out as some of them would be by your deaf-and-dumb sulks. I am fond of you. But don't you go too far. This isn't the time for it. We ought to be thinking of what we've got to do. And I can't let you go out to-night, galloping off to your mother with some crazy tale or other about me. I won't have it. Don't you make any mistake about it: if you will have it that I killed the boy, then you've killed him as much as I."

In sincerity of feeling and openness of statement, these words went far beyond anything that had ever been said in this home, kept up on the wages of a secret industry eked out by the sale of more or less secret wares—the poor expedients devised by a mediocre mankind for preserving an imperfect society from the dangers of moral and physical corruption, both secret, too, of their kind. They were spoken because Mr. Verloc had felt himself really outraged; but the reticent decencies of this home life, nestling in a shady street behind a shop where the sun never shone, remained apparently undisturbed. Mrs. Verloc heard him out with perfect propriety, and then rose from her chair in her hat and jacket like a visitor at the end of a call. She advanced towards her husband, one arm extended as if for a silent leave-taking. Her net veil dangling down by one end on the left side of her face gave an air of disorderly formality to her restrained movements. But when she arrived as far as the hearthrug, Mr. Verloc was no longer standing there. He had moved off in the direction of the sofa, without raising his eyes to watch the effect of his tirade. He was tired, resigned in a truly marital spirit. But he felt hurt in the tender spot of his secret weakness. If she would go on sulking in that dreadful, overcharged silence—why then she must. She was a master in that domestic art. Mr. Verloc flung himself heavily upon the sofa, disregarding as usual the fate of his hat, which, as if accustomed to take care of itself, made for a safe shelter under the table.

He was tired. The last particle of his nervous force had been expended in the wonders and agonies of this day full of surprising failures coming at the end of a harassing month of scheming and insomnia. He was tired. A man isn't made of stone. Hang everything! Mr. Verloc reposed characteristically, clad in his outdoor garments. One side of his open overcoat was lying partly on the ground. Mr. Verloc wallowed on his back. But he longed for a more perfect rest—for sleep—for a few hours of delicious forgetfulness. That would come later. Provisionally he rested. And he thought: "I wish she would give over this damned nonsense. It's exasperating."

There must have been something imperfect in Mrs. Verloc's sentiment of regained freedom. Instead of taking the way of the door she leaned back, with her shoulders against the tablet of the mantelpiece, as a wayfarer rests against a fence. A tinge of wildness in her aspect was derived from the black veil hanging like a rag against her cheek, and from the fixity of her black gaze where the light of the room was absorbed and lost without the trace of a single gleam. This woman, capable of a bargain the mere suspicion of which would have been infinitely shocking to Mr. Verloc's idea of love, remained irresolute, as if scrupulously aware of something wanting on her part for the formal closing of the transaction.

On the sofa Mr. Verloc wriggled his shoulders into perfect comfort, and from the fullness of his heart emitted a wish which was certainly as pious as anything likely to come from such a source.

"I wish to goodness," he growled huskily, "I had never seen Greenwich Park or anything belonging to it."

The veiled sound filled the small room with its moderate volume, well adapted to the modest nature of the wish. The waves of air of the proper length, propagated in accordance with correct mathematical formulas, flowed around all the inanimate things in the room, lapped against Mrs. Verloc's head as if it had been a head of stone. And incredible as it may appear, the eyes of Mrs. Verloc seemed to grow still larger. The audible wish of Mr. Verloc's overflowing heart flowed into an empty place in his wife's memory. Greenwich Park. A park! That's where the boy was killed. A park—smashed branches, torn leaves, gravel, bits of brotherly flesh and bone, all spouting up together in the manner of a firework. She remembered now what she had heard, and she remembered it pictorially. They had to gather him up with the shovel. Trembling all over with irrepressible shudders, she saw before her the very implement with its ghastly load scraped up from the ground. Mrs. Verloc closed her eyes desperately, throwing upon that vision the night of her eyelids, where after a rainlike fall of mangled limbs the decapitated head of Stevie lingered suspended alone, and fading out slowly like the last star of a pyrotechnic display. Mrs. Verloc opened her eyes.

Her face was no longer stony. Anybody could have noted the subtle change on her features, in the stare of her eyes, giving her a new and startling expression—an expression seldom observed by competent persons under the conditions of leisure and security demanded for thorough analysis, but whose meaning could not be mistaken at a glance. Mrs. Verloc's doubts as to the end of the bargain no longer existed; her wits, no longer disconnected, were working under the control of her will. But Mr. Verloc observed nothing. He was reposing in that pathetic condition of optimism induced by excess of fatigue. He did not want any more trouble—with his wife too—of all people in the world. He had been unanswerable in his vindication. He was loved for himself. The present phase of her silence he interpreted favourably. This was the time to make it up with her. The silence had lasted long enough. He broke it by calling to her in an undertone:

"Winnie."

"Yes," answered obediently Mrs. Verloc the free woman. She commanded her wits now, her vocal organs; she felt herself to be in an almost preternaturally perfect control of every fibre of her body. It was all her own, because the bargain was at an end. She was clear-sighted. She had become cunning. She chose to answer him so readily for a purpose. She did not wish that man to change his position on the sofa, which was very suitable to the circumstances. She succeeded. The man did not stir. But after answering him she remained leaning negligently against the mantelpiece in the attitude of a resting wayfarer. She was unhurried. Her brow was smooth. The head and shoulders of Mr. Verloc were hidden from her by the high side of the sofa. She kept her eyes fixed on his feet.

She remained thus mysteriously still and suddenly collected till Mr. Verloc was heard with an accent of marital authority, and moving slightly to make room for her to sit on the edge of the sofa.

"Come here," he said in a peculiar tone, which might have been the tone of brutality, but was intimately known to Mrs. Verloc as the note of wooing.

She started forward at once, as if she were still a loyal woman bound to that man by an unbroken contract. Her right hand skimmed slightly the end of the table, and when she had passed on towards the sofa the carving knife had vanished without the slightest sound from the side of the dish. Mr. Verloc heard the creaky plank in the floor, and was content. He waited. Mrs. Verloc was coming. As if the homeless soul of Stevie had flown for shelter straight to the breast of his sister, guardian, and protector, the resemblance of her face with that of her brother grew at every step, even to the droop of the lower lip, even to the slight divergence of the eyes. But Mr. Verloc did not see that. He was lying on his back and staring upwards. He saw partly on the ceiling and partly on the wall the moving shadow of an arm with a clenched hand holding a carving knife. It flickered up and down. It's movements were leisurely. They were leisurely enough for Mr. Verloc to recognise the limb and the weapon.

They were leisurely enough for him to take in the full meaning of the portent, and to taste the flavour of death rising in his gorge. His wife had gone raving mad—murdering mad. They were leisurely enough for the first paralysing effect of this discovery to pass away before a resolute determination to come out victorious from the ghastly struggle with that armed lunatic. They were leisurely enough for Mr. Verloc to elaborate a plan of defence involving a dash behind the table, and the felling of the woman to the ground with a heavy wooden chair. But they were not leisurely enough to allow Mr. Verloc the time to move either hand or foot. The knife was already planted in his breast. It met no resistance on its way. Hazard has such accuracies. Into that plunging blow, delivered over the side of the couch, Mrs. Verloc had put all the inheritance of her immemorial and obscure descent, the simple ferocity of the age of caverns,* and the unbalanced nervous fury of the age of bar-rooms. Mr. Verloc, the Secret Agent, turning slightly on his side with the force of the blow, expired without stirring a limb, in the muttered sound of the word "Don't" by way of protest.

Mrs. Verloc had let go the knife, and her extraordinary resemblance to her late brother had faded, had become very ordinary now. She drew a deep breath, the first easy breath since Chief Inspector Heat had exhibited to her the labelled piece of Stevie's overcoat. She leaned forward on her folded arms over the side of the sofa. She adopted that easy attitude not in order to watch or gloat over the body of Mr. Verloc, but because of the undulatory and swinging movements of the parlour, which for some time behaved as though it were at sea in a tempest. She was giddy but calm. She had become a free woman with a perfection of freedom which left her nothing to desire and absolutely nothing to do, since Stevie's urgent claim on her devotion no longer existed. Mrs. Verloc, who thought in images, was not troubled now by visions, because she did not think at all. And she did not move. She was a woman enjoying her complete irresponsibility and endless leisure, almost in the manner of a corpse. She did not move, she did not think. Neither did the mortal envelope of the late Mr. Verloc reposing on the sofa. Except for the fact that Mrs. Verloc breathed, these two would have been perfectly in accord—that accord of prudent reserve without superfluous words, and sparing of signs, which had been the foundation of their respectable home life. For it had been respectable, covering by a decent reticence the problems that may rise in the practice of a secret profession and the commerce of

---

*Age of cavemen (from the French *l'âge des cavernes*).

shady wares. To the last its decorum had remained undisturbed by unseemly shrieks and other misplaced sincerities of conduct. And after the striking of the blow, this respectability was continued in immobility and silence.

Nothing moved in the parlour till Mrs. Verloc raised her head slowly and looked at the clock with inquiring mistrust. She had become aware of a ticking sound in the room. It grew upon her ear, while she remembered clearly that the clock on the wall was silent, had no audible tick. What did it mean by beginning to tick so loudly all of a sudden? Its face indicated ten minutes to nine. Mrs. Verloc cared nothing for time, and the ticking went on. She concluded it could not be the clock, and her sullen gaze moved along the walls, wavered, and became vague, while she strained her hearing to locate the sound. Tick, tick, tick.

After listening for some time Mrs. Verloc lowered her gaze deliberately on her husband's body. Its attitude of repose was so home-like and familiar that she could do so without feeling embarrassed by any pronounced novelty in the phenomena of her home life. Mr. Verloc was taking his habitual ease. He looked comfortable.

By the position of the body the face of Mr. Verloc was not visible to Mrs. Verloc, his widow. Her fine, sleepy eyes, travelling downward on the track of the sound, became contemplative on meeting a flat object of bone which protruded a little beyond the end of the sofa. It was the handle of the domestic carving knife, with nothing strange about it but its position at right angles to Mr. Verloc's waistcoat and the fact that something dripped from it. Dark drops fell on the floor cloth one after another, with the sound of ticking growing fast and furious like the pulse of an insane clock. At its highest speed this ticking changed into a continuous sound of trickling. Mrs. Verloc watched that transformation with shadows of anxiety coming and going on her face. It was a trickle, dark, swift, thin. . . . Blood!

At this unforeseen circumstance Mrs. Verloc abandoned her pose of idleness and irresponsibility.

With a sudden snatch at her skirts and a faint shriek she ran to the door, as if the trickle had been the first sign of a destroying flood. Finding the table in her way she gave it a push with both hands as though it had been alive, with such force that it went for some distance on its four legs, making a loud, scraping racket, whilst the big dish with the joint crashed heavily on the floor.

Then all became still. Mrs. Verloc on reaching the door had stopped. A round hat disclosed in the middle of the floor by the moving of the table rocked slightly on its crown in the wind of her flight.

CHAPTER TWELVE

WINNIE VERLOC, the widow of Mr. Verloc, the sister of the late faithful Stevie (blown to fragments in a state of innocence and in the conviction of being engaged in a humanitarian enterprise), did not run beyond the door of the parlour. She had indeed run away so far from a mere trickle of blood, but that was a movement of instinctive repulsion. And there she had paused, with staring eyes and lowered head. As though she had run through long years in her flight across the small parlour, Mrs. Verloc by the door was quite a different person from the woman who had been leaning over the sofa, a little swimmy in her head, but otherwise free to enjoy the profound calm of idleness and irresponsibility. Mrs. Verloc was no longer giddy. Her head was steady. On the other hand, she was no longer calm. She was afraid.

If she avoided looking in the direction of her reposing husband it was not because she was afraid of him. Mr. Verloc was not frightful to behold. He looked comfortable. Moreover, he was dead. Mrs. Verloc entertained no vain delusions on the subject of the dead. Nothing brings them back, neither love nor hate. They can do nothing to you. They are as nothing. Her mental state was tinged by a sort of austere contempt for that man who had let himself be killed so easily. He had been the master of a house, the husband of a woman, and the murderer of her Stevie. And now he was of no account in every respect. He was of less practical account than the clothing on his body, than his overcoat, than his boots— than that hat lying on the floor. He was nothing. He was not worth looking at. He was even no longer the murderer of poor Stevie. The only murderer that would be found in the room when people came to look for Mr. Verloc would be—herself!

Her hands shook so that she failed twice in the task of refastening her veil. Mrs. Verloc was no longer a person of leisure and irresponsibility. She was afraid. The stabbing of Mr. Verloc had been only a blow. It had relieved the pent-up agony of shrieks strangled in her throat, of tears dried up in her hot eyes, of the maddening and indignant rage at the atrocious part played by that man, who was less than nothing now, in robbing her of the boy. It had been an obscurely prompted blow. The blood trickling on the floor off the handle of the knife had turned it into an extremely plain case of murder. Mrs. Verloc, who always refrained from looking deep into things, was compelled to look into the very bottom of this thing. She saw there no haunting face, no reproachful shade, no vision of remorse, no sort of ideal conception. She saw there an object. That object was the gallows. Mrs. Verloc was afraid of the gallows.

She was terrified of them ideally. Having never set eyes on that last argument of men's justice except in illustrative woodcuts to a certain type of tales, she first saw them erect against a black and stormy background, festooned with chains and human bones, circled about by birds that peck at dead men's eyes. This was frightful enough, but Mrs. Verloc, though not a well-informed woman, had a sufficient knowledge of the institutions of her country to know that gallows are no longer erected romantically on the banks of dismal rivers or on wind-swept headlands, but in the yards of jails. There within four high walls, as if into a pit, at dawn of day, the murderer was brought out to be executed, with a horrible quietness and, as the reports in the newspapers always said, "in the presence of the authorities." With her eyes staring on the floor, her nostrils quivering with anguish and shame, she imagined herself all alone amongst a lot of strange gentlemen in silk hats who were calmly proceeding about the business of hanging her by the neck. That— never! Never! And how was it done? The impossibility of imagining the details of such quiet execution added something maddening to her abstract terror. The newspapers never gave any details except one, but that one with some affectation was always there at the end of a meagre report. Mrs. Verloc remembered its nature. It came with a cruel burning pain into her head, as if the words "The drop given was fourteen feet" had been scratched on her brain with a hot needle. "The drop given was fourteen feet."[1]

These words affected her physically too. Her throat became convulsed in waves to resist strangulation; and the apprehension of the jerk was so vivid that she seized her head in both hands as if to save it from being torn off her shoulders. "The drop given was fourteen feet." No! that must never be. She could not stand *that*. The thought of it even was not bearable. She could not stand thinking of it. Therefore Mrs. Verloc formed the resolution to go at once and throw herself into the river off one of the bridges.[2]

This time she managed to refasten her veil. With her face as if masked, all black from head to foot except for some flowers in her hat, she looked up mechanically at the clock. She thought it must have stopped. She could not believe that only two minutes had passed since she had looked at it last. Of course not. It had been stopped all the time. As a matter of fact, only three minutes had elapsed from the moment she had drawn the first deep, easy breath after the blow, to this moment when Mrs. Verloc formed the resolution to drown herself in the Thames. But Mrs. Verloc could not believe that. She seemed to have heard or read that clocks and watches always stopped at the moment of murder for the undoing of the murderer. She did not care. "To the bridge—and over I go." . . . But her movements were slow.

She dragged herself painfully across the shop, and had to hold on to the handle of the door before she found the necessary fortitude to open it. The street frightened her, since it led either to the gallows or to the river. She floundered over the doorstep head forward, arms thrown out, like a person falling over the parapet of a bridge. This entrance into the open air had a foretaste of drowning; a slimy dampness enveloped her, entered her nostrils, clung to her hair. It was not actually raining, but each gas-lamp had a rusty little halo of mist. The van and horses were gone, and in the black street the curtained window of the carters' eating-house made a square patch of soiled blood-red light glowing faintly very near the level of the pavement. Mrs. Verloc, dragging herself slowly towards it, thought that she was a very friendless woman. It was true. It was so true that, in a sudden longing to see some friendly face, she could think of no one else but of Mrs. Neale, the charwoman. She had no acquaintances of her own. Nobody would miss her in a social way. It must not be imagined that the Widow Verloc had forgotten her mother. This was not so. Winnie had been a good daughter because she had been a devoted sister. Her mother had always leaned on her for support. No consolation or advice could be expected there. Now that Stevie was dead the bond seemed to be broken. She could not face the old woman with the horrible tale. Moreover, it was too far. The river was her present destination. Mrs. Verloc tried to forget her mother.

Each step cost her an effort of will which seemed the last possible. Mrs. Verloc had dragged herself past the red glow of the eating-house window. "To the bridge—and over I go," she repeated to herself with fierce obstinacy. She put out her hand just in time to steady herself against a lamp-post. "I'll never get there before morning," she thought. The fear of death paralysed her efforts to escape the gallows. It seemed to her she had been staggering in that street for hours. "I'll never get there," she thought. "They'll find me knocking about the streets. It's too far." She held on, panting under her black veil.

"The drop given was fourteen feet."

She pushed the lamp-post away from her violently, and found herself walking. But another wave of faintness overtook her like a great sea, washing away her heart clean out of her breast. "I will never get there," she muttered, suddenly arrested, swaying lightly where she stood. "Never."

And perceiving the utter impossibility of walking as far as the nearest bridge, Mrs. Verloc thought of a flight abroad.

It came to her suddenly. Murderers escaped. They escaped abroad. Spain or California. Mere names. The vast world created for the glory of man was only a vast blank to Mrs. Verloc. She did not know which way to turn. Murderers had friends, relations, helpers—they had knowledge. She had nothing. She was the most lonely of murderers that ever struck a mortal blow. She was alone in London, and the whole town of marvels and mud, with its maze of streets and its mass of lights, was sunk in a hopeless night, rested at the bottom of a black abyss from which no unaided woman could hope to scramble out.

She swayed forward, and made a fresh start blindly, with an awful dread of falling down; but at the end of a few steps, unexpectedly, she found a sensation of support, of security. Raising her head, she saw a man's face peering closely at her veil. Comrade Ossipon was not afraid of strange women, and no feeling of false delicacy could prevent him from striking an acquaintance with a woman apparently very much intoxicated. Comrade Ossipon was interested in women. He held up this one between his two large palms, peering at her in a business-like way till he heard her say faintly, "Mr. Ossipon!" and then he very nearly let her drop to the ground.

"Mrs. Verloc!" he exclaimed. "You here!"

It seemed impossible to him that she should have been drinking. But one never knows. He did not go into that question, but attentive not to discourage kind fate surrendering to him the widow of Comrade Verloc, he tried to draw her to his breast. To his astonishment she came quite easily, and even rested on his arm for a moment before she attempted to disengage herself. Comrade Ossipon would not be brusque with kind fate. He withdrew his arm in a natural way.

"You recognised me," she faltered out, standing before him, fairly steady on her legs.

"Of course I did," said Ossipon with perfect readiness. "I was afraid you were going to fall. I've thought of you too often lately not to recognise you anywhere, at any time. I've always thought of you—ever since I first set eyes on you."

Mrs. Verloc seemed not to hear. "You were coming to the shop?" she said nervously.

"Yes; at once," answered Ossipon. "Directly I read the paper."

In fact, Comrade Ossipon had been skulking for a good two hours in the neighbourhood of Brett Street, unable to make up his mind for a bold move. The robust anarchist was not exactly a bold conqueror. He remembered that Mrs. Verloc had never responded to his glances by the slightest sign of encouragement. Besides, he thought the shop might be watched by the police, and Comrade Ossipon did not wish the police to form an exaggerated notion of his revolutionary sympathies. Even now he did not know precisely what to do. In comparison with his usual amatory speculations this was a big and serious undertaking. He ignored how much there was in it, and how far he would have to go in order to get hold of what there was to get—supposing there was a chance at all. These perplexities checking his elation, imparted to his tone a soberness well in keeping with the circumstances.

"May I ask you where you were going?" he inquired in a subdued voice.

"Don't ask me!" cried Mrs. Verloc with a shuddering, repressed violence. All her strong vitality recoiled from the idea of death. "Never mind where I was going. . . ."

Ossipon concluded that she was very much excited but perfectly sober. She remained silent by his side for a moment, then all at once she did something which he did not expect. She slipped her hand under his arm. He was startled by the act itself certainly, and quite as much, too, by the palpably resolute character of this movement. But this being a delicate affair, Comrade Ossipon behaved with delicacy. He contented himself by pressing the hand slightly against his robust ribs. At the same time he felt himself being impelled forward, and yielded to the impulse. At the end of Brett Street he became aware of being directed to the left. He submitted.

The fruiterer at the corner had put out the blazing glory of his oranges and lemons, and Brett Place was all darkness, interspersed with the misty haloes of the few lamps defining its triangular shape, with a cluster of three lights on one stand in the middle. The dark forms of the man and woman glided slowly arm in arm along the walls with a loverlike and homeless aspect in the miserable night.

"What would you say if I were to tell you that I was going to find you?" Mrs. Verloc asked, gripping his arm with force.

"I would say that you couldn't find any one more ready to help you in your trouble," answered Ossipon, with a notion of making tremendous headway. In fact, the progress of this delicate affair was almost taking his breath away.

"In my trouble!" Mrs. Verloc repeated slowly.

"Yes."

"And do you know what my trouble is?" she whispered with strange intensity.

"Ten minutes after seeing the evening paper," explained Ossipon with ardor, "I met a fellow whom you may have seen once or twice at the shop perhaps, and I had a talk with him which left no doubt whatever in my mind. Then I started for here, wondering whether you—— I've been fond of you beyond words ever since I set eyes on your face," he cried, as if unable to command his feelings.

Comrade Ossipon assumed correctly that no woman was capable of wholly disbelieving such a statement. But he did not know that Mrs. Verloc accepted it with all the fierceness the instinct of self-preservation imparts to the grip of a drowning person. To the widow of Mr. Verloc the robust anarchist was like a radiant messenger of life.

They walked slowly, in step. "I thought so," Mrs. Verloc murmured faintly.

"You've read it in my eyes," suggested Ossipon with great assurance.

"Yes," she breathed out into his inclined ear.

"A love like mine could not be concealed from a woman like you," he went on, trying to detach his mind from material considerations such as the business value of the shop, and the amount of money Mr. Verloc might have left in the bank. He applied himself to the sentimental side of the affair. In his heart of hearts he was a little shocked at his success. Verloc had been a good fellow, and certainly a very decent husband as far as one could see. However, Comrade Ossipon was not going to quarrel with his luck for the sake of a dead man. Resolutely he suppressed his sympathy for the ghost of Comrade Verloc, and went on.

"I could not conceal it. I was too full of you. I daresay you could not help seeing it in my eyes. But I could not guess it. You were always so distant. . . ."

"What else did you expect?" burst out Mrs. Verloc. "I was a respectable woman——"

She paused, then added, as if speaking to herself, in sinister resentment: "Till he made me what I am."

Ossipon let that pass, and took up his running.

"He never did seem to me to be quite worthy of you," he began, throwing loyalty to the winds. "You were worthy of a better fate."

Mrs. Verloc interrupted bitterly:

"Better fate! He cheated me out of seven years of life."

"You seemed to live so happily with him." Ossipon tried to exculpate the lukewarmness of his past conduct. "It's that what's made me timid. You seemed to love him. I was surprised—and jealous," he added.

"Love him!" Mrs. Verloc cried out in a whisper full of scorn and rage. "Love him! I was a good wife to him. I am a respectable woman. You thought I loved him! You did! Look here, Tom——"

The sound of this name thrilled Comrade Ossipon with pride. For his name was Alexander, and he was called Tom by arrangement with the most familiar of his intimates. It was a name of friendship— of moments of expansion. He had no idea that she had ever heard it used by anybody. It was apparent that she had not only caught it, but had treasured it in her memory—perhaps in her heart.

"Look here, Tom! I was a young girl. I was done up. I was tired. I had two people depending on what I could do, and it did seem as if I couldn't do any more. Two people—mother and the boy. He was much more mine than mother's. I sat up nights and nights with him on my lap, all alone upstairs, when I wasn't more than eight years old myself. And then—— He was mine, I tell you. . . . You can't understand that. No man can understand it. What was I to do? There was a young fellow——"

The memory of the early romance with the young butcher survived, tenacious, like the image of a glimpsed ideal in that heart quailing before the fear of the gallows and full of revolt against death.

"That was the man I loved then," went on the widow of Mr. Verloc. "I suppose he could see it in my eyes too. Five-and-twenty shillings a week,[3] and his father threatened to kick him out of the business if he made such a fool of himself as to marry a girl with a crippled mother and a crazy idiot of a boy on her hands. But he would hang about me, till one evening I found the courage to slam the door in his face. I had to do it. I loved him dearly. Five-and-twenty shillings a week! There was that other man—a good lodger. What is a girl to do? Could I've gone on the streets? He seemed kind. He wanted me, anyhow. What was I to do with mother and that poor boy? Eh? I said yes. He seemed good-natured, he was free-handed, he had money, he never said anything. Seven years— seven years a good wife to him, the kind, the good, the generous, the—— And he loved me. Oh yes. He loved me till I sometimes wished myself—— Seven years. Seven years a wife to him. And do you know what he was, that dear friend of yours? Do you know what he was? . . . He was a devil!"

The superhuman vehemence of that whispered statement completely stunned Comrade Ossipon. Winnie Verloc turning about held him by both arms, facing him under the falling mist in the darkness and solitude of Brett Place, in which all sounds of life seemed lost as if in a triangular well of asphalt and bricks, of blind houses and unfeeling stones.

"No; I didn't know," he declared, with a sort of flabby stupidity, whose comical aspect was lost upon a woman haunted by the fear of the gallows, "but I do now. I—I understand," he floundered on, his mind speculating as to what sort of atrocities Verloc could have practised under the sleepy, placid appearances of his married estate. It was positively awful. "I understand," he repeated, and then by a sudden inspiration uttered an "Unhappy woman!" of lofty commiseration instead of the more familiar "Poor darling!" of his usual practice. This was no usual case. He felt conscious of something abnormal going on, while he never lost sight of the greatness of the stake. "Unhappy, brave woman!"

He was glad to have discovered that variation; but he could discover nothing else. "Ah, but he is dead now," was the best he could do. And he put a remarkable amount of animosity into his guarded exclamation. Mrs. Verloc caught at his arm with a sort of frenzy. "You guessed, then, he was dead," she murmured, as if beside herself. "You! You guessed what I had to do. Had to!"

There were suggestions of triumph, relief, gratitude in the indefinable tone of these words. It engrossed the whole attention of Ossipon to the detriment of mere literal sense. He wondered what was up with her, why she had worked herself into this state of wild excitement. He even began to wonder whether the hidden causes of that Greenwich Park affair did not lie deep in the unhappy circumstances of the Verlocs' married life. He went so far as to suspect Mr. Verloc of having selected that extraordinary manner of committing suicide. By Jove! that would account for the utter inanity and wrong-headedness of the thing. No anarchist manifestation was required by the circumstances. Quite the contrary; and Verloc was as well aware of that as any other revolutionist of his standing. What an immense joke if Verloc had simply made fools of the whole of Europe, of the revolutionary world, of the police, of the press, and of the cocksure Professor as well! Indeed, thought Ossipon, in astonishment, it seemed almost certain that he did! Poor beggar! It struck him as very possible that of that household of two it wasn't precisely the man who was the devil.

Alexander Ossipon, nicknamed the Doctor, was naturally inclined to think indulgently of his men friends. He eyed Mrs. Verloc hanging on his arm. Of his women friends he thought in a specially practical way. Why Mrs. Verloc should exclaim at his knowledge of Mr. Verloc's death, which was no guess at all, did not disturb him beyond measure. Women often talked like lunatics. But he was curious to know how she had been informed. The papers could tell her nothing beyond the mere fact: the man blown to pieces in Greenwich Park not having been identified. It was inconceivable on any theory that Verloc should have given her an inkling of his intention—whatever it was. This problem interested Comrade Ossipon immensely. He stopped short. They had gone then along the three sides of Brett Place, and were near the end of Brett Street again.

"How did you first come to hear of it?" he asked in a tone he tried to render appropriate to the character of the revelations which had been made to him by the woman at his side.

She shook violently for a while before she answered in a listless voice:

"From the police. A chief inspector came. Chief Inspector Heat he said he was. He showed me——"

Mrs. Verloc choked. "Oh, Tom, they had to gather him up with a shovel."

Her breast heaved with dry sobs. In a moment Ossipon found his tongue.

"The police! Do you mean to say the police came already? That Chief Inspector Heat himself actually came to tell you?"

"Yes," she confirmed in the same listless tone.

"He came. Just like this. He came. I didn't know. He showed me a piece of overcoat, and—— Just like that. 'Do you know this?' he said."

"Heat! Heat! And what did he do?"

Mrs. Verloc's head dropped. "Nothing. He did nothing. He went away. The police were on that man's side," she murmured tragically. "Another one came too."

"Another—another inspector, do you mean?" asked Ossipon, in great excitement, and very much in the tone of a scared child.

"I don't know. He came. He looked like a foreigner. He may have been one of them Embassy people."

Comrade Ossipon nearly collapsed under this new shock.

"Embassy! Are you aware what you are saying? What Embassy? What on earth do you mean by Embassy?"

"It's that place in Chatham Square. The people he cursed so. I don't know. What does it matter!"

"And that fellow, what did he do or say to you?"

"I don't remember. . . . Nothing. . . . I don't care. Don't ask me," she pleaded in a weary voice.

"All right. I won't," assented Ossipon tenderly. And he meant it too, not because he was touched by the pathos of the pleading voice, but because he felt himself losing his footing in the depths of this tonebrous* affair. Police! Embassy! Phew! For fear of adventuring his intelligence into ways where its natural lights might fail to guide it safely he dismissed resolutely all suppositions, surmises, and theories out of his mind. He had the woman there, absolutely flinging herself at him, and that was the principal consideration. But after what he had heard nothing could astonish him any more. And when Mrs. Verloc, as if startled suddenly out of a dream of safety, began to urge upon him wildly the necessity of an immediate flight on the Continent, he did not exclaim in the least. He simply said with unaffected regret that there was no train till the morning, and stood looking thoughtfully at her face, veiled in black net, in the light of a gas-lamp veiled in a gauze of mist.

Near him, her black form merged in the night, like a figure half chiselled out of a block of black stone. It was impossible to say what she knew, how deep she was involved with policemen and Embassies. But if she wanted to get away, it was not for him to object. He was anxious to be off himself. He felt that the business, the shop so strangely familiar to chief inspectors and members of foreign Embassies, was not the place for him. That must be dropped. But there was the rest. These savings. The money!

"You must hide me till the morning somewhere," she said in a dismayed voice.

"Fact is, my dear, I can't take you where I live. I share the room with a friend."

He was somewhat dismayed himself. In the morning the blessed 'tecs would be out in all the stations, no doubt. And if they

---

*Dark, obscure.

once got hold of her, for one reason or another she would be lost to him indeed.

"But you must. Don't you care for me at all—at all? What are you thinking of?"

She said this violently, but she let her clasped hands fall in discouragement. There was a silence, while the mist fell, and darkness reigned undisturbed over Brett Place. Not a soul, not even the vagabond, lawless, and amorous soul of a cat, came near the man and the woman facing each other.

"It would be possible, perhaps, to find a safe lodging somewhere," Ossipon spoke at last. "But the truth is, my dear, I have not enough money to go and try with—only a few pence. We revolutionists are not rich."

He had fifteen shillings[4] in his pocket. He added:

"And there's the journey before us, too—first thing in the morning at that."

She did not move, made no sound, and Comrade Ossipon's heart sank a little. Apparently she had no suggestion to offer. Suddenly she clutched at her breast, as if she had felt a sharp pain there.

"But I have," she gasped. "I have the money. I have enough money. Tom! Let us go from here."

"How much have you got?" he inquired, without stirring to her tug; for he was a cautious man.

"I have the money, I tell you. All the money."

"What do you mean by it? All the money there was in the bank, or what?" he asked incredulously, but ready not to be surprised at anything in the way of luck.

"Yes, yes!" she said nervously. "All there was. I've it all."

"How on earth did you manage to get hold of it already?" he marvelled.

"He gave it to me," she murmured, suddenly subdued and trembling. Comrade Ossipon put down his rising surprise with a firm hand.

"Why, then—we are saved," he uttered slowly.

She leaned forward, and sank against his breast. He welcomed her there. She had all the money. Her hat was in the way of very marked effusion; her veil too. He was adequate in his manifestations, but no more. She received them without resistance and without abandonment, passively, as if only half sensible. She freed herself from his lax embrace without difficulty.

"You will save me, Tom," she broke out, recoiling, but still keeping her hold on him by the two lapels of his damp coat. "Save me. Hide me. Don't let them have me. You must kill me first. I couldn't do it myself—I couldn't, I couldn't—not even for what I am afraid of."

She was confoundedly bizarre, he thought. She was beginning to inspire him with an indefinite uneasiness. He said surlily, for he was busy with important thoughts:

"What the devil *are* you afraid of?"

"Haven't you guessed what I was driven to do?" cried the woman. Distracted by the vividness of her dreadful apprehensions, her head ringing with forceful words, that kept the horror of her position before her mind, she had imagined her incoherence to be clearness itself. She had no conscience* of how little she had audibly said in the disjointed phrases completed only in her thought. She had felt the relief of a full confession, and she gave a special meaning to every sentence spoken by Comrade Ossipon, whose knowledge did not in the least resemble her own. "Haven't you guessed what I was driven to do?" Her voice fell. "You needn't be long in guessing then what I am afraid of," she continued, in a bitter and sombre murmur. "I won't have it! I won't! I won't! I won't! You must promise to kill me first!" She shook the lapels of his coat. "It must never be!"

He assured her curtly that no promises on his part were necessary, but he took good care not to contradict her in set terms, because he had had much to do with excited women, and he was inclined in general to let his experience guide his conduct in preference to applying his sagacity to each special case. His sagacity in this case was busy in other directions. Women's words fell into water,[5] but the shortcomings of timetables remained. The insular nature of Great Britain obtruded itself upon his notice in an odious form. "Might just as well be put under lock and key every night," he thought irritably, as nonplussed as though he had a wall to scale with the woman on his back. Suddenly he slapped his forehead. He had by dint of cudgelling his brains just thought of the Southampton-St. Malo service.[6]

---

*That is, conception.

The boat left about midnight. There was a train at 10.30. He became cheery and ready to act.

"From Waterloo. Plenty of time. We are all right after all. . . . What's the matter now? This isn't the way," he protested.

Mrs. Verloc, having hooked her arm into his, was trying to drag him into Brett Street again.

"I've forgotten to shut the shop door as I went out," she whispered, terribly agitated.

The shop and all that was in it had ceased to interest Comrade Ossipon. He knew how to limit his desires. He was on the point of saying "What of that? Let it be," but he refrained. He disliked argument about trifles. He even mended his pace considerably on the thought that she might have left the money in the drawer. But his willingness lagged behind her feverish impatience.

The shop seemed to be quite dark at first. The door stood ajar. Mrs. Verloc, leaning against the front, gasped out:

"Nobody has been in. Look! The light—the light in the parlour."

Ossipon, stretching his head forward, saw a faint gleam in the darkness of the shop.

"There is," he said.

"I forgot it." Mrs. Verloc's voice came from behind her veil faintly. And as he stood waiting for her to enter first, she said louder: "Go in and put it out—or I'll go mad."

He made no immediate objection to this proposal, so strangely motived. "Where's all that money?" he asked.

"On me! Go, Tom! Quick! Put it out. . . . Go in!" she cried, seizing him by both shoulders from behind.

Not prepared for a display of physical force, Comrade Ossipon stumbled far into the shop before her push. He was astonished at the strength of the woman, and scandalised by her proceedings. But he did not retrace his steps in order to remonstrate with her severely in the street. He was beginning to be disagreeably impressed by her fantastic behaviour. Moreover, this or never was the time to humour the woman. Comrade Ossipon avoided easily the end of the counter, and approached calmly the glazed door of the parlour. The curtain over the panes being drawn back a little, he, by a very natural impulse, looked in, just as he made ready to turn the handle. He looked in without a thought, without intention, without curiosity of any sort. He looked in because he could not help looking in. He looked in, and discovered Mr. Verloc reposing quietly on the sofa.

A yell coming from the innermost depths of his chest died out unheard and transformed into a sort of greasy, sickly taste on his lips. At the same time the mental personality of Comrade Ossipon executed a frantic leap backwards. But his body, left thus without intellectual guidance, held on to the door handle with the unthinking force of an instinct. The robust anarchist did not even totter. And he stared, his face close to the glass, his eyes protruding out of his head. He would have given anything to get away, but his returning reason informed him that it would not do to let go the door handle. What was it—madness, a nightmare, or a trap into which he had been decoyed with fiendish artfulness? Why—what for? He did not know. Without any sense of guilt in his breast, in the full peace of his conscience as far as these people were concerned, the idea that he would be murdered for mysterious reasons by the couple Verloc passed not so much across his mind as across the pit of his stomach, and went out, leaving behind a trail of sickly faintness—an indisposition. Comrade Ossipon did not feel very well in a very special way for a moment—a long moment. And he stared. Mr. Verloc lay very still meanwhile, simulating sleep for reasons of his own, while that savage woman of his was guarding the door— invisible and silent in the dark and deserted street. Was all this some sort of terrifying arrangement invented by the police for his especial benefit? His modesty shrank from that explanation.

But the true sense of the scene he was beholding came to Ossipon through the contemplation of the hat. It seemed an extraordinary thing, an ominous object, a sign. Black, and rim upward, it lay on the floor before the couch as if prepared to receive the contributions of pence from people who would come presently to behold Mr. Verloc in the fullness of his domestic ease reposing on a sofa. From the hat the eyes of the robust anarchist wandered to the displaced table, gazed at the broken dish for a time, received a kind of optical shock from observing a white gleam under the imperfectly closed eyelids of the man on the couch. Mr. Verloc did not seem so much asleep now as lying down with a bent head and looking insistently at his left breast. And when Comrade Ossipon had made out the handle of the knife he turned away from the glazed door, and retched violently.

The crash of the street door flung to made his very soul leap in a panic. This house with its harmless tenant could still be made a trap of—a trap of a terrible kind. Comrade Ossipon had no settled conception now of what was happening to him. Catching his thigh against the end of the counter, he spun round, staggered with a cry of pain, felt in the distracting clatter of the bell his arms pinned to his side by a convulsive hug, while the cold lips of a woman moved creepily on his very ear to form the words:

"Policeman! He has seen me!"

He ceased to struggle; she never let him go. Her hands had locked themselves with an inseparable twist of fingers on his robust back. While the footsteps approached, they breathed quickly, breast to breast, with hard, laboured breaths, as if theirs had been the attitude of a deadly struggle, while, in fact, it was the attitude of deadly fear. And the time was long.

The constable on the beat had in truth seen something of Mrs. Verloc; only, coming from the lighted thoroughfare at the other end of Brett Street, she had been no more to him than a flutter in the darkness. And he was not even quite sure that there had been a flutter. He had no reason to hurry up. On coming abreast of the shop he observed that it had been closed early. There was nothing very unusual in that. The men on duty had special instructions about that shop: what went on about there was not to be meddled with unless absolutely disorderly, but any observations made were to be reported. There were no observations to make; but from a sense of duty and for the peace of his conscience, owing also to that doubtful flutter of the darkness, the constable crossed the road, and tried the door. The spring latch, whose key was reposing for ever off duty in the late Mr. Verloc's waistcoat pocket, held as well as usual. While the conscientious officer was shaking the handle, Ossipon felt the cold lips of the woman stirring again creepily against his very ear:

"If he comes in, kill me—kill me, Tom."

The constable moved away, flashing as he passed the light of his dark lantern,* merely for form's sake, at the shop window. For a

---

*Handheld lamp with a shutter or screen for covering the light.

moment longer the man and the woman inside stood motionless, panting, breast to breast; then her fingers came unlocked, her arms fell by her side slowly. Ossipon leaned against the counter. The robust anarchist wanted support badly. This was awful. He was almost too disgusted for speech. Yet he managed to utter a plaintive thought, showing at least that he realised his position.

"Only a couple of minutes later and you'd have made me blunder against the fellow poking about here with his damned dark lantern."

The widow of Mr. Verloc, motionless in the middle of the shop, said insistently:

"Go in and put that light out, Tom. It will drive me crazy."

She saw vaguely his vehement gesture of refusal. Nothing in the world would have induced Ossipon to go into the parlour. He was not superstitious, but there was too much blood on the floor; a beastly pool of it all round the hat. He judged he had been already too near that corpse for his peace of mind—for the safety of his neck, perhaps!

"At the meter* then! There. Look. In that corner."

The robust form of Comrade Ossipon, striding brusque and shadowy across the shop, squatted in a corner obediently; but this obedience was without grace. He fumbled nervously—and suddenly in the sound of a muttered curse the light behind the glazed door flickered out to a gasping, hysterical sigh of a woman. Night, the inevitable reward of men's faithful labours on this earth, night had fallen on Mr. Verloc, the tried revolutionist—"one of the old lot"—the humble guardian of society; the invaluable Secret Agent Δ of Baron Stott-Wartenheim's dispatches; a servant of law and order, faithful, trusted, accurate, admirable, with perhaps one single amiable weakness: the idealistic belief in being loved for himself.

Ossipon groped his way back through the stuffy atmosphere, as black as ink now, to the counter. The voice of Mrs. Verloc, standing in the middle of the shop, vibrated after him in that blackness with a desperate protest.

"I will not be hanged, Tom. I will not——"

---

*Device regulating the delivery of gas to a building.

She broke off. Ossipon from the counter issued a warning: "Don't shout like this," then seemed to reflect profoundly. "You did this thing quite by yourself?" he inquired in a hollow voice, but with an appearance of masterful calmness which filled Mrs. Verloc's heart with grateful confidence in his protecting strength.

"Yes," she whispered, invisible.

"I wouldn't have believed it possible," he muttered. "Nobody would." She heard him move about, and the snapping of a lock in the parlour door. Comrade Ossipon had turned the key on Mr. Verloc's repose; and this he did not from reverence for its eternal nature or any other obscurely sentimental consideration, but for the precise reason that he was not at all sure that there was not some one else hiding somewhere in the house. He did not believe the woman, or rather he was incapable by now of judging what could be true, possible, or even probable in this astounding universe. He was terrified out of all capacity for belief or disbelief in regard of this extraordinary affair, which began with police inspectors and Embassies and would end goodness knows where—on the scaffold for some one. He was terrified at the thought that he could not prove the use he made of his time ever since seven o'clock, for he had been skulking about Brett Street. He was terrified at this savage woman who had brought him in there, and would probably saddle him with complicity, at least if he were not careful. He was terrified at the rapidity with which he had been involved in such dangers—decoyed into it. It was some twenty minutes since he had met her—not more.

The voice of Mrs. Verloc rose subdued, pleading piteously: "Don't let them hang me, Tom! Take me out of the country. I'll work for you. I'll slave for you. I'll love you. I've no one in the world. . . . Who would look at me if you don't?" She ceased for a moment; then in the depths of the loneliness made round her by an insignificant thread of blood trickling off the handle of a knife, she found a dreadful inspiration to her—who had been the respectable girl of the Belgravian mansion, the loyal, respectable wife of Mr. Verloc. "I won't ask you to marry me," she breathed out in shamefaced accents.

She moved a step forward in the darkness. He was terrified at her. He would not have been surprised if she had suddenly produced another knife destined for his breast. He certainly would have made no resistance. He had really not enough fortitude in him just then to tell her to keep back. But he inquired in a cavernous, strange tone: "Was he asleep?"

"No," she cried, and went on rapidly. "He wasn't. Not he. He had been telling me that nothing could touch him. After taking the boy away from under my very eyes to kill him—the loving, innocent, harmless lad. My own, I tell you. He was lying on the couch quite easy—after killing the boy—my boy. I would have gone on the streets to get out of his sight. And he says to me like this: 'Come here,' after telling me I had helped to kill the boy. You hear, Tom? He says like this: 'Come here,' after taking my very heart out of me along with the boy to smash in the dirt."

She ceased, then dreamily repeated twice: "Blood and dirt. Blood and dirt." A great light broke upon Comrade Ossipon. It was that half-witted lad then who had perished in the park. And the fooling of everybody all round appeared more complete than ever—colossal. He exclaimed scientifically, in the extremity of his astonishment: "The degenerate—by Heavens!"

"Come here." The voice of Mrs. Verloc rose again. "What did he think I was made of? Tell me, Tom. Come here! Me! Like this! I had been looking at the knife, and I thought I would come then if he wanted me so much. Oh yes! I came—for the last time. . . . With the knife."

He was excessively terrified at her—the sister of the degenerate—a degenerate herself of a murdering type . . . or else of the lying type. Comrade Ossipon might have been said to be terrified scientifically in addition to all other kinds of fear. It was an immeasurable and composite funk, which from its very excess gave him in the dark a false appearance of calm and thoughtful deliberation. For he moved and spoke with difficulty, being as if half frozen in his will and mind—and no one could see his ghastly face. He felt half dead.

He leaped a foot high. Unexpectedly Mrs. Verloc had desecrated the unbroken reserved decency of her home by a shrill and terrible shriek:

"Help, Tom! Save me! I won't be hanged!"

He rushed forward, groping for her mouth with a silencing hand, and the shriek died out. But in his rush he had knocked her over. He felt her now clinging round his legs, and his terror reached its culminating point, became a sort of intoxication, entertained delusions, acquired the characteristics of delirium tremens.* He positively saw snakes now. He saw the woman twined round him like a snake, not to be shaken off. She was not deadly. She was death itself—the companion of life.

Mrs. Verloc, as if relieved by the outburst, was very far from behaving noisily now. She was pitiful.

"Tom, you can't throw me off now," she murmured from the floor. "Not unless you crush my head under your heel.[7] I won't leave you."

"Get up," said Ossipon.

His face was so pale as to be quite visible in the profound black darkness of the shop; while Mrs. Verloc, veiled, had no face, almost no discernible form. The trembling of something small and white, a flower in her hat, marked her place, her movements.

It rose in the blackness. She had got up from the floor, and Ossipon regretted not having run out at once into the street. But he perceived easily that it would not do. It would not do. She would run after him. She would pursue him shrieking till she sent every policeman within hearing in chase. And then goodness only knew what she would say of him. He was so frightened that for a moment the insane notion of strangling her in the dark passed through his mind. And he became more frightened than ever! She had him! He saw himself living in abject terror in some obscure hamlet in Spain or Italy; till some fine morning they found him dead too, with a knife in his breast—like Mr. Verloc. He sighed deeply. He dared not move. And Mrs. Verloc waited in silence the good pleasure of her saviour, deriving comfort from his reflective silence.

Suddenly he spoke up in an almost natural voice. His reflections had come to an end.

"Let's get out, or we will lose the train."

"Where are we going to, Tom?" she asked timidly. Mrs. Verloc was no longer a free woman.

"Let's get to Paris first, the best way we can. . . . Go out first, and see if the way's clear."

---

*Delirium accompanied by violent trembling, usually produced by excessive consumption of alcohol and occasionally accompanied by hallucinations.

She obeyed. Her voice came subdued through the cautiously opened door.

"It's all right."

Ossipon came out. Notwithstanding his endeavours to be gentle, the cracked bell clattered behind the closed door in the empty shop, as if trying in vain to warn the reposing Mr. Verloc of the final departure of his wife—accompanied by his friend.

In the hansom they presently picked up, the robust anarchist became explanatory. He was still awfully pale, with eyes that seemed to have sunk a whole half-inch into his tense face. But he seemed to have thought of everything with extraordinary method.

"When we arrive," he discoursed in a queer monotonous tone, "you must go into the station ahead of me, as if we did not know each other. I will take the tickets, and slip yours into your hand as I pass you. Then you will go into the first-class ladies' waiting-room, and sit there till ten minutes before the train starts. Then you come out. I shall be outside. You go in first on the platform, as if you did not know me. There may be eyes watching there that know what's what. Alone you are only a woman going off by train. I am known. With me, you may be guessed at as Mrs. Verloc running away. Do you understand, my dear?" he added, with an effort.

"Yes," said Mrs. Verloc, sitting there against him in the hansom all rigid with the dread of the gallows and the fear of death. "Yes, Tom." And she added to herself, like an awful refrain: "The drop given was fourteen feet."

Ossipon, not looking at her, and with a face like a fresh plaster cast of himself after a wasting illness, said: "By the bye, I ought to have the money for the tickets now."

Mrs. Verloc, undoing some hooks of her bodice, while she went on staring ahead beyond the splashboard, handed over to him the new pigskin pocket-book. He received it without a word, and seemed to plunge it deep somewhere into his very breast. Then he slapped his coat on the outside.

All this was done without the exchange of a single glance; they were like two people looking out for the first sight of a desired goal. It was not till the hansom swung round a corner and towards the bridge[8] that Ossipon opened his lips again.

"Do you know how much money there is in that thing?" he asked, as if addressing slowly some hobgoblin sitting between the ears of the horse.

"No," said Mrs. Verloc. "He gave it to me. I didn't count. I thought nothing of it at the time. Afterwards——"

She moved her right hand a little. It was so expressive, that little movement of that right hand which had struck the deadly blow into a man's heart less than an hour before, that Ossipon could not repress a shudder. He exaggerated it then purposely, and muttered:

"I am cold. I got chilled through."

Mrs. Verloc looked straight ahead at the perspective of her escape. Now and then, like a sable streamer blown across a road, the words "The drop given was fourteen feet" got in the way of her tense stare. Through her black veil the whites of her big eyes gleamed lustrously like the eyes of a masked woman.

Ossipon's rigidity had something businesslike, a queer official expression. He was heard again all of a sudden, as though he had released a catch in order to speak.

"Look here! Do you know whether your—whether he kept his account at the bank in his own name or in some other name?"

Mrs. Verloc turned upon him her masked face and the big white gleam of her eyes.

"Other name?" she said thoughtfully.

"Be exact in what you say," Ossipon lectured in the swift motion of the hansom. "It's extremely important. I will explain to you. The bank has the number of these notes. If they were paid to him in his own name, then when his—his death becomes known, the notes may serve to track us since we have no other money. You have no other money on you?"

She shook her head negatively.

"None whatever?" he insisted.

"A few coppers."*

"It would be dangerous in that case. The money would have then to be dealt specially with. Very specially. We'd have perhaps to lose more than half the amount in order to get these notes changed in a certain safe place I know of in Paris. In the other case—I mean

---

*Pennies.

if he had his account and got paid out under some other name—
say Smith, for instance—the money is perfectly safe to use. You understand? The bank has no means of knowing that Mr. Verloc and,
say, Smith are one and the same person. Do you see how important
it is that you should make no mistake in answering me? Can you
answer that query at all? Perhaps not. Eh?"

She said composedly:

"I remember now! He didn't bank in his own name. He told me
once that it was on deposit in the name of Prozor."

"You are sure?"

"Certain."

"You don't think the bank had any knowledge of his real name?
Or anybody in the bank or——"

She shrugged her shoulders.

"How can I know? Is it likely, Tom?"

"No. I suppose it's not likely. It would have been more comfortable to know. . . . Here we are. Get out first, and walk straight in.
Move smartly."

He remained behind, and paid the cabman out of his own loose
silver. The programme traced by his minute foresight was carried
out. When Mrs. Verloc, with her ticket for St. Malo in her hand,
entered the ladies' waiting-room, Comrade Ossipon walked into
the bar, and in seven minutes absorbed three goes of hot brandy
and water.

"Trying to drive out a cold," he explained to the barmaid, with a
friendly nod and a grimacing smile. Then he came out, bringing
out from that festive interlude the face of a man who had drunk at
the very Fountain of Sorrow. He raised his eyes to the clock. It was
time. He waited.

Punctual, Mrs. Verloc came out, with her veil down, and all
black—black as commonplace death itself, crowned with a few cheap
and pale flowers. She passed close to a little group of men who were
laughing, but whose laughter could have been struck dead by a single
word. Her walk was indolent, but her back was straight, and Comrade
Ossipon looked after it in terror before making a start himself.

The train was drawn up, with hardly anybody about its row of
open doors. Owing to the time of the year and to the abominable
weather there were hardly any passengers. Mrs. Verloc walked slowly

along the line of empty compartments till Ossipon touched her elbow from behind.

"In here."

She got in, and he remained on the platform looking about. She bent forward, and in a whisper:

"What is it, Tom? Is there any danger?"

"Wait a moment. There's the guard."

She saw him accost the man in uniform. They talked for a while. She heard the guard say "Very well, sir," and saw him touch his cap. Then Ossipon came back, saying: "I told him not to let anybody get into our compartment."

She was leaning forward on her seat. "You think of everything. . . . You'll get me off, Tom?" she asked in a gust of anguish, lifting her veil brusquely to look at her saviour.

She had uncovered a face like adamant.* And out of this face the eyes looked on, big, dry, enlarged, lightless, burnt out like two black holes in the white shining globes.

"There is no danger," he said, gazing into them with an earnestness almost rapt, which to Mrs. Verloc, flying from the gallows, seemed to be full of force and tenderness. This devotion deeply moved her—and the adamantine face lost the stern rigidity of its terror. Comrade Ossipon gazed at it as no lover ever gazed at his mistress's face. Alexander Ossipon, anarchist, nicknamed the Doctor, author of a medical (and improper) pamphlet, late lecturer on the social aspects of hygiene to working men's clubs, was free from the trammels of conventional morality—but he submitted to the rule of science. He was scientific, and he gazed scientifically at that woman, the sister of a degenerate, a degenerate herself—of a murdering type. He gazed at her, and invoked Lombroso, as an Italian peasant recommends himself to his favourite saint. He gazed scientifically. He gazed at her cheeks, at her nose, at her eyes, at her ears. . . . Bad! . . . Fatal! Mrs. Verloc's pale lips parting, slightly relaxed under his passionately attentive gaze, he gazed also at her teeth. . . . Not a doubt remained . . . a murdering type. . . . If Comrade Ossipon did not recommend his terrified soul to Lombroso, it

---

*A type of stone or mineral believed to be unbreakable; hence, something rigid, unyielding.

was only because on scientific grounds he could not believe that he carried about him such a thing as a soul. But he had in him the scientific spirit, which moved him to testify on the platform of a railway station in nervous jerky phrases.

"He was an extraordinary lad, that brother of yours. Most interesting to study. A perfect type in a way. Perfect!"

He spoke scientifically in his secret fear. And Mrs. Verloc, hearing these words of commendation vouchsafed to her beloved dead, swayed forward with a flicker of light in her sombre eyes, like a ray of sunshine heralding a tempest of rain.

"He was that indeed," she whispered softly, with quivering lips. "You took a lot of notice of him, Tom. I loved you for it."

"It's almost incredible the resemblance there was between you two," pursued Ossipon, giving a voice to his abiding dread, and trying to conceal his nervous, sickening impatience for the train to start. "Yes; he resembled you."

These words were not especially touching or sympathetic. But the fact of that resemblance insisted upon was enough in itself to act upon her emotions powerfully. With a little faint cry, and throwing her arms out, Mrs. Verloc burst into tears at last.

Ossipon entered the carriage, hastily closed the door and looked out to see the time by the station clock. Eight minutes more. For the first three of these Mrs. Verloc wept violently and helplessly without pause or interruption. Then she recovered somewhat, and sobbed gently in an abundant fall of tears. She tried to talk to her saviour, to the man who was the messenger of life.

"Oh, Tom! How could I fear to die after he was taken away from me so cruelly? How could I! How could I be such a coward!"

She lamented aloud her love of life, that life without grace or charm, and almost without decency, but of an exalted faithfulness of purpose, even unto murder. And, as often happens in the lament of poor humanity, rich in suffering but indigent in words, the truth—the very cry of truth—was found in a worn and artificial shape picked up somewhere among the phrases of sham sentiment.

"How could I be so afraid of death! Tom, I tried. But I am afraid. I tried to do away with myself. And I couldn't. Am I hard? I suppose the cup of horrors was not full enough for such as me. Then when you came . . ."

She paused. Then in a gust of confidence and gratitude, "I will live all my days for you, Tom!" she sobbed out.

"Go over into the other corner of the carriage, away from the platform," said Ossipon solicitously. She let her saviour settle her comfortably, and he watched the coming on of another crisis of weeping, still more violent than the first. He watched the symptoms with a sort of medical air, as if counting seconds. He heard the guard's whistle at last. An involuntary contraction of the upper lip bared his teeth with all the aspect of savage resolution as he felt the train beginning to move. Mrs. Verloc heard and felt nothing, and Ossipon, her saviour, stood still. He felt the train roll quicker, rumbling heavily to the sound of the woman's loud sobs, and then crossing the carriage in two long strides he opened the door deliberately, and leaped out.

He had leaped out at the very end of the platform; and such was his determination in sticking to his desperate plan that he managed by a sort of miracle, performed almost in the air, to slam to the door of the carriage. Only then did he find himself rolling head over heels, like a shot rabbit. He was bruised, shaken, pale as death, and out of breath when he got up. But he was calm, and perfectly able to meet the excited crowd of railwaymen who had gathered round him in a moment. He explained, in gentle and convincing tones, that his wife had started at a moment's notice for Brittany to her dying mother; that, of course, she was greatly upset, and he considerably concerned at her state; that he was trying to cheer her up, and had absolutely failed to notice at first that the train was moving out. To the general exclamation, "Why didn't you go on to Southampton, then, sir?" he objected the inexperience of a young sister-in-law left alone in the house with three small children, and her alarm at his absence, the telegraph offices being closed. He had acted on impulse. "But I don't think I'll ever try that again," he concluded; smiled all round; distributed some small change, and marched without a limp out of the station.

Outside, Comrade Ossipon, flush of safe banknotes as never before in his life, refused the offer of a cab.

"I can walk," he said, with a little friendly laugh to the civil driver.

He could walk. He walked. He crossed the bridge. Later on the towers of the Abbey saw in their massive immobility the yellow bush of his hair passing under the lamps. The lights of Victoria saw him too, and Sloane Square, and the railings of the Park. And Comrade Ossipon once more found himself on a bridge. The river, a sinister marvel of still shadows and flowing gleams mingling below in a black silence, arrested his attention. He stood looking over the parapet for a long time. The clock tower[9] boomed a brazen blast above his drooping head. He looked up at the dial. . . . Half-past twelve of a wild night in the Channel.

And again Comrade Ossipon walked. His robust form was seen that night in distant parts of the enormous town slumbering monstrously on a carpet of mud under a veil of raw mist. It was seen crossing the streets without life and sound, or diminishing in the interminable straight perspectives of shadowy houses bordering empty roadways lined by strings of gas-lamps. He walked through Squares, Places, Ovals, Commons, through monotonous streets with unknown names where the dust of humanity settles inert and hopeless out of the stream of life. He walked. And suddenly turning into a strip of a front garden with a mangy grass plot, he let himself into a small grimy house with a latchkey he took out of his pocket.

He threw himself down on his bed all dressed, and lay still for a whole quarter of an hour. Then he sat up suddenly, drawing up his knees, and clasping his legs. The first dawn found him open-eyed, in that same posture. This man who could walk so long, so far, so aimlessly, without showing a sign of fatigue, could also remain sitting still for hours without stirring a limb or an eyelid. But when the late sun sent its rays into the room he unclasped his hands, and fell back on the pillow. His eyes stared at the ceiling. And suddenly, they closed. Comrade Ossipon slept in the sunlight.

CHAPTER THIRTEEN

THE enormous iron padlock on the doors of the wall cupboard was the only object in the room on which the eye could rest without becoming afflicted by the miserable unloveliness of forms and the poverty of material. Unsaleable in the ordinary course of business on account of its noble proportions, it had been ceded to the Professor for a few pence by a marine dealer* in the east of London. The room was large, clean, respectable, and poor with that poverty suggesting the starvation of every human need except mere bread. There was nothing on the walls but the paper, an expanse of arsenical green, soiled with indelible smudges here and there, and with stains resembling faded maps of uninhabited continents.

At a deal table near a window sat Comrade Ossipon, holding his head between his fists. The Professor, dressed in his only suit of shoddy tweeds, but flapping to and fro on the bare boards a pair of incredibly dilapidated slippers, had thrust his hands deep into the over-strained pockets of his jacket. He was relating to his robust guest a visit he had lately been paying to the Apostle Michaelis. The Perfect Anarchist had even been unbending a little.

"The fellow didn't know anything of Verloc's death. Of course! He never looks at the newspapers. They make him too sad, he says. But never mind. I walked into his cottage. Not a soul anywhere. I had to shout half a dozen times before he answered me. I thought he was fast asleep yet, in bed. But not at all. He had been writing his book for four hours already. He sat in that tiny cage in a litter of manuscript. There was a half-eaten raw carrot on the table near him. His breakfast. He lives on a diet of raw carrots and a little milk now."

"How does he look on it?" asked Comrade Ossipon listlessly.

*Dealer in second-hand nautical goods.

"Angelic. . . . I picked up a handful of his pages from the floor. The poverty of reasoning is astonishing. He has no logic. He can't think consecutively. But that's nothing. He has divided his biography into three parts, entitled—'Faith, Hope, Charity.'[1] He is elaborating now the idea of a world planned out like an immense and nice hospital, with gardens and flowers, in which the strong are to devote themselves to the nursing of the weak."

The Professor paused.

"Conceive you this folly, Ossipon? The weak! The source of all evil on this earth!" he continued with his grim assurance. "I told him that I dreamt of a world like shambles, where the weak would be taken in hand for utter extermination.

"Do you understand, Ossipon? The source of all evil! They are our sinister masters—the weak, the flabby, the silly, the cowardly, the faint of heart, and the slavish of mind. They have power. They are the multitude. Theirs is the kingdom of the earth. Exterminate, exterminate![2] That is the only way of progress. It is! Follow me, Ossipon? First the great multitude of the weak must go, then the only relatively strong. You see? First the blind, then the deaf and the dumb, then the halt and the lame—and so on. Every taint, every vice, every prejudice, every convention must meet its doom."

"And what remains?" asked Ossipon in a stifled voice.

"I remain—if I am strong enough," asserted the sallow little Professor, whose large ears, thin like membranes, and standing far out from the sides of his frail skull, took on suddenly a deep red tint.

"Haven't I suffered enough from this oppression of the weak?" he continued forcibly. Then tapping the breast-pocket of his jacket: "And yet I *am* the force," he went on. "But the time! The time! Give me time! Ah! that multitude, too stupid to feel either pity or fear. Sometimes I think they have everything on their side. Everything—even death—my own weapon."

"Come and drink some beer with me at the Silenus," said the robust Ossipon after an interval of silence pervaded by the rapid flap, flap of the slippers on the feet of the Perfect Anarchist. The latter accepted. He was jovial that day in his own peculiar way. He slapped Ossipon's shoulder.

"Beer! So be it! Let us drink and be merry, for we are strong, and to-morrow we die."[3]

He busied himself with putting on his boots, and talked mean-while in his curt, resolute tones.

"What's the matter with you, Ossipon? You look glum and seek even my company. I hear that you are seen constantly in places where men utter foolish things over glasses of liquor. Why? Have you abandoned your collection of women? They are the weak who feed the strong—eh?"

He stamped one foot, and picked up his other laced boot, heavy, thick-soled, unblacked, mended many times. He smiled to himself grimly.

"Tell me, Ossipon, terrible man, has ever one of your victims killed herself for you—or are your triumphs so far incomplete—for blood alone puts a seal on greatness? Blood. Death. Look at history."

"You be damned," said Ossipon, without turning his head.

"Why? Let that be the hope of the weak, whose theology has in-vented hell for the strong. Ossipon, my feeling for you is amicable contempt. You couldn't kill a fly."

But rolling to the feast on the top of the omnibus the Professor lost his high spirits. The contemplation of the multitudes thronging the pavements extinguished his assurance under a load of doubt and un-easiness which he could only shake off after a period of seclusion in the room with the large cupboard closed by an enormous padlock.

"And so," said over his shoulder Comrade Ossipon, who sat on the seat behind,—"and so Michaelis dreams of a world like a beau-tiful and cheery hospital?"

"Just so. An immense charity for the healing of the weak," as-sented the Professor sardonically.

"That's silly," admitted Ossipon. "You can't heal weakness. But, after all, Michaelis may not be so far wrong. In two hundred years doctors will rule the world. Science reigns already. It reigns in the shade maybe—but it reigns. And all science must culminate at last in the science of healing—not the weak, but the strong. Mankind wants to live—to live."

"Mankind," asserted the Professor with a self-confident glitter of his iron-rimmed spectacles, "does not know what it wants."

"But you do," growled Ossipon. "Just now you've been crying for time—time. Well, the doctors will serve you out your time—if you are good. You profess yourself to be one of the strong—because you

carry in your pocket enough stuff to send yourself and, say, twenty
other people into eternity. But eternity is a damned hole. It's time
that you need. You—if you met a man who could give you for certain ten years of time, you would call him your master."

"My device is: No God! No master,"[4] said the Professor sententiously as he rose to get off the 'bus.

Ossipon followed. "Wait till you are lying flat on your back at the
end of your time," he retorted, jumping off the footboard after the
other. "Your scurvy, shabby, mangy, little bit of time," he continued
across the street, and hopping on to the curbstone.

"Ossipon, I think that you are a humbug," the Professor said,
opening masterfully the doors of the renowned Silenus. And when
they had established themselves at a little table he developed further this gracious thought. "You are not even a doctor. But you are
funny. Your notion of a humanity universally putting out the
tongue and taking the pill from pole to pole at the bidding of a few
solemn jokers is worthy of the prophet. Prophecy! What's the good
of thinking of what will be!" He raised his glass. "To the destruction
of what is," he said calmly.

He drank and relapsed into his peculiarly close manner of silence.
The thought of a mankind as numerous as the sands of the seashore,
as indestructible, as difficult to handle, oppressed him. The sound of
exploding bombs was lost in their immensity of passive grains without an echo. For instance, this Verloc affair. Who thought of it now?

Ossipon, as if suddenly compelled by some mysterious force,
pulled a much-folded newspaper out of his pocket. The Professor
raised his head at the rustle.

"What's that paper? Anything in it?" he asked.

Ossipon started like a scared somnambulist.

"Nothing. Nothing whatever. The thing's ten days old. I forgot it
in my pocket, I suppose."

But he did not throw the old thing away. Before returning it to
his pocket he stole a glance at the last lines of a paragraph. They
ran thus: "*An impenetrable mystery seems destined to hang for ever
over this act of madness or despair.*"

Such were the end words of an item of news headed: "Suicide of
Lady Passenger from a Cross-Channel Boat." Comrade Ossipon was
familiar with the beauties of its journalistic style. "*An impenetrable

mystery seems destined to hang for ever. . . ." He knew every word by heart. *"An impenetrable mystery. . . ."* And the robust anarchist, hanging his head on his breast, fell into a long reverie.

He was menaced by this thing in the very sources of his existence. He could not issue forth to meet his various conquests, those that he courted on benches in Kensington Gardens,[5] and those he met near area railings,* without the dread of beginning to talk to them of an "impenetrable mystery destined . . ." He was becoming scientifically afraid of insanity lying in wait for him amongst these lines. *"To hang for ever over."* It was an obsession, a torture. He had lately failed to keep several of these appointments, whose note used to be an unbounded trustfulness in the language of sentiment and manly tenderness. The confiding disposition of various classes of women satisfied the needs of his self-love, and put some material means into his hand. He needed it to live. It was there. But if he could no longer make use of it, he ran the risk of starving his ideals and his body. . . . *"This act of madness or despair."*

"An impenetrable mystery" was sure "to hang for ever" as far as all mankind was concerned. But what of that if he alone of all men could never get rid of the cursed knowledge? And Comrade Ossipon's knowledge was as precise as the newspaper man could make it—up to the very threshold of the *"mystery destined to hang for ever . . ."*

Comrade Ossipon was well informed. He knew what the gangway man of the steamer had seen: "A lady in a black dress and a black veil, wandering at midnight alongside, on the quay. 'Are you going by the boat, ma'am?' he had asked her encouragingly. 'This way.' She seemed not to know what to do. He helped her on board. She seemed weak."

And he knew also what the stewardess had seen: A lady in black with a white face standing in the middle of the empty ladies' cabin. The stewardess induced her to lie down there. The lady seemed quite unwilling to speak, and as if she were in some awful trouble. The next the stewardess knew she was gone from the ladies' cabin. The stewardess then went on deck to look for her, and Comrade

---

*Fence surrounding the area, or basement courtyard, which was used by servants as an access to the house and the street.

Ossipon was informed that the good woman found the unhappy lady lying down in one of the hooded seats. Her eyes were open, but she would not answer anything that was said to her. She seemed very ill. The stewardess fetched the chief steward, and those two people stood by the side of the hooded seat consulting over their extraordinary and tragic passenger. They talked in audible whispers (for she seemed past hearing) of St. Malo and the Consul there, of communicating with her people in England. Then they went away to arrange for her removal down below, for indeed by what they could see of her face she seemed to them to be dying. But Comrade Ossipon knew that behind that white mask there was struggling against terror and despair a vigour of vitality, a love of life that could resist the furious anguish which drives to murder and the fear, the blind, mad fear, of the gallows. He knew. But the stewardess and the chief steward knew nothing, except that when they came back for her in less than five minutes the lady in black was no longer in the hooded seat. She was nowhere. She was gone. It was then five o'clock in the morning, and it was no accident either. An hour afterwards one of the steamer's hands found a wedding ring left lying on the seat. It had stuck to the wood in a bit of wet, and its glitter caught the man's eye. There was a date, 24th June 1879, engraved inside. "*An impenetrable mystery is destined to hang for ever. . . .*"

And Comrade Ossipon raised his bowed head, beloved of various humble women of these isles, Apollo-like* in the sunniness of its bush of hair.

The Professor had grown restless meantime. He rose.

"Stay," said Ossipon hurriedly. "Here, what do you know of madness and despair?"

The Professor passed the tip of his tongue on his dry, thin lips, and said doctorally:

"There are no such things. All passion is lost now. The world is mediocre, limp, without force. And madness and despair are a force. And force is a crime in the eyes of the fools, the weak and the silly who rule the roost. You are mediocre. Verloc, whose affair the

---

*Golden, like the hair of Apollo, the mythical Greek god of the sun, who was also the epitome of masculine beauty.

police has managed to smother so nicely, was mediocre. And the police murdered him. He was mediocre. Everybody is mediocre. Madness and despair! Give me that for a lever, and I'll move the world.[6] Ossipon, you have my cordial scorn. You are incapable of conceiving even what the fat-fed citizen would call a crime. You have no force." He paused, smiling sardonically under the fierce glitter of his thick glasses.

"And let me tell you that this little legacy they say you've come into has not improved your intelligence. You sit at your beer like a dummy. Good-bye."

"Will you have it?" said Ossipon, looking up with an idiotic grin.

"Have what?"

"The legacy. All of it."

The incorruptible Professor only smiled. His clothes were all but falling off him, his boots, shapeless with repairs, heavy like lead, let water in at every step. He said:

"I will send you by and by a small bill for certain chemicals which I shall order to-morrow. I need them badly. Understood—eh?"

Ossipon lowered his head slowly. He was alone. *"An impenetrable mystery . . ."* It seemed to him that suspended in the air before him he saw his own brain pulsating to the rhythm of an impenetrable mystery. It was diseased clearly. . . . *"This act of madness or despair."*

The mechanical piano near the door played through a valse cheekily, then fell silent all at once, as if gone grumpy.

Comrade Ossipon, nicknamed the Doctor, went out of the Silenus beer-hall. At the door he hesitated, blinking at a not too splendid sunlight—and the paper with the report of the suicide of a lady was in his pocket. His heart was beating against it. The suicide of a lady—*this act of madness or despair.*

He walked along the street without looking where he put his feet; and he walked in a direction which would not bring him to the place of appointment with another lady (an elderly nursery governess putting her trust in an Apollo-like ambrosial head). He was walking away from it. He could face no woman. It was ruin. He could neither think, work, sleep, nor eat. But he was beginning to drink with pleasure, with anticipation, with hope. It was ruin. His revolutionary career, sustained by the sentiment and trustfulness of many women, was menaced by an impenetrable mystery—the mystery of a human brain pulsating wrongfully to the rhythm of journalistic phrases: ". . . *Will hang for ever over this act* . . . (it was inclining towards the gutter) . . . *of madness or despair*. . . ."

"I am seriously ill," he muttered to himself with scientific insight. Already his robust form, with an Embassy's secret-service money (inherited from Mr. Verloc) in his pockets, was marching in the gutter as if in training for the task of an inevitable future. Already he bowed his broad shoulders, his head of ambrosial locks, as if ready to receive the leather yoke of the sandwich board.* As on that night, more than a week ago, Comrade Ossipon walked without looking where he put his feet, feeling no fatigue, feeling nothing, seeing nothing, hearing not a sound. *"An impenetrable mystery* . . ." He walked disregarded. . . . *"This act of madness or despair."*

And the incorruptible Professor walked too, averting his eyes from the odious multitude of mankind. He had no future. He disdained it. He was a force. His thoughts caressed the images of ruin and destruction. He walked frail, insignificant, shabby, miserable — and terrible in the simplicity of his idea calling madness and despair to the regeneration of the world. Nobody looked at him. He passed on, unsuspected and deadly, like a pest in the street full of men.

---

*Used for hanging advertising placards over the shoulders of persons hired to be walking billboards.

Endnotes

While I have drawn from many different sources in producing the notes for this edition of The Secret Agent, *I am especially indebted to the scholars whose earlier work has provided a rich store of information regarding the novel. The studies most frequently consulted include Norman Sherry's* Conrad's Western World *(Cambridge: Cambridge University Press, 1970), which provides detailed accounts of the historical backgrounds of* The Secret Agent; *and Bruce Harkness and S. W. Reid's authoritative edition of Conrad's novel (Cambridge: Cambridge University Press, 1990), which contains an invaluable textual study in addition to their extremely useful notes.*

—Tatiana M. Holway

Dedication

1. *To H. G. Wells:* Novelist, journalist, popular sociologist, and historian, H. G. Wells (1866–1946) is now best remembered for works such as *The Time Machine* (1895), *The Invisible Man* (1897), and *The War of the Worlds* (1898), which he called "scientific romances." The novels to which Conrad refers, *Love and Mr. Lewisham* (1900) and *Kipps: The Story of a Simple Soul* (1905), represent Wells's forays into more realistic fiction and are seriocomic treatments of the fortunes of their lower-middle-class protagonists. Conrad admired the early popular fiction of the "historian of ages to come," and he was grateful for the attention that Wells, already an important man of letters, bestowed in a largely favorable review on *An Outcast of the Islands* (1896), Conrad's second novel.

Author's Note

1. (p. 3) *a period of mental and emotional reaction:* Conrad began writing the work that would eventually become *The Secret Agent* in early 1906, when he was still feeling exhausted from the effort of writing *Nostromo* (1904), his most ambitious novel to date, which, contrary to his hopes, had a poor critical reception as well as poor sales. As was often the case, Conrad was also afflicted with a variety of physical ailments during this period.

2. (p. 3) *The actual facts are that I began this book impulsively and wrote it continuously*: In fact, the composition of this novel proceeded erratically. In the beginning, it was not a book at all. Originally conceived as a short story entitled "Verloc," the work was expanded to novel length in 1906, while the Conrad family lived in a variety of places both abroad and in England. During the novel's serialization in an American journal in late 1906, Conrad realized it needed further revision and expansion, and he pursued that intention as best he could in the course of 1907, when both his sons, one aged nine, the other barely a year old, were seriously ill, and his wife suffered from crippling leg injuries. "I seem to move, talk, write in a sort of quiet nightmare that goes on and on" (June 7, 1907), he confessed to a friend. For additional information on the composition of *The Secret Agent*, see Note on the Text and This Edition.

3. (p. 3) *so little reproof amongst so much intelligent and sympathetic appreciation*: Praise for *The Secret Agent* appeared in *The Times Literary Supplement* and *The Spectator* and, most importantly, from Edward Garnett (1868–1936), a highly influential publishers' reader, who had been encouraging Conrad from the beginning of his career as a writer and who wrote a highly laudatory review in *The Nation*, for which Conrad was especially grateful. The general reception of *The Secret Agent* was, however, mixed. Alongside favorable notices were some that were considerably less so, with reviewers reproaching Conrad for both his subject matter and his style. Excerpts from some contemporary reactions can be found in the Comments and Questions section of this edition; a wider sampling appears in *Conrad: The Critical Heritage*, edited by Norman Sherry (London: Routledge and Kegan Paul, 1973), as well as in *The Secret Agent: A Selection of Critical Essays*, edited by Ian Watt (London: Macmillan, 1973).

4. (p. 4) *man may smile and smile*: Conrad echoes Shakespeare's Hamlet: "That one may smile, and smile, and be a villain!" (act 1, scene 5), Hamlet observes upon learning of his father's murder by his uncle.

5. (p. 4) *that remote novel,* Nostromo, *. . . and the profoundly personal* Mirror of the Sea: *Nostromo* was published in 1904. *The Mirror of the Sea*, a collection of sketches and essays, some of which are autobiographical in nature, was written largely between 1904 and 1906 and published in the fall of 1906. Conrad also had other writing in hand at the time, including work on what would become *Chance* (1914) and *Victory* (1915).

6. (p. 5) *a few words uttered by a friend*: The friend was Ford Madox Ford, who collaborated with Conrad on a number of works, including *The Inheritors* (1901) and *Romance* (1903). Ford's familiarity with anarchist activities came partly through his cousins, Olive, Helen, and Arthur Rossetti, who ran an anarchist press from the basement of their home. The Rossetti sisters also published a memoir, under the pseudonym "Isabel Meredith," entitled *A Girl Among the Anarchists* (1903), which Conrad consulted while writing *The Secret Agent*, and two earlier stories concerned with anarchism, "The Informer" and "An Anarchist" (written in 1905–1906 and included in the 1908 collection, *A Set of Six*).

7. (p. 5) *the already old story of the attempt to blow up the Greenwich Observatory:* The incident occurred on February 15, 1894, when Martial Bourdin, a young Frenchman who apparently sought to blow up the Royal Observatory in Greenwich Park, was instead fatally injured by the explosion of the dynamite he was carrying. Although the "Greenwich Outrage," as it came to be known, attracted considerable attention from the police and the press, Bourdin's motives were never explained. However, the fact that shortly before the explosion Bourdin had been in the company of his brother-in-law, an anarchist named H. B. Samuels, led many to conclude that the incident was part of an anarchist plot.

8. (p. 5) *a blood-stained inanity of so fatuous a kind:* Conrad's representation of the incident inspired the idea of the *acte gratuit,* or the gratuitous crime, elaborated in *Lafcadio's Adventures* (1914) by André Gide, an admirer of Conrad who supervised the translation of his works into French. A discussion of Gide's *acte gratuit* can be found in the Introduction (p. xxxii).

As for Conrad's own sources of inspiration—they are many and various. A famous passage from *Macbeth* is broadly, typically, and inconclusively suggestive:

> . . . Out, out, brief candle!
> Life's but a walking shadow, a poor player,
> That struts and frets his hour upon the stage,
> And then is heard no more. It is a tale
> Told by an idiot, full of sound and fury,
> Signifying nothing (act 5, scene 5)

9. (p. 5) *"Oh, that fellow was half an idiot. His sister committed suicide afterwards":* In *Joseph Conrad: A Personal Remembrance* (1924), Ford claimed that Conrad invented the detail about suicide. "What the writer [Ford] really said to Conrad was: 'Oh that fellow was half an idiot! His sister murdered her husband afterwards and was allowed to escape by the police.' " Although Ford's account is questionable (among other things, Samuels was not murdered, but lived into the 1930s and was survived by his wife), he was undoubtedly one of several important sources of information for this novel. Some of Conrad's complex attitudes toward and statements about such sources are discussed in the Introduction (pp. xxviii–xxx and lxxxiii–lxxxiv).

10. (p. 6) *the rather summary recollections of an Assistant Commissioner of Police:* Conrad refers to *Sidelights on the Home Rule Movement* (1906), written by Sir Robert Anderson, who was also Director of the Criminal Investigation Department of the Metropolitan Police (1888–1901). The memoir treats Anderson's experiences investigating the Fenian (Irish Home Rule) movement, some of whose members were responsible for a variety of notorious terrorist acts in London and elsewhere. Conrad probably consulted Anderson's book when he undertook the revision of the earlier version of *The Secret Agent,* since the volume was not published until late 1906.

11. (p. 6) *the dynamite outrages in London, away back in the eighties:* Invented in 1866, dynamite soon became the weapon of choice for terrorist action. In the 1880s London was the scene of numerous attempts on government offices, railroad stations, cultural institutions, and so on, many of them perpetrated by Fenians. One response to these outrages, as they were called, was the "dynamite romance," a sub-genre of that sensation fiction popular at the time. While Conrad himself sought a popular audience for *The Secret Agent* (which, in the event, did not sell particularly well when it was published), he was at the same time annoyed by the sensational and unauthorized advertisement of his novel as "A Tale of Diplomatic Intrigue and Anarchist Treachery" by the American journal where it was first serialized.

12. (p. 6) *Sir William Harcourt then:* Sir William Harcourt, who held the office of Home Secretary from 1880 to 1885, was, to many of Conrad's readers, a recognizable model for Sir Ethelred in the novel. While Harcourt was Home Secretary before both the so-called "Greenwich Outrage" (1894) and the date of the action of the novel (1886), his tenure did coincide with some of the "dynamite outrages" described in the previous note. Apart from such instances of chronological complications that arise in the many and various connections between Conrad's novel and events and texts outside it (see also, for example, chapter 2, note 17, below), there are also the multiple temporal complications and innovations of Conrad's narrative, which are addressed in the Introduction (p. xxxvii and note on page lxi).

13. (p. 7) *my solitary and nocturnal walks all over London in my early days:* In his *Notes on Life and Letters* (1921), Conrad describes his first encounters with what he referred to as a "Dickensian" London, which he continued to explore on foot in the 1880s and 1890s, when he lodged in the city between voyages. The London of *The Secret Agent* owes much to these walks, as well as to the representation of the city in Dickens's later novels. These backgrounds and influences are discussed at greater length in the Introduction (pp. xix–xx and note on page xxxvi).

14. (p. 8) *Mr. Vladimir himself:* In a letter written in October of 1907, Conrad indicated that this character was based on a certain General Selivertsov, a Russian director of secret police who sought to repress nihilist activity and was shot and killed in Paris in 1890. Conrad's antipathy for Russian police methods dates far back to his childhood, when his family was sent into exile by Russian authorities for his father's involvement in Polish nationalist activities.

15. (p. 8) *revolutionary refugees in New York:* These were members of the Clan-na-Gael, a branch of the Fenian movement centered in America, where proponents of the Irish Home Rule movement sought support for their cause against Britain among recent Irish immigrants.

16. (p. 9) *Lately, circumstances . . . have compelled me to strip this tale of the literary robe:* In March of 1920, a year before he wrote this Author's Note, Conrad had completed a stage adaptation of *The Secret Agent.* The play ultimately opened in London in the fall of 1922, had a poor critical reception, and closed after a little over a week.

Chapter One

1. (p. 10) *Mr. Verloc:* Conrad appears to have drawn on many sources in creating Mr. Verloc. One who may have influenced the introductory portrait of the character was a former friend, Adolf Krieger, whom Conrad met in London and who assisted him in many ways in the 1880s and 1890s. Among the various similarities between Krieger and Mr. Verloc is the fact that Krieger frequently made trips abroad for unspecified purposes—so much so that rumor held that he was a spy of some sort. For other sources for Mr. Verloc, particularly in his role as a secret agent, see chapter two, note 15.

2. (p. 10) *the era of reconstruction:* During the 1870s and 1880s, vast urban projects, including the building of the Victoria Embankment and the construction of broad new thoroughfares such as Charing Cross Road, were under way. One of their purposes, and effects, was the razing of unsavory neighborhoods and slums.

3. (p. 10) *nondescript packages . . . closed yellow paper envelopes . . . ancient French comic publications:* While the "nondescript packages in wrappers like patent medicines" are likely to hold some potion promising virility (or else some treatment for venereal disease), the "closed yellow paper envelopes" probably contain pornographic photographs or contraceptives (which were used more to prevent disease than as birth control). The description of the "comic publications" as "French" draws as much on the characteristic Victorian association of France with anything risqué as it does on the fact that legislation restricting the publication of pornography in Britain meant that much of it was produced abroad and smuggled into the country. The sale of anarchist publications alongside that of the other wares in Mr. Verloc's shop is discussed in the Introduction (p. xx–xxi).

4. (p. 10) The Torch, The Gong—*rousing titles: The Torch: A Revolutionary Journal of Anarchist Communism* was the title of an actual anarchist publication printed in the 1890s by Olive, Helen, and Arthur Rossetti, youthful cousins of Ford Madox Ford, in the basement of their London home (see Author's Note, note 6). Although *The Gong* is a fictitious title, it rings true to several extra-textual sources. One was *The Bell (Kolokol)*, an important Russian publication-in-exile which was produced largely by the democratic liberal and socialist Alexander Herzen; the supreme anarchist Bakunin contributed to it, and for a short period his conspiratorial accomplice, the arch-terrorist Sergei Nechaev, gained editorial control of its pages. Other actual anarchist papers with "rousing titles" like *The Gong* include *The Alarm*, which was published in London in 1896 (a weekly of the same name appeared in Chicago and in New York in the 1880s), as well as *The Tocsin*. (See Franco Venturi, *Roots of Revolution: A History of the Populist and Socialist Movements in Nineteenth-Century Russia* [London: Phoenix Press, 2001], pp. 90–128 and passim. Eloise Knapp Hay, *The Political Novels of Joseph Conrad: A Critical Study* [Chicago: University of Chicago Press, 1963], p. 237; and Paul Avrich, *Anarchist Portraits* [Princeton: Princeton University Press, 1988], pp. 29 and 179.)

5. (p. 11) *retail value sixpence (price in Mr. Verloc's shop one-and-sixpence):* Mr. Verloc inflates the price of the marking ink 300 percent.

6. (p. 12) *cultivated his domestic virtues:* Widely propounded in the nineteenth century, these virtues find a characteristic expression in John Ruskin's lecture "Of Queens' Gardens," published in *Sesame and Lilies* (1864). There, where he describes the duties of the wifely angel of the hearth, Ruskin also extols the home as "the place of Peace; the shelter not only from all injury, but from all terror, doubt, and division." "So far as the anxieties of the outer life penetrate into it, and the inconsistently-minded, unknown, unloved, or hostile society of the outer world is allowed by either husband or wife to cross the threshold," Ruskin continues, "it ceases to be home."

7. (p. 12) *near Vauxhall Bridge Road . . . the district of Belgravia:* Located south of Hyde Park and Buckingham Palace Gardens, Belgravia was a fashionable residential area developed in the early nineteenth century. Vauxhall Bridge Road, built in 1816 as an approach to the new Vauxhall Bridge over the Thames, borders Pimlico, which was developed in the 1830s and came to be inhabited by a decidedly less fashionable population. Conrad lodged in Pimlico in the 1890s. These and other locations in London as well as in Greenwich that figure in the novel can be found on the maps accompanying this edition of *The Secret Agent.*

8. (p. 12) *He generally arrived in London (like the influenza) from the Continent, only he arrived unheralded by the Press:* In the 1880s and 1890s, reports of outbreaks of the flu in Europe preceded outbreaks in Britain.

9. (p. 14) *Soho:* A crowded area of London, Soho was characterized by its mixed population of artists, foreigners, and radicals, as well as its seedy and disreputable trades. For more on Soho and Conrad's representation of it, see the Introduction (pp. xxi–xxvi).

10. (p. 14) *our excellent system of compulsory education:* The Elementary Education Act of 1870 established the principle that all children should have access to elementary education.

Chapter Two

1. (p. 17) *riding in the Row:* Rotten Row, in Hyde Park, was where ladies and gentlemen rode.

2. (p. 18) *hygienic idleness . . . unhygienic labour:* The term "hygiene," which refers to conditions and practices conducive to health and cleanliness, acquired a further meaning in the nineteenth century, when Victorian reformers and medical practitioners linked physical hygiene with moral hygiene, or purity, and campaigned for the improvement of both, especially among the lower classes.

3. (p. 19) *sellers of invigorating electric belts and . . . inventors of patent medicines:* These quacks hawked products that, whether purporting to remedy impotence or to enhance sexual performance, belong to a milieu that includes the principal wares in Mr. Verloc's shop.

4. (p. 19) *a charioteer at Olympic Games:* The modern Olympic Games were revived in 1896 in Athens. London was the host city for the games scheduled for 1908, the year after *The Secret Agent* was published.

5. (p. 19) *No. 1 Chesham Square:* In the nineteenth century, the Russian Embassy was located in Chesham Place, in Belgravia.

6. (p. 20) *Porthill Street, a street well known in the neighbourhood:* There was, in fact, no such street of that name in Belgravia or elsewhere in London.

7. (p. 20) *London's strayed houses:* In the later nineteenth century, many London streets were renamed and building addresses were changed in response to the needs of the postal service.

8. (p. 21) *Privy Councillor Wurmt:* The German name of this Russian embassy official, along with its meaning (*wurm* is German for "worm"), may have as much to do with Conrad's abhorrence of Prussian and Russian imperialism as with the closeness of relations, diplomatic and otherwise, between Prussia and Russia during portions of the latter half of the nineteenth century.

9. (p. 23) *said in French:* During the eighteenth and nineteenth centuries, French was the language of diplomacy and of polite society in Russia.

10. (p. 23) *Mr. Vladimir, First Secretary:* Conrad's dealings with the Russian Embassy in London in the 1880s, when he was still a Russian subject, may have contributed to the portrait of Mr. Vladimir. For Conrad's own indication of the obscure source for this character, see Author's Note, note 14.

11. (p. 29) *the International Conference assembled in Milan:* Although no such conference was held in Milan, a conference very much like it was called in 1898 in Rome. There, a number of European countries proposed instituting measures aimed at suppressing anarchist activities. British delegates, however, refused to accede to the proposal that anarchists residing in Britain be surrendered to their countries of origin for persecution, and further talks fell apart.

12. (p. 29) *The Future of the Proletariat:* The name of this organization, though fictitious, has an authentic ring to it, given the various (and variable) alliances between revolutionary anarchist, socialist, and communist movements in the later decades of the nineteenth century, as well as the rhetoric they employed. For more on such organizations, their names, and Conrad's representation of them, see the Introduction (pp. xl–xli).

13. (p. 30) *a master plumber:* The idea of the plumber as "the embodiment of fraudulent laziness and incompetency" may owe something to a sketch entitled "Plumbers," written by Charles Dudley Warner and published in *Mark Twain's Library of Humour* (1888).

14. (p. 30) *the symbol* Δ: This symbol may have been connected to the Clan-na-Gael, the American branch of the Fenian movement, whose three leaders were designated by the name "the Triangle," as well as by the symbol itself.

15. (p. 30) *the celebrated agent* Δ: Mr. Verloc's character as a secret agent with multiple allegiances has a number of precedents and partial sources. The career of Eugène François Vidocq (1775–1857), a French criminal-turned-police-informant-turned-detective, may have been suggestive, but there were also other models closer to home. One was H. B. Samuels, a professed anarchist and a brother-in-law of Martial Bourdin, the young man who was killed in the Greenwich explosion (see Author's Note, note 7). While conjecture that Samuels had provided Bourdin with explosives contributed to the idea that the Observatory was the focus of an anarchist plot, the notion that it was not—that, on the contrary, the incident was the result of a police conspiracy,

instigated by Samuels in his role as a secret police agent and with the aim of rousing public indignation about anarchist activity in England—was later promoted by an anarchist named David Nicoll in *The Greenwich Mystery* (1897), a pamphlet Conrad probably read. This pamphlet also mentions a certain Auguste Coulon, who was questioned about the "Greenwich Outrage" and whose dual background (French and Irish), nominal occupation (as a jeweler), purported political affiliation (anarchism), and secret employment (by both a foreign government and the British police) correspond closely enough to Verloc's background and circumstances to suggest that he might also have been a source for this character. (Another is described above, in chapter one, note 1.)

16. (p. 33) *the sacrosanct fetish of to-day is science*: By the late nineteenth century, the influence of science, both as a body of knowledge and as a method of inquiry, had extended far beyond the natural and physical world. Thus, for example, in *The Grammar of Science* (1892), Karl Pearson, a well-known mathematician, statistician, and philosopher of science, asserted not only that science was *the* authoritative mode of knowledge but also that scientific thinking would secure the stability as well as the progress of society. Further exaggerated and popularized, such claims contributed to the scientism that is ironically represented in the novel. See, for example, chapter three, note 7.

17. (p. 33) *"so many presidents have been assassinated"*: Given the date of the action of the novel (1886), Mr. Vladimir's remark is, strictly speaking, anachronistic in that the two presidential assassinations perpetrated by anarchists—that of Sadi Carnot of France in 1894 and of William McKinley of the United States in 1901—occurred later than this date. There were, however, many other instances of anarchist assassinations of officials and royalty in the 1880s and beyond—including, among others, that of Alexander II, Tsar of Russia, in 1881; Antonio Cánovas del Castillo, Prime Minster of Spain, in 1897; Elizabeth, Empress of Austria, in 1898; and Umberto I, King of Italy, in 1900—so that from the perspective of Conrad's audience, Mr. Vladimir's cynical remark about the conventionality of such acts would have amounted to a dreadful truth.

18. (p. 33) *"emotions either of pity or fear"*: The echo here is from *The Poetics*, where Aristotle speaks repeatedly of pity and fear as the proper effects of tragic drama (part 9, section 11; part 11, section 3; and elsewhere). Catharsis, or the purgation of the emotions of pity and fear through tragedy, would, in turn, contribute to the well-being of society.

19. (p. 34) *the National Gallery*: Established in 1824 and located just north of Trafalgar Square, the National Gallery housed a wide-ranging collection of paintings by European and British masters. Although the gallery was never bombed, there was an attempt made in 1884 on another major cultural institution in Trafalgar Square—the Nelson Monument. The cache of dynamite placed at the base of the column was discovered before it exploded.

20. (p. 35) *Greenwich*: Founded in 1675 for purposes of navigation at sea, the Royal Observatory in Greenwich Park is the site of the prime meridian (longitude 0°), which divides the western and eastern hemispheres of the globe and is the position from which distances east and west are measured. Also known as the Greenwich Meridian, the prime meridian became the official

basis for the creation of time zones around the world in 1884. At that time, Greenwich Mean Time, which had already been widely adopted in Britain by the mid-1850s due to the need to coordinate schedules in the rapidly expanding railroad system, was also adopted by twenty-four countries and became, in effect, the global standard for measuring time.

21. (p. 36) *Piccadilly*: Extending from Piccadilly Circus to Hyde Park Corner, Piccadilly was an avenue of grand homes and fashionable clubs in the nineteenth century.

22. (p. 36) *"the whole Lausanne lot"*: Switzerland, including Geneva, Zurich, Lausanne, and other towns, was known as a place of refuge for various radical exiles at the end of the nineteenth century.

23. (p. 39) *Visions of a workhouse infirmary for her child*: Stevie's mother envisions the worst. Workhouses, which were established under the New Poor Law (1834) and sought to discourage the poor from taking advantage of public assistance by making such assistance as meager and unpleasant as possible, were synonymous with harsh privation and degradation in the Victorian era. An infirmary in such a place would have afforded little, if any, relief for the afflicted.

Chapter Three

1. (p. 41) *Michaelis, the ticket-of-leave apostle*: This is another character who appears to have been drawn from several models. While his philosophical pronouncements—such as they are—have Marxist echoes (see chapter three, note 4, below), they also bear some resemblance to the views of Prince Peter Kropotkin (1842–1921), a Russian anarchist who lived in England from the mid-1870s on and wrote *Mutual Aid: A Factor of Evolution* (1902), in which he envisioned a future society based on what he believed to be humanity's innate goodness. Michaelis's views are discussed in greater detail in the Introduction (pp. xlii–xlviii). For other sources for Michaelis, see chapter six, note 2.

2. (p. 41) *Marienbad*: Marienbad is the German name for a fashionable spa located in Bohemia (then part of the Austro-Hungarian Empire; now part of the Czech Republic).

3. (p. 42) *Karl Yundt*: This "terrorist, as he called himself" may be based, in part, on the German terrorist Johann Most, who was notorious more for his bloodthirsty rhetoric than for any specific acts of terror. Most died in March of 1906, while Conrad was writing the novel. Another model for Yundt may have been Mikhail Bakunin (1814–1876), the anarchist leader who advocated spontaneous revolutionary violence. Among other things, Bakunin's supposed example helped to popularize the notion of "Propaganda by Deed," or the idea that committing terrorist acts against the state and society would eventually rouse the oppressed to participate in the revolutionary cause. These matters are taken up in greater detail in the Introduction (pp. xlviii–l).

4. (p. 43) *Struggle, warfare, was the condition of private ownership:* This notion has been fundamental to most radical and leftist thinking from the eighteenth century onward. It is also a basic tenet of Marxism, expressed in such works as *The Communist Manifesto* (1848) by Karl Marx and Friedrich Engels.

5. (p. 44) *Comrade Ossipon:* While no particular individual has been identified as a source for Ossipon, his character derives in part from a widely held view that many, if not most, anarchists were petty scoundrels—self-interested, lazy, parasitical. Conrad's ensuing description of Ossipon's "flattened nose and prominent mouth cast in the rough mould of the negro type" draws on the patently racist criminal theory that Ossipon himself holds and that posited that so-called negroid features were indicative of the criminal and the rapist. (See below, note 7.)

6. (p. 45) *The Corroding Vices of the Middle Classes:* For a detailed description of the sorts of arguments this pamphlet is likely to have propounded, see the Introduction (pp. lii–liii).

7. (p. 45) *Lombroso:* Cesare Lombroso (1836–1909), an Italian physician and criminologist, spelled out his theory associating specific physical features with character traits and deviant behaviors in *Criminal Man* (1876). His views, however, were hardly original. On the contrary, they were very much of a piece with ideas held by Social Darwinists, who sought to link evolution to sociology and developed theories of the progress (or lack thereof) of various races and peoples; with eugenics, the study of heredity and intelligence propounded from the 1870s onward by Francis Galton (among others); and with other purportedly scientific efforts to associate specific forms of so-called deviancy and degeneracy with physical features and, not incidentally, racial, class, and gender "types." Under the circumstances, even if Conrad's readers had never heard of Lombroso (his work was not translated into English until 1911), they would certainly have understood the gist of the reference, behind which there also hovers an allusion to phrenology, a pseudo-science popular in the earlier decades of the nineteenth century. Positing that the moral and intellectual characteristics of an individual could be inferred from the shape of the skull, phrenology, though dignified by the name of "cranioscopy," was also generally derided as "bump-reading."

8. (p. 52) *(no gas was laid upstairs):* Gas lighting, which illuminated most of the major urban thoroughfares in Britain from the early decades of the nineteenth century and then became increasingly widespread in factories, public buildings, theaters, and shops in the middle decades, came to be used in middle- and working-class homes only in the 1890s.

9. (p. 56) *"Shall I put out the light now?":* "Put out the light, and then put out the light" (act 5, scene 2), says Shakespeare's Othello, just before killing Desdemona.

Chapter Four

1. (p. 57) *the be-spectacled, dingy little man:* In describing the Professor's physical appearance, Conrad refers again to current ideas about criminal "types" and specifically anarchists, who were believed to be characterized by poor

sight and such simian characteristics as the "flat, large ears" that "departed widely from the sides of [the Professor's] skull." (See chapter three, note 7.) Sources for the Professor are, however, much more complex. See, for example, note 3, below; chapter five, note 3; and especially the extended discussion of this famous character in the Introduction (pp. lxxiv–xci).

2. (p. 58) *Islington*: A borough north of London, Islington underwent rapid development in the mid-nineteenth century, becoming an industrial area known for its swelling population and its slums.

3. (p. 60) *"I've it always by me"*: The Professor's tactics resemble those of a Fenian terrorist nicknamed "Dynamite Dillon," who was active in the 1880s and evaded arrest by carrying dynamite on his person. The Professor's obsession with developing a " 'really intelligent detonator' " for his device, which is described a little further on in the novel (pp. 61–62), harks back to an earlier version of this character, also named "the Professor," who appears in Conrad's story "The Informer" (written in 1906). Taking up this connection, the historian Paul Avrich has suggested that yet another original for the Professor in *The Secret Agent* was a certain Professor Mezzeroff, a chemist and an anarchist, who was devoted to developing explosives and who also carried dynamite in his pocket ("Conrad's Anarchist Professor: An Undiscovered Source," *Labor History* 18 [Summer 1977], pp. 397–402).

4. (p. 62) *the renowned Silenus Restaurant*: In naming this fictitious restaurant, Conrad draws on the fact that Silenus, a companion to Dionysus (the Greek god of tragedy and of wine, as well as the object of important religious celebrations), was himself both a notorious drunk and famed for his wisdom.

5. (p. 64) *rosy sheet*: Ossipon's newspaper is probably *The Sporting Times*; it was printed on pink paper and was popularly known as "the Pink 'Un." Chief Inspector Heat also reads this newspaper (see chapter nine, pp. 170 and 173).

6. (p. 64) *"There isn't much so far"*: The initial press reports of the explosion that left Martial Bourdin fatally mutilated in Greenwich Park were nearly as brief as the account Ossipon summarizes, though some were quite sensational as well.

7. (pp. 66–67) *"the disintegration of the old morality would have set in in its very temple"*: The remark refers to the story of Jesus and the moneychangers in the temple, which appears in all the Gospels. Matthew, for example, recounts how "Jesus went into the temple of God, and cast out all them that sold and bought in the temple, and overthrew the tables of the moneychangers," saying, "My house shall be called the house of prayer; but ye have made it a den of thieves" (21:12–13). John sums up: "The zeal of thine house hath eaten me up" (2:17). See also Mark 11:15–17 and Luke 19:45–48.

8. (p. 67) *"Latorre, Moser, and all that old lot"*: The individuals in this instance are apparently fictitious.

9. (p. 69) *"A fashionable publisher has offered him five hundred pounds for a book"*: The sum is considerable. Conrad, for example, received only £200 as an advance for *Lord Jim* (1900). By the time he was writing *The Secret Agent*, his earnings from his writings amounted to £650 a year, which was more than a comfortable middle-class income at the time, but considerably less than Conrad, who was plagued by debt, needed to live.

Endnotes

10. (p. 71) *"The Blue-Bells of Scotland"*: A popular song in the nineteenth century, "The Blue Bells of Scotland" recounts the love of the singer for a "Highland laddie" who goes off to war. The song concludes: "Oh no, true love will be his guard and bring him safe again, / For it's oh, my heart would break if my Highland lad were slain."

Chapter Five

1. (p. 74) *like a meeting in a side corridor of a mansion full of life*: The echo here is from the New Testament: "In my Father's house are many mansions" (John 14:2).

2. (p. 74) *Chief Inspector Heat of the Special Crimes Department*: This character may be based in part on Chief Inspector Melville of the Criminal Investigation Department (established in 1878), a figure who was well known to the public as an expert in terrorist activities and who was involved in the investigation of the Greenwich explosion. Heat also bears an interesting resemblance to Inspector Bucket, a prominent character in Dickens's *Bleak House* (1852–1853).

3. (p. 75) *his superiority over all the multitude of mankind*: Conrad's description of the Professor's egomania, along with the comparison of the Professor to Caligula, has been said to have been influenced by Max Nordau's identification, in *Degeneration* (1898), of Caligula as the very type of egomaniac: "In its extreme degree of development, egomania leads to that folly of Caligula," or the individual who "believes himself above all restraints of morality and law, and wishes the whole of humanity had one single head that he might cut it off." Whether or not Conrad was familiar with Nordau's work, it is certainly of a piece with that of other late-nineteenth-century studies of so-called deviant and degenerate types. (See above, chapter three, note 7.)

4. (p. 76) *the hospital*: The remains have been brought to the Royal Hospital for Seamen at Greenwich, an institution founded in the late seventeenth century for the relief and support of disabled naval veterans.

5. (p. 80) *no man is a hero to his valet*: The saying is attributed to Anne de Cornuel, a seventeenth-century Frenchwoman known for her witty aphorisms. Conrad appears to have tinkered with the logic of this statement in his subsequent comment: "or else the heroes would have to brush their own clothes."

6. (p. 89) *Gravesend*: Located at the mouth of the Thames, about 20 miles east of London, and easily accessible by train from the mid-1840s onward, Gravesend was a popular seaside destination for the middle and working classes.

Chapter Six

1. (p. 90) *The lady patroness*: This character may have been suggested by Baroness Angela Burdett-Coutts (1814–1906), an extremely wealthy and renowned philanthropist and social reformer in Victorian Britain, who championed many

diverse causes, including improving the condition of the poor and of the working classes. Like the fictional lady, Burdett-Coutts opened her home (located on Stratton Street, just off Piccadilly, in the wealthy district of Mayfair) to all manner of persons, distinguished in many professions and walks of life.

2. (p. 91) *a rather mad attempt to rescue some prisoners from a police van*: The crime for which Michaelis was imprisoned recalls an incident in Manchester in 1867, when a group of Fenians, seeking to rescue their comrades, attacked a police van and killed a constable, who, like the one in the novel, was a married man and the father of three. And, as in the novel, so in life, the incident aroused considerable public outrage. At the same time, Michaelis's status as a ticket-of-leave prisoner, made much of by society, is similar to that of another Fenian, Michael Davitt, who, upon his conditional release, made much of the hardship he suffered in prison in an autobiographical pamphlet entitled *Leaves from a Prison Diary, or Lectures to a Solitary Audience* (1885), and was, in turn, regarded with sympathy by the public. For discussion of further dimensions of Michaelis's solitary condition, see the Introduction (pp. xliii–xliv).

3. (p. 98) *The Assistant Commissioner of Police*: Like Chief Inspector Heat, the Assistant Commissioner also derives in part from contemporary sources: Sir Howard Vincent, who held the post of Assistant Commissioner and Director of the Special Crimes Department from 1878 to 1884, and Sir Robert Anderson, who held these offices from 1888 to 1901 and wrote *Sidelights on the Home Rule Movement* (1906), the book to which Conrad refers in his preface. (See Author's Note, note 10.)

4. (p. 99) *the bullet head*: It appears that the shape of Chief Inspector Heat's head is not unlike that of the violent criminal, who, according to phrenologists, displayed the tell-tale "sugar cone head," or "murder bump," as it became popularly—and derisively—known. (See above, chapter three, note 7.)

5. (p. 101) *Alfred Wallace . . . his famous book on the Malay Archipelago*: A naturalist who developed a theory of evolution independently of Darwin, Alfred Russel Wallace (1823–1913) wrote *The Malay Archipelago: The Land of the Orang-Utan, and the Bird of Paradise, a Narrative of Travel, with Studies of Man and Nature* (1869). Conrad consulted the book when writing *Lord Jim* (1900), *The Rescue* (1920), and a number of other works in between.

6. (p. 102) *like a Book of Revelation in the history of mankind*: The biblical Revelation of St. John foretells the end of human history, which precedes the Second Coming of Christ.

7. (p. 106) *"A fool and his job are soon parted"*: "A fool and his money are soon parted" is the more common form of the saying.

8. (p. 107) *the name of Brett Street*: Although there was no Brett Street in Soho or anywhere else in London, for that matter, the name "Brett" is nonetheless resonant: it was the name of the police constable who was killed by Fenians in the incident to which the character of Michaelis has been linked. (See above, chapter six, note 2.)

9. (p. 109) *Guildhall Banquet*: The Lord Mayor of London's annual banquet was held on the Lord Mayor's Day, November 9, at Guildhall, the center of London's civic government.

10. (p. 109) *gone off with her to Margate for a week*: The Verlocs honeymoon at a well-known seaside resort which became an especially popular destination for

the lower and middle-classes from the mid-1840s onward, when train service made it readily and cheaply accessible. William Frith's famous painting *Ramsgate Sands* (1854) depicts the scene at a similar resort at mid-century.

11. (p. 110) *Dover:* Located on the English Channel, roughly 70 miles southeast of London, Dover was, and is, a main port of departure for and arrival from the Continent.

12. (p. 111) *Charing Cross and Victoria:* Opened in 1864, Charing Cross Station quickly became one of the busiest railroad stations in London. Victoria Station, built a few years earlier, was a central depot for trains traveling south, to resort areas and to Dover.

Chapter Seven

1. (p. 114) *the great Personage:* In both his physical appearance and his ancient lineage, Sir Ethelred resembles Sir William Harcourt, who was, according to Conrad, the original for this character. (See Author's Note, p. 6).

2. (p. 119) *Ambassador . . . to the Court of St. James:* Although St. James Palace was no longer the residence of the sovereign, the British Court was still referred to as the Court of St. James, and ambassadors to Britain, who were received at Buckingham Palace, continued to be thus designated.

3. (p. 120) *Toodles:* The name of this private secretary, which echoes "Noodle," the name for a fool, and especially a political one, also harks back to the roster of Cabinet members in Dickens's *Bleak House*—from Boodle, Coodle, Doodle, and so on, to Noodle, Poodle, and Quoodle (chapter 12). It also recalls the name of Paul Dombey's wet-nurse, Polly Toodle, in Dickens's earlier *Dombey and Son* (1846–1848).

4. (p. 122) *Palace Yard:* New Palace Yard, located to the north of Westminster Hall, gave access to the Members' Entrance to the House of Commons.

5. (p. 122) *"Not so many British Ministers have been assassinated":* None was, although the Houses of Parliament and Westminster Hall were among the targets during the "dynamite outrages" of the 1880s. (See Author's Note, note 11.)

6. (p. 123) *his own departmental buildings:* These would probably be the buildings that constituted New Scotland Yard, which were located on the Embankment. The original building called "New Scotland Yard," which became police headquarters in 1890, soon proved inadequate to house the Metropolitan Police, and an adjacent building was constructed in 1895.

7. (p. 125) *the Italian restaurant is such a peculiarly British institution:* Restaurants, in contradistinction to eating houses or dining rooms in private clubs, became popular in Britain in the mid-nineteenth century. While there were a number of well-known, opulent, Continental-style restaurants located in fashionable areas of London by the 1870s, many more relatively inexpensive eateries were opened by European immigrants in Soho and attracted a mixed clientele. The peculiarities of the Italian restaurant in Conrad's novel are discussed in the Introduction (pp. xxi–xxiii).

Chapter Eight

1. (p. 128) *almshouses founded by a wealthy innkeeper for the destitute widows of the trade*: Privately funded lodgings for the poor, almshouses, though a last resort, were a better alternative than the notorious Victorian public workhouse. (See chapter two, note 23.)

2. (p. 128) *"half-crowns and five shillings almost every day this last week"*: With half-crowns being the equivalent of 2 shillings and sixpence, and with 20 shillings making up a pound, Winnie Verloc's mother has spent a considerable sum on transportation—close to, if not more than, what amounted at the time to a week's wages in the lower ranks of semi-skilled working-class occupations.

3. (p. 129) *the Charity*: One of hundreds of charitable institutions established in Victorian Britain, the Benevolent Institution of Licensed Victuallers (also known as the Licensed Victuallers' Benevolent Asylum) was founded in 1827 "to receive and maintain for life necessitous aged members, and their wives or widows." To this end, the charity erected nearly 200 houses on 6 acres of grounds in Peckham, a rural area south of London that underwent rapid development in later decades of the nineteenth century and became known for cheap housing.

4. (p. 131) *the proverb that "truth can be more cruel than caricature," if such a proverb existed*: It does, in effect, but the proverb is usually worded "Truth is stranger than fiction."

5. (p. 132) *Whitehall*: By the late nineteenth century, this broad thoroughfare, which led toward the Houses of Parliament, was coming to be dominated by government buildings, including the Treasury building the cab passes. Consequently, the name "Whitehall" itself eventually became synonymous with the administrative operations of the British government as a whole.

6. (p. 132) *"You musn't. . . . It hurts"*: Stevie's reaction recalls a scene in Fyodor Dostoevsky's *Crime and Punishment* (1866), in which Raskolnikov dreams of a horrifying incident in his childhood wherein he witnessed an old mare being beaten to death (part 1, chapter 5). The final mental breakdown of the philosopher Friedrich Nietzsche (1844–1900) after seeing a horse beaten in Turin in 1899 might also be connected to this scene in *The Secret Agent*. For discussions of Conrad's complex relationships both to Dostoevsky and to Nietzsche, see the Introduction (pp. xxxiii–xxxiv and lxxxv–xci).

7. (p. 132) *St. Stephen's*: Parliament sat in St. Stephen's Chapel in the Palace of Westminster from the sixteenth century until fire destroyed it in 1834. Remnants of the palace were incorporated in the new Houses of Parliament, constructed over the next thirty years.

8. (p. 132) *the bridge*: The cab crosses Westminster Bridge on its route south toward the charity almshouses.

9. (p. 139) *like Virgil's Silenus, who, his face smeared with the juice of berries, discoursed of Olympian Gods to the innocent shepherds of Sicily*: The story is recounted in the Sixth Eclogue by Virgil (50–19 B.C.). For Silenus, see chapter four, note 4, as well as the discussion of this figure in the Introduction (pp. lxxxviii–xci).

10. (p. 139) *the steed of apocalyptic misery:* Alluding to the horses that prefigure the Apocalypse in the Book of Revelation (famously represented in Albrecht Dürer's 1498 woodcut engraving, *The Four Horsemen of the Apocalypse*), this description also glances in particular at the "pale horse" that figures prominently in the biblical account: "behold a pale horse: his name that sat on him was Death, and Hell followed with him" (6:8).

11. (p. 144) *"the police . . . are there so that them as have nothing shouldn't take anything away from them who have":* Winnie's remark, which reflects a common working-class view of the police, also echoes, in reverse, the sort of thing she is likely to have heard during the revolutionaries' meetings in the shop— especially "Property is theft," a famous anarchist slogan coined by Pierre-Joseph Proudhon (1809–1865).

12. (p. 145) *the salt of passion in her tasteless life:* The description suggests Jesus's address to his disciples and the persecuted multitudes: "Ye are the salt of the earth: but if the salt has lost his savour, wherewith shall it be salted? it is thenceforth good for nothing, but to be cast out, and to be trodden under foot of men" (Matthew 5:13).

13. (p. 147) *dismal thoughts . . . crowded urgently round him, like a pack of hungry black hounds:* This image, which owes something to Cerberus, the mythical watchdog of Hades, also touches on various related moments in Milton's *Paradise Lost* (1667): to the representation of the figure of Sin, surrounded by "Hell Hounds" that "never ceasing bark'd / With wide Cerberean mouths full loud" (book 2, lines 654–655); to Satan's vision of the "Dogs of Hell" that advance "To waste and havoc yonder world" (book 10, lines 616–617) after the Fall; and especially to Satan's own crucial realization, "Which way I fly is Hell; myself am Hell" (book 4, line 75).

14. (p. 147) *things do not stand much looking into:* Winnie's belief finds an echo in "Burnt Norton" (1935), the first of T. S. Eliot's *Four Quartets* (1943): "human kind / Cannot bear very much reality." For another connection between Eliot's four-part poem and Conrad's novel, see note 25 to the Introduction.

Chapter Nine

1. (pp. 151–152) *wifely talk, as artfully adapted, no doubt, to the circumstances of this return as the talk of Penelope to the return of the wandering Odysseus. Mrs. Verloc, however, had done no weaving during her husband's absence:* In Homer's *Odyssey*, Penelope puts off answering her suitors' proposals of marriage during the ten years that her husband, Odysseus, spends wandering after the Trojan Wars by promising an answer when the shroud that she weaves by day—and secretly unravels at night—is finished. Characterized throughout the epic as "circumspect," Penelope remains silent upon Odysseus's return, when he disguises himself as a beggar whom she does not recognize to be her husband and whom only hospitality requires her to acknowledge (book 19).

2. (p. 152) *a cottage in the country, somewhere on the London, Chatham, and Dover line:* The cottage is in Kent, where Conrad lived, on and off, from 1898 through much of 1907.

3. (p. 154) *the clutches of black care, that perhaps prefers to sit behind a horseman:* The echo comes most directly from the *Odes* of Horace (65–8 B.C.): "Black care is seated behind the horseman" (book 3, line 40). However, Verloc's frame of mind also suggests the black horse of the Apocalypse: "and he that sat on him had a pair of balances in his hand" (Revelation 6:5).

4. (p. 164) *Continental Hotel:* There were a number of hotels of that name in London.

Chapter Ten

1. (p. 176) *the very centre of the Empire on which the sun never sets:* This was a commonplace about the British Empire, especially in the later decades of the nineteenth century, when imperial expansion grew rapidly and extensively, and Britain gained possession of territories on nearly every continent.

2. (p. 177) *"all the fishes of the sea":* Toodles alludes to the passage in Genesis where God blesses Noah and tells him that the "dread of you shall be upon every beast of the earth, and upon every fowl of the air, upon all that moveth upon the earth, and upon all the fishes of the sea: into your hand are they delivered" (9:2).

3. (p. 177) *"a sprat is also thrown away sometimes in order to catch a whale":* The Assistant Commissioner plays on the expression "Throw a sprat to catch a mackerel," meaning to give away something trifling for much greater returns.

4. (p. 178) *the Explorers':* Although the club is fictitious, the name is similar to that of the Travellers' Club, an exclusive institution founded in 1819 and frequented by diplomats, among others. Many clubs such as the Travellers' were located on Pall Mall or in the adjacent district of St. James's.

Chapter Eleven

1. (p. 189) *the Cheshire Cheese:* This was a common name for a pub. Mr. Verloc's Cheshire Cheese is undoubtedly not Ye Olde Cheshire Cheese, a famous pub frequented by many generations of men of letters.

2. (p. 196) *writing on the wall:* Daniel interprets the biblical writing on the wall, "Mene, mene, tekel, upharsin," for Belshazzar, the king of the Chaldeans: "Thou art weighed in the balances, and art found wanting" (Daniel 5:27). Belshazzar is slain that night.

3. (p. 196) *"What's done can't be undone":* Mr. Verloc echoes Shakespeare's Lady Macbeth, who observes, after the murder of Duncan: "Things without all remedy / Should be without regard: what's done, is done" (act 3, scene 2).

4. (p. 204) *among men whose flesh is grass; modest, like the life of violets:* The description draws on several sources. One is the Bible: "For all flesh is as grass, and all the glory of man as the flower of grass. The grass withereth, and the flower thereof falleth away" (1 Peter 1:24; see also Isaiah 40:6). Another is a literary commonplace about the modesty of shade-loving violets as expressed, for example, in "She Dwelt Among the Untrodden Ways," in which Wordsworth compares Lucy, the maiden of the poem, to "A violet by a mossy stone / Half hidden from the eye!" The situation Conrad describes may also allude to the warning to Ophelia that Hamlet's professions of love are like "A violet in the youth of primy nature, / Forward, not permanent, sweet, not lasting" (*Hamlet*, act 1, scene 3).

5. (p. 205) *in the likeness of funereal baked meats:* "The funeral bak'd meats / Did coldly furnish forth the marriage tables," remarks Hamlet (act 1, scene 2), upon the recent murder of his father and remarriage of his mother.

Chapter Twelve

1. (p. 217) *"The drop given was fourteen feet":* Winnie understandably exaggerates. While the extent of the drop varied from person to person, with hangmen determining just how long it should be in order to be fatal, 14 feet was considerably more than necessary.

2. (p. 218) *Mrs. Verloc formed the resolution to go at once and throw herself into the river off one of the bridges:* In popular legend, suicide by drowning was a common fate of fallen women. This fate is depicted in such iconic Victorian works as George Cruikshank's *The Drunkard's Children* (1848) and Augustus Egg's *Past and Present* (1858).

3. (p. 223) *Five-and-twenty shillings a week:* At the end of the nineteenth century, this was the average wage for those who, like Winnie's young butcher, were engaged in semi-skilled occupations, and it was very close to poverty.

4. (p. 227) *fifteen shillings:* This is a meager sum—a week's earnings at the very bottom of the pay scale and therefore hardly enough to get by on.

5. (p. 228) *Women's words fell into water:* The observation is a variation on the proverb "Women's words are fleeting."

6. (p. 228) *the Southampton—St. Malo service:* This cross-Channel ferry service, departing from Southampton, a port located approximately 60 miles southwest of London, and arriving in St. Malo, on the coast of Brittany, in France, was accessible by train from Waterloo Station.

7. (p. 235) *"Not unless you crush my head under your heel":* Winnie's declaration has multiple echoes. On the one hand, it refers to an earlier description of "the salt of passion in [Winnie's] tasteless life" (p. 145), with its allusion to Jesus's saying that the "good for nothing" are "to be cast out, and to be trodden under foot of men" (Matthew 5:13). On the other, the declaration Winnie makes to the man she momentarily thinks of as her savior has several sources, including the passage in Genesis in which God curses the serpent and says, "I will put enmity between thee and the woman, and between thy seed and her seed; it shall bruise thy head, and thou shalt bruise his heel" (3:14–15). Conrad may also be indirectly referring to Milton's providential reinterpretation of this passage in *Paradise Lost*, where it is Eve's "Seed"—that is, Jesus—that "shall bruise / The Serpent's head" (book 10, lines 1031–1032).

8. (p. 236) *the bridge:* This is the Waterloo Bridge, which, according to legend, was favored by suicides. It is "The Bridge of Sighs" in Thomas Hood's 1844 poem of that name.

9. (pp. 241–242) *the Abbey . . . The lights of Victoria . . . Sloane Square . . . the Park . . . a bridge . . . The clock tower:* Ossipon walks in a circle, moving southwest from Westminster Abbey to Victoria Station and Sloane Square; then north toward Hyde Park; and then east, until he makes his way back to Westminster Bridge, from which he sees Big Ben, the enormous clock on the tower of the Palace of Westminster.

Chapter Thirteen

1. (p. 244) *'Faith, Hope, Charity':* These are the principal Christian virtues, according to Paul. "And now abideth faith, hope, charity, these three; but the greatest of these is charity" (1 Corinthians 13:13). Michaelis's scheme for his biography and the future also suggests an earlier passage from Paul: "And though I have the gift of prophecy, and understand all mysteries, and all knowledge; and though I have all faith, so that I could remove mountains, and have not charity, I am nothing" (1 Corinthians 13:2).

2. (p. 244) *"They are the multitude. Theirs is the kingdom of the earth. Exterminate, exterminate!":* The allusion is both to Jesus speaking before the "multitudes"—"Blessed are the meek: for they shall inherit the earth" (Matthew 5:5)—and to Kurtz's famous pronouncement in *Heart of Darkness*—"Exterminate all the brutes" (chapter 2). The latter idea was also put forth by the anarchist Johann Most, a model for Karl Yundt. (See above, chapter three, note 3.)

3. (p. 244) *"Let us drink and be merry, . . . to-morrow we die":* The Professor echoes Isaiah before the fall of Jerusalem: "Let us eat and drink; for tomorrow we shall die" (22:13).

4. (p. 246) *"No God! No master":* This was a common expression among political and social radicals in the latter part of the nineteenth century.

5. (p. 247) *those that he courted on benches in Kensington Gardens:* Ossipon probably meets servants and nannies for the rich in this well-known park, located just west of Hyde Park.

6. (p. 249) *"Give me that for a lever, and I'll move the world":* The Professor adapts a saying attributed to Archimedes (287–212 B.C.): "Give me a place to stand, and with a lever I will move the whole world." Conrad used the Professor's full remark—"Madness and despair! Give me that for a lever, and I'll move the world"—as an epigraph to the French edition of *The Secret Agent*. He also returned to Archimedes's lever in his preface to *A Personal Record* (1912): "Don't talk to me of your Archimedes' lever. . . . Give me the right word and the right accent and I will move the world."

Inspired by
The Secret Agent

A loose adaptation of *The Secret Agent*, Alfred Hitchcock's *Sabotage* (Sheperd, Gaumont–British Pictures, 1936) is set in London in the 1930s and features a movie theater as the front for Mr. Verloc's shady operations, which include the sabotaging of the electrical supply to portions of the city. Although Hitchcock's film does involve international conspiracies not unlike those that figure in Conrad's novel, *Sabotage* omits characters and complications central to the original, introduces new ones, especially in the form of an unlikely love interest that develops between Winnie Verloc and a police detective, and, most crucially, repeatedly foregrounds the critical event that occurs off-stage, as it were, in the text—namely, the explosion of the bomb that kills Stevie, which Hitchcock represents in harrowing, sensational sequences that recur throughout the film. Nonetheless, the taut, menacing atmosphere of *The Secret Agent* is palpable in *Sabotage*, however different the medium and the circumstances through which it is conveyed, and the moments of dark humor Hitchcock injects complement the ironic sensibility of Conrad's novel. (With Oskar Homolka, Sylvia Sidney, and John Loder; released in the United States as *A Woman Alone*.)

Like Hitchcock, Christopher Hampton chose to make the central, though absent, event of the novel graphically explicit in his film of *The Secret Agent* (Twentieth Century Fox, 1996): what we learn, secondhand, in Conrad's text about Stevie's remains in Greenwich Park is gruesomely depicted in Hampton's version. Otherwise, this movie attempts to be largely faithful to the original and restricts itself to relatively minor revisions, leaving out the figure of the Assistant Commissioner, for example, while emphasizing the sexual relations between Winnie and Verloc, as well as Winnie and Ossipon. The spectacle of Robin Williams playing the Professor (in an uncredited role) is, however, peculiar. Best perhaps in its evocation of period atmosphere, this rendition of Conrad's novel is largely lacking in both irony and dramatic tension. (With Bob Hoskins, Patricia Arquette, and Gerard Depardieu.)

Comments & Questions

In this section, we aim to provide the reader with an array of perspectives on the text, as well as questions that challenge those perspectives. The commentary has been culled from sources as diverse as reviews contemporaneous with the work, letters written by the author, literary criticism of later generations, and appreciations written throughout the work's history. Following the commentary, a series of questions seeks to filter Joseph Conrad's The Secret Agent *through a variety of points of view and bring about a richer understanding of this enduring work.*

Comments

A. N. MONKHOUSE

Of course this work is extremely interesting, and it breaks fresh ground. *Nostromo* brought a change of continents, but it was still concerned with romantic adventurers; it would be an ingenious definition of romance that should include the Secret Agent and his companions. We associate Mr. Conrad with memorable experiences of thrilling adventure, of heroical tension, of the glowing East; we seem to be losing something very precious when he compels us to the grim comedy of anarchism. *The Secret Agent* absorbs, but it does not exalt, as did the tragedy of *Lord Jim* or the revelation of 'Youth'; there is nothing that warms our heart like Captain MacWhirr or startles our imagination like the defiance of the dying Jew in *Nostromo*. It is close and fine, but it does not often flash upon us, and it seems that interests are somehow less associated with sympathies than they were. Some very solid, ugly things are described, and if Mr. Conrad's people must always be human, his revolutionaries and their opponents are not engaging. The amiabilities of the anarchists are generally effaced, and they have no very deep enthusiasms. They are strangely wanting in ideals, and, half-desperate as they are, they remain the prey of vanity. Mr. Conrad approaches them with a nimble and even whimsical humour.

—from an unsigned review in the *Manchester Guardian* (September 12, 1907)

THE TIMES LITERARY SUPPLEMENT

Mr. Joseph Conrad, by a stroke of fine humour, has appended to his new book, *The Secret Agent*, a history of anarchists and spies, the sub-title 'A Simple Tale'; and in thinking it over we have suddenly realized that a part at least of this great novelist's mission is to remind his readers how simple men really are, even when they are the destroyers of society or their pursuers. To show how narrow a gulf is fixed between the maker of bombs and the ordinary contented citizen has never before struck a novelist as worth while, the subterranean world in which the terrorists live having up to the present time been considered by him merely as a background for lurid scenes and hair-raising thrills. And then comes Mr. Conrad with his steady, discerning gaze, his passion for humanity, his friendly irony, and above all his delicate and perfectly tactful art, to make them human and incidentally to demonstrate how monotonous a life can theirs also be. Stevenson just dipped into this nether world, bringing away only what was needed for his more or less sensational purpose; it was left for Mr. Conrad once again to hold the lantern that was to light every cranny; just as it was left for him fully to illumine the darkest places of the forecastle, the swamps of the Congo, and the mysteries of the heart of the revolutionary, the Ishmael, the derelict, and the coward. Englishmen cannot be too grateful that this alien of genius, casting about for a medium in which to express his sympathy and his knowledge, hit upon our tongue. *The Secret Agent* is more of a portrait gallery than a story, although it is a story too, and a really exciting one. It is notable, we think, chiefly for the portrait of the Professor the maker of bombs, Mr. Verloc the spy, and Chief Inspector Heat, of Scotland-yard, hunter of men; but there is no one scamped in it; all are made vivid, and their interaction is marvellously managed. The logic of the story is of iron. We do not consider *The Secret Agent* Mr. Conrad's masterpiece; it lacks the free movement of 'Youth' and the terrible minuteness of *Lord Jim*, while it offers no scope for the employment of the tender and warm fancy that made 'Karain' so memorable; but it is, we think, an advance upon *Nostromo*, its immediate predecessor. That canvas was a little overcrowded, while in *The Secret Agent* one's way is clear throughout. But the Professor is its triumph. It is the Professor who principally increases Mr. Conrad's reputation, already of the highest.

—September 20, 1907

COUNTRY LIFE

The Secret Agent, subjected to any test that can be imagined, will not entitle the author to a place beside Scott and Thackeray. One would begin by saying something about his selection of characters, although it may be said that the first, second, third and last essential is that they should be interesting. Unless the creations of an author's brain seize the attention and exercise the mind of his readers they are not worth considering at all; but a less amusing set of people never filled the imaginary world of a novelist than have been chosen for the pages of *The Secret Agent*. There used to be an old song of which the refrain, if we remember rightly, was: 'It's naughty, but it's nice.' Now, Mr. Conrad, in this book, is naughty, without being at all nice. His chief male character is a Mr. Verloc, a sort of spy and informer in the service of revolutionists. In portraying him the author appears to have taken M. Zola as model, for he introduces him with a certain kind of respectability, making him decent in his indecency, and honest in his dishonesty. The thing strikes us at once as a paradox. The sort of shop kept by Mr. Verloc is one where shady photographs, obscene literature and other articles of a similar kind are sold. The people who keep such places are, generally speaking, the most unmitigated blackguards who hold on to the edges of civilization. The man, however, as depicted by Mr. Conrad might have been an honest plasterer or stonemason, who has even gone on the path of respectability so far as to get married, instead of forming one of the slight and fleeting attachments which are more common in the order to which he belongs. His wife—and thereby hangs a tale—is the daughter of a woman who has kept a boarding-house and is the widow of a low type of licensed victualler or publican. The man is a very dull dog who, apparently, has a gift for spouting in parks and places where

Socialists assemble, but shows very little trace indeed of eloquence in the conversations he holds with the various people during the course of this story. Indeed, it would appear as if Mr. Conrad had set himself the impossible task of trying to make dulness interesting, for he lets Verloc only use a hoarse whisper in private, instead of a voice that was said to carry over the greater extent of Hyde Park; and he is distinguished, more than in any other way, by an utter lack of wit and *esprit*. . . .

If Mrs. Verloc had been interesting, the tale would have been so as well; but, if possible, she is still duller than her husband. This fact is emphasised by the very bad style in which Mr. Conrad tells his story. You can tell a great writer at once, because his analysis is all done, as it were, behind the curtain. He makes his people speak and act, and leaves the reader to judge what is passing in their minds. The course followed by Mr. Conrad is exactly the opposite of this. In page after page he discourses fluently about the ideas that were coursing through the brain of a woman who never spoke at all. . . .

Critics generally have agreed that even very great authors, such as Fielding, made a mistake in keeping to the example of Cervantes, and introducing short stories into the middle of their novels. Mr. Conrad is not guilty of that mistake, but of one equally inartistic, and that is the fault of bringing in minor and unessential characters and making far too much of them. It is best to give specific examples, so that any reader can, if he wishes, turn up the book and see for himself, or herself, how far these strictures are justified. Let us take Chapter VIII as an example. It tells us how Mrs. Verloc's mother went about to get admitted to an almshouse. The incident in itself is well enough, and might be helpful in developing the character of Mrs. Verloc; but considering that the woman never comes into the story again, the enormously-drawn-out tale of her departure must be considered as an excrescence, was not wanted in the slightest. Again, the characters of the Assistant Commissioner, the Inspector of Police, and the Minister, whose portrait seems to be intended as a burlesque of the late Sir William Harcourt, are all unnecessary to the picture, and might have been left out, or their parts curtailed, to very great advantage. In fact, if Mr. Conrad was aiming at art and immortality instead of at filling up a definite number of pages, he could have reduced his story to a tenth part of its present dimensions, and still rather added to than taken away from its merits. The book might fairly be described as a study of murder, by a writer with a personality as egotistical as that of Mr. Bernard Shaw, only lacking in the wit and humour which goes some way to justify the existence of the latter.

—from a review signed Z. (September 21, 1907)

ARNOLD BENNETT

A certain amount of reading has been done lately. Conrad's *The Secret Agent*. A sort of sensationalism sternly treated on the plane of realistic psychology. A short story written out to the length of a novel. Nothing but a single episode told to the last drop. The Embassy scenes did not appear to me to be quite genuine, but rather a sincere effort to imagine events for which the author had nothing but psychological data of a general order. But the domestic existence of the spy, and the character of his wife—the 'feel' of their relations, very masterly indeed, also the invention of the idiot brother-in-law for the doing of the crime. On the other hand, the contrivance of the mother-in-law's departure, though the departure was in itself excellent, seemed clumsy; and the final scenes between the wife and the anarchist after her husband's death rather missed fire in their wildness; they fail, not in the conception but in execution. On the whole, coming after *Nostromo*, the book gives a disappointing effect of slightness.

—from a journal entry dated September 25, 1907

EDWARD GARNETT

Mr. Conrad's achievement in his novels and tales of seamen's life in the Eastern seas, was, in fact, a poet's achievement; he showed us the struggle of man's passionate and wilful endeavour, cast against the background of nature's infinity and passionless purpose. And in *The Secret Agent* Mr. Conrad's ironical insight into the natural facts of life, into those permanent animal instincts which underlie our spiritual necessities and aspirations, serves him admirably in place of the mysterious backgrounds of tropical seas and skies to which he has accustomed us. He goes down into the dim recesses of human motive, but though his background is only the murky gloom of old London's foggy streets and squares, the effect is none the less arresting. His character sketches of Michaelis, the ticket-of-leave apostle of anarchism, of Karl Yundt, the famous terrorist, the moribund veteran of dynamite wars, 'who has been a great actor in his time, on platforms, in secret assemblies, in private interviews,' but who has never, strange to say, put his theories into practice; of Comrade Ossipon, who lives by exploiting the servant-girls whom his handsome face has seduced; and of the Professor, the dingy little man whose ferocious hatred of social injustice inspires him with a moral force that makes both his posturing comrades and the police shudder, acutely conscious, as they are, that he has both the will and the means to shatter a streetful of people to bits—these character sketches supply us with a working analysis of anarchism that is profoundly true, though the philosophical anarchism of certain creative minds is, of course, out of the range of the author's survey. And not less well done is the scrutiny of the official *morale* and personal incentives that govern the conduct of those guardians of social order, Chief Inspector Heat and the Assistant-Commissioner of Police. The two men, who have different ends in view, typify the daily conflict between Justice as a means and Justice as an end, which two are indeed rarely in harmony.

But Mr. Conrad's superiority over nearly all contemporary English novelists is shown in his discriminating impartiality which, facing imperturbably all the conflicting impulses of human nature, refuses to be biassed in favour of one species of man rather than another. Chief Inspector Heat, the thief-taker and the guardian of social order, is no better a man than the inflexible avenger of social injustice, the Professor. The Deputy Commissioner of Police, though a fearless and fine individual, moves our admiration no more than does the child-like idealist, Michaelis, who has been kept in prison for fifteen years for a disinterested act of courage. Whether the spy, Mr. Verloc, is more contemptible than the suave and rosy-gilled favourite of London drawing-rooms, M. Vladimir, is as difficult a point to decide as whether the latter is less despicable than the robust seducer of women, the cowardly Comrade Ossipon. And, by a refined stroke of irony, the innocent victim of anarchist propaganda and bureaucratic countermining is the unfortunate and weak-witted lad, Stevie, whose morbid dread of pain is exploited by the bewildered *agent provocateur*, Mr. Verloc, in his effort to serve the designs of his Embassy, and preserve both his situation and his own skin. Finally, as an illustration of our author's serene impartiality, we may mention that the real heroine of the story is concealed in the trivial figure of Mr. Verloc's mother-in-law, whose effacement of self for the sake of her son, Stevie, is the cause contributory to his own and her daughter's ruin. For Mr. Verloc, growing desperate, sends the half-witted lad with an infernal machine to blow up Greenwich Observatory, and, Stevie perishing, Mr. Verloc is attacked by his wife in a fit of frenzy and killed.

While the psychological analysis of the characters' motives is as full of acumen as is the author's philosophical penetration of life, it is right to add that Mr. Verloc and his wife are less convincing in their actions than in their meditations. There is a hidden weakness in the springs of impulse of both these figures, and at certain moments they become automata. But such defects are few. Mr. Conrad's art of suggesting the essence of an atmosphere and of a character in two or three pages has never been more strikingly illustrated than in *The Secret Agent*. It has the profound and ruthless sincerity of the great Slav writers mingled with the haunting charm that reminds us so often of his compatriot Chopin.

—from an unsigned review in the *Nation* (September 28, 1907)

GLASGOW NEWS

It is not an irrelevant reflection upon *The Secret Agent* that its author, Joseph Conrad, is of Polish birth. Nor is that reflection forced upon one by the fact that the book deals with the underworld of revolutionary intrigue with an authority of first-hand, almost instinctive knowledge, which is something entirely different from the crudely sensational and improbable imaginings of the average English novelist who writes of underground Russian politics. There is much more in the author's origin than that. For the fact is that he has imported into English literature a quality, a mood, a temperament which has never appeared in it before—something perhaps entirely alien to our national genius, at any rate something which we can only parallel in the great Russian writers. That something, not easily defined, may be suggested as a spirit of complete and impassive sincerity, a dry north light in which nothing escapes, nothing is forced or exaggerated or obscured, in which everything appears exactly as it is in its own shape and place. The author never takes a side, never betrays any of the personal feeling, the sentiment or humour or geniality or cynicism or contempt or bitterness that British writers either parade or visibly attempt to suppress—nothing but tranquil comprehension and passionless statement. At the utmost there is a grave irony, or a faint tinge of melancholy, as of one brooding without resentment over the futility and pettiness of human efforts and desires. But this is a new note in our literature—Hardy's sombre tragedy is something quite different—so new that one does not feel it British at all; it is Slavonic. And surely it is a strange accident that has thrown this great writer, imbued with the genius of a race so different from our own, into using our language as his medium of expression, and using it with the power and grace of a born master.

—October 3, 1907

STAR

Another book that emerges from the inky torrent is *The Secret Agent* by Mr. Joseph Conrad. Its imaginative force is terrible. It is the first book in which Mr. Conrad has put London into his magic crucible. The soul of London is not easily transmuted into literature, and few of our novelists have managed to achieve the alchemy of vision. The realists have all failed. Since Dickens no novelist has caught the obscure haunting grotesquerie of London. Now Mr. Conrad has caught it, and caught it as wonderfully as he caught the magic of the Malay forest and the magic of the sea. He stirs and mixes London into his characters, although they are nearly all alien anarchists. You feel its fat, foul, heavy, mysterious presence behind these strange dim folk who move like fish in a dingy aquarium. Verloc, the foreign spy, and his wife, and the idiot boy, and the sensual Ossipon, and the horrible old Professor, are all alive. The murder of Verloc is one of the most intensely dramatic murders in fiction. Its imaginative realism is amazing. Mr. Conrad's pictorial gift is diabolical. He makes you see the whole scene. The moment of the crime is intolerably visible. You see Verloc seeing the shadow of the arm with the clenched hand holding the carving-knife. You think out the plan of defence which he thinks out. You feel that there was not time for him to move, although there was time for him to think. You hear the ticking which is not the ticking of the clock, for the clock has stopped, and you shudder when you realise with Mrs. Verloc that it is the sound of the drops of blood falling on the floor-cloth, with a sound of trickling growing fast and furious like the pulse of an insane clock. But the most ghastly piece of pictorial imagination is Mr. Verloc's round hat on the floor which rocks slightly on its crown in the wind of her flight. That is a stroke of genius. It is the fine art of murder in fiction.

—October 5, 1907

STEWARD EDWARD WHITE
The book has to do with anarchists, diplomats, policemen and stodgy middle-class English people. Of the lot, all but the Professor with his n*th* power explosive are either opéra bouffe or treated as such. In that we touch the chief fault of the book. Mr. Conrad sketches for us a half-dozen characters from the standpoint of delicately satiric contempt, the sort of contempt that refuses to take seriously either the motives, temperaments or actions of the specimens at which it laughs. . . . The Secret Agent himself pays 'visitations' which 'set in with great severity.' He is 'steady like a rock—a soft kind of rock.' The diplomat has 'the air of a preternaturally thriving baby that will not stand nonsense from anybody.' The three anarchists gathered in the little back shop are cowardly, fat, decrepit, futile. Probably they were so, and Mr. Conrad intends to show just these qualities in apposition to the swift terror of the dynamite outrage. But he overdoes it. One feels that after the fall of the curtain they will go forth to the consumption of beer—real beer, not the property beer they drink in the book.

And then, without any real reason for it, we are offered mangled flesh scooped up with a shovel, and gentlemen with carving knives in their bosoms, and abandoned crazy ladies leaping from channel steamers.

The only excuse for a book with a 'disagreeable ending,' so-called, is an exact realism that makes the tragedy inevitable from the first. Witness 'The Heart of Darkness.' When an author's personal bias is permitted in any way to intrude, it weakens by just so much the convincing quality of his work. . . .

With it all is Mr. Conrad's marvellous faculty of fixing a scene in suspension as by a flash of lightning, his power of bringing out a character by a multiplicity of little touches, the insight that has made his work a delight. The imaginative reader can see readily enough what he is after. Only he has not done it.

—from the *Bookman* (January 1908)

F. R. LEAVIS
The Secret Agent is truly classical in its maturity of attitude and the consummateness of the art in which this finds expression. . . . The irony of *The Secret Agent* is not a matter of an insistent and obvious 'significance' of tone, or the endless repetition of a single formula. The tone is truly subtle—subtle with the subtlety of the theme; and the theme develops itself in a complex organic structure. The effect depends upon an interplay of contrasting moral perspectives, and the rich economy of the pattern they make relates *The Secret Agent* to *Nostromo*: the two works, for all the great differences between them in range and temper, are triumphs of the same art—the aim of *The Secret Agent*, of course, confines the range, and the kind of irony involves a limiting detachment (we don't look for the secrets of Conrad's soul in *The Secret Agent*). . . .

—from *The Great Tradition* (1948)

Questions

1. Although it is Mr. Verloc who is the chief secret agent in this novel, what other characters behave as secret agents, too? What kinds of secrets do they harbor? How does secrecy itself affect human relationships in this novel?

2. Again, while it is Mr. Verloc who is explicitly, albeit secretly, designated by the symbol Δ, triangular relationships can be found throughout *The Secret Agent*. What are some of them, and how do they represent and develop the theme of trust and its betrayal in the novel?

3. One of Winnie Verloc's prominent characteristics is her belief that "things do not stand much looking into" (p. 147). What kinds of "things" might those be? Why has Winnie not "looked into" them in the course of her married life with Mr. Verloc? What might have happened if she had? What happens when, near the end of the novel, she does?

4. In 1884, two years before the date specified for the fictional action of *The Secret Agent* and ten years before the "Greenwich Outrage" actually occurred, Greenwich Mean Time was officially adopted by twenty-four countries and became, in effect, the global standard for the measurement of time. In what ways does the fact of such standardization resonate in this novel about anarchism? How is time represented in *The Secret Agent*? How is time treated in the organization of the narrative itself? And how is the form the narrative takes related to the symbolic representation of time in the novel?

5. Terrorism, though largely identified with the character of the Professor and, to a lesser degree, Karl Yundt, appears in many other shapes and forms in this novel. What are some? How, more generally, do fear and anxiety figure in the conception and the effect of *The Secret Agent*?

6. Conrad's representation of anarchists and anarchism in *The Secret Agent*, though once thought to be unrealistic by some reviewers and critics, has been shown to be quite accurate historically. More recently, it has also been thought to be prescient. In what ways does this early twentieth-century novel speak to our condition in the early twenty-first?

For Further Reading

Biographical Works and Letters

Baines, Jocelyn. *Joseph Conrad: A Critical Biography*. New York: McGraw-Hill, 1960.

Batchelor, John. *The Life of Joseph Conrad: A Critical Biography*. Oxford: Blackwell, 1994.

Karl, Frederick R. *Joseph Conrad: The Three Lives*. New York: Farrar, Straus, and Giroux, 1979. An extensive study of Conrad's life and work.

——, and Laurence Davies, eds. *The Collected Letters of Joseph Conrad*. 8 vols. Cambridge: Cambridge University Press, 1983–.

Meyer, Bernard. *Joseph Conrad: A Psychoanalytic Biography*. Princeton, NJ: Princeton University Press, 1967.

Meyers, Jeffrey. *Joseph Conrad: A Biography*. New York: Charles Scribner's Sons, 1991.

Najder, Zdzislaw. *Joseph Conrad: A Chronicle*. New Brunswick, NJ: Rutgers University Press, 1983.

Ray, Martin, ed. *Joseph Conrad: Interviews and Recollections*. London: Macmillan, 1990.

Watts, Cedric. *Joseph Conrad: A Literary Life*. London: Macmillan, 1989.

Critical Studies

Fleishman, Avrom. *Conrad's Politics: Community and Anarchy in the Fiction of Joseph Conrad*. Baltimore: Johns Hopkins University Press, 1967.

Guérard, Albert J. *Conrad the Novelist*. Cambridge, MA: Harvard University Press, 1958.

Hay, Eloise Knapp. *The Political Novels of Joseph Conrad: A Critical Study*. Chicago: University of Chicago Press, 1963.

Howe, Irving. *Politics and the Novel.* New York: Meridian, 1957.

Kaplan, Carola, Peter Mallios, and Andrea White, eds. *Conrad in the Twenty-First Century.* New York: Routledge, 2005.

Leavis, F. R. *The Great Tradition: George Eliot, Henry James, Joseph Conrad.* London: Chatto and Windus, 1948.

Najder, Zdzislaw. *Conrad in Perspective: Essays on Art and Fidelity.* Cambridge: Cambridge University Press, 1997.

Sherry, Norman, ed. *Conrad: The Critical Heritage.* London: Routledge and Kegan Paul, 1973.

——. *Conrad's Western World.* Cambridge: Cambridge University Press, 1971.

Stape, J. H., ed. *The Cambridge Companion to Joseph Conrad.* Cambridge: Cambridge University Press, 1996.

Watt, Ian. *Conrad in the Nineteenth Century.* Berkeley: University of California Press, 1979.

——, ed. *Conrad, The Secret Agent: A Selection of Critical Essays.* Casebook Series. London: Macmillan, 1973.

Literary and Historical Contexts

Harrison, Michael. *London by Gaslight, 1861–1911.* Dubuque, IA: Gasogene Press, 1987.

Houen, Alex. *Terrorism and Modern Literature.* New York: Oxford University Press, 2002.

Laqueur, Walter. *A History of Terrorism.* New Brunswick, NJ: Transaction Press, 2001.

Melchiori, Barbara Arnett. *Terrorism in the Late Victorian Novel.* London: Croom Helm, 1985.

Internet Resources

The Joseph Conrad Society of America. www.engl.unt.edu/~jgpeters/Conrad/index.html

The Joseph Conrad Society (UK). http://www.josephconradsociety.org/

Victorian London. www.victorianlondon.org

The Victorian Web. www.victorianweb.org

Look for the following titles, available now and forthcoming from
BARNES & NOBLE CLASSICS .

Visit your local bookstore for these fine titles.

Adventures of Huckleberry Finn	Mark Twain	1-59308-000-X	$4.95
The Adventures of Tom Sawyer	Mark Twain	1-59308-068-9	$4.95
The Age of Innocence	Edith Wharton	1-59308-143-X	$5.95
Alice's Adventures in Wonderland and Through the Looking-Glass	Lewis Carroll	1-59308-015-8	$5.95
Anna Karenina	Leo Tolstoy	1-59308-027-1	$8.95
The Art of War	Sun Tzu	1-59308-017-4	$7.95
The Awakening and Selected Short Fiction	Kate Chopin	1-59308-001-8	$4.95
The Brothers Karamazov	Fyodor Dostoevsky	1-59308-045-X	$9.95
The Call of the Wild and White Fang	Jack London	1-59308-200-2	$5.95
Candide	Voltaire	1-59308-028-X	$4.95
A Christmas Carol, The Chimes and The Cricket on the Hearth	Charles Dickens	1-59308-033-6	$5.95
The Collected Poems of Emily Dickinson		1-59308-050-6	$5.95
The Complete Sherlock Holmes, Vol. I	Sir Arthur Conan Doyle	1-59308-034-4	$7.95
The Complete Sherlock Holmes, Vol. II	Sir Arthur Conan Doyle	1-59308-040-9	$7.95
The Count of Monte Cristo	Alexandre Dumas	1-59308-151-0	$7.95
Daniel Deronda	George Eliot	1-59308-290-8	$8.95
David Copperfield	Charles Dickens	1-59308-063-8	$7.95
The Death of Ivan Ilych and Other Stories	Leo Tolstoy	1-59308-069-7	$7.95
Don Quixote	Miguel de Cervantes	1-59308-046-8	$9.95
Dracula	Bram Stoker	1-59308-114-6	$6.95
Emma	Jane Austen	1-59308-089-1	$4.95
Essays and Poems by Ralph Waldo Emerson		1-59308-076-X	$6.95
The Essential Tales and Poems of Edgar Allan Poe		1-59308-064-6	$7.95
Frankenstein	Mary Shelley	1-59308-115-4	$4.95
Great American Short Stories: from Hawthorne to Hemingway		1-59308-086-7	$7.95
Great Expectations	Charles Dickens	1-59308-006-9	$4.95
Gulliver's Travels	Jonathan Swift	1-59308-132-4	$5.95
Hard Times	Charles Dickens	1-59308-156-1	$5.95
Heart of Darkness and Selected Short Fiction	Joseph Conrad	1-59308-021-2	$4.95
The Histories	Herodotus	1-59308-102-2	$6.95
The House of Mirth	Edith Wharton	1-59308-153-7	$6.95
Howards End	E. M. Forster	1-59308-022-0	$6.95
The Hunchback of Notre Dame	Victor Hugo	1-59308-047-6	$5.95
The Idiot	Fyodor Dostoevsky	1-59308-058-1	$7.95
The Importance of Being Earnest and Four Other Plays	Oscar Wilde	1-59308-059-X	$6.95
The Inferno	Dante Alighieri	1-59308-051-4	$6.95
Jane Eyre	Charlotte Brontë	1-59308-007-7	$4.95
Jude the Obscure	Thomas Hardy	1-59308-035-2	$6.95
The Jungle Books	Rudyard Kipling	1-59308-109-X	$5.95
The Jungle	Upton Sinclair	1-59308-008-5	$4.95
The Last of the Mohicans	James Fenimore Cooper	1-59308-137-5	$5.95
Leaves of Grass: First and "Death-bed" Editions	Walt Whitman	1-59308-083-2	$9.95
Les Misérables	Victor Hugo	1-59308-066-2	$9.95
Little Women	Louisa May Alcott	1-59308-108-1	$6.95

(continued)

Main Street	Sinclair Lewis	1-59308-036-0	$5.95
Mansfield Park	Jane Austen	1-59308-154-5	$5.95
The Metamorphosis and Other Stories	Franz Kafka	1-59308-029-8	$6.95
Moby-Dick	Herman Melville	1-59308-018-2	$9.95
My Ántonia	Willa Cather	1-59308-202-9	$5.95
Narrative of the Life of Frederick Douglass, an American Slave		1-59308-041-7	$4.95
Notes From Underground, The Double and Other Stories	Fyodor Dostoevsky	1-59308-037-9	$4.95
O Pioneers!	Willa Cather	1-59308-205-3	$5.95
The Odyssey	Homer	1-59308-009-3	$5.95
Oliver Twist	Charles Dickens	1-59308-206-1	$6.95
The Origin of Species	Charles Darwin	1-59308-077-8	$7.95
Paradise Lost	John Milton	1-59308-095-6	$7.95
Persuasion	Jane Austen	1-59308-130-8	$5.95
The Picture of Dorian Gray	Oscar Wilde	1-59308-025-5	$4.95
The Portrait of a Lady	Henry James	1-59308-096-4	$7.95
A Portrait of the Artist as a Young Man and Dubliners	James Joyce	1-59308-031-X	$6.95
Pride and Prejudice	Jane Austen	1-59308-201-0	$5.95
The Prince and Other Writings	Niccolò Machiavelli	1-59308-060-3	$5.95
The Red Badge of Courage and Selected Short Fiction	Stephen Crane	1-59308-119-7	$4.95
Republic	Plato	1-59308-097-2	$6.95
Robinson Crusoe	Daniel Defoe	1-59308-360-2	$5.95
The Scarlet Letter	Nathaniel Hawthorne	1-59308-207-X	$4.95
Sense and Sensibility	Jane Austen	1-59308-125-1	$5.95
Sons and Lovers	D. H. Lawrence	1-59308-013-1	$7.95
The Souls of Black Folk	W. E. B. Du Bois	1-59308-014-X	$5.95
The Strange Case of Dr. Jekyll and Mr. Hyde and Other Stories	Robert Louis Stevenson	1-59308-131-6	$4.95
A Tale of Two Cities	Charles Dickens	1-59308-138-3	$5.95
Tao Te Ching	Lao Tzu	1-59308-256-8	$5.95
The Three Musketeers	Alexandre Dumas	1-59308-148-0	$8.95
The Time Machine and The Invisible Man	H. G. Wells	1-59308-032-8	$4.95
Tom Jones	Henry Fielding	1-59308-070-0	$8.95
Treasure Island	Robert Louis Stevenson	1-59308-247-9	$4.95
The Turn of the Screw, The Aspern Papers and Two Stories	Henry James	1-59308-043-3	$5.95
Twenty Thousand Leagues Under the Sea	Jules Verne	1-59308-302-5	$5.95
Uncle Tom's Cabin	Harriet Beecher Stowe	1-59308-121-9	$7.95
Vanity Fair	William Makepeace Thackeray	1-59308-071-9	$7.95
Villette	Charlotte Brontë	1-59308-316-5	$7.95
The Voyage Out	Virginia Woolf	1-59308-229-0	$6.95
Walden and Civil Disobedience	Henry David Thoreau	1-59308-208-8	$5.95
The War of the Worlds	H. G. Wells	1-59308-085-9	$3.95
Wuthering Heights	Emily Brontë	1-59308-044-1	$4.95